MVFOL

D0037962

Debbie Macomber is a #1 *New York Times* bestselling author and a leading voice in women's fiction worldwide. Her work has appeared on every major bestseller list, with more than 170 million copies in print, and she is a multiple award winner. Hallmark Channel based a television series on Debbie's popular Cedar Cove books. For more information, visit her website, debbiemacomber.com.

USA TODAY bestselling author **Delores Fossen** has had more than one hundred novels published, with millions of copies of her books in print worldwide. She's received the Booksellers' Best Award and the RT Reviewers' Choice Best Book Award, and was a finalist for the prestigious RITA® Award. In addition, she's had nearly a hundred short stories and articles published in national magazines. Married to an air force colonel, Delores is the mother of four children and has lived in England and all over the United States. She's had a variety of careers and jobs: an air force captain, a special-ed teacher and a rehab counselor. None was as fun or challenging as the time she spent as a stay-at-home mom. You can get updates about Delores's books or contact her through her website at www.deloresfossen.com.

#1 *New York Times* **Bestselling Author**

DEBBIE MACOMBER

THE WYOMING KID

ISBN-13: 978-1-335-80430-3

The Wyoming Kid

Copyright © 2019 by Harlequin Books S.A.

The publisher acknowledges the copyright holders of the individual works as follows:

The Wyoming Kid
Copyright © 2006 by Debbie Macomber

The Horseman's Son
Copyright © 2008 by Delores Fossen

Recycling programs for this product may not exist in your area.

This edition published by arrangement with Harlequin Books S.A.

For questions and comments about the quality of this book, please contact us at CustomerService@Harlequin.com.

HARLEQUIN®
www.Harlequin.com

Printed in U.S.A.

CONTENTS

THE WYOMING KID   9
Debbie Macomber

THE HORSEMAN'S SON   243
Delores Fossen

Also available from Debbie Macomber

Blossom Street

The Shop on Blossom Street
A Good Yarn
Susannah's Garden
Back on Blossom Street
Twenty Wishes
Summer on Blossom Street
Hannah's List
The Twenty-First Wish
  (in The Knitting Diaries)
A Turn in the Road

Cedar Cove

16 Lighthouse Road
204 Rosewood Lane
311 Pelican Court
44 Cranberry Point
50 Harbor Street
6 Rainier Drive
74 Seaside Avenue
8 Sandpiper Way
92 Pacific Boulevard
1022 Evergreen Place
Christmas in Cedar Cove
  (5-B Poppy Lane and
  A Cedar Cove Christmas)
1105 Yakima Street
1225 Christmas Tree Lane

Dakota Series

Dakota Born
Dakota Home
Always Dakota
Buffalo Valley

The Manning Family

The Manning Sisters
  (The Cowboy's Lady and
  The Sheriff Takes a Wife)

The Manning Brides
  (Marriage of Inconvenience
  and Stand-In Wife)
The Manning Grooms
  (Bride on the Loose and
  Same Time, Next Year)

Christmas Books

A Gift to Last
On a Snowy Night
Home for the Holidays
Glad Tidings
Christmas Wishes
Small Town Christmas
When Christmas Comes
  (now retitled Trading
  Christmas)
There's Something About Christmas
Christmas Letters
The Perfect Christmas
Choir of Angels
  (Shirley, Goodness and Mercy,
  Those Christmas Angels and
  Where Angels Go)
Call Me Mrs. Miracle

Heart of Texas

Texas Skies
  (Lonesome Cowboy and
  Texas Two-Step)
Texas Nights
  (Caroline's Child and
  Dr. Texas)
Texas Home
  (Nell's Cowboy and
  Lone Star Baby)
Promise, Texas
Return to Promise

Midnight Sons

Alaska Skies
  (*Brides for Brothers* and
  The Marriage Risk)
Alaska Nights
  (*Daddy's Little Helper* and
  Because of the Baby)
Alaska Home
  (*Falling for Him,*
  Ending in Marriage and
  Midnight Sons and Daughters)

This Matter of Marriage
Montana
Thursdays at Eight
Between Friends
Changing Habits
Married in Seattle
  (*First Comes Marriage* and
  Wanted: Perfect Partner)
Right Next Door
  (*Father's Day* and
  The Courtship of Carol Sommars)
Wyoming Brides
  (*Denim and Diamonds* and
  The Wyoming Kid)
Fairy Tale Weddings
  (*Cindy and the Prince* and
  Some Kind of Wonderful)
The Man You'll Marry
  (*The First Man You Meet* and
  The Man You'll Marry)
Orchard Valley Grooms
  (*Valerie* and *Stephanie*)
Orchard Valley Brides
  (*Norah* and *Lone Star Lovin'*)
The Sooner the Better
An Engagement in Seattle
  (*Groom Wanted* and
  Bride Wanted)
Out of the Rain
  (*Marriage Wanted* and
  Laughter in the Rain)
Learning to Love
  (*Sugar and Spice* and
  Love by Degree)

You…Again
  (*Baby Blessed* and
  Yesterday Once More)
The Unexpected Husband
  (*Jury of His Peers* and
  Any Sunday)
Three Brides, No Groom
Love in Plain Sight
  (*Love 'n' Marriage* and
  Almost an Angel)
I Left My Heart
  (*A Friend or Two* and
  No Competition)
Marriage Between Friends
  (*White Lace and Promises* and
  Friends—And Then Some)
A Man's Heart
  (*The Way to a Man's Heart*
  and *Hasty Wedding*)
North to Alaska
  (*That Wintry Feeling* and
  Borrowed Dreams)
On a Clear Day
  (*Starlight* and
  Promise Me Forever)
To Love and Protect
  (*Shadow Chasing* and
  For All My Tomorrows)
Home in Seattle
  (*The Playboy and the Widow*
  and *Fallen Angel*)
Together Again
  (*The Trouble with Caasi* and
  Reflections of Yesterday)
The Reluctant Groom
  (*All Things Considered*
  and *Almost Paradise*)
A Real Prince
  (*The Bachelor Prince*
  and *Yesterday's Hero*)
Private Paradise
  (in *That Summer Place*)

Debbie Macomber's
  Cedar Cove Cookbook
Debbie Macomber's
  Christmas Cookbook

THE WYOMING KID

Debbie Macomber

To the Peninsula Chapter
of Romance Writers of America—gutsy girls all.

Chapter 1

His truck shuddering as he hit a rut, Lonny Ellison pulled into the ranch yard at Spring Valley and slammed on the brakes. He jumped out of the cab, muttering furiously. In pure frustration, he kicked the side of his Ford Ranger with one scuffed boot. His sister, who was hanging clothes on the line, straightened and watched him approach. No word of greeting, not even a wave, just a little smile. As calm as could be, Letty studied him, which only irritated him more. He blamed her for this. She was the one who had her heart set on Lonny's dating that…that woman. She was also the one who'd been busy trying to do some matchmaking—not that she'd had any success. She'd even promised a year ago that she wouldn't do it again. Ha!

It wasn't like Lonny to let a woman rattle him, but

Joy Fuller certainly had. This wasn't the first time, either. Oh, no. Far from it.

He had plenty of cause to dislike her. Two years ago, when she'd moved to Red Springs to take a teaching job, he'd gone out of his way to make her feel welcome in the community. They'd gone out a few times, and they'd argued—he couldn't even remember why—and he hadn't spoken to her until Letty came back on the scene last summer. He'd—briefly—rediscovered some interest in her, but it hadn't ended well. Now *this!* Friend of Letty's or not, he wasn't about to let Joy Fuller escape the consequences of what she'd done.

What bothered him most was the complete disrespect Joy had shown him and his vehicle. Why, his truck was in prime condition, his pride and— No, under the circumstances, he couldn't call it his pride and *joy.* But he treasured that Ford almost as much as he did his horse.

"What's gotten into you?" Letty asked, completely unruffled by his actions.

"Why did it have to be *her?* Again?"

"And who would that be?" his sister asked mildly.

"Your…your teacher friend. She—" Lonny struggled to find the words. "It's outrageous!"

Letty's expressive eyes widened and she gave a deep sigh. "Okay, what did Joy do this time?"

"Here!" He motioned toward the front of his pickup so his sister could see for herself.

"Oh, oh. This sounds like déjà vu." Letty scanned the bumper. "Looks like it, too."

He pointed, his finger shaking as he directed her attention to the most recent dent.

"Where?" Letty asked, bending over to examine it more carefully, squinting hard.

"There." If she assumed that being obtuse was amusing him, she was wrong. He stabbed his finger at it again. All right, he'd admit the truck had its share of nicks and dents. The pickup could use a new front fender, and a paint job wouldn't be a bad idea, but in no way did that minimize what Joy had done.

"Oh, give it up, Lonny. This thing is ready for the scrap heap."

"You're joking, aren't you? There's at least another decade left in the engine." He should've known better than to discuss this with his sister. As he'd learned to his sorrow, women always stuck together.

"You don't mean this tiny little dent, do you?" she asked, poking it with her finger.

"Tiny little dent!" he repeated, shocked that she didn't see this for what it was.

"Come on," Letty said, "and just tell me what Joy supposedly did." She shook her head. "I don't understand why you're so upset."

To say he was *upset* was an understatement. He was fit to be tied, and it was Joy Fuller's fault. Lonny liked to think of himself as an easygoing guy. Very rarely did a woman, any woman, rile him the way Joy had. Not only that, she seemed to enjoy it.

"Joy Fuller ran a stop sign," he explained. "Just like she did last year. Different stop sign, though," he muttered in disgust. "Not that it makes things any better."

"Joy crashed into you?"

"Almost. By the grace of God, I was able to avoid a collision, but in the process I hit the pole."

"Then this really *is* déjà vu," Letty said delightedly.

That was not the response he was looking for.

Lonny jerked the Stetson off his head and smacked it hard against his thigh. Wincing, he went on with his story. "Then Joy gets out of her car, tells me she's *sorry* and asks if there's any damage."

"Gee, I hope you slugged her for that," Letty murmured, rolling her eyes.

Lonny decided to ignore the sarcasm. "I showed her the dent," he said, not even trying to keep the indignation out of his voice. "She said there were even more dents on my truck than last year, so how could she tell which one she'd caused?" His voice rose as his agitation grew.

"What did you say next?" Letty asked.

Lonny stared down at the ground. "We…argued." That was Joy's fault, too. Just like last year. She seemed to expect him to tell her that all was forgiven. Well, he wasn't forgiving her anything, least of all the damage she'd caused.

When he hadn't fallen under her spell once again— as she'd obviously expected—their argument had quickly heated up. Within minutes her true nature was revealed. "She said my truck was a piece of crap." Even now the statement outraged him. Lonny looked at his Ford, muttering, "That's no way for a lady to talk. Not only did Joy insult my vehicle, she insulted *me*."

This schoolteacher, this city slicker, had no appreciation of country life. That was what you got when the town hired someone like Joy Fuller. You could take the woman out of the city but there was plenty of city left in her.

"Why don't you let Joy's insurance take care of it?" Letty said in that soothing way of hers. "It was really nice of you to let it go last year."

Lonny scowled. Joy had a lot to atone for as far as he was concerned, and he wasn't inclined to be as generous this time. "And get this. She tried to buy me off—again!" Even now, the suggestion offended him.

Letty raised her eyebrows and Lonny muttered, "She said she'd give me fifty bucks."

"So she didn't increase her offer? Wasn't that the amount she wanted to give you before?"

His sister's mouth quivered, and if he didn't know better, Lonny would've thought she was laughing. "You refused?" she murmured.

"Oh, yeah," he told her. "I'm gonna get an estimate from the body shop. Fifty bucks," he spat. "Fifty bucks!"

"Hmm." Letty grinned. "Seems to me Joy's managed to get your attention. Hasn't she?"

Lonny decided to ignore that comment, which he considered unworthy of his sister. All right, he had some history with Joy Fuller, most of it unpleasant. But the past was the past and had nothing to do with the here and now. "I wrote down her license plate number." He pulled a small piece of paper from his shirt pocket and brandished it under her nose. "This time I *am* going to report her to the police."

"You most certainly will not!" Letty snatched the paper out of his hand. "Joy is one of my best friends and I won't let you treat her so rudely."

His sister hadn't encountered the same side of the teacher he had. "You haven't seen that evil look about her—I suspect she normally keeps that PT Cruiser in the garage and travels by broomstick."

His sister didn't appreciate his attempt at humor. "Oh, for heaven's sake, Joy plays the organ at church on Sundays, as you very well know. Don't try to pretend you don't."

"That's all a front," he said darkly.

"You have unfinished business with Joy, which is why you're blowing this *incident* out of all proportion."

Lonny thought it best to ignore that comment, too. He'd finished with Joy a long time ago—and she with him—which suited him just fine. "I'd say she's one scary woman. Mean as a rattlesnake." He gave an exaggerated shiver. "Probably shrinks heads as a hobby."

Letty had the grace to smile. "Would you stop it? Joy's probably the sweetest person I've ever met."

"*Sweet?*" Lonny hadn't seen any evidence of a gentle disposition, not in the past year, and not now. He shuddered to think he'd once wanted to marry Joy. Man, had he dodged *that* bullet.

Hands on her hips, Letty shook her head sadly. "Come in and have some iced tea."

"Nah. You go on without me." Shaking his head, he strolled toward the barn. Joy Fuller was his sister's friend. One of her best friends. That meant he had to seriously question Letty's taste—and good sense. Years ago, when he was young and foolish, Lonny had ridden broncos and bulls and been known as The Wyoming Kid. He darn near got himself killed a time or two. But he'd rather sit on one of those beasts again than tangle with the likes of Joy Fuller.

Chapter 2

Joy Fuller glanced out the window of her combination third-and-fourth-grade classroom and did a quick double take. It couldn't be! But it was—Lonny Ellison. She should've known he wouldn't just let things be. The real problem was that they'd started off on the wrong foot two years ago. She'd been new to the community, still learning about life in Red Springs, Wyoming, when she'd met Lonny through a mutual acquaintance.

At first they'd gotten along well. He'd been a rodeo cowboy and had an ego even bigger than that ridiculously big belt buckle he'd shown her. Apparently, she hadn't paid him the homage he felt was his due. After a month or two of laughing, with decreasing sincerity, at his comments about city slickers, the joke had worn thin. She'd made it clear that she wasn't willing to be another of his buckle bunnies and soon after, they'd agreed not to see each other anymore. Not that their relationship was serious, of course; they'd gone out for dinner and dancing a few times—that was about it. So she hadn't thought their disagreement was a big deal, but apparently it had been to Lonny. It seemed no woman had ever spoken her mind to the great and mighty Wyoming Kid before.

Lonny had said he appreciated her honesty, and that was the last she'd heard from him. Joy had been surprised by his reaction. However, if that was how he felt, it was fine with her. He hadn't asked her out again and she hadn't contacted him, either. She saw him around town now and then, but aside from a polite nod or a cool "hello," they'd ignored each other. It was a rather disappointing end to what had begun as a promising relationship. But that was nearly two years ago and she was long past feeling any regrets. Their minor collision soon after Letty's return had seemed fitting somehow, the perfect finishing touch to their so-called relationship.

Then she'd had to miss that blasted stop sign the other day—but at least it was a different one, not the sign she'd missed last year, the one at Oak and Spruce. Naturally he had to be the one who slammed into the post. Again. The shock and embarrassment still upset her. Worse, Joy hadn't recovered yet from their verbal exchange. Lonny was completely and totally unreasonable, and he'd made some extremely unpleasant accusations. All right, in an effort to be fair, she'd admit that Lonny Ellison was easy to look at—tall and rangy with wide, muscular shoulders. He had strikingly rich, dark eyes and a solid jaw, and he reminded her a little of a young Clint Eastwood. However, appearances weren't everything.

Letty, who was a romantic, had wanted to match Joy with her brother. Letty had only moved back to the area a year ago and at first she hadn't realized that they'd already dated for a brief time. Joy had done her best to explain why a relationship with Lonny just wouldn't work. He was too stubborn and she was…well, a woman had her pride. They simply weren't compatible. And if she hadn't known that before, their first near-collision had proven it. This second one just confirmed it.

She peeked surreptitiously out the window again. Lonny was leaning against his rattletrap truck, ankles crossed to highlight his dusty boots. Chase Brown, Letty's husband, and Lonny owned adjoining ranches and shared a large herd of cattle. According to Letty, that was a recent enterprise; they'd joined forces last fall and were now raising hormone-free cattle. In any case, one would think a working rancher had better things to do than hang around outside a schoolyard. He was there to pester her; she was convinced of it. His lanky arms were crossed and his head bowed, with his Stetson riding low on his forehead, as if he didn't have a care in the world. His posture resembled that neon sign of a cowpoke in downtown Vegas, she thought.

She knew exactly why Lonny had come to the school. He was planning to cause her trouble. Joy rued the day she'd ever met the man. He was rude, unreasonable, juvenile, plus a dozen other adjectives she didn't even want to *think* about in front of a classroom full of young children.

Children.

Sucking in a deep breath, Joy returned her attention to her class, only to discover that all the kids were watching her expectantly. Seeing Lonny standing outside her window had thrown her so badly that she'd forgotten she was in the middle of a spelling test. Her students were waiting for the next word.

"Arrogant," she muttered.

A dozen hands shot into the air.

"Eric," Joy said, calling on the boy sitting at the front desk in the second row.

"Arrogant isn't one of our spelling words," he said, and several protests followed.

"This is an extra-credit word," she said. Squinting, she glared out the window again.

No sooner had the test papers been handed in than the bell rang, signaling the end of the school day. Her students dashed out the door a lot faster than they'd entered, and within minutes, the entire schoolyard was filled with youngsters. As luck would have it, she had playground duty that afternoon. This meant she was required to step out of the shelter of the school building and into the vicinity of Lonny Ellison.

Because Red Springs was a ranching community, most children lived well outside the town limits. Huge buses lumbered down country roads every morning and afternoon. These buses delivered the children to school and to their homes, some traveling as far as thirty miles.

Despite Lonny's dire predictions, Joy was surprised by how successfully she'd adjusted to life in this small Wyoming community. Born and raised in Seattle, she'd hungered for small-town life, eager to experience the joys of living in a close, family-oriented community. Red Springs was far removed from everything familiar, but she'd discovered that people were the same everywhere. Not exactly a complicated insight, but it was as profound as it was simple. Parents wanted the best for their children in Red Springs, the same way they did back home. Neighbors were friendly if you made the effort to get to know them. Wyoming didn't have the distinctive beauty associated with Puget Sound and the two mountain ranges; instead, it possessed a beauty all its own. Joy had done her research and was fascinated to learn that this was the land where dinosaurs had once roamed and where more than half the world's geysers were located, in Yellowstone National Park. Much of central Wyoming had been an ancient inland sea, and she'd gone on a few fossil-hunting expeditions with friends from school.

It was true that Joy didn't have access to all the amenities she did in a big city. But she'd found that she could live without the majority of convenient luxuries, such as movie theaters and the occasional concerts. Movies went to DVD so quickly these days, and if the small theater in town didn't show it, Joy could rent it a few months after its release, via the internet.

As for shopping, virtually everything she needed was available online. Ordering on the internet wasn't the same as spending the day at the mall, but that, too, had its compensations. If Joy couldn't step inside a shopping mall, then she didn't squander her money on impulse buys.

The one thing she did miss, however, was her family and friends. She talked to her parents every week, and regularly emailed her brother and her closest friends. At Christmas or during the summer, she visited Seattle to see everyone. Several of her college classmates were married now. Three years after receiving her master's in education, Joy was still single. While she was in no rush, she did long for a husband and family of her own one day. Red Springs was full of eligible men; unfortunately, most of them were at least fifty. The pickings were slim, as Letty was eager to remind her. She'd dated, but none of the men had interested her the way Lonny once had.

Since there was no avoiding it, Joy left the school and watched as the children formed neat rows and boarded the buses. She folded her arms and stood straight and as tall as her five-foot-ten-inch frame would allow. Thankfully she'd chosen her nicest jumper that morning, a denim one with a white turtleneck. She felt she needed any advantage she could get if she had to face Lonny Ellison. The jumper had buckle snaps and crisscrossed her shoulders, helping to disguise her slight build.

"Ms. Fuller, Ms. Fuller," six-year-old Cricket Brown shouted, racing across the playground to her side. The little girl's long braids bounced as she skipped over to Joy. Her cherub face was flushed with excitement.

"Hello, Cricket," Joy said, smiling down at the youngster. She'd witnessed a remarkable change in the little girl since Letty's marriage to Chase Brown. Despite her friendship with Letty, Joy wasn't aware of all the details, but she knew there was a lengthy romantic history between her and Chase, one that had taken place ten years earlier. Letty had moved away and when she'd returned, she had a daughter and no husband.

Letty was gentle, kind, thoughtful, the exact opposite of her brother. Out of the corner of her eye, Joy noticed he was striding toward her.

Cricket wasn't in the lineup for the bus, which explained Lonny's presence. He'd apparently come to pick up his niece. Preferring to ignore him altogether, Joy turned her back to avoid looking in Lonny's direction. The students were all aboard the waiting buses. One had already pulled out of the yard and was headed down the street.

"My uncle Lonny's here." Cricket grinned ecstatically.

"I know." Joy couldn't very well say she hadn't seen him, because she had. The hair on the back of her neck had stood on end the minute he'd parked outside the school. The radar-like reaction her body continued to have whenever he made an appearance confused and annoyed her.

"Look! He's coming now," Cricket cried, waving furiously at her uncle.

Lonny joined the two of them and held Joy's look for a long moment. Chills ran down her spine. It was too much to hope that Lonny would simply collect Cricket and then be on his way, too much to hope he wouldn't mention the stop sign incident. The *second* stop sign incident. Oh, no, this man wouldn't permit an opportunity like that to pass him by.

"Mr. Ellison," she said, unwilling to blink. She kept her face as expressionless as possible.

"Ms. Fuller." He touched the brim of his Stetson with his index finger.

"Yes?" Crossing her arms, she boldly met his gaze,

preferring to let him do the talking. She refused to be intimidated by this ill-tempered rancher. She'd made one small mistake and run a stop sign, causing a *minor* near-accident. The stop sign at Grove and Logan was new and she'd been so accustomed to not stopping that she'd sailed through the intersection.

She'd driven at the legal speed limit, forgetting about the newly installed stop sign. She'd noticed it at the last possible second; it was already too late to stop but she'd immediately slowed down. Unfortunately, Lonny Ellison had entered the same intersection at the same time and they'd experienced a *trivial* mishap. Once again, Joy had been more than willing to admit that she was the one at fault, and she would gladly have accepted full responsibility if he hadn't behaved like an escaped lunatic. In fact, Lonny had carried this incident far beyond anything sane or reasonable. Not that—based on past experience—this was surprising.

It didn't help that he was a good five inches taller than she was and about as lean and mean as a wolverine. Staring up at him now, she changed her mind about his being the slightest bit attractive. Well, he *could* be if not for his dark, beady eyes. Even when Joy and Lonny had dated he hadn't smiled all that often, and only at his own jokes, which were usually about city slickers and absurd rodeo exploits. Since then, he seemed to wear a perpetual frown, glaring at her as if she were a stinkbug he wanted to stomp.

"I got the estimate on the damage to my truck," he announced, handing her a folded sheet.

Damage? What damage? The dent in his fender was barely visible. Joy concluded it was better not to ask.

"I'll take a look at it," she said, struggling not to reveal how utterly irritating she found him. As far as she could see, his precious truck was on its way to the scrap yard.

"You'll want to pay particular attention to the cost of repairing that section of the fender," he added.

She might as well pay him off and be done with it. Unfolding the yellow sheet, she glanced down. Despite her best efforts to refrain from any emotion, she gasped. "This is a joke, right?"

"No. You'll see I'm not asking you to replace the *whole* bumper."

"They don't replace half a bumper or even a small section. This…this two hundred and fifty dollars seems way out of line."

"A new bumper, plus installation, costs over five hundred dollars. Two hundred and fifty is half of that."

Joy swallowed hard. Yes, she'd been at fault, and yes, it wasn't the first time, but even dividing the cost of the bumper, that amount was ridiculous. She certainly hadn't done five hundred dollars' worth of damage— or even fifty dollars, in her opinion.

To his credit, Lonny had done an admirable job of preventing any serious repercussions. She'd been badly shaken by the incident, which could easily have been much worse, and so had Lonny. She'd tried to apologize, sincerely tried, but Lonny had leaped out of his pickup in a rage.

Because he'd been such a jerk about it, Joy had responded in anger, too. From that moment on, they'd had trouble even being civil to each other. Joy was convinced his anger wasn't so much about this so-called accident as it was about their former relationship. He was the one who'd broken it off, not her. Well, okay, it'd been a mutual decision.

Now he was insisting that a mere scratch would cost hundreds of dollars to repair. It was hard to tell which dent the collision had even caused. His truck had at least ten others just like it, including the one from last year's *incident,* and most of them were much worse. She suspected he was punishing her for not falling under the spell of the Great Rodeo Rider. *That* was the real story here.

Joy marched over to where Lonny had parked his vehicle. "You can't expect me to pay that kind of money for one tiny dent." She gestured at the scratched and battered truck. "That's highway robbery." She stood her ground—easy to do because she didn't *have* an extra two hundred and fifty dollars. "What about all the other dents? They don't seem to bother you, but this one does. And why is that, I wonder?"

Anger flashed from his eyes. "That *tiny dent* does bother me. So does the other *tiny dent* you caused. But what bothers me more is unsafe drivers. In my view, you should have your driver's license revoked."

"I forgot about the stop sign," Joy admitted. "And I've apologized a dozen times. I don't mean to be difficult here, but this just seems wrong to me. You're angry about something else entirely and we both know what that is."

"You're wrong. This has nothing to do with you and me. This is about my truck."

"Who do you think you're kidding?" she burst out. "You're angry because I'm a woman with opinions that didn't happen to agree with yours. You didn't want a relationship, you wanted someone to flatter your ego and I didn't fall into line the way other women have." She'd never met any of those women, but she'd certainly heard about them....

His eyes narrowed. "You're just a city girl. I'm surprised you stuck around this long. If you figure that arguing will convince me to forget what you did to my truck, you're dead wrong." He shook his head as if she'd insulted him.

Joy couldn't believe he was going to pursue this.

"You owe me for the damage to my vehicle," he insisted.

"You...you..." she sputtered at the unfairness of it all. "I'm not paying you a dime." If he wanted to be unreasonable, then she could be, too.

"Would you rather I had my insurance company contact yours?"

"Not really."

"Then I'd appreciate a check in the amount of two hundred and fifty dollars."

"That's practically blackmail!"

"Blackmail?" Lonny spat out the word as if it left a bad taste in his mouth. "I went to a lot of time and effort to get this estimate. I wanted to be as fair and amicable as possible and *this* is what I get?" He threw his arms up as if completely disgusted. "You're lucky I was willing to share the cost with you, which I didn't have to do."

"You think you're being *fair?*"

"Yes." He nodded. "I only want to be fair," he said in self-righteous tones.

Joy relaxed. "Then fifty dollars should do it."

Lonny's eyes widened. "Fifty dollars won't even begin to cover the damage."

"I don't see you rushing out for estimates on any of the other damage to your truck." She pointed at a couple of deep gouges on the driver's door. "And they had nothing to do with *me*."

"I admit I was responsible for those," he said. "I'll get around to taking care of them someday."

"Apparently *someday* has arrived and you're trying to rip me off."

They were almost nose to nose now and tall as he was, Joy didn't even flinch. This man was a Neanderthal, a knuckle-dragging throwback who didn't know the first thing about civility or common decency.

"Ms. Fuller? Uncle Lonny?"

The small voice of a child drifted through the fog of Joy's anger. To her horror, she'd been so upset, she'd forgotten all about Cricket.

"You're yelling," the little girl said, staring up at them. Her expression was one of uncertainty.

Joy immediately crouched down so she was level with the six-year-old. "Your uncle Lonny and I let our emotions get the better of us," she said and laughed as if it was all a joke.

Frowning, Cricket glanced from Joy to her uncle. "Uncle Lonny says when you aren't teaching school you shrink heads. When I asked Mommy about it, she said Uncle Lonny didn't mean that. You don't really shrink heads, do you?"

Lonny cleared his throat. "Ah, perhaps it's time we left, Cricket." He reached for the little girl's hand but Cricket resisted.

"Of course I don't shrink heads," Joy said, standing upright. Her irritation continued to simmer as she met Lonny's gaze. "Your uncle was only teasing."

"No, I wasn't," Lonny muttered under his breath.

Joy sighed. "*That* was mature."

"I don't care what you think of me. All I want from you is two hundred and fifty dollars to pay for the damage you did to my truck."

"My fifty-dollar offer stands anytime you're willing to accept it."

His fierce glare told her the offer was, and would remain, unacceptable.

"If you don't cooperate, I'll go to your insurance company," he warned.

If it came to that, then so be it. Surely a claims adjuster would agree with her. "You can threaten me all you want. Fifty dollars is my best offer—take it or leave it."

"I'll leave it." This was said emphatically, conviction behind each syllable.

Joy handed him back the written estimate. "That's perfectly fine by me. You can contact me when you're prepared to be reasonable."

"You think *I'm* the one who's being unreasonable?" he asked, sounding shocked and hurt.

She rolled her eyes. Lonny should've had a career as a B-movie actor, not a bull-rider or whatever he'd been. Bull *something*, anyway.

"As a matter of fact, I do," she said calmly.

Lonny had the audacity to scowl.

This man was the most outrageous human being she'd ever had the misfortune to meet. Remembering the child's presence, Joy bit her tongue in an effort to restrain herself from arguing further.

"You haven't heard the last of me," he threatened.

"Oh, say it isn't so," Joy murmured ever so sweetly. If she never saw Lonny Ellison again, it would be too soon.

Lonny whirled around and opened the door on the passenger side for his niece.

"Be careful not to scratch this priceless antique," Joy called out to the little girl.

After helping Cricket inside, Lonny closed the door. "Very funny," he said. "You won't be nearly as amused once your insurance people hear from mine."

Joy was no longer concerned about that. Her agent would take one look at Lonny Ellison's beaten-up vehicle and might, if the cowpoke was lucky, offer him fifty bucks.

Whatever happened, he wasn't getting a penny more out of her. She'd rather go to jail.

Chapter 3

"You've got a thing for Ms. Fuller, don't you?" Cricket asked as she sat beside Lonny in the cab of his truck. "That's what my mommy says."

Lonny made a noncommittal reply. If he announced his true feelings for the teacher, he'd singe his niece's ears. Joy was right about something, though. His anger was connected to their earlier relationship, if he could even call it that. The first few dates had gone well, and he'd felt encouraged. He'd been impressed with her intelligence and adventuresome spirit. For a time—more than once, actually—he'd even thought Joy might be the one. But it became apparent soon enough that she couldn't take a joke. That was when her uppity, know-it-all, schoolmarm side had come out. She seemed to think his ego was the problem. Not so! He was a kidder and she had no sense of humor. He'd been glad to end it right then and there.

His sister had tried to play the role of matchmaker after she returned to Red Springs and became friends with Joy. Lonny wasn't interested, since he'd had a private look into the real Joy Fuller, behind all her sweetness and charm.

"Mom says sometimes people who really like each other pretend they don't, 'cause they're afraid of their feelings," Cricket continued, sounding wise beyond her years. He could hear the echo of Letty's opinions in her daughter's words.

Leave it to a female to come up with a nonsensical notion like that.

"Do you like Ms. Fuller the way Mom said?" Cricket asked again.

Lonny shrugged. That was as much of a comment as he cared to make. He was well aware of his sister's opinions. Letty hoped to marry him off. He was thirty-five now, and the pool of eligible women in Red Springs was quickly evaporating. His romantic sister had set her sights on him and Joy, but as far as he was concerned, hell would freeze over first.

Lonny figured he'd had his share of women on the rodeo circuit and he had no desire for that kind of complication again. Most of those girlfriends had been what you'd call short-term— some of them *very* short-term. They'd treated him like a hero, which was gratifying, but he'd grown bored with their demands, and even their adulation had become tiresome after a while. Since he'd retired eight years earlier, he'd lived alone and frankly, that was how he liked it.

Just recently he'd hired Tom, a young man who'd drifted onto his ranch. That seemed to be working out all right. Tom had a room in the barn and kept mostly to himself. Lonny didn't want to pry into his business, but he had checked the boy's identification. To his relief, Tom was of age; still, he seemed young to be completely on his own. Lonny had talked to the local sheriff and learned that Tom wasn't wanted for any crimes. Lonny hoped that, given time, the boy would trust him enough to share what had prompted him to leave his family. For now, he was safer living and working with Lonny than making his own way in the world.

Despite his sister's claims, Lonny was convinced that bringing a woman into his life would cause nothing but trouble. First thing a wife would want to do was update his kitchen and the appliances. That stove had been around as long as he could remember—his mother had cooked on it   and he didn't see any need to buy another. Same with the refrigerator. Then, as soon as a wife had sweet-talked him into redoing the kitchen, sure as hell she'd insist on all new furniture. It wouldn't end there, either. He'd be forking out for paint and wallpaper and who knows what. After a few months he wouldn't even recognize his own house— or his bank account. No, sir, he couldn't afford a wife, not with the financial risk he and Chase were taking by raising their cattle without growth hormones.

A heifer took five years to reach twelve hundred pounds on the open range, eating a natural diet of grass. By contrast, commercial steers, who were routinely given hormones, reached that weight in eighteen to twenty months. That meant he and Chase were feeding and caring for a single head of beef nearly three years longer than the average cattleman. Penned cattle were corn-fed and given a diet that featured protein supplements. Lonny had seen some of those so-called supplements, and they included chicken feathers and rot like that. Furthermore, penned steers were on a regimen of antibiotics to protect them from the various diseases that ran rampant in such close quarters.

Yup, they were taking a risk, he and Chase, raising natural beef, and the truth was that Lonny was on a tight budget. But he could manage, living on his own, even with Tom's wages and the room and board he provided. Lonny was proud of their cattle-ranching venture; not only were they producing a higher quality beef, for which the market was growing, but their methods were far more humane.

Cricket sang softly to herself during the rest of the ride. Lonny pulled into the long dirt drive that led to Chase and Letty's place, leaving a plume of dust in his wake.

When he neared the house, he was mildly surprised to find Chase's truck parked outside the barn. His sister had phoned him a couple of days earlier and asked him to collect Cricket after school. Letty had an appointment with the heart specialist in Rock Springs, sixty miles west of Red Springs. Chase had insisted on driving her. Of course Lonny had agreed to pick up his niece.

Letty had undergone heart surgery a little less than a year ago. While the procedure had been a success, she required regular physicals. Lonny was happy to help in any way he could. He knew Letty was fine health-wise, and in just about every other way, too. In fact, he'd never seen his sister happier. Still, it didn't do any harm to have that confirmed by a physician.

As soon as he brought the truck to a stop, Cricket bounded out of the cab and raced off to look for her mother. Lonny climbed out more slowly and glanced around. He walked into the barn, where Chase was busy with his afternoon chores. For a while, he'd had an older ranch hand working with him, but Mel had retired in December. Now the two of them, Chase and Lonny, managed alone, with the addition of Tom's help.

"Cricket's with you?" Chase asked, looking up from the stall he was mucking out.

Lonny nodded. "Letty asked me to pick her up today."

Straightening, Chase leaned against the pitchfork and slid back the brim of his hat. "Why'd she do that?" he asked, frowning slightly. "The school bus would've dropped her off at your place. No need for you to go all the way into town."

"I had other business there," Lonny said, but he didn't explain that his real reason had to do with Joy Fuller and the money she owed him.

"Hey, Lonny," Letty called. Bright sunlight spilled into the barn as Letty swept open the door. Cricket stayed close to her mother's side. "I wondered if I'd find you here."

"I thought you might want your daughter back," he joked. "How'd the appointment go?"

"Just great." She raised her eyebrows. "Cricket tells me you got into another argument with Joy."

He frowned at his niece. He should've guessed she'd

run tattling to her mother. "The woman's being completely unreasonable. Personally, I don't know how you can get along with her."

"Really?" Letty exchanged a knowing look with her husband.

"Just a minute here!" Lonny waved his finger at them. "None of that."

"None of what?" His sister was the picture of innocence.

"You know very well what I mean. You've got this sliver up your fingernail about me being attracted to your friend, and how she'd be the perfect wife."

"As I've said before, you protest too much." Letty seemed hard put to keep from rubbing her hands together in satisfaction. His sister was in love and it only made sense, he supposed, for her to see Cupid at work between him and Joy. Only it wasn't happening. He didn't even like the woman. And she didn't like him.

Not that there was any point in saying another word. Arguing with his sister was like asking an angry bronc not to throw you. No matter what Lonny said or did, it wouldn't change Letty's mind. Despite his brief and ill-fated romance with Joy, something—he couldn't imagine what—had convinced his softhearted little sister that he was head-over-heels crazy about *Ms*. Fuller.

"What did you say to her this time?" Letty demanded.

"Me?"

"Yes, you!" She propped her hands on her hips, and judging by her stern look, there'd be no escaping the wrath of Letty. The fact that Joy had managed to turn his own sister against him was testament to the evil power she possessed.

"If you must know, I took her the estimate for the damage she did to my truck."

"You're kidding!" Letty cried. "You actually got an estimate?"

"Damn straight I did." Okay, so maybe he was carrying this a bit far, but someone needed to teach the woman a lesson, and that someone might as well be him.

"But your truck…"

Lonny already knew what she was going to say. It was the same argument Joy had given him. "Yes, there are plenty of other dents on the bumper—including the *previous* one she caused. All I'm asking is that she make restitution for the *second* one. I don't understand why everyone wants to argue about this. She caused the dent. The least she can do is pay to have it fixed."

"Lonny, you've got to be joking."

He wasn't. "What about assuming personal responsibility? You'd think a woman teaching our children would *want* to make restitution." According to Letty, the entire community thought the sun rose and set on Ms. Fuller. Not him, though. He'd seen the woman behind those deceptive smiles.

"What did Joy have to say to that?" Chase asked, and his mouth twitched in a smile he couldn't quite hide.

Lonny resisted the urge to ask his brother-in-law what he found so darned amusing. "She made me an insulting offer of fifty dollars. The woman's nuts if she thinks I'll accept that."

Letty uttered a rather unfeminine-sounding snort. "I can't say I blame her."

"What about my truck? What about me? That woman's carelessness nearly gave me a heart attack!"

"You said she apologized."

Granted, after the accident, Joy had been all sweet and apologetic. However, it didn't take long for her dark side to show, just like it had a year ago.

Since everyone was taking sides with Joy, Lonny considered dropping the entire matter. Or he considered it for a moment, anyway... When he presented Joy with the bill, he'd hoped she'd take all the blame and tell him how sorry she was...and sound as if she meant it. At that point, he would've felt good about absolving her and being magnanimous. He'd figured they could talk like adults, maybe meet for a friendly drink—see what happened from there.

That, however, wasn't how things had gone. Joy had exploded. His impetuous little fantasy shriveled up even more quickly than it had appeared, to be replaced by an anger that matched hers.

"What are you planning to do now?" Letty asked, checking her watch.

Lonny looked to his brother-in-law and best friend for help, but Chase was staying out of this one. There was a time Chase would've leaped to Lonny's defense. Not now; marriage had changed him. "I don't know yet. I was thinking I should file a claim with her insurance company." He didn't actually plan to do that, but the threat sounded real and he'd let Letty believe he just might.

"Don't even think about it," his sister snapped.

He shrugged, afraid now that he was digging himself into a hole. But pride demanded he not back down.

"One look at your truck and I'm afraid the adjuster would laugh," Chase told him.

That hole was getting deeper by the minute.

Shaking her head, Letty sighed. "I'd better call Joy and see if she's okay."

Lonny stared at her. "Why wouldn't she be okay?"

Letty patted his shoulder. "Sometimes you don't know how intimidating you can be, big brother."

As Lonny stood there scratching his head, wondering how everything had gotten so confused, Letty walked out of the barn.

Utterly baffled, Lonny muttered, "Did I hear her right? Is she actually going to phone Joy? Isn't that like consorting with the enemy? What about family loyalty, one for all and all for one, that kind of stuff?"

Chase seemed about to answer when Letty turned back. "Do you want to stay for dinner?" she asked.

Invitations on days other than Sunday were rare, and Lonny had no intention of turning one down. He might be upset with his sister but he wasn't stupid. Letty was a mighty fine cook. "Sure."

A half hour or so later, Lonny accompanied his brother-in-law to the house. After washing up, Chase brought out two cans of cold beer. Then, just as they had on so many other evenings, the two of them sat on the porch, enjoying the cool breeze.

"The doc said Letty's going to be all right?" Lonny asked his friend.

Chase took a deep swallow of beer. "According to him, Letty's as good as new."

That was what Lonny had guessed. His sister had come home after almost ten years without telling him why. Her heart was in bad shape, and she'd needed an expensive surgery, one she couldn't afford. She'd trusted Lonny to raise Cricket for her if she died. Cricket's father had abandoned Letty before the little girl was even born. Letty hadn't told Lonny any more than that, and he'd never asked. Thankfully she'd had the surgery, for which Chase had secretly paid, and it'd been successful. She'd been married to him since last summer. Even for a guy as cynical about marriage as Lonny, it was easy to see how much she and Chase loved each other. Cricket had settled down, too. For the first time in her life, the little girl had a father and a family. Lonny was delighted with the way everything had turned out for his sister and his best friend.

"You like married life, don't you?" he asked. Although he knew the answer, he asked the question anyway. Lonny couldn't think of another man who'd be completely honest with him.

Chase looked into the distance and nodded.

"Why?"

Chase smiled. "Well, marriage definitely has its good points."

"Sex?"

"I'm not about to discount that," his friend assured him, his smile widening. "But there's more to marriage than crawling into bed with a warm body."

"Such as?"

Chase didn't take offense at the question, the way another guy might have. "I hadn't realized how lonely it was around this place since my dad died," Chase said.

His expression was sober and thoughtful as he stared out at the ranch that had been in his family for four generations. "Letty and Cricket have given me purpose. I have a reason to get out of bed in the morning—a reason other than chores. That's the best I can explain it."

Lonny leaned back and rested his elbows on the step. He considered what his friend had said and, frankly, he didn't see it. "I like my life the way it is."

Chase nodded. "Before Letty returned, I thought the same thing."

At least *one* person understood his feelings.

"Is it okay if I join you?" Letty asked from behind the screen door before moving on to the porch. She held a glass of lemonade.

"Sure, go ahead," Lonny said agreeably.

His sister sat on the step beside Chase, who slid his arm around her shoulders. She pressed her head against him, then glanced at Lonny.

"Did you phone her?" he muttered. It probably wasn't a good idea to even ask, but he had to admit he was curious.

"I will later," Letty said. "I was afraid if I called her now, she might be too distressed to talk."

"I'm the one who's distressed," he muttered, not that anyone had asked about *his* feelings.

Letty ignored the comment. "You've really got a thing for her, don't you?"

"No, I don't." Dammit, he wished his sister would stop saying that. Even his niece was parroting her words. Lonny didn't want to argue with Letty, but the fact was, he knew his own feelings. "I can guess what you're thinking and I'm here to tell you, you're wrong."

"You seem to talk about her quite a bit," she said archly.

No argument there. "Now, listen, I want you to give me your solemn word that you won't do anything stupid."

"Like what?" Letty asked.

"Like try to get me and Joy together again. I told you before, I'm not interested and I mean it."

"You know, big brother, I might've believed you earlier, but I don't anymore."

Not knowing what to say, Lonny just shook his head. "I want your word, Letty. I'm serious about this."

"Your brother doesn't need your help." Chase kissed the top of her head.

"He's right," Lonny said.

"But—"

"I don't need a woman in my life."

"You're lonely."

"I've got plenty of friends, plus you guys practically next door," he told her. "Besides, Tom's around."

At this reminder of the teenage boy living at the ranch, Letty asked, "How's that going?"

Lonny shrugged. "All right, I guess." He liked the kid, who was skinny as a beanpole and friendly but still reserved. "He's a hard worker."

Letty reached for Chase's hand. "It was good of you to give him a job."

Lonny didn't think of it that way. "I was looking for seasonal help. He showed up at the right time." When Lonny found him in the barn, Tom had offered to work in exchange for breakfast. The kid must've been half-starved, because he gobbled down six eggs, half a pound of bacon and five or six slices of toast, along with several cups of coffee. In between bites, he brushed off Lonny's questions about his history and hometown. When Lonny mentioned that he and Chase were hoping to hire a ranch hand for the season, Tom's eyes had brightened and he'd asked to apply for the job.

"I'm worried about you," his sister lamented, refusing to drop the subject. "You do need someone."

"I do not."

Letty studied him for a long moment, then finally acquiesced. "Okay, big brother, you're on your own."

And that was exactly how Lonny wanted it.

Chapter 4

Tom Meyerson finished the last of his nightly chores and headed for his room in the barn. Stumbling onto this job was the best thing that'd happened to him in years. He'd been bone-weary and desperate when Lonny Ellison found him sleeping in his barn. That day, three months ago now, he'd walked twenty or twenty-five miles, and all he'd had to eat was an apple and half a candy bar. By the time he saw the barn far off in the distance, he'd been thirsty, hungry and so exhausted he could barely put one foot in front of the other. He didn't think he'd make it to the next town by nightfall, so he'd hidden in the barn and fallen instantly asleep.

Life had been hell since his mother died. The doctor had said she had a weak heart, and Tom knew why: his dad had broken it years before. His father was a no-good drunk. There'd been nothing positive in Tom's life except his mother. Fortunately, he was an only child, so at least there wasn't a younger brother or sister to worry about. Shortly after he graduated from high school last spring, nearly a year ago, it became apparent that his father's sole interest in him was as a source of beer money. He'd stolen every penny Tom had tried to save.

The last time his money had mysteriously disappeared, Tom had confronted his father. They'd had a vicious argument and his old man had kicked him out of the house. At first Tom didn't know what to do, but then he'd realized this was probably for the best. He collected what was due him from the hardware store where he worked part-time and, with a little less than fifty dollars in his pocket, started his new life. He'd spent twenty of those dollars on a bus ticket to the town of Red Springs, then walked from there. All Tom wanted was to get away from Thompson, Wyoming, as far and fast as he could. It wasn't like his father would be looking for him.

Life on the road was hard. He'd hitchhiked when he could, but there'd been few vehicles on the routes he'd traveled. Most of the time he'd hoofed it. He must have walked a hundred miles or more, and no matter what happened, he never wanted to go back.

When Lonny Ellison discovered him, Tom was sure the rancher would file trespassing charges. Instead, Lonny had given him a job, a room and three square meals a day, which was more than he'd had since his mother's death.

The phone in the barn rang, and Tom leaped out of his bunk where he'd been reading yesterday's paper and hurried to answer it. Lonny wasn't back from town yet, because his truck wasn't parked out front.

He lifted the receiver and offered a tentative "Hello."

A short silence followed. "Tom?"

Tom's heart began to pound. It was Michelle, a girl he'd met at the feed store soon after he'd started working for Lonny. Like him, she was shy and although they hadn't said more than a few words to each other, he enjoyed seeing her. Whenever he went to the store with Lonny, she made an excuse to come out of the office and hang around outside.

"Hi." Tom couldn't help being excited that she'd phoned.

"You didn't come in this afternoon," Michelle said, sounding disappointed.

Tom had looked forward to seeing her all week, only to be thwarted. "Lonny decided to drive into town by himself." Tom had searched for an excuse to join him, but none had presented itself, so he'd stayed on the ranch. He liked the work, although he'd never lived on a ranch before, and Lonny and Chase were teaching him a lot.

His afternoon had been spent repairing breaks in the fencing along the road. The whole time he was doing that, he was thinking about Michelle and how pretty she was.

"I wondered," Michelle whispered, then hesitated as if there was more she wanted to tell him.

Her father owned Larson's Feed, and she helped out after school. The last time he was in town, he'd casually mentioned that he'd be back on Tuesday and hoped to see her then. He wanted to ask her out on a date but didn't have any way of getting into Red Springs without borrowing Lonny's truck and he was reluctant to ask. Lonny had already done plenty for him, and it didn't seem right to take advantage of his generosity.

"Lonny had to pick up his niece after school," Tom added.

"Oh."

Michelle didn't appear to be much of a conversationalist, which could be a problem because he wasn't, either.

"I was hoping, you know..." She let the rest fade. Then, all at once, she blurted out, "There's a dance the last day of school. It's a pretty big deal. The whole town throws a festival and the high school has this big dance and I was wondering if you'd go with me."

She said it all so fast, she couldn't possibly have taken a breath. After she finished speaking, it took Tom a few seconds to realize what she'd asked him. He felt an immediate surge of regret.

The silence seemed endless as he struggled with what to tell her. In the end, he told the simple truth. "I can't."

"Why not?"

Tom didn't want to get into that. "I just...can't." He hated to disappoint her, but there was nothing more he could say.

"I shouldn't have asked... I wouldn't have, but— Oh, never mind. I'm sorry...." With that, she hung up as if she couldn't get off the line fast enough.

Tom felt wretched. He didn't have the clothes he'd need for a dance; in fact, he'd never attended a dance in his life, even in high school. Those kinds of social events were for other kids. He was sorry to refuse Michelle, sorrier than she'd ever know, but there wasn't any alternative.

As he returned to his room, Tom lay back on the hard mattress and tucked his hands behind his head, staring up at the ceiling. It would've been nice, that school dance with Michelle. All they'd done so far was talk a few times. The thought of holding her in his arms imbued him with a sense of joy—a joy that was new and unfamiliar to him.

Tom gave himself a mental shake. He might as well forget about the dance right then and there, because it wasn't going to happen.

Just back from school, Joy was still furious over her confrontation with Lonny Ellison. The man had his nerve. In an effort to forget that unfortunate episode, Joy tried to grade the spelling-test papers, but she soon discovered she couldn't concentrate. The only thing she seemed able to do with all this pent-up anger was pace her living room until she'd practically worn a pattern in the carpet.

When the phone rang, Joy nearly jumped out of her skin. Her heart still hadn't stopped hammering when she picked up the portable telephone on the kitchen counter.

"Joy, it's Letty. Lonny dropped Cricket off and he's beside himself. What happened?"

"Your brother," Joy answered from between gritted teeth, "is the most egotistical, unpleasant, arrogant man I've ever met." Then she proceeded to describe the entire scene in the schoolyard, which was burned in her memory.

"You mean to say you didn't *really* come after him with a pitchfork?" Letty asked.

"Is that what he said?" Joy asked. She wouldn't put it past Lonny to fabricate such a ridiculous story.

"No, no, I was just teasing," Letty assured her. "But I will say his version of events is only vaguely similar to yours."

"He's exaggerating, of course."

"I'm sorry," Letty said, sounding genuinely contrite. "My guess is Lonny's still attracted to you and isn't sure how to deal with it. What went wrong with you two, anyway?"

"I don't know, and furthermore, I don't care." That wasn't completely true. She did care and, despite her annoyance at his current attitude, wished the situation between them was different.

Letty hesitated briefly before she continued. "I have no idea how else to explain my brother's behavior. All I can tell you is that this isn't like Lonny."

"In other words, it's me he dislikes," she said starkly.

"No," Letty said. "Just the opposite. I think this is his nutty way of getting back together with you. Like I said, he's attracted to you. There's no question in my mind about that."

Her ego would like to believe it, but she'd seen the look in Lonny's eyes and it wasn't admiration or attraction.

"Lonny can be a little stubborn but—"

"A little?" Joy broke in. "A *little?*"

"I apologize on his behalf," Letty said. "I'm hoping

you'll be able to look past his perverse behavior and recognize the reason for it. Be gentle with him, okay? I'm fairly certain my brother is smitten."

"He's *what?*"

"Smitten," Letty repeated. "It's an old-fashioned word, one my mother would've used. It means—well, you know what it means. The sad part is, Lonny isn't smart enough to figure this out."

"Then I hope he never does, because any spark of interest I might've felt toward him is dead. No one's ever made me so mad!" Joy felt her anger regain momentum and crowd out her other feelings for Lonny.

"You're *sure* you're not interested in my brother?"

"Positive. I don't want to see him again as long as I live. Every time I do, my blood pressure rises until I feel like my head's going to explode. I've never met a more irritating man in my life."

Letty's regretful sigh drifted through the phone line. "I was afraid of that."

They spoke for a few more minutes and then Joy replaced the receiver. She felt better after talking to Letty—only she wasn't sure why. Maybe venting her aggression with someone who understood both her and Lonny had helped. It would be nice, flattering really, if all this craziness was indeed related to Lonny's overpowering attraction, as Letty seemed to think, but Joy doubted it.

She hadn't been on a date in so long that she was actually considering one of those online dating services. School would be out in a couple of weeks; this summer, when she had some free time, Joy planned to develop a social life. She didn't have a strategy yet, beyond the vague possibilities offered by the internet, nor did she have much romantic experience. Her only serious romance had been with Josh Howell in her last year of college. Their relationship was relegated to casual-friends status after she'd accepted the teaching job in Wyoming. They'd kept in touch, usually by email. Since she'd moved away, he'd been involved in an increasingly serious relationship. She hadn't heard from him in more than two months, and Joy surmised that his current girlfriend was soon to become his wife.

Josh lived in Seattle, where he worked for an investment firm. He went on—in detail—about the woman he was seeing every time he emailed her. Lori Something-or-Other was apparently blonde, beautiful and a power to be reckoned with in the investment industry. Or maybe it was insurance… In any case, Joy sometimes wondered why he kept in touch with her at all when he was so enamored of someone else.

She microwaved a frozen entrée for dinner, ate while watching the national news, corrected her spelling papers and then logged on to the internet. She immediately noticed Josh's email. How ironic that she'd get this message when she'd just been thinking about him!

From: Josh Howell
Sent: May 16
To: Joy Fuller
Subject: I'm going to be in your area!
Hi, Joy,
We haven't exchanged emails in a while, and I was wondering what you've been up to lately. The company's sending me on a business trip to Salt Lake City, which

I'm combining with a few vacation days. When I looked
at the map, I noticed that Red Springs isn't too far away.
I'd love to stop by and catch up with you. After the
conference, I'll rent a car, and I should be in your area
the first or second of June. Would that work for you?
Look forward to hearing from you! I've missed your
emails.
Love,
Josh
P.S. Did I mention that Lori and I broke up?

With her hand pressed to her mouth to contain her
surprise and happiness, Joy read the email twice. Josh
wasn't seeing Lori anymore! Interesting that he'd mentioned it in a postscript, as if he'd almost forgotten the
fact. This made her wonder. Had she misinterpreted
the extent of his feelings for the other woman? Did he
still see Joy as more than just a friend? Was he suggest-
ing they might want to pick up the relationship where
they'd left off? She was certainly open to the possibility. Josh was a man who knew how to treat a woman.
He could teach Lonny Ellison a thing or two.

Another interesting fact—Josh had said he'd be in
the area, but Red Springs was a little out of his way.
Like about two hundred miles… Not that she was com-
plaining. What she suspected, what she wanted to believe, was that he'd go a *lot* out of his way in order to
see her.

Joy quickly emailed Josh back. In the space of a
single evening, her emotions had veered from fury to
eager anticipation. Earlier she'd had to resist the urge to
burst into tears, and now she was bubbling with delight.

Just before hitting Send, Joy paused. Maybe she should phone Josh instead. It wouldn't hurt. Calling him meant he'd know without a doubt how pleased she was to hear from him.

She hesitated, suddenly worried that she might seem too eager. But she was. In fact, she was thrilled....

Her mind made up, she reached for the phone. If he didn't answer, she could always send the email she'd already composed. Receiver in hand, Joy realized she no longer remembered his number. She'd written it down, but had no idea exactly where. Still, she found it easily enough, at the very back of her personal phone directory. In pencil, which implied that she'd expected to erase it....

Josh answered right away.

"Josh, it's Joy. I just opened your email."

"Joy!" She could hear the smile in his voice.

"I'd love it if you came to Red Springs, but I need to warn you we're in the middle of nowhere. Well, not really... There *are* other towns, but they're few and far between." She was chattering, but it felt so good to talk to him. "One of my teaching friends said we may not be at the end of the world, but you can see it from here."

Josh responded with a husky laugh. "How are you?"

"Great, just great." Especially now that she'd heard from him.

"Do those dates work for you?" he asked.

Joy had been so excited, she hadn't even checked the calendar. A glance at the one on her desk showed her that June first fell on a Thursday and the second...

"June second is the last day of school," she told him, her hopes deflating.

"That's fine. I'll take you out to dinner and we can celebrate."

"There's a problem. On the evening of the last day, we have a carnival. The whole town shows up. It's sort of a big deal, and this year they've even managed to get a real carnival company to set up rides. Everyone's looking forward to it."

"So we'll attend the carnival."

That sounded good, except for one thing. "I'm working the cotton candy machine." She'd taken that task the year before, too. While it'd been fun, she'd worn as much of the sugary pink sweetness as she'd managed to get onto the paper tubes.

"Not to worry, I'll find something to occupy myself while you're busy. If the school needs another volunteer, sign me up. I'm game for just about anything."

"You'd do that?" This was better than Joy would have dreamed. "Thanks! Oh, Josh, I can't tell you how glad I am to hear from you."

"I feel the same way."

"I'm sorry about you and Lori," she said, carefully broaching the subject.

His hesitation was only slight; still, Joy noticed. "Yeah," he said. "Too bad it didn't work out."

He didn't supply any details and Joy didn't feel it would be right to question him. Later, when they were able to meet and talk face-to-face, he'd probably be more comfortable discussing the circumstances of their parting.

"How's life in cowboy town?" Josh asked, changing the subject. When she'd been offered the teaching position, he'd discouraged her from accepting it. Josh had told her she shouldn't take the first job offered. He was convinced that if she waited, there'd be an opening in the Seattle area. He couldn't understand why Joy had wanted to get away from the big city and live in a small town.

The truth was, she loved her job and Red Springs. This was the second year of a two-year contract and, so far, she'd enjoyed every minute. That didn't mean, however, that she wouldn't be willing to move if the opportunity arose—such as renewing a promising relationship, with the hope of a marriage proposal in the not-so-distant future.

"They seem to grow cowboys by the bushel here," she said with a laugh. "Most of the kids are comfortable in the saddle by the time they're in kindergarten. I like Red Springs, but I'm sure that to outsiders, the town isn't too impressive. There are a couple of nice restaurants, the Mexican Fiesta and Uncle Dave's Café, but that's about it."

He murmured a noncommittal response.

"The town seemed rather bleak when I first arrived." She didn't mention the disappointing relationship with Lonny Ellison—then or now. "That didn't last long, though. It's the people here who are so wonderful." With one exception, she mused. "We've got a motel— I'll make you a reservation—a couple of bars, a great church, a theater and—"

"Do you still play the church organ?"

"I do." She was surprised he'd remembered that.

"Anything else I should know about Red Springs?"

"Not really. I'll be happy to give you the grand tour." The offer was sincere. She'd love showing off the town and introducing him to the friends she'd made. "Maybe we can visit a real working ranch—my friend Letty's, for example. We could even do that on horseback."

"Don't tell me you're riding horses yourself?"

"I have," she answered, smiling. "But I don't make a habit of it." Getting onto the back of a horse had been daunting the first time, but Joy discovered she rather enjoyed it. Well…she didn't hate it. Her muscles had been sore afterward and she hadn't felt the urge to try it again for quite a while. She'd gone out riding with friends three times in the last nine months, and that was enough for her.

"I don't suppose any of those cowpokes have caught your interest," Josh said casually.

Lonny Ellison flashed across her mind. She squeezed her eyes shut, unnerved by the vividness of his image.

"So there *is* someone else," Josh said when she didn't immediately respond.

"No." She nearly swallowed her tongue in her eagerness to deny it. "Not at all."

"Good," Josh said. It seemed he'd decided to accept her denial at face value, much to Joy's relief. She *wasn't* interested in Lonny Ellison, so she hadn't lied. Annoyed by him, yes. Interested? No, no, no! "I'll be in touch again soon," he was saying.

"I'll see you in a couple of weeks." Joy could hardly wait.

Chapter 5

Saturday morning, Lonny woke in a surprisingly good mood. For some reason, he'd dreamed about Joy Fuller, although it'd been several days since he'd run into her. He was reluctant to admit it, but he hadn't been nearly as annoyed by their confrontation as he'd let her believe.

He frowned at the thought. Could it be that Letty was right and he was still attracted to Joy? Nah. Still, the possibility stayed in his mind. One thing was certain; he'd felt invigorated by their verbal exchanges and he seemed to think of her all too frequently.

He poured his first cup of coffee and stepped outside, taking a moment to appreciate the early-morning sunlight that greeted him. A rooster's crowing accentuated the feeling of peace and contentment. This was his world, the only place he wanted to be.

The one thing that troubled him on what should've

been a perfect spring day was the way Joy Fuller lingered in his mind. He couldn't stop remembering how pretty she was and how animated she got when she was all riled up. He shouldn't be thinking about her at all, though. He had chores to do, places to be and, most importantly, cattle to worm. But with Tom's help, they'd make fast work of it. Chase had already done some of the herd the day before.

It was unfortunate that he and Joy had gotten off on the wrong foot, he thought as he scattered grain for the chickens. He discovered a dozen eggs waiting for him, and that made him smile.

But he was irritated when he found himself continuing to smile—smiling for no real reason. Well, there *was* a reason and her name was Joy Fuller and that was even worse. He was a little unnerved by his own amusement at the way she'd reacted to his outrageous comments. He'd never had any intention of contacting his insurance company or hers, and in the light of day, he realized how irrational he'd sounded. But even if *he* knew he wasn't following through with that threat, she didn't.

He almost laughed out loud at the image of her sputtering and gesticulating the day of their accident. Okay, *incident.* She wasn't likely to forgive him for making such a fuss over that fender-bender.

He collected the eggs and returned to the house. With an efficiency born of long practice, he scrambled half a dozen eggs, fried bacon and made toast. In the middle of his domestic efforts, Tom came in. They sat down to breakfast, exchanging a few words as they listened to the radio news, then headed out.

The morning sped by, and they finished the worming by eleven o'clock. Lonny drove into Red Springs to do errands; normally Tom liked to join him, but he'd been keeping to himself lately. During the past few days, he'd seemed more reserved than usual. Whatever the problem, the boy chose not to divulge it, which was fine. If and when he wanted to talk, Lonny was willing to listen.

Tom didn't have much to say at the best of times. The kid put in a good day's work, and that was all Lonny could expect. If Tom preferred to stay at the ranch, that was his business. Come to think of it, though, Tom had been mighty eager to get into town every chance he got—until recently. Lonny suspected Michelle Larson at the feed store had something to do with that. He couldn't help wondering what was going on there. It was probably as obvious as it seemed—a boy-girl thing. In that case, considering his own relationship difficulties, he wouldn't have much advice to offer.

As he drove toward town, Lonny turned the radio up as loud as he could stand it, listening to Johnny and Willie and Garth, even singing along now and then. As he approached the intersection at Grove and Logan, he remembered reading in the *Red Springs Journal* that the new stop sign had caused a couple of accidents in the past week. Real accidents, too, not just minor collisions. If this continued, the town was likely to order a traffic light. There was already one on Main Street, and in his opinion, one light was enough.

The first of his errands took him to the feed store. Lonny backed his pickup to the loading dock and tossed in a fifty-pound sack of chicken feed. The owner's daughter hurried out as soon as he pulled into the lot. When Michelle saw that he was alone, her face fell and she wandered back into the store.

Lonny paid for his purchase and stayed to have a cup of coffee with Charley Larson. They talked about the same things they always discussed. The weather, followed by the low price of cattle and the prospects for naturally raised beef. Then they rounded off their conversation with a few comments about the upcoming community carnival.

Lonny wasn't really surprised when Charley asked him, "What do you know about that hand you hired?"

"Tom?" Lonny said with a shrug. "Not much. He's of age, if that's what you're wondering. I checked, and as far as I can see, he's not in any trouble. He keeps to himself and he's a hard worker. What makes you ask?" Although Lonny could guess.

Charley glanced over his shoulder toward the store. "My Michelle likes him."

"That bother you?"

"Not in the least," Charley muttered. "I think Michelle might've asked him to the school dance. He seems to have turned her down."

So *that* was the reason Tom was so gloomy these days. Lonny couldn't imagine why he'd said no to Michelle when he was so obviously taken with the girl. Apparently his hired hand was as inept at relationships as Lonny was himself. Granted, he'd never had difficulties during his rodeo days, but Joy Fuller was a different proposition altogether. "I'll ask Tom about it and get back to you."

Charley hesitated. "If you do, be subtle about it, okay? Otherwise, Michelle will get upset with me."

"I will," Lonny promised, considering his options.

There was the school carnival, for starters. Lonny figured he'd go around suppertime—and while he was at it, he'd bring Tom. The dance was later that night, so if Tom was already in town, he'd have no excuse not to attend. These events weren't for another two weeks, but his sister had roped him into volunteering for the cleanup committee, which meant he'd be picking up trash and sweeping the street. She'd said something about him frying burgers with Chase, too. There was no point in arguing with her. Besides, he enjoyed the festivities.

Last year Joy had been working the cotton candy machine. He'd hoped to have a conversation with her, but he hadn't done it. For one thing, she'd been constantly busy, chatting with a crowd of people who all seemed to like her and have lots to say. For another, he'd felt uncharacteristically tongue-tied around her. He sure didn't want a bunch of interested onlookers witnessing his stumbling, fumbling attempts at conversation.

When he'd finished talking to Charley and climbed into the cab of his pickup, Lonny noticed a flash of green outside the town's biggest grocery store, situated across the street.

Lonny's eyes locked on Joy Fuller's green PT Cruiser. She pulled into the lot, parked and headed into the store.

Groceries were on Lonny's list of errands. Nothing much, just the basics. Unexpectedly, the happy feeling he'd experienced while driving into town with the radio blasting came over him again. A carefree, what-the-hell feeling...

Lonny parked and jumped out of his pickup. His steps were light as he entered the store and grabbed a cart. His first stop was the vegetable aisle. It was too soon to expect much produce from Letty's garden. Last year, she'd seen to it that he got healthy portions of lettuce, green beans, fresh peas and zucchini. He was counting on her to do the same this summer. Until then, he had no choice but to buy a few vegetables himself.

Glancing around, he was disappointed not to see Joy. He tossed a bag of carrots in his cart, then threw in some lettuce and made his way to the meat department. She wasn't there. So he wheeled his cart to the back of the store, to the dairy case. He'd heard that a lot of women ate yogurt. But Joy wasn't in that section, either.

Then he heard her laugh.

Lonny smiled. The sound came from somewhere in the middle of the store. Turning his cart around, he trotted toward the frozen food. He should've known that was where he'd find her.

Here was proof that, unlike Letty, who cooked for her family, Joy didn't take much time to prepare meals. Neither did he, come to think of it—breakfast was his one and only specialty—which was why dinner invitations from Letty were appreciated. Tom and Lonny mostly fended for themselves. A can of soup or chili, a sandwich or two, was about as fancy as either of them got.

Sure enough, the instant Lonny turned into the aisle, he saw Joy. Her back was to him, and the three Wilson kids were chatting with her, along with their mom, Della. Lonny had gone to school with Della Harrison; she'd married Bobby Wilson, a friend of his, and had three kids in quick succession. Lonny didn't know whether to envy Bobby and Della or pity them.

He strolled up to the two women. "Hi, Della," he said, trying to seem casual and nonchalant. He nodded politely in Joy's direction and touched the brim of his Stetson.

The smile faded from Joy's face. "Mr. Ellison," she returned primly.

Lonny had trouble keeping his eyes off Joy. He had to admit she looked mighty fine in a pair of jeans. Both women gazed at him expectantly, and he didn't have a clue what to say next. Judging by her expression, Joy would rather be just about anywhere else at that moment.

"Good to run into you, Lonny," Della said pleasantly. "Bobby was saying the other day that we don't see near enough of you."

"Yeah, we'll get together soon." Lonny manufactured an anxious frown. "But I've been having problems with my truck. I had an accident recently and, well, it hasn't run the same since."

"Really?" Della asked.

"That's right," he said, wondering if he'd overdone the facade of wounded innocence.

"Ms. Fuller is my teacher," a sweet little girl announced proudly.

Della was looking suspiciously from him to Joy. Lonny decided that was his cue to move on, and he would have, except that he made the mistake of glancing into Joy's grocery cart. It was just as he'd expected—frozen entrées. Only she'd picked the diet ones. She didn't need to be on any diet. In fact, her figure was about as perfect as a woman's could get. No wonder she'd snapped at him and been so irritable. The woman was starving herself.

"That's what you intend to eat this week?" he asked, reaching for one of the entrées. He felt suddenly hopeful. If she was hungry, the way he suspected, then she might accept an invitation to dinner. They could talk everything out over enchiladas and maybe a Corona or two at the Mexican Fiesta. Everything always seemed better on a full stomach.

"What's wrong with that?" she demanded, yanking the frozen entrée out of his hand and tossing it back in her cart.

"You shouldn't be on a diet," he insisted. "If that's what you're having for dinner, it's no wonder you're so skinny—or so mad."

"Lonny," Della gasped.

Oh, boy, he'd done it again. That comment hadn't come out quite as he'd intended. "I—you… I—" He tried to backtrack, but all he could manage was a bad imitation of a trout. As usual, his mouth had operated independently of his brain.

He turned to Della, but she glared at him with the same intensity as Joy. Instinct told him to hightail it out of the store before he made the situation worse than it already was.

"I didn't mean that like it sounded," he muttered. "You look fine for being underweight." Again he glanced at Della for help, but none was forthcoming.

"You're a little on the thin side, that's all. Not much, of course. In fact, you're just about right."

"It's a male problem," Della said, speaking to Joy. She scowled. "They don't know when to keep their mouths shut."

"Uh, it was nice seeing you both," he said. He'd thought he was complimenting her, but to his utter astonishment, Joy's eyes had filled with tears.

Lonny's gut twisted. He couldn't imagine what he'd said that was bad enough to make her cry. "Joy, I..."

Della looked at him with open contempt. He swallowed, not knowing how to fix this mess. He was aghast as Joy abruptly left the aisle, her grocery cart rattling.

"See what you've done?" Della hissed at him under her breath. "You idiot."

"What's wrong with Ms. Fuller?" the little girl asked. "What did that man do?" She focused her blue eyes on him and had he been a lesser man, Lonny would've backed off. If looks could kill, his sister would be planning his burial service about now.

"I—I didn't mean anything," Lonny stammered, feeling as low as a man could get.

"You're hopeless," Della said, shaking her head.

The girl shook her head, too, eyes narrowed.

"I...I—"

"The least you can do is apologize." Della's fingers gripped the cart handle.

"I tried." He motioned helplessly.

"You didn't try hard enough." With that Della sped away, her children in tow. The little girl marched to the end of the aisle, then turned back and stuck her tongue out at him.

A sick feeling attacked the pit of his stomach. He should've known better. He'd decided not to pursue a relationship with Joy and then, next thing he knew, he was trying to invite her for dinner. He couldn't even do *that* without making a mess of it.

He felt dreadful, worse than dreadful. He'd actually made Joy cry, but God's honest truth, he couldn't believe a little comment like that was worthy of tears.

He walked up to the front of the store only to see Joy dash out, carrying two grocery bags. Abandoning his cart, he hurried after her.

"Joy," he called, sprinting into the parking lot.

At the sound of his voice she whirled around and confronted him. "In case you hadn't already guessed, I'm not interested in speaking to you."

"I—ah…" In his entire life, Lonny had never backed down from a confrontation. Served him right that the first time it happened would be with a woman.

"You were trying to embarrass me. Trying to make me feel stupid."

"I…I—" For some reason, he couldn't make his tongue form the words in his brain.

"You poked fun at me, called me skinny. Well, maybe I am, but—"

"You aren't," he cried. "I just said that because…because it didn't look like you were eating enough and I thought maybe I could feed you."

"Feed me?"

"Dinner."

"Just leave me alone!" Joy left him and bolted for her car.

Lonny exhaled sharply. Following her was probably a bad idea—another in a long list of them. He would've preferred to simply go home, but he couldn't make himself do it. Unable to come up with any alternative, Lonny jogged after her. He wouldn't sleep tonight if he didn't tell her how sorry he was.

He knew she'd heard his footsteps, because the instant she set the groceries in the Cruiser's trunk, she whirled around. They were practically nose to nose. "I don't need you to feed me or talk to me or anything else," she said. "All I want you to do is *leave me alone.*"

"I will, only you have to listen to me first." Darn, this was hard. "I didn't mean to suggest you were unattractive, because you are."

"Unattractive?" she cried. "I'm *unattractive?* This is supposed to be an apology? Is that why you decided not to see me two years ago? You thought I was too skinny?"

"No, no, I meant you're attractive." Could this possibly get any worse? "Anyway, that has nothing to do with now. Can't you just accept my apology? Are you always this hotheaded?"

Eyes glistening, she turned and slammed the trunk lid. The noise reverberated around the parking lot.

Nothing he said was going to help; the situation seemed completely out of his control. "I think you're about as beautiful as a girl can get." There, he'd said it.

She stared at him for a long moment. "What did you say?"

"You're beautiful," he repeated. He hadn't intended to tell her that, even if it was true. Which it was.

The fire in her eyes gradually died away, replaced

by a quizzical look that said she wasn't sure she could believe him. But then she smiled.

Lonny felt a burst of sheer happiness at that smile.

She glanced down at the asphalt. "When I was growing up, I had knobby knees and skinny legs and I was teased unmercifully. The other kids used to call me Skel. Short for skeleton."

That explained a lot.

"I had no idea."

"You couldn't have," she assured him. "When you said I was skinny, it brought back a lot of bad memories."

In an effort to comfort her, Lonny pulled her close. That was when insanity took over for the second time that day. Even knowing they were in the middle of town in the grocery-store parking lot, even knowing she'd told him in no uncertain terms to leave her alone, Lonny bent forward and kissed her.

Kissing Joy felt good. She seemed to be experiencing the same wonderful sensation, because she didn't object. He knew he was right when she wound her arms around his neck and she opened to him, as naturally as could be.

Lonny groaned. They kissed with a passion that was as heated as any argument they'd ever had. He wanted to tell her again how sorry he was, how deeply he regretted everything he'd said, and he prayed his kisses were enough to convey what was in his heart.

Then all at once Joy's hands were pushing him away. Caught off guard, Lonny stumbled back. He would've landed squarely on his butt if not for some quick shuffling.

"What did you do *that* for?" She brought one hand to her mouth.

"I don't know," he admitted quietly. "I wanted to tell you I was sorry, and that seemed as good a way as any."

She backed toward the driver's door as if she didn't trust him not to reach for her a second time.

He might have, too, if he'd felt he had the slightest chance of reasoning with her—or resuming their previous activity.

"Well, don't do it again."

"Fine," he said. She made it sound as if that kiss had been against her will. Not so. She could deny it, but he knew the truth. Joy Fuller had wanted that kiss as much as he had.

Chapter 6

Joy couldn't figure out how that kiss had ever happened. As she drove home, she touched her finger to her swollen lips. What shocked her most was how much she'd *enjoyed* his kiss. They'd kissed before, back in their dating days, but it certainly hadn't affected her like this. Her irritation rose. Lonny Ellison had insulted her, and in response, she'd let him *kiss* her?

Upset as she was, Joy nearly ran through the stop sign at Grove and Logan. Again. She slammed on her brakes hard, which jolted her forward with enough force to lock her seat belt so tightly she couldn't breathe. Just as quickly, she was thrown back against the seat. When she did manage to catch her breath, she exhaled shakily as her pulse hammered in her ears.

Once she got home, Joy unpacked her groceries and tried hard to put that ridiculous kiss out of her mind.

The fact that Lonny had apologized was a lame excuse for what he'd done—what she'd allowed. Standing in her kitchen, Joy covered her face with both hands. For heaven's sake, they'd been in a parking lot! Anyone driving by or coming out of the store might have witnessed that...that torrid scene.

Her face burned at the mere thought of it. She'd worked hard to maintain a solid reputation in the community, and now Lonny Ellison and her own reckless behavior threatened to destroy it.

Thankfully, her afternoon was busy; otherwise she would've spent the rest of the day worrying. She had choir practice at two o'clock at the church and there was a carnival committee meeting at school immediately following that. Joy's one desperate hope was that no one she knew had been anywhere near the grocery store that morning.

By the time she arrived at the church, her stomach was in turmoil. As she took her place at the organ, she surreptitiously watched the choir members. Fortunately, no one seemed to pay her any particular attention. That was promising, although she supposed the last person they'd say anything to would be her. Once she was out of sight, the gossip would probably spread faster than an August brush fire.

To her relief, practice went well. Joy stayed on when everyone had left and played through the songs, which helped settle her nerves. Music had always had a calming effect on her, and that was exactly what she needed.

Kissing in public. Dear heaven, what was she thinking? Of course, that was the problem. She *hadn't* been thinking. All reason had flown from her brain. But regardless of her own role in this, she cast the greater part of the blame at Lonny Ellison's feet. His sole purpose in commenting on her diet had been to embarrass her.

At three, the school parking lot started to fill up for the meeting. The committees had been formed months earlier, and their main purpose now was to raise funds for the end-of-school carnival. Bringing in professional carnival rides had put a definite strain on their limited budget. But everyone in town was excited about it, and the committee would do whatever was necessary to finance the rides, for which they planned to charge only a nominal fee.

A number of women had already gathered in the high school gymnasium when Joy slipped into the meeting. She sat in the back row, where she was soon joined by Letty Brown. Involuntarily, Joy tensed, afraid Lonny might have mentioned their kiss to his sister. Apparently not, because Letty smiled at her, and they made small talk for several minutes. That didn't prove anything, though.

"When's the last time you talked to your brother?" Joy asked when she couldn't stand the suspense anymore.

Letty frowned. "A couple of days ago. Why?"

It demanded all of Joy's acting skills to give a nonchalant shrug. "No reason."

A moment later, Doris Fleming banged the gavel to bring the meeting to order. After the preliminaries and the reading of the minutes, Doris announced, "I have all the game prizes ordered, I've paid for the carnival, and—I'm shocked to tell you—our finances have been entirely depleted. We need to raise funds and we need to do it fast, otherwise we'll have no operating budget. We still have to buy food, drinks and so forth."

Janice Rothchild's hand shot into the air. "We could do a bake sale. That's always good for raising money."

A few women groaned. Muttering broke out until Doris banged the gavel again.

"A bake sale's always been our best money-raiser," Janice reminded the other women. She should know because she'd been the carnival treasurer for as long as Joy had been in town.

"Well, yes, Della's pies sell out right away, and Florence Williams's sourdough biscuits, too, of course."

"Don't forget Sally's chocolate cake," Myrtle Jameson shouted out. "That's one of the first to go. But last year, *everything* sold out in under two hours."

"Order, please," Doris said. She held her index finger to her lips. "Myrtle, you're right. Remember how, at the last bake sale, there was a line outside the door even before we opened? And, Betty," she said, pointing her gavel at a woman who sat in the front row. "Tell the ladies what happened to you."

Betty Sanders, who was well into her eighties, stood, using her cane for balance. "One of the men stopped me in the parking lot and bought all my butterhorn rolls the second I got out of my car."

"See what I mean?" Janice said, looking around for confirmation. "That's why I suggested we do a bake sale. They're *very* popular."

"I have another idea," Letty said, leaping to her feet.

The women twisted around to see who was speaking. "If the bake sale's so popular and we sell out right away, why don't we auction off the baked goods?"

Letty sat back down and the room instantly erupted into discordant chatter.

Doris pounded the gavel and Joy could see that she was keen on Letty's idea.

"That's a fabulous suggestion," Doris said. "We'd raise a lot more cash—and our treasury could sure use it."

"But where would we hold an auction?" someone called out. "Especially at this late date? Don't forget, the carnival's only two weeks away."

A variety of suggestions followed. Finally someone else brought forth the idea of having the auction during Friday-night bingo at the community center. Expressions of approval rippled across the room.

"An auction's a perfect idea." Joy leaned close in order to whisper to her friend.

"I don't know why someone hasn't thought of it before," Letty said, shrugging off the praise.

"Bingo is the most popular event of the week," Lois Franklin reminded the group. "And Bill told me he always needs entertainment for intermission. I know he'll welcome this idea."

"It helps that you're married to him," Doris said, chuckling. "So we can count on holding the auction at bingo?"

Lois nodded. "I'll make sure of it." And she would, since Bill was the caller—and the man in charge of bingo in Red Springs.

"It's as good as done, then," Doris said. "Thank you, Lois."

"When?" another woman asked. "Next Friday?"

Doris glanced around. "Does a week give everyone enough time to get the word out?"

There were nods of assent.

Although she'd hoped to remain inconspicuous during this meeting, Joy didn't feel she could keep silent. She raised her hand and stood. "That only gives us seven days—including today—to let people know." They'd need to have signs made and posted around town right away.

After another round of muttered rumblings, Doris slammed the gavel yet again. "That's true, but there's nothing we can do about it. The bake sale auction is set for next Friday night."

"We'll tell everyone," Betty said, leaning on her cane.

"No problem." Honey Sue Jameson got to her feet. "I'll make it my business to tell the entire town about this." Honey Sue was Myrtle's daughter-in-law. She and her husband, Don, owned the local radio station, so she was on the radio every morning, announcing the news and reading the farm report. Honey Sue had come by her name because her voice was as sweet and smooth as honey. Although Joy had no interest in the price of beef or soybeans, she sometimes tuned in just to hear Honey Sue, who could actually make a list of prices sound almost poetic.

"That's terrific," Doris said, beaming at the prospect of filling the committee's coffers. "I'll put out sheets of paper for sign-up lists. Ladies, please indicate what you're bringing and how you can help publicize our bake sale."

"Just a minute," Betty said, returning everyone's attention to the front of the room. "Who'll be the auctioneer?"

"We could always ask Don," Lois Franklin suggested.

"If he won't do it, I will," Honey Sue volunteered.

Once again Doris nodded her approval.

"Will the name of whoever contributed the baked item be mentioned?" someone else wanted to know.

Doris frowned. "I…" She looked to Honey Sue for advice. "What do you think?"

Honey Sue smiled. "I don't suppose it could hurt."

"The name of the donor will be announced at the time the baked item is brought up for auction," Doris stated decisively.

"That might generate even higher bids," Letty murmured. "Chase is crazy for Betty's butterhorn rolls. He doesn't know it, but Betty gave me the recipe. I just haven't gotten around to baking them yet."

Joy whispered in Letty's ear. "So it was Chase who stopped her in the parking lot?"

"I'm not sure, but knowing Chase, it probably was."

Several sheets of paper were set up on the front table, and the women stepped forward to write down their donations.

Joy and Letty joined the line. "What are you going to bake?" Joy asked her friend.

"Pecan pie," Letty said without hesitation. "What about you?"

Several ideas ran through Joy's mind. No doubt

Lonny thought she purchased frozen entrées because she didn't know how to cook. Well, that wasn't the case. She should arrive with Cherries Jubilee, toss on the brandy and light it up. She could just imagine Lonny Ellison's expression when he saw flames leaping into the air. Or perhaps Baked Alaska. That would make a point, too.

"I haven't decided yet," she murmured.

"Remember the last time you watched Cricket for me?" Letty said. "The two of you baked peanut butter cookies. They were wonderful."

"You think so?" Joy didn't mean to sound so insecure. The cookies were fine, but they didn't provide the dramatic statement she was hoping to make. She shouldn't worry about impressing anyone, least of all Lonny. Still, the thought flitted through her mind. She would derive great satisfaction from seeing his face when she presented Crêpes Suzette.

Joy didn't have a single thing to prove to Lonny, or anyone else for that matter, and yet she *wanted* to impress him. It was all about pride. This…this cowpoke was taking up far too much of her time and energy. She didn't want to be attracted to him. Josh was coming back into her life and he was someone she knew, someone she felt comfortable with. Lonny made her angry every time she thought about him, he'd embarrassed her publicly more than once, *and* they had absolutely nothing in common.

"Peanut butter cookies are so…" Joy paused, searching for the right word. "*Ordinary,*" she finished.

Letty grinned. "In case you haven't noticed, most everyone around these parts prefers ordinary. We're a meat-and-potatoes kind of community. You won't see anyone signing up to bring Crêpes Suzette."

"Ah…" So much for that idea.

"It's a lesson I learned when I came back after living in California all those years," Letty went on. "I didn't need to impress anyone. All I had to do was be myself."

Even though Joy longed to see the look on Lonny's face when the auctioneer brought forth her fabulously exclusive dessert and read her name, she realized she'd only embarrass herself. No one would bid on it; no doubt they'd feel sorry for her, the city girl who'd tried to show off her superior baking skills.

"Peanut butter cookies it is," she said with a sigh.

Letty reached the front of the line and wrote down pecan pie. Joy added her cookies to the list, noticing that only one other woman had offered to bake them.

Letty waited for her, and together they walked to the parking lot. Several other cars were pulling out.

"Is something going on between my brother and you?" Letty asked unexpectedly.

Joy almost couldn't swallow her gasp of alarm. "Wh-what do you mean?"

"Well, you *did* ask about him," Letty said. "You wanted to know if I'd talked to my brother recently."

"Oh, that." Joy brushed off the question. "No reason." It was the same response she'd made earlier, but she couldn't come up with a more inventive excuse on the spur of the moment.

Letty regarded her as if she knew there *was* a reason. "Well, regardless, we'll see him soon enough."

"We will?" Joy widened her eyes. She'd sincerely hoped to avoid him.

"Of course," Letty said matter-of-factly. "You can bet he'll be at the auction." And with that simple statement, she both confirmed Joy's fears and ignited her hopes.

Chapter 7

Lonny had plenty to do around the ranch. Early in the afternoon, after he got back from town, he rode out to the herd, seeking any cattle that showed signs of sickness. Chase had found one heifer with a runny nose and isolated her for the time being.

Lonny felt a sense of pride as his gaze fell on the rows of wheat, stretching as far as the eye could see. The stalks were still slender and light green. He and Chase had planted three hundred acres, another three hundred in soybeans and nearly that much in natural grasses. The wheat was grown for grazing and for seed. They grew everything their cattle ate. The herd now numbered about four hundred, and their goal was to eventually increase it to fifteen hundred head.

A herd that size would take years to develop, depending on the public's response to natural beef. He had to believe that once health-conscious consumers realized they had a choice, they'd prefer a product devoid of potentially harmful chemicals. Both Chase and Lonny had staked their financial future on this hope.

Thinking about their plans for the herd distracted him from Joy Fuller—but not for long. Following that scene this morning, he was half-afraid his sister might be right. He *was* attracted to Joy. He had been earlier, too, when they'd first dated, only it had all blown up in his face. The woman was opinionated and argumentative—but then, so was he. Together, they were like a match striking tinder. Saturday's kiss had shown him how quickly that could lead to combustion.

He understood now why he'd reacted so irrationally at the time of the accident. He knew why he'd insisted she take responsibility for the damage to his truck. The truth had hit him squarely between the eyes when he kissed her. It shook him, mainly because he didn't *want* to be attracted to Joy. They'd already tried a relationship and he'd decided it wasn't going to work. It wouldn't this time, either, and now…now, he thought, looking over the cattle scattered across the green land, he had other considerations, other worries.

Tom came into view on Dolly, the brown-and-white mare he preferred to ride. He was unusually mature for nineteen and, to Lonny's relief, didn't require much supervision. He gave Tom a few instructions, then rode back to the barn. He should check the fence line, which needed continual attention. Yet whenever he started a task, he had to struggle not to get sidetracked by thoughts of Joy…and that kiss.

Twice he'd actually climbed inside his truck, intend-

ing to go into town so he could talk to her. He didn't
know what he could possibly say that would make a
shred of difference. He was convinced that she'd enjoyed their kiss as much as he had, but she'd insisted
she didn't want him touching her.

For a moment there, for one of the most wonderful
interludes of his life, she'd kissed him back. Then she'd
suddenly broken it off.

Once he'd finished rubbing down his horse, Lonny
walked resolutely toward the truck. He would go to Joy,
he decided, take his hat off and ask if they could talk
man to man—no, that wouldn't work. Man to woman,
then. They'd clear up past misunderstandings and perhaps they could start fresh.

He'd apologize, too, for the way he'd behaved after
the accident, and tell her she didn't need to pay him a
dime to repair that dent. It added character to his truck,
he'd say. He wouldn't mention their kiss, though. If he
apologized, he'd be lying and she'd see right through
him.

Determined now, even though it was already late afternoon, he got into his pickup. It was at this point that
he'd changed his mind twice before. But based on his
frustrating inability to forget about Joy for more than a
few minutes, he could only conclude that it wouldn't do
any good to stick around the ranch. In his current emotional state, he wasn't worth a plugged nickel, anyway.

The twenty-minute drive into town seemed to pass
in five. Before he had a chance to think about what
he intended to say, he'd reached Joy's house. At least
he assumed she still lived in the same place she'd
rented when she moved to town. He parked outside

and clutched the steering wheel for probably three minutes before he found the gumption to walk to the front door. Checking the contents of the mailbox confirmed that this was, indeed, her home.

Lonny wasn't fond of eating crow and he was about to swallow a sizable portion. He was willing to do it, though, if that would set things straight between him and Joy.

Squaring his shoulders, he cleared his throat and removed his Stetson. He shook his head in case his hair was flat, took a deep breath and braced his feet apart. Then he rang her doorbell.

Nothing.

He pressed it again, harder and longer this time.

Still nothing.

Lonny peeked in the front window. There didn't appear to be anyone home. Now that he thought about it, her little green PT Cruiser was nowhere in sight.

Disappointed, Lonny went back to his own vehicle. It seemed important to let her know he'd made an effort to contact her. Digging around in his glove compartment, he found a slip of paper—an old gas station receipt—and a pencil stub. He spent a moment thinking about what to say. After careful consideration, he wrote: *I came to talk. I think we should, don't you? Call me. Lonny J. Ellison.* Then he wrote down his phone number.

He'd added his middle initial so she'd realize he was serious. His father had chosen Jethro as his middle name, and he usually avoided any reminder of it. For Joy, he'd reveal his embarrassing secret—because if she asked what the *J* stood for, he'd tell her.

As he pulled away from the curb and turned the corner, he glanced in his rearview mirror and saw her green car coming from the opposite direction.

Lonny made a quick U-turn and parked just out of sight. Leaning over his steering wheel, he managed to get a glimpse of Joy's front porch. Sure enough, it was her.

His best course of action, he decided, was to wait and see what happened when she found his note.

Lonny watched Joy walk slowly toward the house. He noticed that her shoulders were hunched as if she wasn't feeling well. She opened the screen door and the slip of paper he'd tucked there dropped to the porch.

Lonny almost called out, afraid she hadn't seen it. She had, though. Bending down, she picked up the note he'd folded in half. He held his breath as she read it. Then he saw her take his heartfelt message, crumple it with both hands and shove it inside her pocket. After that, she unlocked the front door, slammed it shut and drew her drapes.

Lonny sighed. Perhaps now wasn't a good time to approach her, after all.

On the drive back to his ranch, Lonny wondered how his plan could have gone so wrong. Joy's reaction to his note made it clear that she wasn't interested in anything he had to say. He could take a hint. But in his opinion, she wasn't being honest with herself; otherwise, she would've acknowledged how much she'd liked that kiss. Fine. He could deal with it.

The rest of the day was shot, so Lonny stopped at Chase and Letty's. As soon as his truck rolled into the yard, Cricket came running out of the house, bouncing down the porch steps.

Lonny was out of his vehicle just in time to catch her in his arms and swing her around. Now, *this* was a gratifying reception—exactly the type he'd hoped to get from Joy. That, however, was not to be.

"Mom's baking pecan pie," Cricket announced.

"For dinner?" he asked, setting his niece down on the ground.

Cricket frowned. "I don't think so."

"Your mommy makes the best pecan pie I ever tasted." If he hung around awhile, she might offer him a piece.

Chase stepped out of the barn, wiping his brow with his forearm. "What are you doing here?" he asked. "I thought you were going to finish the worming."

"Good to see you, too," Lonny teased. They'd been best friends their entire lives. Friends, partners, neighbors—and now, brothers-in-law. "Tom and I finished the worming early." Early enough to race into town and make an idiot of himself over Joy. But that was information he planned to keep private.

"Aren't you and Tom driving the herd to the lower pasture this weekend?"

"I decided against it," Lonny said. "There's still plenty of grass in the upper pasture. I meant to tell you...."

Letty came out onto the back porch and waved when she saw him. "Hi, Lonny," she said. She didn't look as if she'd been baking.

"What's this I hear about a pecan pie?" he asked, moving closer. If he was lucky, she'd offer him a piece *and* invite him to dinner. In that case, he'd casually bring up the subject of Joy and get his sister's opinion. Maybe he needed a woman's perspective.

"I'm not baking the pie until later in the week. It's for an auction. Want to stay for dinner? I'm just setting the table."

"What're you making?"

"Roast chicken, scalloped potatoes, green bean casserole."

He grinned. "It'd be my pleasure." Letty's cooking was downright inspired, and this meal reminded him of one their mother might have made. Toward the end of her life, though, she'd taken more interest in quilting than in the culinary arts. Letty had inherited their mother's abilities in the kitchen, and she could do artistic stuff, too—singing and knitting and other things, like the dried herb wreath that hung on the kitchen door.

"I'll wash up and join you in a few minutes," Chase said.

"Cricket, go add another place setting to the table," Letty instructed her daughter.

"Can Uncle Lonny sit next to me?"

"I wouldn't sit anywhere else," Lonny said as the six-year-old followed her mother up the steps.

"Were you in town today?" Letty asked.

Lonny paused, unsure how much to tell his sister. "I just made a quick trip," he said cautiously. He'd actually made two trips, but he didn't point *that* out.

"Did you happen to run into Joy?"

He froze in midstep. "Why do you ask?"

Letty eyed him speculatively. "What is it with you

two?" she demanded, hands on hips. "I asked Joy about you and she clammed right up."

"Really?" Lonny played it cool. If she wasn't talking, then he wasn't, either. He didn't know how many people had caught sight of the spectacle they'd made of themselves—and whether someone had tattled to Letty.

"I wish you and Joy would talk," she said, in the same sisterly tone she'd used when they were kids. "It's ridiculous the way you keep circling each other. *One* of you needs to be adult enough to discuss this."

"I agree with you." His response seemed to surprise her. What Letty didn't know was that Lonny had already tried, and it hadn't gotten him anywhere. He held open the screen door. "It's obvious," he said, tossing Letty a cocky smile. "The woman wants me."

"The only thing that's obvious to me, big brother, is that you're so in love with her you can't think straight."

He laughed that off—but he was man enough to admit there was *something* between him and Joy. However, exactly what it was and how deep it went, not to mention how he should handle it, remained a mystery.

Letty walked into the kitchen and got him a cup of coffee. "You tried talking to her?"

Lonny took the mug and shook his head. He hadn't spoken to Joy, not technically; he'd left her a note. Rather than explain, he didn't answer the question. "Tell me about the auction. What's it for?"

Letty studied him as he added sugar to his coffee. "I signed up to bring a pecan pie for a bake sale auction. The carnival committee needs operating capital, and we have to raise it quickly."

"You aren't going to sell the goodies the way you

normally do?" That was a disappointment. An auction would drive up the prices. Lonny had a sweet tooth and he was generally first in line for a bake sale. This pie might prove to be expensive.

"If you want the pecan pie, you're going to have to bid on it like everyone else," his sister gleefully informed him. "Otherwise, you'll have to wait until next Thanksgiving."

Head down, Lonny muttered a few words he didn't want Cricket or his sister to hear.

"I was at a meeting about the bake sale this afternoon," Letty said as he leaned his hip against the kitchen counter. "Joy was there, too."

That remark caught his attention; Lonny suddenly lifted his head and realized his little sister had just baited him. He'd fallen for it, too, hook, line and sinker. In an effort to cover his interest, he laughed. "You're telling me Joy's contributing to the bake sale?" Apparently his sister was unaware that the woman's meals came from the freezer section of the grocery store.

His sister didn't see the humor in it, so he felt he needed to enlighten her. "Do you seriously think she can bake?"

"Why not?" Letty asked, eyebrows raised.

Lonny could see he was getting more involved in the subject than was really prudent. He considered telling Letty about seeing Joy earlier, then promptly decided against it. With a quick shrug, he said, "Oh, nothing."

Lonny wondered what was taking Chase so long to wash up. He could use a diversion. Sighing, he thought he might as well get Letty's advice now. The hell with being sensible or discreet. "I blew it with Joy," he said in a low voice.

His confession didn't come easy. Before he could think better of it, Lonny described the incident inside the store—stopping short of the kiss. It wasn't that he was opposed to telling his sister the full truth...eventually. If he and Joy had been seen, the gossip would find its way to Letty soon enough; in fact, he was surprised she hadn't heard anything yet. But that kiss was special. For as long as possible, he wanted to keep those moments to himself.

"You said *what?*" his sister exploded after listening to the whole sad story.

Lonny pulled out a chair and sat down. "I feel bad about it now. She said she got teased about being thin as a kid, and I stepped in it with both feet."

"Lonny!"

It didn't help having his sister yell at him. He knew he'd made a mistake; she didn't need to beat up on him all over again. Della and her daughters had done an adequate job of that already.

"I apologized," he muttered, rubbing his hands over his eyes. "Well, I tried."

Letty frowned.

"What?" he snapped. If Chase didn't arrive soon, he'd go and search for the guy himself.

"Here's what you're going to do," his sister said, speaking slowly and clearly, as though he were hard of hearing—or deficient in understanding.

"Now, Letty..."

"You're going to bid on Joy's peanut butter cookies." His sister wouldn't allow him to interrupt. Letty was still frowning, her eyes narrowed. "And you're going to be the highest bidder."

"Okay." That much he could do.

She nodded, evidently approving his willingness to fall in with her scheme. Well, he supposed she couldn't get him into worse trouble with Joy than he was now.

"And then," Letty continued, "you're going to *taste* Joy's cookies and declare they're the best you've ever had in your entire life."

"I am?" This seemed a little overboard to Lonny.

"Yes, you will, and you're going to mean it, too."

Lonny wasn't so sure about that, but he'd hear his sister out. He'd asked for her opinion, and the least he could do was listen.

Fortunately, Chase clattered down the stairs at that moment, putting a temporary end to Letty's career as a romantic adviser.

Chapter 8

Wednesday afternoon Joy hurried home from school, planning to do some baking. She'd spent far too much time reading through cookbooks and searching websites on the internet, looking for a spectacular dessert that would knock the boots off a certain rancher.

Every time she found a recipe she was sure would impress Lonny, Joy remembered the scorn in his eyes when he'd picked up her frozen dinner. He'd probably fall over in a dead faint when he realized that not only could she bake, she was good at it.

Since she'd wasted so many hours on research, Joy had yet to make her peanut butter cookies, a recipe handed down from her grandmother. This recipe was an old family favorite.

She turned on the radio and arranged her ingredients. Flour, sugar, peanut butter… She lined them up along the counter in order of use. Bowls, measuring cups and utensils waited on the kitchen table; the oven was preheating and the cookie sheet greased. She was nothing if not organized.

The doorbell rang just as she was measuring the flour. Joy set the bag down and hurried into the front hall, curious to find out who her visitor might be.

Letty stood there, with Cricket at her side, and Joy immediately opened the screen door. "Come in," she said, glad of the company.

"Thanks," Letty said, smiling as she stepped into the house. "I was in town to buy pecans and thought I'd come over and see how you're doing."

"I'm baking," Joy announced. "Or at least, I'm getting started."

Letty hesitated. "I don't want to interrupt...."

"I haven't actually begun, so your timing's perfect," she said, ushering Letty and Cricket into the kitchen.

"Can I play on your computer?" Cricket asked when her mother sat down at the table.

Joy glanced at Letty, who nodded, and Cricket loped eagerly toward the spare bedroom. Apparently, Chase had taught her solitaire.

With a sweep of her hand, Letty indicated the half-dozen cookbooks Joy had spread out on the table and on two of her four chairs. In addition, she had a six-inch stack of recipes she'd printed off the internet.

"What's all this?" Letty asked, as Joy cleared a chair and sat down across from her.

"Dessert recipes," Joy admitted a bit sheepishly.

Letty reached for one on the stack she'd gotten off the internet. "Cannoli?" she read, and Joy watched her friend's face as she scanned the directions. "This sounds complicated."

Joy had thought so herself. "I could probably manage it, but I was afraid I'd waste a lot of time shaping them and then I'd need to fill them, too. Besides, they're deep-fried and I don't know how well they'd keep."

"You said you were baking peanut butter cookies."

"I am," Joy was quick to tell her, motioning toward the counter, "but I also wanted to bring something more…impressive. I'm a good cook and…" She let the rest fade. Since Letty was Lonny's sister, she couldn't very well confess what she was trying to prove and why. The less Letty knew about her most recent encounter with Lonny, the better.

"Tiramisu?" Letty cocked her head as she read the recipe title in a cookbook that was open directly in front of her. She looked skeptical when she returned her attention to Joy.

"I rejected that one, too," Joy confessed. "I wasn't sure I could get all the ingredients without having to drive into Red Rock or Cheyenne."

"Baklava?" Letty asked next, pointing at another recipe.

"I had no idea whether anyone in town would even know what that was," Joy said. "There isn't a large Greek population in the area, is there?"

"No." Letty confirmed what Joy already suspected.

"The Raspberry Truffle Torte Bombe had possibilities," Joy said, gesturing at yet another of the cookbooks. "However, I was afraid the ice cream would melt."

"Joy, what's wrong with peanut butter cookies?" Letty asked.

"Nothing. I just wanted to bake more than one thing."

"Then bake a cake, and not a chocolate truffle one, either," she said, reaching for another of the pages Joy had printed out. "Just a plain, simple cake. That'll generate more interest than anything with melting ice cream in the middle."

"It will?"

Letty nodded and seemed surprised that she had to remind Joy of the obvious. "You've been part of this community long enough to know this," she said mildly. "You don't need to impress anyone."

Least of all Lonny Ellison, Joy mused. "You're right," she agreed. Actually, she was relieved. Although she was willing to try, she wasn't convinced she could pull off a culinary masterpiece before Friday night. She was a little out of practice.

She shouldn't be thinking about Lonny at all. Josh would be here soon, and there'd be a chance to renew that relationship.

"You're bringing more than the pecan pie, though, aren't you?" Joy asked, determined not to think about either man.

Letty nodded. "Chase suggested I bake a Lemonade Cake, which is one of his favorites. I suspect he wants to bid on it himself." She smiled as she said it.

Joy envied Letty the warm, loving relationship she had with her husband. She couldn't imagine Chase saying or doing any of the things Lonny Ellison had said and done to her. More and more, she thought about their earlier relationship and how they'd walked away from each other after some ridiculous, forgettable argument. Maybe she was partly to blame. If she was honest, she'd have to admit there was no *maybe* about it. And, still being honest, she regretted the lost opportunity. But it was too late, especially with Josh showing up.

Letty and Chase shared a special love story, and now that they were married, it seemed as if they'd always been together. Chase had loved Letty from the time he was a teenager; in fact, he'd loved her enough to let her leave Wyoming without guilt so she could pursue her dream of becoming a singer. For almost ten years Letty had worked hard at creating a musical career, with moderate success, getting fairly steady gigs as a background singer and doing a few commercials that still paid residuals from time to time. When she returned to Wyoming, she came back with a daughter and a heart ailment that threatened to shorten her life. She'd been born with it but had never known there was a problem; it had been discovered during her pregnancy. She'd come home, possibly to die, or at least that was what she'd believed. But she'd had the required surgery and could live a normal life now.

"Other than cookies, what do you enjoy baking?" Letty asked.

Because she lived alone and generally cooked for one, Joy hadn't done much baking since her arrival in Red Springs. Before college, she used to spend hours in the kitchen, often with her mother. "My mom taught me a great apple pie recipe," Joy said after a moment.

"Then bake an apple pie."

Apple pie—it felt as if a weight had been lifted from

her shoulders. "That's what I'll do," she said triumphantly.

"My brother's got a real sweet tooth," Letty murmured.

Joy shrugged, implying that was of little concern
to her. She supposed this was Letty's way of remind-
ing her that Lonny would be attending the auction. Joy
wasn't sure how to react.

Her feelings on the subject of Lonny were decidedly mixed, and no one else had ever had such a con-
fusing effect on her. Joy genuinely liked all the people
who were close to him—Letty, of course, and Chase,
who was Lonny's best friend. Not to mention Cricket,
who talked nonstop about her wonderful uncle Lonny.
He was obviously popular with the other ranchers
and townsfolk, too. In other words, no one except her
seemed to have a problem with him.

She was tempted to ask Letty about it. She hesitated, unsure how to introduce her question, but before
she could say anything, Letty said it was time she left.

"Thanks for coming over," Joy said as she walked
Letty and Cricket to the front door.

"Bake that pie," Letty advised yet again. "*After* you
make those cookies."

"I will," Joy promised.

"See you Friday night. Do you want Chase and me
to pick you up?"

Joy shook her head. "Honey Sue called and asked
me to help with the setup, so I'll need to be there early."

Letty nodded, and Joy was grateful she had an excuse for declining the ride. If Lonny came into town for

the auction, he'd sit with the couple, and if she joined them, too, the situation might be awkward for everyone.

Joy didn't want to think about Lonny anymore, but it was hard to avoid. She'd found his message in her screen door on Saturday, after the carnival committee meeting. At the time she'd been so angry and upset, she'd tossed it without even considering his suggestion. But perhaps he was right. Perhaps it would be a good idea to clear the air. Then again, to what end? They'd already learned that their personalities and beliefs were diametrically opposed, and that wasn't likely to change. Besides, Josh was coming. No, she'd better forget about Lonny—once she'd impressed him with her culinary aptitude.

The evening news was on when Joy finished baking a double batch of the peanut butter cookies. This was a tried and true recipe, tested a million times over the years, and there was no question that these were some of her best. They came out of the oven looking perfect. Her grandmother had used fork tines to create a crisscross pattern on each one, and Joy followed tradition. Once they'd cooled, she carefully arranged them in a couple of tin boxes left over from Christmas and stored them in the cupboard until Friday night.

Just as she was flipping through her family cookbook, searching for her grandmother's apple pie recipe, the phone rang. The interruption annoyed her. She'd been fantasizing about the bidding war over the cookies and the apple pie and was busy picturing Lonny's shocked face, an image she wanted to hold on to as long as she could.

"Hello," she answered on the third ring, hoping her frustration wasn't evident.

"Joy, it's Josh."

Caught up as she was in her dream world, it took her a second to remember who Josh was.

"Josh! Hi," she said quickly.

"Am I calling at a bad time?"

"No, no, of course not." It wasn't as if she could admit she'd been obsessively thinking about another man.

"Is someone there?" Josh asked after a brief hesitation.

"No, what makes you ask?"

"You sound preoccupied."

"I'm in the middle of baking."

"You bake?" He asked this as if it were a big joke.

She sighed. Not another one. "Yes, I know how to bake." Joy was unable to keep the irritation out of her voice. "I didn't mean that the way it came across," she added hastily. "There's a bake sale auction in town this Friday and—well, never mind, it isn't important."

Those remarks were followed by a short pause. "Joy," he said solemnly, "are you involved with anyone?"

"Involved, as in a relationship?" She made her voice as light and carefree as possible. "No, not at all. I already told you that. Why do you ask?"

"I got the impression you might be."

She laughed as if she found his statement humorous. Fortunately, this sounded more genuine than her previous denial. "No, Josh, I'm not involved, I promise you, but the fact that you asked has definitely brightened my day. Okay, there was someone early on, two years ago, but we only went out for a few months and then decided to drop the whole thing."

"Really?"

"Yes, it was nothing," she assured him. "Wait until you see Red Springs," she continued excitedly. "It's small-town America, just the way I always thought it would be. Everyone's so friendly and caring."

"It seems like a nice place," he said politely.

"It is. The folks around here are good salt-of-the-earth people."

"Actually…" He paused again. "I, uh, wondered if it might be a little boring—hardly any restaurants or clubs. I mean, what do you do for entertainment? Besides, I thought you were a city girl."

"I am…. I was. And for entertainment, we have bingo and the county fair and—"

"If you had the opportunity, you'd move back to the city, right?" He made it more statement than question.

"Oh, sure," she responded without much consideration. Almost as soon as the words were out of her mouth, she wondered if that was true. Joy loved Wyoming and everything she'd learned about life in a town like Red Springs. She'd made friends and felt she'd become part of the community.

"I phoned to let you know my travel plans have been confirmed," Josh said. He seemed to expect her to comment.

Joy tore her gaze away from the empty pie tin. "That's good news," she said, adding, "I look forward to seeing you," although that seemed oddly formal. Tucking the portable phone between her shoulder and ear, she walked over to the refrigerator and opened the bottom bin, where she found a bag of Granny Smith apples. She counted out six.

"Joy?"

If Josh had asked her something, she hadn't heard it. "I'm sorry, I missed what you said."

"Perhaps I should call another time. Or I'll email you."

"Fine," she said.

"Bye."

She set the apples on the counter. "Bye," she echoed, and realized Josh had hung up. He hadn't even waited until she'd said goodbye. Then again, maybe she'd kept *him* waiting a little too long.

Chapter 9

"Are you going into town?" Tom asked Lonny late Friday afternoon as they rode toward the barn.

"I guess so," Lonny said. He'd been in the saddle from dawn, they both had, and he wasn't in any mood to shower and drive all the way into Red Springs. He'd prefer something cold to drink and a long hot soak. Still, Letty would have his hide if he didn't show up for that auction. The entire town would be there. The bake sale auction had been hyped on the radio all week by Honey Sue Jameson, and Chase told him the original idea had been Letty's. Nope, he wouldn't dare disappoint her, or he'd have Chase mad at him, too. Not to mention that it was his one chance to make things right with Joy.

"If you do, could I tag along?" Tom asked.

This surprised Lonny, since Tom didn't often ask for

favors. Little by little, he'd revealed some of what his home life had been like. Lonny knew it was a sign of trust that the boy had confided in him at all. Based on what Tom had said, he was much better off not living with his father. Lonny wanted to help him in whatever way he could. Tom was smart and should be in college or trade school. The best person to talk to was a high school counselor—or maybe Joy. She related well to kids and knew a lot more than he did about scholarships and educational opportunities.

Tom had a real knack for horsemanship and an intuitive connection with animals. His patience and skill impressed Lonny; without much difficulty he could see Tom as a veterinarian. He'd mentioned it one evening and Tom had gotten flustered and quickly changed the subject. Later Tom had said it was best not to get his hopes up about anything like that. He had no chance of ever going to school, no matter how long he worked or how much money he saved. But Lonny felt there had to be a solution, and he was determined to find it.

"You can come along if you want," Lonny told him. He didn't ask for an explanation but suspected Tom's interest had to do with Michelle Larson. Which reminded him—he'd promised Charley Larson he'd speak to the boy about that dance.

"Thanks," Tom mumbled as he headed off to his room in the barn.

"Be ready in an hour," Lonny shouted after him.

Tom half turned, nodding.

Lonny finished tending to Moonshine, his gelding, and then hurried into the house for a long, hot shower. The mirror was fogged when he got out and began to shave. Normally he took care of that in the morning, but tonight he wanted his skin to be smooth in case— his thoughts came to a shuddering halt. In case he had the opportunity to kiss Joy again. It wasn't likely to happen, but he couldn't help hoping. He frowned. He'd rather tussle with a porcupine, he told himself, than cross her again.

Lonny snickered out loud. That wasn't true and it was time he fessed up. Not once had he stopped thinking about Joy. She was on his mind every minute of every day. It was her face, her eyes, that he saw when he drifted off to sleep at night, and her rose-scented perfume he thought about. When he woke in the morning, the first thing that popped into his mind was the memory of holding her and the kisses they'd shared. She was there all the times in between, too. Lonny didn't like it. Not thinking about her was a losing battle, so he figured he'd give in and try to win her over. As he'd told Letty, he'd blown it with Joy. Lonny Ellison wasn't a quitter, though. He hadn't gotten all those rodeo buckles by walking away from a challenge, and he wasn't about to start now. Not that he'd compare Joy Fuller to an ornery bull or an angry bronc. Well, not really. He chuckled at the thought.

By the time he'd shaved—fortunately without nicking himself—changed into a clean pair of Levi's and a stiff new shirt Letty had bought him last Christmas, Lonny figured he was well on his way to showing off his better side. No matter what Joy said or did, Lonny was determined not to lose his temper.

Tom was outside, leaning against the pickup, when Lonny stepped out of the house and bounded down the back steps. The boy had dressed in his best clothes, too. As soon as Lonny appeared, Tom hopped into the passenger seat.

"You goin' to the bake auction?" Lonny asked conversationally.

Tom had the window rolled down, his elbow resting on the narrow ledge. "I was thinking about it," he admitted.

"Me, too. I got a hankering for something sweet."

Tom didn't comment.

"Nothing like home-baked goods."

Tom offered him a half smile and nodded in agreement.

"Will Michelle Larson be there?" Lonny asked. That question got an immediate rise out of Tom. He jerked his elbow back inside the truck and straightened abruptly.

"Maybe," he answered, glaring at Lonny as if he resented the question. "What about Ms. Fuller?"

That caught Lonny unawares. Apparently Tom knew more about him than he'd assumed. "I suppose she might be," he grumbled in reply. His hired hand's message had been received, and Lonny didn't ask any further questions.

In fact, neither of them said another word until they reached town. Lonny suspected there'd be a good audience for the charity event, but he hadn't expected there'd be so much traffic around the community center that he'd have trouble getting a parking spot. As soon as they found a vacant space—ten minutes later—and parked, Tom climbed out of the truck. With a quick wave, he disappeared into the crowd.

Lonny didn't know how Tom intended to get home, but if his hired hand wasn't worried about it, then he wasn't, either.

When Lonny entered the community center, it was hard to tell there was a bingo game in progress. People roamed about the room, chatting and visiting, while Bill Franklin struggled to be heard over the chatter. A table, loaded with a delectable display of homemade goodies, was set up on stage.

Bill did his best to call out the bingo numbers but ended up having to shout into the microphone. This was possibly the biggest turnout for a bingo event in Red Springs history.

Goldie Frank stood up and shouted, "Bingo!" then proceeded to wave her card wildly.

Bill seemed downright relieved. There was scattered applause as Goldie came forward to accept her prize.

"That's the end of the first round of bingo for the evening," Bill said loudly, the sound system reverberating as he did. "There will now be a baked goods auction to raise funds for the carnival. Don Jameson from 1050 AM radio is our auctioneer."

That announcement was followed by another polite round of applause. Don Jameson stepped up to the front of the room and Bill handed him the microphone.

Lonny saw Letty and Chase and noticed there was an empty chair at their table. Weaving his way through the crowd, he took the opportunity to search for Joy, trying not to be too obvious. He half hoped she'd be sitting with his sister. She wasn't. When he did find her, she was with Carol Anderson. The two women sat near the back, and Joy seemed to be enjoying herself, chatting animatedly with Carol and her husband.

Lonny nearly stumbled over his own feet. It'd been nearly a week since he'd seen Joy. For the life of him, he couldn't remember her being that pretty. He took a second look. Hot damn! His sister was easy on the eyes and so were other women in town; Joy, however, was striking. In fact, she was beautiful.

"Lonny?" Someone tugged at his sleeve.

Letty's voice broke into his thoughts, and he realized he'd stopped dead in the middle of the room, staring at Joy Fuller with his mouth practically hanging open.

"Chase and I saved you a seat."

Despite Letty's insistent tone, he couldn't drag his eyes from Joy. Unfortunately she happened to glance up just then. The room's noise seemed to fade as they stared at each other.

A few seconds later, Joy narrowed her eyes and deliberately turned away. He blinked and finally dropped his gaze.

"Lonny," his sister said again, tugging at his arm. "Did you hear me?"

"I'm coming," he muttered. He didn't need to look back at Joy to know she was watching him. He could sense that she didn't want him there.

Her attitude didn't bode well for any conciliatory effort on his part. Still, he was up to the challenge, no matter how difficult she made it.

After exchanging greetings with Chase, Lonny took the chair next to Letty and focused his attention on the table of baked goods. As he studied the display, it occurred to him that he might not know what Joy had baked.

"Those peanut butter cookies look appetizing, don't they?" his sister whispered, leaning toward him.

"I suppose." Plenty of the other goodies did, as well.

"The apple pie, too."

There appeared to be several apple pies.

"The pie closest to the front is the one you should notice."

"Oh." It took Lonny longer than it should have to understand what his sister was trying to tell him. He brightened. "Peanut butter, you say."

Letty winked and he smiled back conspiratorially.

Generally speaking, a cookie was a cookie, as far as Lonny was concerned. Right then and there, however, he had the worst hankering for peanut butter. Of course, they could've been made with sawdust and Lonny wouldn't have cared.

The first item up for auction was Betty Sanders's butterhorn rolls. Chase made the first bid of twenty dollars for the entire batch. Another hand went up, and there were three or four other bids in quick succession. In the end Chase got the rolls but it cost him nearly fifty bucks.

He stood and withdrew his wallet, grumbling all the while that he preferred it when he could meet Betty in the parking lot and buy what he wanted before anyone else had a chance.

The next item up was a coconut cake baked by Mary and Michelle Larson. It didn't come as any surprise when Tom made the opening bid. Two or three others entered the bidding, but just when it seemed that Tom was about to walk away with the cake, someone else doubled the bid. Lonny whirled around and saw that it was Al Brighton's boy, Kenny, who'd stepped in at the last minute. Kenny got to his feet, glaring across the room at Tom, who stood at the back of the hall. Tom shrugged and bid again. The room watched as the two teenage boys squared off. When the bid reached a hundred dollars, Mary Larson hurried up to the stage and whispered in Don Jameson's ear.

"Mary has offered to bake a second coconut cake," Don announced, "so you can each have one. Is that agreeable?"

Kenny's body language said it wasn't. He looked at Tom, and Tom nodded.

"All right," Kenny conceded with bad grace.

Don's gavel hit the podium as he said into the microphone, "Two coconut cakes for one hundred dollars each."

The room erupted into chaotic noise.

"This is getting a little rich for my blood," Letty whispered to Lonny.

As luck would have it, Joy's peanut butter cookies came on the auction block next. Don hadn't even begun to describe them when Lonny's hand shot into the air. "Fifty dollars," he called out.

The room went quiet.

After the two previous bids, no one seemed interested in raising the amount and that suited him just fine. Lonny sighed with relief.

"Fifty-one," a female voice said.

Frowning, Lonny craned his neck to see who was

bidding against him. To his utter astonishment, it was Joy Fuller.

"Sixty," he shouted, annoyed that she'd do this.

"Sixty-one," was her immediate response.

Don glanced from one to the other. "Just a minute, Ms. Fuller, aren't you the one who donated these cookies?"

"I am," she told him. "Now I want them back."

What she wanted was to make sure Lonny didn't buy them. "What's she doing that for?" he asked his sister.

Letty looked as puzzled as he did. "I don't have a clue."

"Seventy dollars," Lonny offered. If she wanted to bid him up, then there was nothing he could do about it, except to keep going. The money would benefit the community. His sister seemed to think this would help in his efforts to settle his dispute with Joy, so her bidding against him made no sense.

"Seventy-one," she called back.

Letty frowned and covered Lonny's hand with her own. "Let Joy have them," she whispered.

"But…" Lonny hated to lose, and it bothered him to let her have those cookies. Surely Joy could see what he was trying to do here! Lonny didn't understand her actions; still, he figured he should trust Letty. He backed down so Joy could have the winning bid on her own peanut butter cookies.

He saw her come forward and collect the cookies. Then she immediately made her way to the exit.

"I'll be right back," he whispered to Letty as he quickly got up and followed.

It took him a few minutes to find her in the community center parking lot, which was dark and quiet. Lonny could hear the auction taking place inside, could hear Don's amplified voice and the din of laughter and bursts of applause. By the time he reached her, Joy had unlocked her car.

"Joy, wait," Lonny called. Then, thinking he should tread lightly, he amended his greeting. "Ms. Fuller." He felt as if he were back in grade school and didn't like it.

She tensed, standing outside her little green PT Cruiser. Her purse and the tin of cookies were inside, resting on the passenger seat.

"What do you want *now?*" she demanded, crossing her arms.

She was already mad at him, and he hadn't done a damned thing wrong. "Why'd you do that?" he asked, genuinely curious. "Why'd you bid against me?"

She didn't answer him; instead she asked a question of her own. "Why can't you just leave me alone?"

"I don't know," he said with a shrug. "I guess I've gotten used to having you around."

She cracked a smile. "I couldn't let you buy those cookies."

"Why not?" Lonny didn't get this at all. Frowning, he shoved his hands inside his jeans pockets. "Do you dislike me that much?"

Her eyes shot up to meet his and she slowly shook her head. "No." Her voice was barely audible. "I don't dislike you, Lonny. I never have. It's just that—"

"Is it because I called you skinny?"

She assured him that wasn't the reason. "And it isn't because of the accident," she said. "Either one."

"Do you mind giving me a clue, then?"

For a moment he thought she was going to ignore his question. "I forgot the salt," she finally told him.

"Excuse me?"

"The salt," she said, more loudly this time. "Just before the auction today, I took out a cookie to sample. I hadn't tasted one earlier and when I did, I realized what I'd done. It was too late to withdraw them or to bake a new batch." She sighed despondently. "I was working so hard to impress you and then to do something stupid like that..."

She wanted to impress him? This was exactly the kind of news he'd been hoping to hear. He propped one foot against her car bumper. "Really?"

Her gaze narrowed. "Get that smug look off your face," she snapped.

Now he knew why she'd given him the evil eye earlier. That had been a warning not to bid on her cookies, only he hadn't been smart enough to figure it out. Actually he was glad he'd bid; at least he'd shown her how interested he was.

Her eyes glistened as if she were about to cry. Lonny had dealt with his share of difficult situations over the years. He'd delivered calves in the middle of a lightning storm, dealt with rattlesnakes, faced drunken cowboys—but he couldn't handle a weeping woman.

"I would've eaten every one of those cookies and not said a word," he told Joy. Then, wanting to comfort her, he gently drew her into his arms.

Joy stared wordlessly up at him. She started to say something, then stopped. Frankly he'd rather she didn't speak because he could tell from the look in her eyes that she wanted the same thing he did. He brought his mouth to hers.

He heard her moan or maybe that was him. This—holding her in his arms, kissing her—was what he'd been thinking about all week, what he'd been dreaming about, too.

Her mouth was soft and pliable and responsive. She raised her arms and circled his neck, and that was all the encouragement Lonny needed. Immediately he deepened the kiss, locking his arms around her waist.

She moaned again, quietly at first, and then a bit louder. Lonny pulled her tight against him so she'd know exactly what she was doing to him and how much he wanted her.

Suddenly, without the slightest hint, she broke off the kiss and took two paces back. At first Lonny was too stunned to react. He stared at her, hardly knowing what to think.

She was frowning. "That shouldn't have happened," she muttered.

"Why not?" He found her reaction incomprehensible because his was entirely the opposite. As far as he was concerned, this was the best thing that had happened to him in two years.

"We—we don't get along."

"It seems to me we're getting along just great. Okay, so we had a rocky start, an argument or two, but we're over that. I'm willing to give it another shot if you are."

"I...I—"

She seemed to be having a problem making up her mind. That got him thinking she could use a little help, so he kissed her again.

When the kiss ended, he gave her a questioning look; wide-eyed, she blinked up at him.

Just to be on the safe side, he brought her into his embrace a third time. Once he'd finished, she was trembling in his arms.

"Let me know when you decide," he whispered, then turned and walked away.

Pleased with himself, Lonny strolled toward his pickup. As he neared the Ford, he saw his ranch hand leaning against the fender, head lowered.

"You ready to go?" Lonny asked.

Tom nodded, climbing into the truck. Only when the interior light went on did Lonny notice that he had a bloody nose. A bruise had formed on his cheek, too.

"You been fighting?" he asked, shocked by the boy's appearance.

Tom didn't answer.

"What happened?"

Tom remained silent.

"You don't want to talk about it?"

Tom shrugged.

"I'm guessing this involves a woman," Lonny said, starting the engine. His guess went further than that— Michelle Larson and Kenny Brighton were part of the story. Was Michelle having trouble choosing between Tom and Kenny? It struck him as highly possible. Because he knew from the events of this evening that women seldom seemed to know what they wanted.

Chapter 10

Joy couldn't believe she'd let Lonny Ellison kiss her again—and again. She didn't understand why she hadn't stopped him. It was as if her brain had gone to sleep or something and her body had taken over. As she lay in bed on Saturday morning after a restless night's sleep, she was aghast at her own behavior. Groaning, with the blankets pulled all the way up to her chin, she relived the scene outside the community center.

She could only imagine what Lonny must be thinking. She hadn't even been able to answer a simple question! He'd as much as said he was willing to start their relationship over and asked if she wanted that, too. She should've said she didn't want anything to do with him, although her heart—and her hormones—were telling her *yes*.

As soon as they were kissing—okay, be honest, *heat-*

edly kissing—she'd panicked. First, she and Lonny Ellison had nothing in common, and second…well, second— She put a halt to her reasoning because the truth was, she had no logical explanation for her response to his kisses. It wasn't like this two years ago. Okay, their kisses back then had been pleasant but not extraordinary. Not at all.

Maybe she'd gone without tenderness or physical affection for too long. That, however, wasn't true. She'd received no shortage of invitations and had dated various men in the past year. There'd been Earl Gross and Larry Caven and George Lewis. And Glen Brewster. She'd dated all four of them for short periods of time. She'd kissed each of them, too. Unfortunately, there hadn't been any spark and they'd seemed to recognize it just as Joy had. She remained friendly with all of them, and they with her. Of course, two years ago, there hadn't been what she'd call sparks with Lonny Ellison, either. Unless that referred to their arguments….

Now Lonny was back in her life and this couldn't have come at a worse time. Not only would Josh be visiting, he seemed interested in resuming their relationship. Once he was in town and they'd had a chance to talk, she'd know if there was a chance for them. Until then, she'd have to deal with her ambivalent feelings for Lonny.

Tossing aside her covers, she prepared a pot of coffee and while she waited, she logged on to her computer. She checked her email, scrolling down the entries, and paused when she came to a message from Josh. Another entry caught her attention, too, one from Letty. She read Letty's first.

From: Letty Brown
Sent: Saturday, May 27, 6:45 a.m.
To: Joy Fuller
Subject: Where Did You Go?

Joy:
I looked for you last night after the auction and couldn't
find you. My brother disappeared about the same time
you did.

Joy groaned and wondered if anyone else had noticed that they'd both left just after the bidding on her
peanut butter cookies.

In case you're wondering, the auction was a big hit.
Your apple pie sold for $30.00 to Clem Russell, but
the highest price paid for any one item was Myrtle
Jameson's chocolate cake, which went for a whopping
$175.00. (Unless you count the Larsons' coconut cake,
which sold twice, to Tom and Kenny Brighton.) All in all,
we raised more than a thousand dollars, which makes
this the most successful fund-raising event ever. I wish
you'd been there to the end.

Is everything all right? My brother didn't cause any
problems, did he? Oh, did you hear about the fight?
Tom, Lonny's ranch hand, got beaten up—three against
one. Apparently Kenny and a couple of other boys were
involved. I think it might've had something to do with
Michelle Larson. Did you see or hear anything? That
happened around the time you left. Bill Franklin broke
it up and told Chase about it later.

I'll be in town later this morning. If I have time, I'll

drop by. Chase and Lonny will be gone most of the day, since they're moving the cattle, trying to get the herd to the best pastureland.
Hope to catch up with you later.
Letty

Joy quickly answered her friend and told Letty she'd be in and out of the house all day, so if she did stop by Joy couldn't guarantee she'd be home. In her response, Joy ignored the subject of the auction and why she'd left.

Joy said she didn't know about the teenagers fighting; she didn't add that she'd heard something as she hurried to the parking lot. That was just before Lonny caught up with her. Needless to say, she didn't mention that, either. The less said about Friday night, the better.

As she hit the Send key, Joy realized she was avoiding her friend because of Lonny. That was a mistake. Letty had become her best friend in Red Springs, and Joy was determined not to let Letty's brother come between them.

At least Letty's email assured her that Lonny would be on the range all day. Knowing there was no possibility of running into him, she was free to do her errands without worrying about seeing him every time she turned a corner.

Her first order of business was stocking up on groceries. Last week, in her effort to escape Lonny, she'd purchased the bare essentials and fled. Now she was out of milk, bread, peanut butter and almost everything else.

After downing a cup of coffee, Joy dressed in jeans

and a light blue cotton shirt. At a little after nine, she headed out the door, more carefree than she'd felt in weeks. As usual, she saw a number of her students and former students on Main Street and in the grocery store. She enjoyed these brief interactions, which reminded her how different her life was compared to what it would've been if she'd stayed in Seattle.

Not until she'd loaded her groceries did she remember that she hadn't even read or responded to Josh's email. It was only natural to blame that on Lonny, too. Preoccupied with him as she was, she'd forgotten all about Josh.

One thing was certain—this kissing had to stop. Both times they'd been standing in a parking lot, exposed to the entire community.

Oh, no!

The potential for embarrassment overwhelmed her as she slammed the trunk lid of her PT Cruiser. There'd been a fight near the community center—which meant people had been outside, maybe more than a few. So it was possible that…oh, dear…that someone had seen her and Lonny wrapped in each other's arms. At the time it had seemed so…so private. There they were, the two of them, in this…this passionate embrace, practically devouring each other. Her face burned with mortification.

No—she was overreacting. People kissed in public all the time. Red Springs was a conservative town, but she hadn't done anything worthy of censure. The only logical course of action was to put the matter out of her mind. If, by chance, she and Lonny had been seen, no one was likely to ask her about it.

"Hello, Ms. Fuller." Little Cassie Morton greeted her as she skipped past Joy.

Cassie had been her student the year before and Alicia, her mother, was a classroom volunteer. Joy liked Alicia and appreciated the many hours she'd helped in class.

"Hi," Joy said cheerfully. "I see you two are out and about early on this lovely Saturday morning."

"We're going grocery shopping," Cassie explained, hopping from one foot to the other. The nine-year-old never stood still if she could run, jump or skip.

Smiling, Alicia strolled toward Joy. "Looks like you and Lonny Ellison are an item these days," the other woman said casually as she reached inside her purse and withdrew a sheaf of store coupons.

"Who told you that?" Joy asked, hoping to sound indifferent and perhaps slightly amused.

Alicia glanced up. "You mean you aren't?"

"I…I used to date Lonny. We went out a couple of years ago, but that's it." Joy nearly stuttered in her rush to broadcast her denial.

"Really?" Alicia's face took on a confused expression. "Sorry. I guess I misunderstood."

Joy hurried after her. "Who said we were seeing each other, if you don't mind my asking?"

"No one," Alicia told her. "I saw Lonny watching you at the auction last night and he had the *look,* if you know what I mean. It was rather sweet."

"Lonny?" Joy repeated with forced joviality. "I'm sure he was staring at someone else."

Alicia shrugged. "Maybe. You could do worse, you know. Folks around here are fond of Lonny. People still talk about his rodeo days. The Wyoming Kid was one of the best bull-riders around before he retired. I think he was smart to get out while he could still walk." She flashed a quick grin. "Actually, he was at the top of his form. That takes courage, you know, to give up that kind of money and fame. His dad wasn't doing well, so he was needed at home. Lonny came back, and he hasn't left since. I admire him for that."

"I do, too," Joy said, and it was true. She'd heard plenty about Lonny's successes, riding broncs as well as bulls. In fact, when they first dated, he'd proudly shown her his belt buckles. He wasn't shy about letting her know exactly how good he'd been. And yet, he'd abandoned it all in order to help his family. Walked away from the fame and the glory without question when his parents needed him. But he'd never mentioned *that* to her, not once.

"Lonny's a real sweetheart," Alicia said warmly.

Joy nodded, unable to come up with an appropriate response, and returned to her car. Her next stop was the cleaners, where she picked up her pink pantsuit, the one she planned to wear the day Josh arrived. From there, she went to Walmart for household odds and ends. By the time she'd finished, it was after twelve, and Joy was famished.

Eating a container of yogurt in front of her computer, she logged back on to the internet and answered Josh. He'd be in Red Springs in six days. There was a lot riding on this visit—certainly for her, and maybe for him, too.

The rest of her day was uneventful. In between weekly tasks like mopping the kitchen floor and dealing with accumulated clutter, she did three loads of wash, mowed her lawn and washed her car. By dinnertime, she was pleasantly tired. She wouldn't have any problem sleeping tonight; she'd made sure of it.

The phone rang only once, late in the afternoon. It was Patsy Miller, president of the PTA. Patsy asked Joy if she'd be willing to serve as a chaperone for the high school's end-of-the-year dance.

"I'll have company," she explained reluctantly, hating to turn Patsy down. Patsy had provided consistent support to every teacher in town, and Joy wanted to repay that.

"Bring your guest," Patsy suggested.

"You wouldn't mind?"

"Not at all."

"That would be great. I'll ask him and let you know." As soon as Joy hung up, she went back on-line and told Josh about the dance. It would be the perfect end to a perfect day, or so she hoped. Joy couldn't think of any better way to show him the town she'd grown to love than to have him accompany her to the carnival and then the dance.

Climbing into bed, Joy went instantly to sleep—the contented sleep of a hardworking woman.

The next morning, she discovered that Josh had answered her two emails. Both the carnival and the dance sounded like fun to him, he said. He emphasized how eager he was to see her again—a mutual feeling, she thought with a smile.

When Joy arrived at church on Sunday morning, her spirits were high. Sitting in the front pew for easy access to the organ, Joy couldn't see who was and wasn't in attendance. Normally she wouldn't care. But her weekend so far had been relatively stress-free, and she wanted to keep it that way. If Lonny Ellison was at church, she needed to know for her own self-protection.

When the opening hymns were over, Joy slid off the organ bench and took the opportunity to scan the congregation. Letty and Chase sat in a middle pew; Crickct would be at the children's service in the church basement.

Without being obvious—at least she hoped not—Joy took one more look around the congregation. As far as she could tell, there was no Lonny. It seemed to her that he usually attended, so perhaps he'd decided to stay away for a week to give them both some much-needed breathing space. Her sense of well-being increased.

At the end of the announcements and just before the sermon, the choir, all dressed in their white robes, gathered at the front of the church. Joy returned to the organ bench and poised her hands over the keyboard, her eyes focused on Penny Johnson, the choir director. With a nod of her head, Penny indicated that Joy should begin.

Just as she lowered her hands, she glanced over her shoulder at the church doors. At that very instant, they opened and in stepped Lonny Ellison. He stood at the back, staring directly at her. Naturally there weren't any seats available except in front; everyone knew you had to come early if you wanted to sit in the back. After a slight hesitation, Lonny started up the left-hand side— the side where Joy sat. She watched him and nearly faltered. It took all her control to play the first chord.

He'd *planned* this, darn him. Joy didn't know how

he'd managed it, but he'd timed his entrance to coincide with the music. He'd done it to unnerve her and he'd succeeded. This exact thing had happened last year, too; thanks to him she'd faltered and missed a couple of notes. Anger spread through her like flames in dry grass.

When she turned the sheet music, she inadvertently turned two pages instead of one. Her mistake was immediately obvious. He'd done it again! Penny threw her a shocked look and to her credit, Joy recovered quickly. She hoped Penny was the only person who'd noticed. Still, Joy cringed in embarrassment and her heart pounded loudly. Thud. Thud. Thud. It seemed, to her ears, like a percussive counterpoint to the chords she was playing.

The rest of the service remained a blur in Joy's mind. She didn't hear a word of Pastor Downey's sermon. Not a single word.

Thankfully, the closing song was "What a Friend We Have in Jesus," which she could've played in her sleep. As the congregation filed out, Joy finished the last refrain. She took several minutes to turn off the organ and cover the keyboard, then collect her sheet music and Bible. Normally she finished two or three minutes after the church emptied; however, this Sunday, she was at least six minutes longer than usual.

By now, she hoped, Lonny Ellison would be gone.

He wasn't.

Instead, he stood on the lawn by the church steps—waiting for her. He was chatting with a couple of other ranchers, but Joy wasn't fooled. He'd purposely hung around to talk to her.

When she walked down the steps, he broke away from his group.

Joy froze, one foot behind her on the final step, the other on the sidewalk. With a fierce look, she dared him to utter even a word. It was a glare she'd perfected in the classroom, and it obviously worked as well on adult men as it did on recalcitrant little boys. Lonny stopped dead in his tracks.

Then, as if she hadn't a care in the world, Joy casually greeted her friends and left.

Chapter 11

Sunday morning before he drove to church, Lonny had come into the barn to ask Tom if he wanted to attend services with him. Tom had gone a couple of Sundays, mainly because he'd hoped to see Michelle. The bruise on his cheek had turned an ugly purple and was even more noticeable now. Still, it looked worse than it felt. Kenny had sucker punched him with the aid of two of his friends, who'd distracted Tom.

Tom had declined Lonny's invitation. He didn't want Michelle to see the bruise, didn't want her to think Kenny was tougher than he was.

Tom hated fights, but he wouldn't back down from one, either. Kenny had started it, and while Tom might be small and wiry, he knew how to defend himself. He guessed Kenny Brighton had gotten the shock of his life when Tom's first punch connected. In fact, he would've smiled at the thought—except that it hurt to smile. If Bill Franklin hadn't broken up the fight, Tom would've won, despite the assistance provided by Kenny's friends. His drunk of an old man had taught him a thing or two in that department; by the time he was fifteen, Tom had learned to hold his own. Even three to one, he figured he'd stand a chance.

Lonny drove off, and Tom busied himself sweeping the barn floor. Ten mintues later, he heard another car coming down the drive and glanced out. When he saw who it was, he sucked in his breath.

Michelle.

He hesitated, then reluctantly stepped into the yard. He stood there stiffly, hands tucked in his back pockets.

She parked the car and when she got out, he realized that she'd brought him the coconut cake, protected by a plastic dome like the kind they had in diners. Catching sight of him, she frowned. Her pretty blue eyes went soft with concern as she looked at the bruise on his cheek. "Oh, Tom," she said, walking toward him.

She reached out to stroke his cheek, but he averted his face, jerking his chin away before she could touch him. At his rejection, pain flashed in her eyes. "I—I brought the cake you bought at the bake sale."

"Thanks." He took it carefully from her hands.

He figured she'd leave then, but she didn't.

"I'll put it in the house," he mumbled.

"Okay."

Tom hurried into the kitchen, depositing the cake on the table. She and her mother had done a good job with it, making it almost double the size of the one Kenny had claimed Friday night. That pleased Tom.

"What are you still doing here?" he asked gruffly when he returned to the yard. He didn't want her to know how happy he was to see her—despite his injury and his disfigured face.

"I came to find out if Kenny hurt you."

She should worry about the other guy, not him, he thought defiantly. "He didn't."

Her eyes refused to leave his face and after a moment, she nearly dissolved into tears. "I'm so sorry, Tom."

"For what? You weren't to blame."

"Yes, I was," she cried, and her voice quavered. "It was all my fault."

Tom shook his head, angry that she'd assume responsibility. Kenny Brighton was the jerk, not Michelle.

"Kenny asked me to the dance and I told him no. He wanted to know why I wouldn't go with him and I…I said I…I was going with you."

Tom felt his throat close up. "I already told you I can't take you to the dance." He didn't mean to sound angry, but he couldn't help it.

"I know, and I'm truly sorry, but I had to tell Kenny *something,* otherwise he'd pester me. He wouldn't leave me alone until I gave in and I…I know I shouldn't have lied. But because I did, he had it in for you and when you bid on the cake, he was mad and started that fight."

She was crying openly now. The tears ran down her face and Tom watched helplessly. He'd only seen one other woman cry—his mother—and he hadn't been able to stand it. He'd always tried to protect her, to comfort her. So Tom did what came naturally, and that was to hold Michelle.

They'd never touched. All their relationship amounted to was a few conversations at the feed store. He'd liked other girls back home, but he'd never had strong feelings for any of them the way he did Michelle.

When she slipped so easily into his arms, it was all Tom could do to hold in a sigh. She brought her arms about his waist and pressed her face against his shirt. Tom shyly put his own arms around her and rested his jaw against her hair. She smelled fresh and sweet and he'd never felt this good.

Michelle sniffled, then dropped her arms. He did the same. "I should go," she whispered.

Tom didn't say anything to stop her, but he didn't want her to leave.

She started walking toward her car. "I didn't tell my parents where I was going and…" She kept her head lowered and after a short pause blurted out, "Why won't you go to the dance with me?"

Dread sat heavily on his chest. "I…can't."

"You don't like me?"

He laughed, not because what she asked had amused him, but because it was so ludicrous, so far removed from the truth. "Oh, I like you."

She gazed up at him and he swore her eyes were the pure blue of an ocean he'd never seen, and deep enough to dive straight into. "I like you, too," she told him in a whisper. "I like you a *lot.* I wait for you every week, just hoping you'll stop by with Lonny. Dad thinks I'm working all these extra hours because I'm saving money for college. That's not the real reason, though. I'm there on the off-chance you'll come into town."

Although he was secretly thrilled, Tom couldn't

allow her to care for him. He had nothing to offer her. He had no future, and his past…his past was something he hoped to keep buried for the rest of his life. "I'm nothing, Michelle, you hear me? Nothing."

"Don't say that," she countered with a firmness that surprised him. "Don't *ever* say that, because it's not true. I've seen you with people and with animals, too. You're respectful and caring and kind. You don't want anyone to see it, but you are. You're not afraid of work, either. Kenny comes to the store with his dad, but he lets other people load up the truck. You're the first one there, willing to help. I've noticed many things about you, Tom. *Many* things," she emphasized. "You're as honorable as my father."

That appeared to be the highest compliment she could pay him. Tom didn't say it, but he'd noticed many things about Michelle Larson, too. What he liked most was the way she believed in him. No one ever had, except his mother. By the time she died, though, she'd been beaten down and miserable. Tom had been determined to get away from the man who'd done that to her—his father—the man who'd tried to destroy him, too. There was no turning back now.

The pressure on his chest increased. "I'll see what I can do about that dance," he said. He couldn't make her any promises. More than anything, he wanted to go there with Michelle. More than anything he wanted an excuse to hold her again, and smell her hair and maybe even kiss her.

"Thank you," she whispered.

Then before he could stop her, she pressed the palm of her hand against his cheek. His jaw still ached a bit. Not much; just enough to remind him that Kenny Brighton was a dirty fighter and not to be trusted. Taking her wrist, Tom brought her hand to his lips and kissed it.

Michelle smiled and it seemed—it really did—as if the sun had come out from behind a dark cloud and drenched him in warmth and light. But when she left soon afterward, the sensation of buoyant happiness quickly died. He should never have told her he'd think about the dance.

An hour later, Lonny returned from church and without a word to Tom marched directly into the house. Tom didn't know what was wrong and Lonny hadn't confided in him. Lonny was fair and a good boss, but he hadn't been in a particularly good mood for the last week or so. Not that it made him rude or unpleasant. Just kind of remote.

At twelve-thirty, Tom went inside. They took turns preparing meals, and this one was his. Tom found Lonny sitting at the kitchen table, his head in his hands, almost as if he was praying.

"You feel okay?" Tom asked, wondering what he could do to help.

Lonny shrugged. "I guess."

Tom opened the refrigerator and took out a slab of cheese. Grilled cheese sandwiches were easy enough. That and a can of soup would take care of their appetites.

"How many sandwiches you want?" he asked.

"Just one."

Tom nodded and took bread out of the plastic container on the kitchen counter. "I heard there's going to be a dance in town," he said, hoping he sounded casual and only vaguely interested.

"You thinking of going?" Lonny asked, showing the first hint of curiosity.

Tom shrugged, imitating Lonny. "I was thinking about it. Only…" He didn't finish.

"Only what?"

Tom lifted his shoulders again. "All I brought with me is work clothes." That was all he had, period, but he didn't mention that part.

Lonny stood up from the table and looked Tom up and down. "How much you weigh?"

Tom told him, as well as he could remember.

"That's about right. I've got an old suit you're welcome to have if it fits you."

Tom's heart shot straight into his throat. No one had ever given him anything without expecting something in return. "I'll pay you for it—I insist. How much you want for that suit? If it fits," he qualified.

"Fine, pay if you want," Lonny agreed. "I'll take a big fat slice of that as payment," he said, gesturing toward the coconut cake.

Tom grinned, satisfied with his response. "You got it."

"Fair trade. If you need a ride into town Friday night, let me know."

Tom laid the bread, butter side down, in the heated pan. "I'd appreciate it."

"You taking Michelle Larson to that dance?" Lonny asked next.

With his back to the other man, moving the sandwiches around with a spatula, Tom smiled. "Like I said, I was thinking about it."

"You do that. She's a good girl."

"I know." He frowned then, because having something decent to wear was just the first hurdle. It didn't come easy, letting anyone know how inadequate he was when it came to a situation like this. He glanced over his shoulder and saw that Lonny was watching him. "I've never been to a dance before," he muttered.

"You'll enjoy yourself," Lonny said, reaching for a knife and a couple of plates to serve slices of the cake.

"I said, I've never been to a dance before," Tom repeated, louder this time. He turned around to properly face his employer.

Lonny frowned and looked mildly guilty about slicing into Tom's coconut cake. "There's nothing to worry about. They might have a real band, or there could be someone playing CDs—I'm not sure how it'll work this year. The school will arrange to have a few adults there as chaperones."

It was plain that Tom would need to spell it out for him. "I don't know how to dance," he murmured, breaking eye contact. "What am I supposed to do when the music starts?"

"Ah." Lonny nodded sagely. "I see your problem."

"Do *you* know how to dance?" He wouldn't come right out and ask, but if Lonny volunteered to teach him, Tom would be willing to take lessons, as long as they didn't interfere with work.

"Me, dance?" Lonny asked in a jovial tone. "Not really. Mostly I fake it."

"Anyone can do that?" Tom wasn't sure he believed this.

"I do. I just sort of shuffle my feet and move my arms around a lot and no one's ever said anything. You like music, don't you?"

Tom did. He listened to the country-western station on the radio. "What kind of music do they play at school dances?"

The question appeared to be difficult because it took Lonny a long time to answer. "Regular music," he finally said.

Tom didn't know what regular music was. He frowned.

"I've got some old movies in the living room somewhere that you might want to watch. They might help you."

"What kind of movies?"

Lonny thought about that for a few minutes. "There's a couple with John Travolta and one with Kevin Bacon. Hey, that movie might interest you because it's got a farm boy in it who doesn't know how to dance, either. Kevin knows a few moves and takes him under his wing. It's a good movie, great music. Why don't you watch it?"

"Okay." Tom would do just about anything to keep from making a fool of himself in front of Michelle. He needed to learn quickly, too; the dance was only five days away.

The phone rang then, and Lonny went into the other room to answer it. While he was on the phone, Tom finished preparing the cheese sandwiches. He heated a can of tomato soup and had it dished up and on the table by the time Lonny returned.

When Lonny came back into the kitchen, he was frowning.

"Problems?" Tom asked, instantly alert.

Lonny shook his head. "I'm going to volunteer as a chaperone at that dance."

Tom's suspicions were instantly raised. "Any particular reason?"

Lonny bit into his grilled cheese sandwich and nodded. "Sounds like Kenny Brighton might be looking for trouble, especially if you turn up with Michelle."

Tom bristled. "I can take care of myself."

"I don't doubt it, but Kenny will think twice about starting something if I'm there."

Tom didn't like the idea of Lonny having to hang around the school dance because of him.

Lonny seemed to sense his reaction. "What about Michelle?" he added. "How's *she* going to feel if Kenny beats up on you again?"

Tom saw the wisdom of what Lonny was saying. "You'd do that for me?" he asked.

"I offered, didn't I?"

Tom's chest tightened, and he stared down at his plate while he struggled with the emotion that hit him out of nowhere. This rancher, whom he'd known for only a few months, was more of a parent to him than his own father had ever been.

"Let me see about that suit," Lonny said when he'd eaten his lunch. He set his dirty dishes in the sink and went upstairs; within minutes he'd returned, holding out a perfectly good brown suit.

"What do you think?" Lonny asked.

The suit was far better than Tom had expected. It

didn't look as if it'd ever been worn. "What I think is I should give you that entire coconut cake."

Lonny laughed. "Go try this on, and if there's any of that cake left when you get back, consider yourself fortunate."

Tom already knew he was fortunate. He didn't need a slice of coconut cake to tell him that.

Chapter 12

Letty and Chase often invited Lonny, and now Tom, to join them for dinner on Sunday evenings. Tom had accepted twice, but this week he declined. Before Lonny left, Tom asked if it would be all right if he watched a few of those movies Lonny had mentioned earlier.

Lonny had no objection to that. He smiled as he pulled out of the yard in his pickup and headed for Chase and Letty's. He was glad to be able to help the boy, hoping it worked out, with the dance and Michelle and all.

Lonny drove the short distance to Chase's ranch, still feeling confused about Joy. He counted on Letty to have some insights on what he should do about his feelings for her. He knew he could be stubborn, but until recently he hadn't recognized how much his attitude had cost him. For nearly two years, he'd allowed his relationship with Joy to lie fallow. During that time he'd watched her develop friendships in the community, and he knew that everything he'd accused her of was wrong. She was no city slicker; from the first, she'd done her best to become part of the community. Lonny hadn't wanted to accept that because she'd wounded his pride. He'd wanted her to fail just to prove how right he was. It bothered him to admit that, but it was the truth. He swallowed hard and his hands tightened around the steering wheel. Because of his stubbornness, he'd done a great disservice to Joy—and to himself.

Plain and simple, Lonny was attracted to Joy—more than attracted. Their kisses over the past few days confirmed what he already knew. Another uncomfortable truth: not once in the last two years had Joy been far from his thoughts. Following their most recent traffic *incident*—as she'd correctly described it—the potency of that attraction had all but exploded in his face.

Lonny could acknowledge it now. For two years he'd been in love with Joy. The near-collision had simply brought everything to the surface, and it explained his overreaction to the events of that afternoon. He grinned, thinking about the way he'd stormed at her as if she'd nearly caused a fatal accident. No wonder she was wary of him.

Deep in thought, Lonny missed the turnoff to Spring Valley Ranch. He must've driven here ten thousand times and not once overshot the entrance. The fact that he had today said a lot about his preoccupation with Joy.

As Lonny drove into the yard, he noticed that Chase was giving Cricket a riding lesson on Jennybird. The little girl rode her pony around the corral while Chase held the lead rope. Chase gave him a quick wave and continued his slow circuit. Meanwhile, Letty sat in a rocking chair on the porch, watching.

Lonny crossed the yard and joined his sister, claiming the chair next to hers.

Letty raised her glass of lemonade in greeting. "Tom won't be coming?" she asked.

Lonny shook his head. "Not tonight."

Letty stood and went inside the house, reappearing a minute later with a second glass of lemonade, which she handed him.

"Thanks." Lonny took a long, thirst-quenching drink, then set down the glass with a disconsolate sigh.

Letty turned to him. "What's wrong?"

His state of mind obviously showed more than Lonny had realized. Rather than blurt out what was troubling him, he shrugged. "I've been doing some thinking about Joy and me."

His sister sat down again and started rocking. "I've been telling you for a whole year that you're an idiot." Her smile cut the sharpness of her words.

"I can't disagree," he muttered. Even after being in the rodeo world and dating dozens of women, he was as naive as a twelve-year-old kid about romancing a woman like Joy.

"Listen," he said, deciding to speak openly with his sister. "Would you be willing to advise me? Maybe you could even help me—speak to Joy on my behalf." He wouldn't normally ask that of Letty, and requesting this kind of favor didn't come easy.

Letty hesitated; she rocked back and forth, just the

way their mother used to. When she spoke he heard her regret. "Lonny, as much as I'd like to, I can't do that."

He nodded. Actually, that was what he'd expected, but it didn't hurt to ask.

"I'll be happy to offer my opinion, though."

He made a noncommittal sound. Letty had never been shy about sharing her opinions, especially when they concerned him.

"There's something you should probably know. Something important I learned just today."

He tensed. "About Joy?"

Letty sipped her lemonade. "Josh Howell contacted her."

"The college boyfriend?" Lonny's jaw tightened. Right now, this was the worst piece of news he could hear. When they'd first started dating, Joy had casually mentioned Josh a few times; Lonny had read between the lines and understood that this relationship had played an important role in her past.

She'd stayed in touch with Josh and although their romance had cooled, Joy still had feelings for the other man. It was early in their own relationship, and Lonny hadn't wanted Joy to think he was the jealous type, so he'd said nothing. But the fact was, he *had* been jealous and he hadn't liked knowing that Joy and this city boy were continuing some kind of involvement, even a diminished one from a distance.

"Well?" Letty pressed. "Doesn't it concern you?"

Lonny made an effort to disguise his views on the matter. "What does Josh want?"

"All I heard is he's coming to visit."

"Here? In Red Springs?"

"That's what she said. My guess is that he wants to revive their relationship."

"She told you that?" His jaw went even tighter.

"Not in so many words, but think about it. Why else would Josh come here? It isn't like he has some burning desire to visit a ranching community. He's coming because of Joy." She paused, tilting her head toward Lonny. "I find his timing rather suspicious, don't you?"

"How?" Lonny asked bluntly.

"Joy's teaching contract is up for renewal."

"So, you think he's hoping to lure her back to Seattle?" His voice fell as he took in the significance of the timing. Right then and there, Lonny decided he wasn't letting her go without a fight. Not physical, of course—that would be stupid and unfair; Josh wouldn't stand a chance against him, if he did say so himself. And knowing Joy, she'd be furious with Lonny and immediately side with the city guy. A physical showdown would be the worst possible move. No, this challenge was mental. Emotional. And it had more to do with convincing Joy than scaring off Josh.

"When will he be here?" he asked urgently.

Letty must've seen that determined look in his eyes, because she reached over and patted his hand reassuringly. "I'm not sure, but I believe it's sometime this week."

He nodded.

"What are you thinking?" she asked.

That should be obvious. "I've only got a few days to talk Joy into staying here." Although he knew darn well that more than talk would be involved...

Letty frowned at him. "Why do you care if she leaves or not?"

Lonny didn't appreciate the question. Nevertheless, he gave her an honest answer. He could pretend he hadn't heard—or he could tell Letty the words that burned to be spoken. "Because I love her."

"I know," Letty replied, leaning back with a satisfied grin. "You have for a long time."

Lonny expected more of an I-told-you-so and was mildly surprised when Letty didn't lay into him for his foolishness or recite a litany of rules on how to persuade Joy to make her life in Red Springs, with him.

"So what are you going to do about it?" Letty asked next.

The answer to that wasn't clear. "I don't know."

Letty frowned again, a worried frown. "Promise me you won't say anything stupid."

"Like what?" he demanded.

She rolled her eyes. "Like you're going to charge her insurance company for the so-called damage to your truck."

"I never really intended to do that. It was a ploy, that's all."

"A ploy to infuriate and anger Joy. Because of it—and because of other stupid things you've said—you have a lot of ground to recover."

Lonny didn't need his sister telling him what he already knew. "I'll talk to her." But that didn't seem to be working, either. He'd left her a note, and she'd thrown it away. Joy wasn't interested in talking to him, yet every time they were together, they ended up in each other's arms. The fact was, those few kisses gave him hope and encouragement. They told him that while Joy might deny it, she *did* have feelings for him, feelings as intense as his were for her. Feelings she wasn't ready to acknowledge.

His sister turned to stare at him as if he were a stranger. "Can I make a suggestion?" she asked.

"Sure." He'd been counting on it.

"A woman likes to know she's wanted and needed and treasured," she told him. Lonny understood what she was saying—that this was exactly how Chase felt about her. Lonny had seen it happen. His friend had come alive the moment Letty returned to Red Springs. It was the same way Lonny felt about Joy. All he had to do now was figure out how to protect her pride, while keeping his own intact.

"I'll tell her," Lonny said, suspecting this might be his only route to Joy.

"Go slow," Letty murmured.

"Slow," he repeated. "But I haven't got time to hang around, not with this other guy hot on her heels."

"Yes, you do, otherwise Joy will assume you're only interested now because Josh is about to make an appearance in her life. She's got to believe your actions are motivated by sincerity, not competitiveness."

"Oh." Letty was right about that, too.

This was getting complicated. "Should I approach her with gifts?" He felt at a distinct disadvantage. Joy wasn't like the girls he'd met in his rodeo days; he'd rarely ever given them gifts, beyond maybe buying them a beer.

Letty nodded approvingly. "That's a good place to start."

Lonny rather liked the idea of bringing Joy things. He had a freezer full of meat, some of his best. None of that hormone-laden stuff sold in the grocery stores, either. He'd explain that his and Chase's cattle were lean, and fed on grass, and he'd make sure she recognized the significance of that. "I could take her some steaks from my freezer," he said, pleased with himself.

"Uh…" Letty cocked her head to one side, as if she was trying to come up with a way to tell him that wasn't quite what she had in mind.

"What?"

"Bringing her a few steaks is a nice thought," his sister informed him. "But women tend to prefer gifts that are more…*personal*."

Lonny cast a desperate look at Letty. "Help me out here."

"Flowers are always nice," she said.

Flowers from a shop were expensive and died within a few days. "What about perfume?"

"Yes, but that poses a problem. Most women have preferences. They develop their own favorites. A particular scent smells different depending on who wears it, you know."

Lonny wasn't sure what his sister had just said, other than that he shouldn't buy perfume. Well, if there was no better alternative, he'd go with her first suggestion. "Flowers I can do."

"Start there."

"I will," he promised. "Then you'll help me figure out what I should get her next?" he said, relying on his sister's assistance. He considered her the strategist; he'd simply follow her directions.

"Don't be in too big a rush," Letty reminded him. "If you run into her by accident, be polite and respectful, and then go about your business."

Lonny saw the brilliance of his sister's words. He hoped he could restrain himself enough to do that. Every time he saw Joy, all he could think about was how much he wanted to hold her and kiss her. It went without saying that there was more to a relationship between a man and a woman than the physical. Mutual desire was important and necessary, but no more so than mutual respect, honesty and genuine caring. He felt all of that for Joy. Unfortunately, it was easier to convey the holding and kissing part.

"Other than getting Joy gifts, what else should I do?"

Letty's brow creased in thought.

"Do I have to learn to talk pretty?" Lonny asked, a bit embarrassed. Like most cowboys, he tended to be plainspoken. Besides, it was hard enough not to trip over his tongue saying normal things to Joy, let alone anything poetic.

"She needs to know how much she means to you," Letty said.

Lonny gestured helplessly as a sick feeling settled in the pit of his stomach. "I'm not sure how to tell her that."

"Tell me what you like about her physically," Letty said. "And I suggest you not say anything about her weight."

"Okay…" A picture of Joy formed in his mind, and he relaxed. "She's just the right height."

"For what?"

Lonny shifted uncomfortably in his seat. "Kissing."

"Okay…anything else?"

"Oh, sure." But now that he'd said it, he couldn't come up with a single thing.

"Do you like her eyes?"

He nodded. "They're blue." He said that so Letty would know he'd been paying attention. "A real pretty shade of blue."

"Good." She clearly approved. "You can tell her that."

"Sort of a Roquefort-cheese blue."

Her face fell.

"That's not a good comparison?" he muttered.

"Think flowers instead," she hinted.

"Okay." But he'd have to give it some consideration. He wasn't that knowledgeable about flowers. Especially *blue* flowers.

"If you can persuade her, you and Joy will make a wonderful couple."

"If?" he repeated, taking offense at the qualifier. His sister seemed to forget that at one time he'd ridden bulls and broncos. It was the sheer force of his determination, along with—of course—his innate skill, that had kept him in prize money. Joy was the biggest prize of his life and he was going to cowboy up and do whatever he had to—even if he got thrown or trampled in the process.

"What took you so long, big brother?" Letty teased. "You've been crazy about Joy for two years."

Earlier, he would've denied that, but the time for pretense was past. "Pride mostly." However, he'd seen the error of his ways. No doubt Letty was happy with his decision, and Lonny's heart felt lighter and more carefree than it had in years. He felt good. Better than good, he felt *terrific*.

Lonny followed his sister's gaze as she watched Chase and Cricket with the spotted pony. He was moved to see how much Chase loved Cricket. He might not be her biological father, but in every way that mattered, Chase was Cricket's daddy.

His sister's eyes grew soft and full of love. One day, if everything went as Lonny hoped, he'd have a son or daughter of his own. It would please him beyond measure if Joy was the mother of his children. The thought quickened a desire so powerful that his chest constricted with emotion. He loved Joy. He sincerely loved her and the sun would fall from the sky before he lost her to anyone, least of all an old boyfriend.

Chapter 13

The alarm rang at six o'clock Monday morning and with a groan, Joy stretched out her arm and flipped the switch to the off position. She was warm and comfortable, and a sense of happiness spread through her. In five days, Josh would be in Red Springs. With her!

He'd phoned on Sunday afternoon, and they'd talked for an hour. Toward the end of their conversation, he'd admitted that Red Springs was two-hundred-plus miles out of his way; in other words, he was letting her know that he wanted to renew their relationship. That meant he'd missed her and was willing to invest time, effort and expense in seeing her again. She felt the glow of that knowledge even now. Lonny drifted into her mind and she made a determined effort to chase him away. Her willingness to accept his kisses—and kiss him back—mortified her.

In fact, it was Lonny's kisses that had prompted her to tell Letty about Josh's visit. Letty would certainly mention it to Lonny, which was exactly what she wanted. It was the coward's way out, she freely admitted that, but she was apprehensive over what might happen when Josh arrived.

She was afraid Lonny might force a confrontation with her, and she hoped this news would discourage him. She didn't *want* to think about Lonny or worry about her reaction to him. She felt so positive about Josh and their future together, and the only person who might ruin that was Lonny.

Josh was thoughtful and generous and as different from Lonny Ellison as a man could get. Just the thought of him incited her to toss aside the warm covers and bolt upright, irritated that this disagreeable rancher kept making unwanted appearances in her life. He was irrational, bad-tempered and, well… It didn't matter, because she wouldn't be having anything more to do with him.

Joy got to school early and had just parked her car in the employee lot when she saw Letty Brown drive to the student drop-off area. Either Letty had business in town this morning, or Cricket had missed the bus.

The back passenger door opened and Cricket popped out, greeted Joy with an exuberant "Hi, Ms. Fuller!" and then skipped over to the playground.

Letty rolled down her car window and waved at Joy.

Joy waved back. Strangely reluctant to see her friend, she trotted over to Letty's car. Thankfully no one had pulled in behind her. In the next twenty minutes the driveway would be seething with activity.

"Morning," Letty said from inside her car.

"Isn't this a beautiful day?" It could be raining buckets and it would still be an absolutely perfect day as far as Joy was concerned. As long as she could avoid seeing, hearing or thinking about one annoying man...

"You seem in a very good mood for a Monday morning."

"I am," Joy said, resting one hand on the window frame.

Letty laughed. "Me, too." She lowered her voice. "Can you keep a secret?"

"Of course."

Letty bit her lip. "Chase doesn't even know. Cricket, either." Then her eyes brightened and she placed her hand on Joy's. "I'm pregnant!"

Joy gasped. "Oh, Letty! That's incredible news!" Because of her medical condition, pregnancy could be a risk. Letty had told Joy that Chase was concerned about the strain a pregnancy would put on her heart.

"I won't say anything to Chase until the doctor officially confirms it," she continued, "but I know my own body. And just to be sure, I took one of those home tests. Chase will want to hear what the doctor says, though."

"But I thought—" Joy closed her mouth abruptly, afraid to say anything about the worries and fears that might accompany a pregnancy.

Letty must have sensed what Joy was thinking, because she added, "I went to see Dr. Faraday, the heart specialist, a little while ago."

Joy remembered that visit. It was the day Lonny had come to pick up Cricket.

"The doc gave me a clean bill of health," Letty exclaimed with unrestrained happiness. "The surgery was one hundred percent successful, and he couldn't see any reason I shouldn't have a second baby."

Joy knew how badly Letty wanted another child. Seeing her friend's wild joy nearly brought tears to her own eyes. "I'm so thrilled for you."

"Now, promise me, not a word to anyone," Letty warned.

"My lips are sealed." Half leaning into the front of the vehicle through the open window, Joy hugged her friend's shoulders. Straightening, she said, "I have some news, too—although it isn't as momentous as yours."

"Is this a secret or am I free to broadcast it?"

"So you're the town crier?"

"No," Letty said with a laugh, "that would be Honey Sue, but I run a close second."

Joy waited a moment for effect, then nearly burst out laughing at the expression on Letty's face. "Josh and I talked for over an hour yesterday, and I'm thinking of moving back to Seattle." She hated to leave Red Springs. But if she and Josh decided to resume their relationship in a serious way, she'd have to return to the Puget Sound area. A few internet inquiries had assured her there were teaching positions available.

The joy faded from Letty's eyes. "You'd actually move back to Seattle for Josh?"

Joy nodded. "Of course, everything hinges on what happens this weekend. But at this point, I'd say there's plenty of reason to believe I would."

Letty made an effort to smile. "I'd hate to see you go."

"I'd hate it, too, but I can't ask Josh to give up his

career and move to Wyoming when there are no job opportunities for him. I can get a teaching position nearly anywhere."

"That makes sense." Letty's words were filled with poorly concealed disappointment.

Joy took a deep breath, realizing this had to be said. "I know you always hoped that things would work out between Lonny and me. Unfortunately that's not the case."

"My brother can be stubborn, that's for sure."

"I can be, too," Joy admitted. "The two of us don't really get along. I feel bad about it, because I genuinely like Lonny. I always have, but it's best to bow out now before either of us gets hurt."

"You're certain about that?" Letty's gaze pleaded with hers.

"Yes," Joy said quickly. Although she was confident and hopeful about her relationship with Josh, she wouldn't leave Red Springs without a few regrets. And one of those regrets was Lonny Ellison....

"When will Josh arrive?" Letty asked.

Joy braced her hands against the window frame. "Friday. He's driving from Salt Lake City and should get here sometime in the afternoon."

"That's...great."

Joy could tell that Letty was trying hard to sound pleased for her; at the same time, the concern in her eyes sent a conflicting message.

"So Josh will be with you at the school carnival?" she asked casually.

"He's looking forward to it, and so am I."

When Letty didn't respond, Joy asked, "Do you

think that'll be a problem?" Although she'd lived in the community for two years, there seemed to be a lot she didn't understand about people's expectations. Perhaps bringing a male friend to what was technically a school function would be frowned upon.

Letty gave her a slight smile. "No, everything's fine. Don't worry."

Joy smiled back but felt tears gather in her eyes.

"I'll miss you," Letty whispered.

"There's always a chance I might not leave," Joy said honestly. "The school board's offered me a new contract and I've asked for time to think it over. I'll know more after this weekend. Oh, I shouldn't have said anything," she muttered fretfully. "It's too soon."

Letty shrugged and then sighed. "We'll keep in touch no matter what happens."

"Absolutely," Joy concurred. "We'll always be friends."

Letty nodded and glanced over her shoulder. Another car had pulled into the school's circular driveway. "You're right, of course. Anyway, I should go."

"See you later," Joy said, stepping back from the curb.

Letty checked her rearview mirror and drove carefully out of the slot.

Joy went on to her class, excited and happy for her friend. Despite his worries, Chase would be ecstatic when Letty told him about her pregnancy. Joy had watched Chase with Cricket and marveled at how deeply he cared for the child. Lonny was a good uncle, too. In time, when he found the right woman, Lonny would make a good father himself. But she didn't want to think about Lonny with another woman and pushed that thought from her mind.

Her day went relatively smoothly, considering that this was the last week of school and the children were restless and eager to be outside. When classes were dismissed that afternoon, Joy drove down Main Street to Franklin Rentals. She needed to double-check that the cotton candy machine would be there in time for the carnival.

"Good afternoon, Joy," Bill Franklin greeted her when she entered the store.

She stepped around air compressors, spray paint equipment and a dozen other machines of uncertain purpose on her way to the counter. "Hello, Bill."

"I bet I know why you're here. Rest assured, everything will be in well before Friday. If not, I'm afraid I'd be ridden out of town on a rail," he said with a laugh.

"Thanks, Bill." She smiled at his mild joke. "I'll tell the other committee members."

"Thanks, Joy."

After another few minutes, she retraced her steps through the maze of equipment that littered the floor.

She was headed toward her car when she saw Lonny Ellison strolling in the direction of Franklin Rentals. She stopped in her tracks.

He saw her, too, and froze.

Neither moved for at least a minute.

Lonny broke out of the trance first and walked, slowly and deliberately, toward her.

Joy's heart felt as if it were attempting to break free of her chest, it pounded that hard and fast. Despite her reaction, she pretended to be unaffected. As Lonny neared, she lowered her head and said in a stiff, formal tone, "Mr. Ellison."

Lonny paused, touching the brim of his Stetson. "Ms. Fuller," he returned just as formally. Then he removed his hat and held it in both hands.

Lonny had stopped a few feet away. Joy stood there, rooted to the sidewalk. She couldn't summon the resolve to take a single step, although her nerves were on full alert and adrenaline coursed through her bloodstream.

"You look…pretty…today," Lonny said after an awkward moment.

Not once had Lonny ever complimented her appearance. Well, except for that embarrassing, backhanded attempt in the grocery store… "Thank you. You do, too."

His eyes widened. "I look…pretty?"

She almost managed a smile. "Not exactly."

"That's a relief."

This was ridiculous, she told herself, the two of them standing in the middle of the sidewalk like this, just staring at each other. "Have a good afternoon," she said abruptly and started to walk away.

"Joy," Lonny choked out.

"Yes?" Joy maintained a healthy distance for fear they'd find an excuse to kiss again, and in broad daylight, too.

He hesitated. "I—I hope the two of us will remain friends."

At first Joy wasn't sure how to respond. His evident sincerity took her by surprise. "I do, too," she finally said.

His eyes crinkled with a half smile and he nodded once, then cleared his throat. "Also, I wish to apologize if I offended you by my actions."

"Actions?"

He lowered his voice. "Those...kisses."

"Oh." Her cheeks instantly flushed with heat. He appeared to be awaiting her response, so she said, "Apology accepted."

"Thank you."

Her car wasn't far away now and when she used the remote to unlock it, Lonny rushed over and held open the driver's door.

Slipping inside the Cruiser, she blinked up at him. "Who are you and what have you done with Lonny Ellison?"

He chuckled. "I'm not nearly as bad as you think."

She wanted to say she doubted that, but it would've been impolite—and untrue.

"I'm through with pretending, Joy," he told her. "I cared about you two years ago, and I care about you now." He took a step back from her vehicle. "I let foolish pride stand in the way and I regret it." Having said that, he smiled, replacing his Stetson. "Have a good evening."

"Thank you, I will." Her fingers trembled as she inserted the key in the ignition. When she looked up again, Lonny was walking into Franklin Rentals.

Joy mulled over their short exchange during her drive home, still feeling confused. There was an unreal quality about it, almost as if she'd dreamed the entire episode. This strained politeness wouldn't last; of that, she was sure. Sooner or later Lonny would return to his dictatorial ways.

She poured herself a glass of iced tea and sat at her kitchen table while she mentally reviewed her day, starting with Letty's news. This evening would be a very special one for Letty and Chase.

Without warning, Joy felt a sharp twinge of emotion. One day that same pleasure would be hers, when she'd be able to tell the man she loved that she was pregnant with his child. A yearning, a deep and silent longing, yawned inside her. She felt the desire to be loved, to experience that kind of love. Out of nowhere, tears filled her eyes and she bit hard on her lower lip, trying to control the emotion.

Someday... She had to believe that someday it would be her turn.

Chapter 14

Tom Meyerson eagerly anticipated Lonny's next trip into Red Springs. Fortunately, he didn't have long to wait. At breakfast on Wednesday morning, Lonny announced that he had several errands to run that afternoon.

"Would you mind if I came along?" Tom asked as nonchalantly as he could. It was a habit from the years of living with his father. If his old man knew that Tom wanted or needed something, he went out of his way to make sure Tom didn't get it. Through the years, Tom had gotten good at hiding his feelings.

He had to see Michelle and talk to her. He wouldn't *ask* Lonny to take him, to make a special trip for him, nor would he borrow the truck. But if Lonny was going anyway... Sure, he could phone Michelle and he probably should have, but he wanted to see her eyes light up when he told her he'd be taking her to the dance, after all. At night, as he drifted into sleep, he imagined her smile and it made him feel good inside.

He waited for Lonny to answer, almost fearing his employer would turn him down.

Lonny shrugged. "As long as you're finished your chores, I don't have a problem with you hitching a ride."

Tom smiled, unable to disguise his happiness. He cleared his throat. "Thanks, I appreciate it."

Lonny slapped him on the back in an affectionate gesture. Before he could stop himself, Tom flinched. After years of avoiding his father's brutal assaults, the reaction was instinctive. He held his breath, hoping Lonny wouldn't comment.

Lonny noticed, all right, but to Tom's relief, didn't say anything. Instead, he checked his watch. "I want to leave around four."

Michelle would be out of school by then and at the store, working in the office for her dad. Happy expectation carried Tom the rest of the day.

He'd watched the movies Lonny had mentioned two or three times each and had practiced a few moves in front of the mirror. No one was going to confuse him with Kevin Bacon or John Travolta, that was for sure. But he didn't feel like a complete incompetent, either.

He'd been listening to the radio more, too, and was beginning to think he could handle a dance. Deep down, he sensed that his mother would be pleased if she knew. Perhaps she did....

At ten to four, Tom changed his shirt and combed his hair. When he came out of the barn, he saw that Lonny was already in the truck.

Tom hopped into the pickup beside him.

Lonny wrinkled his nose and sniffed the air. "That you?" he asked.

Tom frowned; maybe he should've taken the time to shower.

"You're wearing cologne," Lonny chided.

Tom's face turned beet-red, and Lonny chuckled. After a moment, Tom smiled, too, and then he made a loud sniffing sound himself. "Hey, I'm not the only one. Who are *you* going to see?"

Lonny's laughter faded quickly enough, and he grumbled an unintelligible reply.

"I'll bet it's Joy Fuller."

Lonny ignored him, and Tom figured he'd better not push the subject. He'd learned to trust Lonny, but he wasn't sure yet how far that trust went. Still, he found he was gradually lowering his guard. Being with Lonny, talking to him about Michelle, had felt good. He liked Letty and Chase, too. Twice now he'd joined the family for Sunday dinner, and those times were about as close as he'd gotten to seeing a real family in action. He hadn't known it could be like that, hadn't realized people related to each other in such a caring and generous manner. Tom was grateful for whatever circumstances had led him to Red Springs and Lonny's barn. It was, without question, the best thing that had happened to him in his whole life.

"Would you mind if I turned on the radio?" Tom asked as a companionable silence grew between them.

"Go ahead."

Tom leaned forward and spun the dial until he found a country-western station. He looked at Lonny, who nodded. Tom relaxed against the seat and before long, his foot was tapping and his hand was bouncing rhythmically on his knee.

Lonny turned the volume up nearly full blast. After only a moment or two, they were both singing at the top of their lungs. Tom was sure anyone passing them on the highway would cringe, because neither of them could sing on key. Tom didn't care, though. This was about as good as it got for someone like him. Cruising down the highway with the windows open, music blaring—and, for this one day, he didn't have a worry in the world other than what kind of flowers to buy his girl for the dance.

The radio was playing at a more discreet volume by the time they reached the outskirts of Red Springs. Lonny pulled up across from Larson's Feed, and Tom opened the passenger door and jumped out.

"I shouldn't be longer than an hour," Lonny told him.

"I'll wait for you here."

With a toot of his horn, Lonny drove off.

Tom jogged across the street and when he walked into the store, Michelle was behind the cash register, smiling at him.

"Hi," she said shyly.

"Hi," Tom answered, having trouble finding his tongue. She was so pretty, it was hard not to just stand there and stare at her.

"Would you like a Coke?" she asked.

"Uh, sure."

"Dad has some in the office. I'll be right back."

"That's fine." He'd wait all day if she asked him to.

Tom leaned against the long counter, then straightened when Michelle's father came in. Tom immediately removed his hat. "Good afternoon, Mr. Larson."

"Tom," the other man said, inclining his head toward him. Then, as if he had important business to attend to, he left almost as suddenly as he'd appeared.

Michelle was back a minute later, holding two cans of soda. "Dad said it'd be okay if we sat out front," she said. The feed store had a porch with two rocking chairs and a big community bulletin board. The porch had weathered with time, and the red-painted building had seen better days, but there was a feeling of comfort here, and even of welcome.

They sat down, and Tom opened his soda and handed it to Michelle. At first she didn't seem to understand that he was opening hers and they needed to exchange cans. When she did, she offered him the biggest, sweetest smile he'd ever seen. Tom thought he'd be willing to open a thousand pop cans for one of her smiles.

"Did you decide about the dance?" she asked, her eyes wide and hopeful.

Tom took his first swallow of Coke, then lowered his head. When he glanced up, he discovered Michelle watching him closely, and she seemed to be holding her breath. He smiled and said, "It looks like I'll be able to go."

Just as he'd anticipated, Michelle nearly exploded with happiness. "You *can?* Really? You're not teasing me, are you?"

He simply shook his head.

She set her drink aside and pressed her fingers to her lips. "I think I'm going to cry."

"Don't do that," he nearly shouted. Every time he'd

seen tears in his mother's eyes, he'd been shaken and
scared. And he'd always felt it was his duty to make
things right, even though he wasn't the one who'd made
her cry.

"I'm just so happy."

"I am, too." Tom wasn't accustomed to this much
happiness. He felt he should be on his guard, glance
over his shoulder every once in a while, because disappointment probably wasn't far behind.

Michelle picked up her drink. "Thank you," she
whispered.

Tom thought *he* should be thanking her. "I need to
know what color your dress is," he managed to say instead.

Her lips curved in a smile, and her eyes were alight
with joy. "It's pale yellow with little white flowers. It's
the prettiest dress I've ever had. I bought it even before
I asked you to take me to the dance."

Tom made a mental note of the color. He'd ask Letty
what kind of flower he should buy for the corsage. He
didn't know much about flowers—or about any of the
other things that seemed important to women.

He wouldn't even have known about the corsage if
Lonny hadn't mentioned it. That'd brought up a flurry
of questions on Tom's part. Having never attended a
school dance, or any other dance for that matter, he had
no idea what to expect. He was afraid he might inadvertently say or do something embarrassing. He wanted
this one night to be as perfect as he could make it. For
Michelle, yes, and in a way he could barely understand,
for his mother, too.

They sat in silence for a while, and Tom searched

for subjects to discuss. His mind whirled with questions and comments.

"The weather will be nice for the carnival and the dance," Michelle said conversationally.

"That's good."

"Dad says not to worry about—" She hesitated and looked away.

Tom frowned, wondering if Michelle's father had said something derogatory about him. "What?" he asked, his heart sinking. He'd barely spoken more than a few words to Mr. Larson. Her father probably didn't need a reason to dislike him, though. Tom had learned early in life that people often didn't. Being poor, being a drunkard's son—those had been reasons enough back home.

"I thought I should tell you."

"Then do it," Tom said, stiffening.

"Kenny's dad phoned mine last Sunday."

Tom didn't like the sound of this. "About what?"

"Mr. Brighton said Kenny's pretty upset about you seeing me. He said he's afraid if you and I go to the dance together, there might be trouble."

Tom relaxed, grateful this situation didn't involve Mr. Larson's feelings toward him. "Kenny Brighton doesn't scare me."

"It bothered my dad. He's afraid Kenny might try to pull something at the dance. Mostly, he doesn't want me caught in the middle."

Tom hadn't really considered that. "Your dad's right." He hated to suggest it, but he couldn't see any alternative. "Maybe we'd better not attend the dance."

Michelle's reaction was immediate. "No way are we

missing that dance! Not after everything I went through to get you to be my date."

Tom started to protest, but Michelle was adamant. "I'm not letting Kenny Brighton ruin the last dance of high school. And…and you aren't half the man I thought you were if *you* let him. Besides, Dad and I came to an understanding."

Her words stung Tom's pride. "What do you mean, half the man you thought I was?"

She shook her head. "I didn't mean that part."

He eyed her skeptically.

"Don't you want to know how Dad and I compromised?" she asked, obviously eager to tell him.

"All right."

She smiled again, one of those special smiles that made his mouth go dry. "I had to get Mom on my side first, and then the two of us talked to Dad. After a couple of hours, he finally saw reason." She paused long enough to draw in a deep breath. "Dad phoned Lonny last Sunday afternoon and asked him to volunteer as a chaperone for the dance."

"I know." He'd been thinking about it, and although he appreciated Lonny's support, he'd begun to feel a little humiliated. Scowling, he said, "I don't need anyone to do my fighting for me."

"That's just it, don't you see?" Michelle insisted, her eyes pleading with his for understanding. "If Lonny's at the dance, there won't *be* any fight."

Maybe, but Tom wasn't convinced. Kenny and a couple of his friends could come looking for trouble, and if that was the case, Tom wouldn't back down. He didn't want Lonny leaping in to rescue him, either.

Tom would take care of the situation, in his own time and his own way.

"Tom?" Michelle whispered.

He tried to reassure her with a smile, but he didn't think it worked, because her expression grew even more distraught. "Don't worry, okay?" he murmured.

"I can't help it. You have this…this look like you're upset and angry, and it's frightening me."

As much as possible, Tom relaxed. "It'll be fine."

"I shouldn't have said anything. But at least if Kenny does start a fight, Lonny will make sure it's fair." She paused. "I hope there isn't one, though."

Tom didn't respond.

Michelle leaned toward him and took his hand, clasping it between both of hers. Her hold was surprisingly strong.

"Look at me," she pleaded.

At first he resisted. He knew he couldn't refuse her, and he wouldn't put himself in a position where he'd be bound by his word.

"Please," she whispered, raising his hand to her lips and kissing his knuckles.

Hot sensation shot up his arm, straight to his heart. Tom closed his eyes rather than get lost in her completely.

"Don't ask me not to fight, Michelle, because I can't promise you that." His words contained a steely edge as he braced himself against the power she had over him.

"You'll let Lonny chaperone the dance, right?"

He nodded.

"That's all I ask, except…"

"Except what?"

"Except…" She smiled again. "Except that I want you to dance every dance with me."

Now, that was a promise Tom could keep.

Chapter 15

Lonny couldn't stop thinking about his conversation with Joy last Monday afternoon. He'd wanted to tell Letty about it, but hadn't had the chance. What surprised him was the wealth of feeling he'd experienced just seeing her. Perhaps the thought that he might lose her to another man had escalated the intensity of his emotions. He didn't think so, though. These feelings had always been there, hidden by pride, perhaps, but definitely there.

After dropping Tom off at Larson's, he drove over to the school. Joy's car wasn't in the lot. Then he remembered her mentioning something about early dismissal for the rest of the week. That put a dent in his plans. He'd hoped to meet her on the school grounds, figuring they'd be able to talk freely because she'd feel safe in a familiar environment.

He wanted to follow up on their previous conversation. He'd given her a couple of days to contemplate his apology. He hadn't discussed this with his sister, but Lonny felt certain Letty would approve. Lonny was a businessman who preferred to be straightforward and honest in his dealings.

Still, he was prepared to go slow, the way Letty had suggested. He needed to earn Joy's trust all over again. But he believed that she knew him, knew the person he really was.

The more Lonny thought about Joy becoming a part of his life—not just for now, but forever—the stronger his desire to make it happen. They'd have a good marriage, he was sure of it, and, if she was willing, he'd like to start a family soon. He wanted the same happiness Chase and Letty had.

Letty was pregnant. Chase had nearly shouted his ear off Monday night. He'd called after dinner, and when Lonny heard Chase yelling, he'd been afraid some disaster had occurred. It took him a moment to grasp what his friend was telling him—that he was about to become a father and Lonny an uncle for the second time. Apparently Letty had broken the news to Chase over dinner.

Lonny smiled, recalling his reaction. In the same situation, he knew he'd feel exactly the same way. Since he was already at the school, he parked and walked inside, only to find Joy's classroom empty, pretty much as he'd expected.

Lonny tried to decide what to do next. He could always swing by her place, he supposed, climbing back in his truck.

Sure enough, her car was parked on the street in front of her house, and she was in the yard watering her flower beds. She wore denim shorts and a tank top and her feet were bare. The sight of her, dressed so casually, nearly caused him to drive over the curb. She had long, shapely legs and the figure he'd once considered skinny made him practically swallow his tongue.

Lonny parked his truck directly behind her Cruiser and turned off the engine. He hesitated, wondering if he should've gotten Letty's advice first. But it was too late now. Joy had seen him.

She stood there glaring at him and holding the hose as if it were a weapon she might use against him.

Lonny got out of the truck and walked over to the sidewalk by her house.

She still clutched the hose, water jetting out, almost daring him to take one step on her green lawn.

"Good afternoon," he said, as politely as he could. He held his hat in his hands, smiling.

"Hello." Her greeting was cool, her tone uninflected. "What are you doing here?"

That was an important question. If he had his way, his answer would be to start the marriage negotiations.... Well, perhaps *negotiations* wasn't quite the right word. He'd broach the subject directly—except he knew Letty would tell him that was a mistake.

"I stopped by to see how your day went," he answered, hoping he looked relaxed.

"Why?" she asked bluntly, raising the hose. He was just outside the line of fire—or water.

"Put the hose down, Joy."

She slowly lowered it, pointing it at the ground.

"Why are you here?" she demanded again. Despite her hostility, her eyes told him she was pleased he'd come to see her.

"Wait," he said. He ran to his truck and grabbed a large bunch of wildflowers from the passenger seat. He'd picked them by the side of the road; there were yellow ones and blue ones and some pink and white ones, too. He didn't have a vase, so he'd wrapped the stems in a plastic bag with water.

Joy looked as if she didn't know what to say. In the months they'd dated, he'd never brought her flowers.

She was speechless for a long moment. "That was a lovely thing to do." She almost managed a smile— almost.

Joy set the hose on the lawn and hurried to the side of the house to turn off the water. Then she returned to accept his flowers and tucked them in the crook of her arm.

The silence stretched between them.

Feeling naked without his hat, Lonny set it back on his head. "I went to see you at school."

"My last parent-teacher appointment was over by two," she explained.

He nodded.

More silence.

She wasn't in a talkative mood, and once again Lonny recalled his sister's advice about going slow. Hard as it was to walk away, he decided he had to. "I hope you enjoy the flowers," he mumbled, trying to hide his disappointment.

Joy offered him a tentative smile. "Would you care for a glass of iced tea?" she asked in a friendly voice.

"Sure." He tried to sound nonchalant but was secretly delighted. This, finally, was progress. "That would be nice. I'd also like your opinion on something if you don't mind." He had an idea for supplementing his and Chase's income and genuinely wanted to hear what she thought. She had the advantage of living in a ranching community, while having a big-city background, both of which were relevant to his plan. He'd like her advice on how to help Tom, too.

"All right." Joy led the way into her kitchen. The sliding glass door opened onto a patio, which she'd edged with large containers holding a variety of flowers. She retrieved a large jar and arranged the wildflowers—some of which were probably weeds, he thought, slightly embarrassed as he compared them to her array of plants. After filling their glasses, she suggested they enjoy their tea outside.

Lonny held open the sliding glass door and followed her outside. Discussing this idea with her had been a spur-of-the-moment thing. But he sensed that Joy would have a valuable perspective he should hear before he approached Chase and Letty with his suggestion.

He sipped his tea and set the tall glass on the patio table. "I figure by now you've learned something about raising cattle," he began.

"A little," she agreed.

Lonny nodded encouragingly.

"I know you and Chase raise grass-fed cattle versus taking your herd to a feedlot," she continued.

"Right," he said, impressed by her understanding. "Basically, that means the animal's main diet is grass. We supplement it with some other roughage, otherwise there can be problems. Our cattle are leaner and the beef has less saturated fat."

"I think that's admirable."

"The thing is, the economics of ranching, especially with a small herd, just doesn't work anymore. Chase and I are just too ornery to admit it." He smiled as he said that. "I suffer from an unfortunate streak of stubbornness, as you might already know." He let those words sink in, so she'd realize again how much he regretted their past differences. "Now that Letty's pregnant, Chase is worried. He sold off a large chunk of his land. When he did, he figured on buying it back one day, but the truth is, that doesn't seem possible now." Lonny wasn't sure Chase had admitted that even to himself.

"What are you going to do?" Joy asked, sounding concerned.

"I've been giving this a lot of thought. I could always let Tom go. As it is, I'm barely paying him a living wage—I can't afford to. It's hard just to make enough to keep the ranch going." Granted, Lonny still had some savings from his rodeo days, although he'd invested most of that cash in buying their herd.

"Have you considered selling?"

That was probably a solution he *should* consider, but no matter how bad the situation got, he couldn't see himself doing it. "Ranching is more than an occupation—and selling isn't really an option, at least not for me and Chase. This land came to us through our families. It's our inheritance and what we hope to pass on to our children and their children. It's more than land." He didn't know if Joy would understand this part. She hadn't been born into ranching the way he and Chase and Letty had. Perhaps he'd been wrong to bring up the subject. He felt foolish now, uncertain. This wasn't all that different from declaring his feelings for her—and proposing marriage. At least now, she'd know what she was getting when he did ask.

"You said you've got an idea. Does it have to do with this?"

"Yeah. I haven't talked to anyone else about it and, well, it's pretty much off the top of my head."

"Go on," she urged.

"I was looking through a magazine the other day and came across an article about guest ranches. I guess they used to be called dude ranches, and according to this article they're more popular than ever. The owners put people up for maybe a week and take them on cattle drives and so on. I nearly fell off my chair when I saw what they were charging."

Joy frowned thoughtfully. "I've heard of them. Like in that movie *City Slickers?* It came out in the nineties. I really enjoyed it."

"So did I, and the rest of us in town, too. I'm not laughing now, though."

Joy raised her hand. "Do you mean to say—are you actually thinking of taking on a bunch of…city slickers?"

He ducked one shoulder. "I am. I don't have a bunkhouse, but Chase does, and his place is right next to mine. It seems there are people out there willing to pay top dollar for the experience of being on a ranch."

"Sounds promising," Joy said. "How much would it add to your workload?"

"For now, the brunt of the operation would fall on Chase and Letty because they have the facilities to put folks up and I don't." He paused. "The whole idea is still in its infancy."

"For that kind of enterprise, you'd need to have a sociable personality. Which you do. You get along well with people," she said, then added, "with a few exceptions."

He smiled because he knew she was talking about the two of them. "I generally don't have a problem," he said, "unless my pride gets in the way."

"You're not the only one with that problem."

In other words, Joy was acknowledging her part in their falling-out.

"What do you think?" he asked eagerly. He hadn't used this as a ploy to get her to confess her own failings; that wasn't the point. As far as he was concerned, the past was the past, and this was now. They sat on her patio, two friends sharing ideas.

"I love it. I really do." Joy beamed at him. "You'd have to advertise," she said, "when you're ready to launch this."

He smiled back, even more excited now about the guest ranch idea. He couldn't explain why, but it'd seemed right—natural—to discuss it with Joy first.

"I'd like to bring Tom in on the deal," he said, "but only in the summers when he's out of school. That's something I want to talk to you about later."

"Tom's still in school?"

"No, but I hope he'll go to college. We've been looking at scholarships online, and he's already applied for a few in the state. He's definitely got the brains and the drive."

"What about his family?"

Lonny brushed off the question. The truth was, he still didn't know much about Tom's family other than that his mother was dead and his father was a drunk—facts Tom had only recently, and reluctantly, divulged. "He doesn't have any."

"So you're helping him?"

"I'm trying to. Tom deserves a break in life."

"I think you're doing a wonderful thing. And I'd be happy to help in any way I can."

"Thanks." Her praise flustered him. "Getting back to the guest ranch…"

She glanced away. "Letty's a fabulous cook. I imagine part of the attraction would be the meals."

"I'd want to appeal to families," Lonny said, throwing out another idea.

"You'll need activities for children, then," Joy said.

"Yeah." Lonny was glad she'd followed his thought to its logical conclusion.

"I'd be able to help you with that," she told him. "I could write out a list of suggestions."

That was precisely what he'd wanted to hear. "Great!" He could see she was catching his enthusiasm.

"Did you check to see if there are other guest ranches in the area?"

"I did. There are a few in different parts of the state, but there aren't any within a hundred miles of Red Springs." Nor were there any operated by former rodeo champions.

Their eyes met, and Lonny realized they were smiling at each other. Again. Really smiling. "I'd appreciate any help you could give us," Lonny said, forcing himself to look away. He could feel his pulse quickening, and it didn't have anything to do with his excitement about the guest ranch, either.

"If you'll excuse me a moment," Joy said abruptly, "I—I'll get us refills on the tea."

"Sure."

She stood as if she was in a rush and Lonny wondered if he'd said or done something to offend her. On impulse, he downed the last of his tea and hurried inside.

The darkness of her kitchen, after the sunlight outside, momentarily blinded him. When he could focus, he found Joy standing by the sink with her back to him. Letty would be pretty mad if she knew what he was thinking just then. Regardless, Lonny walked up behind Joy and placed his hands lightly on her shoulders.

His heart reacted wildly when she leaned against him, and Lonny breathed in the clean, warm scent of her hair.

"Don't be angry with me," he whispered close to her ear.

"Angry? Why?" she whispered back.

"I want to kiss you again."

She released a soft indefinable moan. Then she turned and slid her arms around his neck. A moment later, his mouth was on hers with a hunger and a need that threatened to overwhelm him. Arms about her waist, he lifted her from the floor and devoured her mouth with his. He couldn't take enough or give enough.

When she tore her mouth from his, he immediately dropped his arms and stepped away, fearing she'd rant at him like she had before, when he'd kissed her in the parking lot.

She didn't.

Instead, she stared up at him with a shocked expression. She'd rested one arm on the counter as if she needed to maintain her balance, and held her free hand over her heart.

Lonny waited. He couldn't even begin to predict what she'd say or do next.

"I...I—thank you for the f-flowers," she stammered. "They're l-lovely."

"Can I take you to dinner?" he asked, not wanting to leave.

She blinked slowly. "It's a little early, isn't it?"

"An early dinner, then." He was finding it difficult to remember Letty's advice about going slow.

She didn't answer for a long time. "Not tonight."

Lonny swallowed his disappointment and nodded. "I guess I'll be going."

"Okay."

Joy walked him to the front door and held open the screen. "Thank you for stopping by."

He touched the brim of his hat and left. But as he approached the truck, his steps grew heavier. He'd completely forgotten about Josh! But then he brightened. Judging by the way she'd kissed him, Joy had, too.

Chapter 16

"Stupid, stupid, stupid!" Joy wanted to bang her head against the wall in frustration. Not only had she invited Lonny Ellison into her home, she'd allowed him to kiss her. *Again*. Worse, she'd practically *begged* him to. Then, complicating matters even more, she'd kissed him back. The man made her crazy and here she was, kissing him with an abandon that had left her nerves tingling. Instead of avoiding him, she was encouraging him.

One hand on her forehead, Joy closed the front door and, for good measure, emphatically turned the lock. She didn't know if she was keeping Lonny out or keeping herself from running after him.

This was a disaster! Josh was due in two days. Two days. Because of their emails and telephone conversations, he was coming with the expectation of resuming their relationship.

Josh was perfect for her. His future was secure, he was handsome and congenial. They had a lot in common and their parents were good friends. At one time, he was everything she'd ever wanted in a man.

At one time—what was she thinking? She'd broken up with Lonny almost two years ago, after a relationship that had lasted barely three months. The fact that he was back in her life now could only be described as bad timing. She didn't want him to invade her every waking moment—or to take up residence in her dreams, as he'd begun to do.

Totally confused about her feelings for Lonny, Joy returned to the kitchen and rearranged the wildflowers in their vase. She was touched by the image of him scrambling in ditches to collect them; it was quite possibly the sweetest gesture she'd ever received from a man. Anyone could call a florist and read off a credit card number, she told herself; not every man would go and pick his own flowers.

When she'd finished, Joy set the bouquet in the center of her kitchen table and stepped back to admire the flowers. Lonny was proud and stubborn, but he'd let her know he was sorry about what had happened two years earlier.

"The jerk," she muttered. "He did that on purpose."

The doorbell rang and Joy went rigid. If it was Lonny again, she didn't want him seeing her like this. She was an emotional mess. And even though she preferred to blame him for that, she knew she couldn't.

"Who is it?" she called out.

"Petal Pushers," Jerry Hawkins shouted back.

The local florist shop! Surprised, Joy unlatched the dead bolt and threw open the door to discover Jerry standing on the front step, holding a lovely floral arrangement protected by cellophane. "Mom asked me to drop these by," he explained.

Sally owned the shop and her son made deliveries after school.

"Who'd be sending me flowers?" Joy asked. Considering her previous thoughts, she was all too conscious of the irony.

"Mom said they're from a man."

Joy's eyes widened as she accepted the arrangement. It consisted of pink lilies, bright yellow African daisies, sweet williams and gladioli, interspersed with greenery and beautifully displayed in an old-fashioned watering can.

"Do I need to sign anything?" she asked.

"No," Jerry was quick to tell her. "Enjoy."

"I will, thank you." She closed the door with her foot and carried the large arrangement into the kitchen, placing it on the counter. As she unpinned the card from the bright yellow ribbon, she shook her head. The flowers had to be from Josh.

She was right. The card read: *I'm looking forward to this weekend. Josh.*

Until that very afternoon, Joy had been looking forward to seeing him, too. No—she still was, but not with the same unalloyed pleasure. She put the formal arrangement next to the glass jar filled with the wildflowers Lonny had brought her. Once again, the irony didn't escape her. Businessman and rancher. One as polished and smooth as the satin ribbon wrapped about the watering can and the other as unsophisticated as… the plastic grocery bag in which he'd presented his flowers.

These were the two men in her life. They didn't know it, but they were fast coming to a showdown. Josh would arrive for the school carnival and, sure as anything, Lonny would be in town at the same time. Already her stomach was in knots. Joy had no idea what to do; the only person she could talk to was Letty.

She waited until she'd calmed down before she reached for the phone and hit speed dial to connect with Letty, who answered on the first ring.

"Joy, it's so good to hear from you," she said enthusiastically.

"Can you talk for a minute?" Joy asked, too unnerved to bother with the normal pleasantries.

"Of course." Letty's voice was concerned. "Is everything all right?"

"No… I don't know," she mumbled before blurting out, "Lonny came by earlier."

Letty's hesitation was long enough for Joy to notice.

"He brought me a bouquet of wildflowers and, Letty, it was just so sweet of him."

"Lonny brought you flowers," Letty repeated, as if she had trouble believing it herself. "Really?"

"Yes. I'm looking at them right now." She didn't mention the second bouquet she was looking at, too. Sighing, Joy sank into a kitchen chair and propped her elbow on the table. She supported her forehead with one hand as she closed her eyes, suddenly feeling tired. "I should've told him Josh was coming. I wanted to, but I didn't." Granted, it would've been a bit awkward when she was in his arms kissing him. *Not* that she planned to mention that scene in the kitchen.

"Joy," her friend gently chastised, "don't you realize how much my brother cares about you?"

She swallowed hard because she did know and it distressed her. "I sort of guessed.... The last couple of times we've met, he's been so cordial and polite. He's even told me he feels sorry about our disagreement, and I never thought he'd do anything like that."

Letty released a deep sigh and said in a soft voice, "I didn't, either. Oh dear, I feel terrible."

Joy's eyes flew open. "Is it the pregnancy?"

"I'm perfectly healthy. No, this has to do with Lonny. He...asked for my help."

"Your help in what?" Joy was already confused and this wasn't making things any easier.

"My brother asked for my advice on how to win you back and... I'm the one who suggested he bring you flowers."

"Oh."

"Lonny's always cared about you, only he was too stubborn to admit it. Now it's hitting him between the eyes. Josh wants you back, too, and you're going to have to make a decision. Either way, someone's going to be disappointed."

"You're right."

Silence fell between them as they both mulled over the significance of this. Letty spoke first.

"Listen, Joy, you're my friend but Lonny's my brother, and I don't think I'm the best person to be talking to about this," she said.

"There isn't anyone else," Joy cried. "Letty, please, just hear me out?"

"I'll try, but you need to know I'm not exactly a neutral observer. It's a mess," she said, "and to some extent I blame myself."

"You didn't do anything."

"I did, though," Letty confessed, sounding thoroughly miserable. "I encouraged Lonny, built up the idea of a relationship with you. You know I think the world of you and in my enthusiasm—well, never mind. None of that's important now."

"Oh dear," Joy murmured. Things seemed to get more complicated all the time.

"Do you still have feelings for my brother?" Letty asked, her voice elevated with what could have been hope.

That was the million-dollar question. "I...I'm not sure." At the moment, Joy was too bewildered to know how she felt about either man.

"Okay, fair enough," Letty said, exhaling a lengthy sigh.

"The thing is, Josh is coming this weekend."

"Believe me, I'm well aware of that," Letty said.

Joy pressed the phone harder against her ear. "I don't want any trouble."

"What do you mean?"

"Lonny's going to the carnival, isn't he?"

"Of course."

"Is there any way you could distract him?" Joy pleaded. "Keep him away until after Josh leaves?" As soon as she said the words, she realized how ridiculous that sounded—as if these two men were a couple of bulls or stallions that had to be separated to prevent a dangerous confrontation.

Letty gave a short, cheerless laugh. "Lonny won't cause any trouble, if that's what you're thinking," she assured Joy. "That's not his style. Besides, he already knows."

"Lonny knows? About Josh?"

"Yes, I told him."

Involuntarily her foot started tapping. "That explains it, then."

"Explains what?"

"The flowers, the apology, everything." So Josh's pending visit was the reason for Lonny's abrupt change in behavior.

"You're wrong," Letty insisted. "He came to talk to me *before* he knew about Josh."

"He did?" That didn't really improve the situation; however, at least it cleared up his motives. "Oh…"

"What?" Letty asked.

"Nothing. Just…he has a wonderful idea for the ranch. He wanted to hear my opinion before he brought it to you and Chase. I think it's brilliant."

"What is it?"

"I can't tell you. Lonny will when he's ready. I like it, though, I really do. I even told him I'd be willing to help. I was sincere about that." However, if her relationship with Josh progressed the way she'd once hoped, that would be impossible. For the first time since he'd contacted her, Joy regretted that he was coming to Red Springs. His timing couldn't have been worse—or better. The problem was, she couldn't decide which.

Letty added, "Don't hurt my brother, Joy. He might

be the most stubborn man you've ever met in your life, but he's decent and hardworking and he genuinely cares for you."

"I know," Joy said, and she meant it. "I'll talk to him tomorrow." She needed time to work out what to say, and yet, no matter how prepared she was, this would be one of the most difficult conversations she'd ever had.

Chapter 17

The next evening, Lonny reflected that his day had gone very well indeed. He'd awakened in a fine mood and it was still with him. He felt inspired, motivated and challenged, all at once. His goal was to win Joy's heart, and he believed he'd made some strides toward it. He wasn't going to let some fast-talking business-man steal her away, even if he was an old boyfriend. Lonny didn't know exactly what Josh did for a living but picturing him as some high-and-mighty company mogul suited his purposes.

Joy loved *him*. She might not realize it yet, but she would soon. His mission was to convince her that she belonged right here in Red Springs—with him.

Lonny hadn't fully appreciated his sister's dating advice until yesterday. Those wildflowers had worked better than he'd ever imagined. He could almost see

Joy's heart melt the instant she laid eyes on that bunch of flowers.

After dinner, feeling good about life in general, Lonny sat out on his porch, in the rocking chair that had once been his father's. He couldn't remember the last time he'd lazed away an evening like this. He sometimes joined Letty and Chase on the porch over at their place, but he seldom sat here on his own. Music sounded faintly from inside the barn, where Tom was practicing his dance moves. Given all the time and effort the boy had put into getting ready for this dance, he should be pretty confident by now.

Lonny relaxed and linked his fingers behind his head. He was feeling downright domestic. He'd waited a lot of years to consider marriage. He hadn't been in any rush to settle down, because marriage meant responsibilities, and he already had enough of those.

Funny, he didn't think like that anymore. He was actually looking forward to living the rest of his life with Joy. Marriage to her was bound to be interesting, not to mention passionate and satisfying in every conceivable way.

So far, his sister's advice to "go slow" had been right on the money. Come Friday, he'd be in town for the carnival and later the dance. He could visualize it now. By this time tomorrow night, he'd be holding her hand and later he'd be dancing with her, and that was all it would take to tell everyone in Red Springs how he felt about Joy Fuller.

A cloud of swirling dust alerted him to the fact that there was a car coming down the long driveway. Lonny stood, and when he did, Joy's PT Cruiser came into view. A sensation of happiness stole over him. The last person he'd expected to see here, at his place, was Joy, and at the same time, she was the one person he most wanted it to be.

He'd hurried down the steps and was walking across the yard as she parked. At that moment, Tom stuck his head out of the barn. He smiled at Lonny and gave him a thumbs-up, then returned to his practicing.

Lonny greeted Joy from halfway across the yard. "This is a pleasant surprise."

Her eyes didn't quite meet his. "Would it be all right if we talked?"

"It would be more than all right." With his hand at the small of her back, he steered her toward the porch. "My parents used to sit out here in the evenings. I'd consider it an honor to have you join me." He hoped she picked up on his subtle hint about the two of them sitting together in the space once reserved for a long-married couple....

Lonny reached for the second rocking chair and dragged it closer to his own. "Can I get you anything? A pillow? Something to drink?" he asked, minding his manners in a way that would've made his mother proud.

"Nothing, thanks," she said before sitting down.

She seemed nervous, but Lonny wanted her to know there wasn't any reason to be. He sat next to her and they both rocked for a few minutes.

"It's quite a coincidence that you should stop by," he commented casually. "I was just thinking about you."

"You were?"

"Yup, I spent most of my day thinking about you." He'd dreamed about her, too, and awakened with the warmest, most delicious feeling. He couldn't recall everything his dream had entailed, but he remembered the gist of it—they were married and there were three youngsters running around. Two boys and a cute little girl. He was feeding the youngest in a high chair, while Joy was busy getting dinner on the table for the rest of the family. She interrupted what she was doing to kiss him—and then the alarm blared.

She frowned. "Lonny, please just listen."

"I'll listen to anything you want to tell me," he said, matching the seriousness of her expression.

She closed her eyes and kept them tightly shut. Lonny turned his chair so they sat facing each other, their knees touching. He took both of her hands and held them in his.

"Joy?" he asked. "What's wrong?"

She opened her eyes and gave him a tentative smile. "You know Josh Howell's coming to town, don't you? My college boyfriend?"

He nodded. "Letty mentioned it." He didn't care. Joy loved *him*—didn't she?—and he loved her. As far as he was concerned, the other man was a minor inconvenience.

"But—"

Rather than listen to her extol Josh's virtues, or even say his name, he leaned forward and gently pressed his lips to hers. Her mouth softened and instantly molded and shaped to his, as if she wanted this as badly as he did. Cradling the back of her neck, he deepened the kiss. The tantalizing sensations tormented and delighted him. Joy, too, he guessed, because after a moment, she twisted her head, breaking the contact.

"I need to talk to you and you're making it impossible," she moaned.

"Good." He wanted her as caught up in this whirlwind of feeling as he was. More importantly, he wanted her to understand that they were meant to be together, the two of them. Josh might be her past, but *he* was her future.

"Please, Lonny, just listen, all right?"

"If you insist." But then he brought his lips back to hers. This second round was even more delectable than the first....

"Please stop! I can't think when you're kissing me," she pleaded and seemed to have difficulty breathing normally.

She wasn't the only one. "It's hard to refuse you anything, but I don't know if I can stop."

"Try. For the sake of my sanity, would you kindly try?"

He pushed his chair back and motioned for her to stand. When she did, his arms circled her waist and he pulled her into his lap. Her eyes widened with surprise. She hardly seemed aware that her arms had slipped around his neck. She stared at him. "Why did you do that?"

"Isn't it obvious?" He longed to have her close, needed her close. She must know how deeply their kisses had affected him.

"I have something important to tell you," she said but without the conviction of earlier.

"Okay," he murmured as he spread soft kisses down the side of her neck. She sighed and inclined her head.

Apparently what she had to tell him wasn't that important, after all.

"I've reached a decision…." Her voice held a soft, beseeching quality.

A sense of exhilaration and triumph shot through him. "Okay, no kissing for…" He checked his watch. "Five minutes, and then all bets are off." He returned his mouth to the hollow of her throat, savoring the feel of her smooth skin.

Joy moved her head to one side. "That's kissing," she said breathlessly.

"I'm staying clear of your lips. Tell me what's so important that you had to drive all the way out here."

She caught his earlobe between her teeth. Hot sensation coursed through him like a powerful electric shock. She was quickly driving him beyond reason, and in self-defense, he seized her by the waist. To his surprise, his hands came upon bare flesh. Her light sweater had ridden up just enough to reveal her midriff. Her skin felt so smooth, so warm…. He'd never intended to take things this far, but now there was no stopping him. He slid his hand higher and cupped her breast. As his palm closed around it, he heard her soft intake of breath.

Joy buried her face in his neck and took several deep breaths. His own breathing had grown labored.

"You keep doing that and I'm going to embarrass us both," he said.

She instantly went still.

"Joy," he said, although he found it difficult to speak at all. "I don't care why you're here or what you came to tell me. I love—"

She brought her index finger to his lips. "Don't say it." Pain flashed from her eyes.

"Okay." He sobered. "I think you'd better explain." He made an effort to focus on her words.

"Josh Howell is coming tomorrow," she said.

"Yes, I know. We talked about that. I'm not worried."

"I've decided not to renew my teaching contract. I'm moving back to the Puget Sound area."

A sense of unreality gripped him. He blinked. "What?"

"I—I've decided not to renew my teaching contract."

When the words did sink in, he stared into her eyes, but she couldn't hold his gaze.

"Say something," she pleaded. "Don't look at me like—like you don't believe I'll do it. I've made my decision."

"Okay," he said, his thoughts chaotic. "That decision is yours to make. I don't want you to go, but I can't kidnap you and keep you in the root cellar until you change your mind."

She frowned unhappily. "I know this upsets you. I haven't told anyone else yet. I wanted to tell you first."

"Any particular reason you're confiding in me?"

She nodded several times. "Considering everything that's happened, I felt I should."

"So you're in love with Josh?"

Joy bit her lip. "I don't know."

"But you've already decided you're leaving with him?" Lonny asked, not understanding her logic. Joy didn't seem to notice that he was still caressing her back.

"I won't leave right away."

"Of course," he agreed quietly.

"Josh and I...we've been talking and emailing and—" She let the rest fade.

"Renewing your acquaintance," he finished.

"Exactly." Her eyes were half-closed as she spoke.

"And you're thinking that because of Josh, you'll leave Red Springs?"

"Yes." Slowly exhaling, she looked directly at him. "The thing is, I hate to go."

"The town will miss you. So will I."

"I'll miss you, too," she whispered.

It was exactly what Lonny had hoped to hear. "Then don't go."

She didn't respond.

"I'm hoping you'll reconsider."

"I...I don't think I can."

"If you stay here, we could get married," he suggested.

Apparently he'd shocked her into speechlessness. "I've been doing a lot of thinking about what went wrong with our relationship earlier," he said, "and I realize now I was the problem."

"You?"

"It was my fault. I reacted the same way then as I did when we had the traffic accident—I mean incident—the first time. And again last month." He grimaced comically. "I guess I'm a slow learner."

"You were unreasonable and high-handed and—"

He stopped her before she could continue with the list of his faults. "I love you, Joy, and I don't want you to move away."

She scrambled off his lap, nearly stumbling in her

eagerness to get off the porch. "You're trying to confuse me!"

"No. I'm telling you right now, it'd be a big mistake to make such an important decision while you're unsure of what you want. That's what I did, and it cost me two years I might've spent with you."

"I...I've already made up my mind."

She was fighting herself just as hard as she was fighting him. He longed to kiss her again, but he knew that would only infuriate her.

"I'm...l-leaving," she said, stuttering as she turned away. "I can see it wasn't a good idea to talk to you about this."

He didn't make a move to stop her. "You might want to straighten your sweater before you go," he said in a reasonable tone.

Embarrassed and flustered, she whirled around and fumbled with her clothes.

It occurred to Lonny that she might have expected a different reaction to her announcement. "Do you want me to be jealous?" he asked. He was prepared to act as if he was, and it wouldn't be that big a stretch. He'd never even met Josh Howell, but he didn't like the man.

"No!" she blurted out irritably.

"Good. Because I will if that's what you want. But truth be told, I'm more confident than ever that we're meant to be together." He smiled at her. "Like I said, we've already lost two years and I'm not planning to repeat that mistake. I hope you aren't, either. We're not getting any younger, you know, and if we're going to have kids..."

That really seemed to upset her, because her eyes

went wide with shock. At least, he hoped it was shock and not horror.

"Joy," he said, staying calm and clearheaded. "We were pretty involved physically a few minutes ago. I can't believe you'd allow a man to kiss you and touch you the way I just did if you didn't have strong feelings for him."

She backed away. "Josh will be here tomorrow, and all I ask is that you leave us alone."

He shrugged. "I'm not making any promises. You'd feel the same if some other gal was stepping in and trying to steal me away."

"I'm not a prize to be won at the carnival. You're so sure of yourself! I should marry Josh just to spite you."

That was an empty threat if he'd ever heard one. "You won't."

She made an exasperated sound and marched down the porch steps, almost tripping in her haste.

"Joy," he said, following her. "I don't want you to leave when you're this upset."

"I have to go!"

"I love you. If you want, I'll be furious and jealous and I'll corner Josh Howell and demand that he get outta town."

She shook her head vigorously. "Don't you dare!"

"I'm serious. I'm not willing to lose you to Josh."

"You've already lost me. I came here to tell you I'm not renewing my teaching contract."

Rather than argue with her, he sighed heavily. "Kiss me goodbye."

That seemed to fluster her more than anything else he'd said. "No!"

"Joy, my parents never went to sleep without settling an argument. That's the advice they always gave newly married couples. I don't want us to get in the habit of parting angry, either."

Aghast, she glared at him. "But we're not a couple!"

"But I believe we *should* be a couple. Because I love you and I know you love me."

She seemed about to burst into tears. "No, I don't. I refuse to love anyone as stubborn...and—"

"Pigheaded," he supplied.

Climbing into the car, she insisted one final time, "I don't love you!" She slammed the door shut and started the engine. A moment later, she tore out of the yard, kicking up a trail of dust.

"Oh, yes, you do," Lonny whispered. "You do love me, Joy Fuller. And I'm going to prove it."

Chapter 18

After the confrontation with Lonny, Joy barely slept that night. The man's arrogance was unbelievable. How dare he insist she was in love with him!

It'd seemed only right that she tell Lonny about her decision. Going to him had been a mistake, though, one that made her question her own sanity. He'd been condescending, and treated her as if she was too feeble-minded to form her own opinions. He'd practically laughed at her! Mortified, Joy wanted to bury her face in her hands.

She'd thought...well, she'd hoped they could part as friends. That was what she'd wanted to tell him. Instead, she'd ended their conversation feeling angry and more certain than ever. To be fair, she had to admit there was definitely a physical attraction between them. But that was his fault, not hers. Well, it wasn't really a question of *fault*. The man could kiss like no one she'd ever known. So of course she'd kissed him back; any red-blooded woman would.

She got out of bed, yawning, unable to stop thinking about last night. Just remembering the way he'd pulled her into his lap and then proceeded to seduce her, had her cheeks burning with embarrassment. As she readied for school, she chose her pink pantsuit. Today was the biggest event of the year in Red Springs. Her eyes already burned from lack of sleep and it was going to be a long, long day. First, the carnival, then the high school dance. On top of all that, Josh would show up sometime around four—when everything was getting started. If she could make it through today without losing her mind or breaking into tears, it would be a miracle.

The last day of school was more of a formality than an occasion to teach. The students were restless and anxious to escape. It was a bittersweet experience for Joy to see her students move on to the next grade. Each one was special to her. Most of the third-graders would be back in this classroom next year as fourth-grade students, and there'd be a group of new, younger kids, as well.

At noon, the bell rang and her pupils dashed out the door, shouting with excitement and glee.

Smiling, Joy walked onto the playground to wave goodbye, thinking this might be her last opportunity. The contract sat at home unsigned. Even now, she wasn't sure what to do. She'd made her decision and then Lonny had kissed her and all at once her certainty had evaporated.

The school buses had already lined up, their diesel engines running. The children formed straggling rows and boarded the buses with far more noise than usual. Most would return with their families for the carnival in a few hours.

As Joy grinned and waved and called out goodbyes, she reflected that her afternoon would be busy, getting everything done before Josh arrived. She'd made a reservation for him at the one and only local motel, the Rest Easy Inn. When she saw Josh, she told herself, she'd know her own feelings, know what was right for her. Joy couldn't help wondering what this weekend would hold for them both. She wished… Her thoughts came to a dead halt. What *did* she wish?

If Josh had contacted her a few months earlier, everything would be different, and yet the only real change in her life was Lonny.

"Goodbye, Ms. Fuller," Cricket said, coming up to Joy and throwing both arms around her waist.

"I'll see you later, won't I?" Joy asked, crouching beside the little girl.

"Oh, yes," Cricket said. "I'm going to ride the Ferris wheel with my daddy, and he said he'd buy me a snow cone and popcorn and cotton candy, too."

"I'll roll you an extra-big cotton candy," Joy promised.

An unfamiliar vehicle pulled into the parking lot. Wary of strangers, Joy narrowed her eyes suspiciously. Then the car door opened and a man stepped out.

"Josh," Joy whispered. He was early—and every bit as handsome as she remembered.

He gazed around as though he wasn't sure where to

go. Staring at him, Joy was again struck by his good looks. She'd been afraid he couldn't possibly live up to her memories—or her expectations. Wrong. He was even *more* attractive now. More everything. He exuded success and ambition.

Joy began walking toward him. "Josh!" She raised her arm high above her head.

As soon as Josh saw her, he smiled broadly and strode toward her. Then they were standing face-to-face and after a moment of smiling at each other, they hugged.

"Hey, let me take a look at you," Josh said, holding her at arm's length. "You've changed," he said, his bright blue eyes meeting hers. "You're more beautiful than ever."

His words embarrassed her a little and she laughed. "I was just thinking the same about you."

"Ms. Fuller, Ms. Fuller," Cricket said. She'd trailed after Joy and now stood there, her eyes as round as pie tins.

"Yes, Cricket?" Joy said, turning away from Josh to focus her attention on the child. "What is it?"

"Who's this man?" Cricket asked with uncharacteristic rudeness.

"This is my friend, Mr. Howell."

Cricket frowned.

"Mr. Howell drove to Red Springs to visit me," Joy elaborated.

"Is he your *boy*friend?" she asked.

Before Joy could answer, Josh did. "Yes, I'm Ms. Fuller's boyfriend." He slipped his arm around Joy's waist and brought her close to his side.

The girl's lower lip shot out. "I'm telling my uncle Lonny." Having made that announcement, Cricket stomped off the playground and boarded the school bus, the last child to do so.

"And just who is Cricket's uncle Lonny?" Josh asked, quirking his eyebrow at her.

"A local rancher," Joy said, not inclined to explain if she didn't have to.

"Really?" Josh didn't sound too concerned, which pleased Joy. She didn't want him to worry. And there was no reason for him to be jealous—was there?

"Did you tell me about 'Uncle' Lonny?" he asked.

"I'm sure I did," Joy said in casual tones. "He owns a ranch about twenty minutes outside town."

"He's not the one you had those near-collisions with, is he?"

"Yes," she cried, surprised Josh had remembered. "That's Lonny. We dated for a while when I first moved to Red Springs—I know I mentioned that in my emails—but we broke up and I haven't had much to do with him since." Because it was bound to happen at some point this evening, she added, "You'll meet him later." She dreaded the prospect, but there was no help for it. Her only hope was that Lonny would ignore both her and Josh, unlikely though that seemed.

"Is your rancher friend still being unreasonable about last month's accident?" Josh asked.

"Actually, he's been pretty decent about it lately. He said I should just forget the whole thing."

"And you have?"

She nodded, more than eager to get off the subject of Lonny. Taking Josh's hand, she smiled up at him.

"Let me finish a few things at school and then maybe we could go to lunch."

"Sure. In the meantime, I'll check into the motel."

"Okay." Releasing his hand, she nodded again. She hadn't expected Josh this soon and she still had loose ends to tie up in her classroom. All the arrangements were in place for tonight. When Letty had learned Josh would be coming, she'd volunteered to take the second half of Joy's shift so she'd have a chance to be with her visitor. From her past experience with the cotton candy machine, Joy knew she'd need time to clean up before the dance, too.

"There's a nice Mexican restaurant on Main Street," she suggested. "I could meet you there in an hour."

"Perfect."

Hands on his hips, Josh looked over at the school. "This is rather a quaint building, isn't it?"

Joy had thought the same thing when she'd first seen the stone schoolhouse, built fifty years earlier, but she'd grown used to it. The school felt comfortable to her, and it evoked an enjoyable nostalgia.

"I love it," she said fondly. "They just don't build schools like this anymore." While the budget called for a new schoolhouse two years from now, Joy would miss this one. Although, of course, it didn't matter because she wouldn't be here.

Josh nodded sympathetically. "I'll see you in an hour, then."

Joy felt light and carefree as she returned to her classroom. She intended to go into this new relationship with Josh wholeheartedly, see where it led. Deep down, though, Joy suspected neither of them was ready for marriage. Still, she wanted to make it work. The spoiler, so to speak, was Lonny Ellison. He arrogantly claimed she was in love with him and…he might not be wrong. Or not completely. But that didn't mean a long-term relationship between them would succeed.

By the time Joy hurried into the restaurant, she was later than she'd planned. She'd left several duties unfinished, which meant she'd have to go back to school in the morning. Because it was almost one-thirty, only a handful of people were in the restaurant.

Josh was seated in a booth, reading the menu, when she slid breathlessly into the bench across from him. She really didn't have time to linger over lunch. She had a hundred things to do before the carnival opened at five.

"Sorry I'm late," she said, glancing around for Miguel so they could order.

Josh reached for her hand. He'd changed out of his business suit and was dressed in slacks and a shirt, with the top two buttons left undone. He looked no less attractive in casual clothes—maybe more so.

"You didn't have any problem finding your way around, did you?" she asked, using a chip to scoop up some salsa. Miguel seemed to be busy in the kitchen.

"You're joking, aren't you?" He laughed as he said it. "There's only one road through town."

There were more, but apparently he hadn't felt any need to investigate the side streets.

"The other end of town is blocked off for the carnival," she reminded him. The motel and restaurant were located at this end of Red Springs.

"Have you decided what you'd like to eat?" she asked.

"I have."

As if he suddenly realized Joy had arrived, Miguel appeared to take their order. "I'll have the luncheon special. I can have the chili relleno baked, right?" Josh asked.

"We cook them the regular way," Miguel said with a heavy accent.

"Baked or fried?" Josh pressed.

Miguel looked to Joy to supply the answer.

"I believe they fry them, Josh," she said.

Josh frowned. "In that case, I'll have the enchilada plate."

Miguel gratefully wrote that down and turned to Joy, who nodded. He went back to the kitchen.

"Aren't you going to order?" Josh asked.

"I already did. I always have the same thing and Miguel knows how I like my tostada salad."

Josh clasped both her hands. "You look fabulous," he said, studying her. "Really fabulous."

She smiled at his words.

"I thought you'd come running home three months after you accepted this job," Josh admitted.

That wasn't exactly a flattering comment, but she let it slide.

"It's hard to believe you actually live here, so far from civilization," he added, glancing around as if he couldn't quite picture her in this setting.

"I remember thinking that when I first got to Red Springs. But it grew on me. I love it now."

"Don't you miss all the great restaurants in Seattle?"

"Well, yes, but…"

"This place is hardly Mexican," Josh murmured under his breath.

"The Mexican Fiesta isn't as fancy as the big chains in Seattle, but I like their food," she said, struggling not to sound defensive. She remembered her first visit to Red Springs. She'd wanted to live in a small community, but it had taken a while to adjust to the lack of amenities. The first time she'd eaten the town's version of Mexican food, she'd had to make an effort not to compare it to her favorite Seattle restaurant.

"We used to have Mexican almost every week," Josh said.

Joy didn't think it had been that often.

He wrinkled his forehead. "If I recall correctly, you used to order chicken enchiladas."

That was definitely some other girl he'd dated. Joy had never really liked enchiladas. He'd probably seen a dozen different women in the last two years, culminating in his now-ended relationship with Lori.

"You'd better tell me how everything's going to work this afternoon," he said. "I hear this town's going to be rocking."

Joy detected a hint of condescension but ignored it. "Everyone within a fifty-mile radius shows up. Ranching's a hard way to make a living these days," she said, remembering her many conversations with Letty. "There are only a few occasions during the year when the community has cause for celebration, and the end of school is one."

"My mother never celebrated my getting out of school for the summer," he joked. "If anything, she was crying in her martini. No more tennis dates for her when Julie and I were underfoot all day."

"A lot of these kids help around the ranch," she explained. "Families are important here. Tradition, too."

Josh's parents had split up and both had remarried by the time he started junior high. Fractured households seemed natural to him, and a community like this, with its emphasis on strong families, would seem an anomaly in his world.

"Everyone's thrilled about the carnival rides," Joy said. "This is the first year we're doing that." The children's excitement at such a modest pleasure wasn't something Josh would understand or appreciate, so Joy didn't bother to explain it further.

For the next few minutes until their lunches arrived, they chatted about Red Springs and her role in the community. Miguel delivered their orders with his usual fanfare, and Joy sensed that Josh was restraining a sarcastic smile. Her tostada salad was exactly the way she liked it, but she noticed that he just stared at his enchiladas.

"A high school dance," he repeated when she reminded him that he'd agreed to chaperone with her. Clearly he was amused.

"Come on, it'll be fun."

"I'm sure it will." His eyes twinkled as he took the first bite of his enchiladas.

"Tell me about your job," she said, wanting to turn the subject away from herself.

Josh had always been easy to talk to, and she was soon immersed in their conversation. He liked working for the investment firm, where he seemed to be advancing quickly. He'd purchased a home in Kirkland, outside Seattle. This she knew from the emails they'd exchanged. He described in some detail what it meant to be a home owner.

As he spoke, Joy realized that, despite her earlier decision, she couldn't imagine living in Seattle again. Josh was proud of his home and she was happy for him, yet she knew that living in Red Springs had changed her. His kind of neighborhood, with its expensive homes and anonymity, was no longer what she wanted. Neither was his social life—company functions and cocktail parties at which barbed remarks passed for wit.

"What if you have to move?" she asked. His company was well-known; with his ambition and energy Josh might be asked to relocate to a different city.

"I like living in Seattle. However, if the firm asked me to change offices, and it came with a big promotion, I'd definitely consider it," he said.

Joy nodded.

"What about you?"

"Me? You mean, would I move if the opportunity arose?"

He seemed intensely interested in her answer. With his elbows propped on the table and his fork dangling over his food, he awaited her response.

"From Red Springs?" She swallowed. "I don't know.... I've settled in nicely and I feel like I'm part of the community." She'd be viewed as a newcomer for the next sixty years, but that didn't bother her.

"If a once-in-a-lifetime opportunity came up, how would you feel?"

"That would depend on the opportunity," she said, sidestepping the question.

The restaurant door opened and sunlight shot into the darkened room. Joy didn't pay much attention until Lonny strolled directly to her table.

"Hello, Joy," he said.

She nearly dropped her fork. Fortunately, she hadn't taken a sip of her water or she could've been in serious danger of choking.

"Lonny." His name was more breath than sound.

"Would you introduce me to your friend?" he asked, staring down at Josh.

"Uh…"

Josh slid out of the booth and stood. "Josh Howell," he said, extending his hand. "And you are?"

Lonny grinned as the two men exchanged handshakes. "Lonny Ellison. I'm the man who's in love with Joy."

Chapter 19

Lonny nearly burst out laughing at the look on Joy's face.

"And how does Joy feel about you?" Josh asked coolly, before she managed to speak.

"She loves me, too, only she's not ready to admit it."

"Lonny!" Her fork fell to the table with a loud clang.

Lonny sent a glance at Josh and winked. "See what I mean?" The other man seemed to be somewhat taken aback but not angry, which boded well.

"What are you *doing* here?" Joy asked when it became apparent that he had no intention of leaving.

"Actually, Betty Sanders sent me to look for you," he told her. "She needs you for something, and Myrtle Jameson said she saw you come in here. There's a carnival that has to be set up, you know."

"I can see word spreads quickly in this town," Josh said, "if people are keeping track of your whereabouts."

Joy grabbed her purse and scrambled out of the booth. "I'll be right back."

As soon as she vacated the seat, Lonny replaced her. He was a bit hungry himself and selected a tortilla chip, dipping it in the salsa. "Take your time," he said non-chalantly. "I'll keep your friend company."

"I...I—" She was sputtering again. "I'll be back in five minutes," she promised Josh, and then returned to the table and kissed his cheek.

That, Lonny thought, was completely unnecessary; it was more as if she had a point to prove. He looked away before she could see how deeply that small display of affection for another man had affected him.

"Nice to meet you, Josh," Lonny said when Joy was gone, "but I can't stay long. My sister's got me helping, too. My hired hand and I are assembling the beanbag toss. You'd think two grown men could put this silly contraption together, wouldn't you? The problem is, the instructions are in Chinese." He left the booth a moment later and started to walk out of the restaurant.

"Do you need help with that?" Josh called after him.

"Thanks, but I think we've got it. A couple of others could use a hand, though."

Josh nodded. "I'll settle up here and be out soon."

"Thanks," Lonny said. Despite the fact that Josh was here to reconnect with the woman *he* loved, Lonny decided he rather liked him. He seemed to be a decent guy.

When he stepped outside, Lonny saw Joy trotting

down the sidewalk, toward the restaurant. She ignored him and kept moving.

"Did you find her?" Tom asked, when Lonny got back to the carnival site. The beanbag toss apparatus was up but balanced precariously, leaning to one side. They had to find a way to stabilize it.

"Cricket and I finished with the Go Fish booth," Chase announced triumphantly, carrying the little girl on his shoulders and joining Lonny and Tom.

Cricket smiled down at them from her perch. "We did a good job, too."

"Cricket," Letty cried, rushing toward them, hands on her hips. "Chase, put her down right this minute."

Lonny was grateful to see his sister. "I saw Joy," he said, striving to sound unconcerned.

Letty lifted her brows in question.

"She was with Josh Howell," Lonny added.

"He *said* he was her boyfriend," Cricket muttered indignantly. "He isn't, is he?" The question was directed at her uncle.

"No way," Lonny assured the little girl.

"Then how come he said that?"

The kid had a point. "He just doesn't know it yet," Lonny explained, not meeting Letty's eyes.

"Ms. Fuller will tell him, won't she?"

"She will soon enough," Lonny said.

"However," Letty cut in, "Ms. Fuller is the one making the decisions, not your uncle Lonny."

Cricket waited for Lonny to agree or disagree. Lonny shrugged. His sister wasn't wrong, but the situation was more complicated than that.

Letty was frowning. "Listen, we don't have time to

stand around discussing Joy's love life. The carnival's about to start."

"All right, all right." Lonny picked up the beanbag toss instructions again. He studied the drawing, turned it around and took another look. Ah, that made more sense....

By five o'clock, the streets of Red Springs were filled to capacity. This was the one time of year when the town got a taste of big-city living, complete with traffic jams. Parking slots were at a premium. Many streets were closed off and teeming with kids and adults alike, all enjoying themselves.

Chase and Lonny took a shift together, grilling hamburgers and serving them as quickly as they were cooked. While he was flipping burgers, Lonny caught a glimpse of Joy out of the corner of his eye. She was strolling through the grounds with Josh, sharing a bag of popcorn and sipping lemonade. He pretended not to notice but his gut tightened, and almost immediately the doubts began chasing each other, around and around. Maybe Josh would convince her, after all. Just as fast, a sense of well-being returned. Joy had as much pride as he did, but she wasn't stupid. She loved him. Lonny believed that...and yet there were a lot of factors he hadn't considered before. Such as the fact that Josh was so likable and that Joy had family and friends in Seattle. Josh could offer her a privileged life. All the reasons marriage to Josh might seem appealing presented themselves to his fevered mind.

Lonny's gut remained in knots until he saw Tom and Michelle stroll past, holding hands. His mood instantly lightened. This was probably Tom's first real date. Tom kept his emotions in check about most things, but he hadn't been able to squelch his enthusiasm for the carnival and the high school dance that was to follow. The kid had his chores finished before the sun was even up. He was ready to leave for town by ten that morning. Lonny had to assign him some extra work to keep him busy and distracted from his nervousness about Michelle. By two o'clock, though, he was dressed and waiting.

Apparently Michelle had informed him it wasn't necessary to wear a suit to the dance, so Tom had given it back to Lonny. The kid's eyes had lit up like Christmas morning when Lonny assured him he didn't need it anymore. He told Tom to keep the suit because he might be able to use it someday. Tom had purchased a new shirt and jeans for the dance and he'd even had his hair cut and he'd polished his black boots to a shine they'd likely never seen before.

Michelle had been good for Tom. She'd talked to him about college, reinforcing Lonny's suggestions, and encouraged him to apply for scholarships. Together Tom and Lonny had worked on completing the online application forms. Lonny felt pleased that Tom was looking beyond his past and toward the future.

In the same way Michelle had helped Tom, Joy had been good for Lonny. While it was true that they'd argued frequently, Joy had taught Lonny some important things about himself. Not the least of which was that he wanted marriage and a family. That was a new aspiration for him.

The moment he and Chase finished their shift, he

planned to seek her out. He couldn't stand by and do nothing while Josh escorted her about town.

Caught up in his own anxiety, he automatically followed Chase and Cricket to the long line of kids waiting for cotton candy. But after a few minutes he realized his sister was the one stirring up the sugary pink confection.

When Letty saw Lonny, she motioned for him to come to the front of the line.

"Don't do it," she said, looking at him sternly. Her mouth was pinched and she resembled their mother more than he'd thought possible.

"Do what?" he asked, playing innocent.

"Don't play games with me, big brother. I know you." All the while she was speaking, Letty rotated the paper cone along the outside of the circular barrel as it produced the cotton candy. "*Stay away from Joy.*" Smiling, she took two tickets from the waiting youngster and handed her the fluffy pink bouquet.

"But—"

"Chasc, don't you *dare* let him go near Joy while she's with Josh."

Chase frowned. "I'm not his babysitter."

"Stay with him. You can do that, can't you?"

Chase obviously wasn't happy about it. "I suppose."

"Good."

"Here, sweetie," she said, giving Cricket a tube of cotton candy. She turned to Lonny again. "Stay out of trouble, okay?"

Feeling like a kid who'd just been reprimanded, Lonny mumbled, "I took your advice earlier. I suppose I can again." He hoped Letty recognized how difficult this was going to be.

His sister narrowed her eyes. "Listen to me, Lonny," she insisted. "You've got to let Joy make up her own mind."

"But..."

"If you push her, you'll lose her. Understand?"

Lonny sighed. What choice did he have?

Chase took Cricket to all the kids' rides and Lonny felt like a third wheel walking around with them. Every now and then, he unexpectedly caught a glimpse of Joy and Josh. Once he saw them deep in conversation, their heads close together as they shared a bag of popcorn. Josh fed Joy a kernel and she smiled up at him as she accepted it.

Lonny's stomach convulsed at the sight. It came to him then that Josh might actually have the upper hand. He'd been so certain earlier, convinced to the core that Joy Fuller loved *him*. Now he wasn't as sure.

Confronted with Joy and Josh looking so comfortable, so intimate, was a rude awakening. Letty seemed to think doing nothing was the best response. It was killing him, but so far he'd managed. Barely.

"You okay?" Chase asked at one point.

"No," Lonny admitted from between clenched teeth. It began to seem that every time he turned a corner, there was Joy with her college boyfriend. When he saw them holding hands, he involuntarily started toward her. Chase grabbed his elbow, stopping him.

"Remember what Letty said," his friend muttered.

"How would *you* feel?" Lonny snapped, glaring at him.

"If I saw Letty holding hands with another man, you mean?" Chase asked. He shook his head. "Same way you're feeling now."

"That's what I thought."

"Josh will be on his way back to Seattle in a day, maybe two, and that'll be the end of it."

With all his heart, Lonny wanted to believe Joy would stay. "But what if she decides to go with him?" he asked. The possibility seemed very real at the moment.

"If she does, then it was meant to be."

Chase sounded so casual about it. So offhand. Apparently the love Lonny had for Joy didn't figure into this. Not according to his friend, anyway. Lonny didn't know how he was supposed to keep his mouth shut and pretend Chase was right. Like hell she'd leave with Josh What's-His-Name! He'd fight for Joy, make her understand how deep his feelings ran. He wasn't a man who gave his heart easily. He wasn't going to stand idly by and watch Josh walk off with her. Not in this lifetime. Not ever.

"You can't force her to marry you," Chase said, his hold tightening on Lonny's elbow.

"Sure I can," Lonny argued, for argument's sake.

Chase's reaction was to laugh.

"All right, all right," Lonny reluctantly agreed. He had to let this play out the way it would. The decision was up to her, and Lonny tried to believe that her good sense—and true feelings—would prevail.

"The dance is in an hour," Chase reminded him.

"Thank God for that." At least there he wouldn't be exposed to the sight of Joy and Josh holding hands and whispering to each other. He'd be able to concentrate on the kids and forget that his life was on the verge of imploding.

The dance was held in the high school gymnasium. Lonny got there early to avoid the risk of seeing Joy with Josh again. There was a limit to how much he could take.

The high school kids had done an admirable job of decorating the basketball court. The student body obviously had enough funds to hire a real band—well, a live band, anyway. They were tuning up, and discordant sounds spilled out the open doors. Groaning, Lonny had to resist plugging his ears. He only hoped Tom appreciated his sacrifice. Actually, he should be the one thanking Tom for an excuse to leave that blasted carnival. No telling how long those festivities would last.

Couples were slowly drifting in. While the guys were dressed in jeans and Western shirts, the girls all seemed to be wearing fancy dresses and strappy high-heeled shoes. If there'd been a dance like this while he was in school, Lonny didn't remember it. As he sat at the back of the gymnasium, guarding the punch bowl, he saw Tom and Michelle arrive.

Charley Larson's daughter was lovely. She wore a corsage on her wrist, and Lonny knew Tom had worried plenty about that white rose. But all his anguish and fretting seemed worth it now. They exuded such innocent happiness, Lonny found himself smiling.

Then, just when he'd started to relax, he saw Joy. He froze with a cup of punch halfway to his mouth. Sure enough, Josh tagged along behind her, one hand on her waist. Lonny felt as if someone had stuck a knife in his back. This dance was supposed to be his escape. Instead, it was fast becoming the scene of his emotional downfall. He didn't know how he'd manage to stand by and do nothing when Josh took Joy in his arms. Joy, the woman Lonny loved and hoped to marry.

The music began in earnest then. The lead singer stepped up to the microphone and announced the first dance.

Lonny set aside his punch and marched across the room.

When Joy saw him she scowled fiercely. "What are *you* doing here?" she demanded. She seemed to be asking that a lot today.

"I'm a chaperone. And you?"

"We're chaperoning, as well," Josh answered on her behalf.

Couples surged onto the dance floor all around them. "I believe this dance is mine," Lonny said and held out his hand to Joy.

She met his gaze without flinching, but didn't respond. She glanced at Josh, as if to ask his permission.

"Would you mind if I danced this number with Joy?" Lonny kept his voice as free of emotion as possible.

"Go ahead."

Lonny half expected Joy to argue with him and was pleasantly surprised when she simply followed him onto the floor. Since this was the first such event Lonny had chaperoned, he didn't know if the adults were allowed to dance. That, however, didn't concern him. If they wanted to fire him, they could. He didn't care. All that mattered was having Joy in his arms again.

He took her hand and she moved reluctantly into

his arms. To his relief, this was a slow dance. Closing his eyes, Lonny brought her against him and noticed how stiff she was.

"I don't know what you think you're doing," she whispered heatedly.

He pretended not to hear. Despite her reluctance, he drew her closer and held her hand in his.

"I'm talking to you," she said. "Could you answer me?"

Lonny ignored her question. A minute or two later, he felt her relax slightly. After that, it didn't take long for her to sigh and begin to move with him.

This was what he wanted, what he *needed.* Her body flowed naturally in motion with his. The fear started to leave him and he tightened his arm around her waist. This was perfect. They even breathed in unison.

Although it was agony not to kiss her when the music stopped, Lonny dropped his arms and stepped back.

"Thank you."

Joy stared at him, her eyes wide and confused.

He held her gaze for a long moment, unable to look away. It was on the tip of his tongue to tell her how much he loved her.

But Joy turned abruptly and walked back to Josh, who stood waiting on the sidelines.

Chapter 20

Joy wanted to argue with Lonny. He'd purposely gone out of his way to embarrass her, first in the restaurant and now on the dance floor. Understandably, Josh had asked plenty of questions this afternoon. Joy had explained her complicated relationship with Lonny as well as she could. He'd listened, but hadn't pressured her. He'd responded as a friend would, and for that she was grateful. Joy had seen Lonny watching them at the carnival. Every time she looked up, he seemed to be there, his eyes following her like a hawk tracking its prey.

Then, to confuse the situation even more, Lonny had to insist on dancing with her. That was when the *real* trouble started. She'd expected him to argue with her, which would've been fine. Joy was more than ready to give him an earful. All afternoon she'd felt his disapproving gaze. And then, when they'd danced…

Even while her mind whirled with an angry torrent of accusations, her body seemed to melt in his arms. Somehow, without her being aware of it, her eyes had closed and her head was pressed against his shoulder. He hadn't uttered a single word. All Lonny had done was hold her, dance with her. When the music stopped, he'd simply released her.

She moved slowly to the edge of the floor.

"I believe the next dance is mine," Josh said as he came forward to claim Joy.

"Yes, of—of course," she stammered. Absorbed in her thoughts, she hadn't noticed Josh approaching her. The music began again.

"That would be…" She couldn't think of the right word. *Nice,* she mused, as Josh took her hand and led her onto the floor. The music was much faster this time, and the dance floor quickly became crowded.

Josh was an accomplished dancer. His movements were flamboyant, energetic but controlled—as good as anything she'd ever seen on TV. The teenagers gathered around him were clapping in time with the music. More and more people came to watch his performance, and it occurred to Joy that he wasn't dancing with *her,* the way Lonny had. They were just occupying the same space. She tried gamely to keep up with him. Joy was impressed with his dancing, all the while disliking the fact that the two of them were the center of attention.

Joy had gone to a number of dances with Josh during their college days, but she couldn't remember his being this smooth or agile. Apparently, it was a recently acquired skill.

The music stopped, and the crowd broke into spon-

taneous applause. Joy couldn't get off the floor fast
enough. Josh followed her, but at a slower pace.

"Where did you learn to dance like that?" Joy asked,
and realized there was a lot about him she no longer
knew. Josh had changed; the thing was, Joy had, too.

"Lori and I went dancing a lot."

"You're great at it," Joy said sincerely. This was
the first real dance she'd attended in two years and
frankly, she could do with a refresher course. Beside
Josh, she'd looked pretty lame, she thought ruefully. But
there just weren't that many opportunities to dance in
Red Springs. Most places served beer in jugs, played
only country-western music and had floors covered
with sawdust.

Josh's smile didn't quite reach his eyes. "I miss it,
you know."

Joy suspected it was more than the dancing Josh
missed, but she kept her opinion to herself.

When she glanced up, she saw that Lonny was
watching her again.

Because she had a job to do, she walked along the
perimeter of the dance floor, her eyes focused on the
dancing couples. Josh strolled beside her. She noticed
Tom, Lonny's hired hand, and Michelle Larson dancing together. Tom appeared awkward and uneasy, con-
centrating heavily on each movement. He was rigid
and held Michelle an arm's length away from him. His
lips moved as he silently counted the steps. Michelle,
bless her, tried her best to follow his lead. They were
a sweet-looking couple.

A moment later, Joy saw that she wasn't the only
one watching Tom and Michelle dance. Kenny Brigh-

ton stood at the outer edge of the dance floor, eyeing the couple, his fists flexing at his sides.

Joy felt it was her duty to waylay trouble before it happened. Trying not to be obvious, she moved toward the other boy, pulling Josh with her, holding his hand.

"Good evening, Kenny," she said. "May I introduce you to my friend Josh Howell?"

Kenny didn't appreciate the interruption in his brooding. He acknowledged her with the faintest of nods, but his gaze didn't waver from Tom and Michelle.

"Kenny's family helped bring the carnival rides to Red Springs," Joy said brightly to Josh, as though this was a feat worthy of mention. "Isn't that right, Kenny?" she added when he didn't respond.

"If you say so," he muttered.

"Is there a problem between you and Tom?" she asked, deciding it was best to confront the issue head-on. Subtlety was getting them nowhere.

For the first time Kenny tore his eyes away from the dancing couple. "Michelle was supposed to be *my* date."

"You mean to say Tom kidnapped her?" she asked, trying to make light of the situation. Her attempt fell decidedly flat.

Kenny wasn't amused. "Something like that. I asked her first and she had some weak excuse for why she couldn't go with me. Next thing I hear, she's coming to the dance with Ellison's ranch hand." He practically spat the last two words.

"That's a woman's prerogative, isn't it?" Joy said, desperately hoping to keep the peace. This was the last official event of the school year, and she didn't want to see it ruined.

Kenny didn't appear to agree with her. "I'm twice the man that hired hand will ever be."

"Kenny, listen, we don't want any trouble here," she said, turning to Josh for help.

Josh nodded. "Why don't you find someone else to dance with," he suggested.

Kenny turned to Josh long enough to cast him a look of disdain. "I don't want to," he said sullenly. Joy could smell alcohol on his breath, strictly forbidden but furtively indulged in by the older boys.

She was afraid of what Kenny might do next, afraid he'd welcome an opportunity to fight Tom again. In his current frame of mind, Kenny might even see Josh as a convenient target, ridiculous though that was.

"Come on," Josh said, urging her away from Kenny. "I don't think you can do any good here."

Joy was reluctant to leave. As she moved past Kenny, she noticed Lonny keeping a close eye on the boy, too. He darted a look in her direction and she nodded, glancing at Kenny. Lonny's faint smile assured her he had matters well in hand.

Joy was astonished at how effectively they were able to communicate with just eye contact. This was a difficult situation with the potential to blow up into a major fracas. At the same time, she had every confidence that Lonny would know how to handle it. Sighing with relief, she patrolled the dance floor, smiling at students she recognized. She exchanged greetings with the other chaperones, and when she introduced Josh, she noted several surprised looks. Lonny wasn't the only one who seemed to think she was linked to him romantically.

"Would you like to dance again?" Josh asked when

they'd made their way completely around the dance floor. They stood near the punch bowl, while Lonny was on the side of the room closest to Kenny. She kept her eyes trained on the boy in case a problem erupted. Not that there was much *she'd* be able to do...

"Joy?" Josh prodded.

"I'm not sure I should," she said.

Although she'd been out on the floor twice, making a spectacle of herself at least once, she was present at this event in an official capacity. She could sense trouble simmering and needed to take her chaperoning duties seriously. Still, she felt bad about abandoning Josh.

"I have to be aware of what's happening and I can't do that if I'm dancing," she murmured, standing on her tiptoes and stretching to look for Kenny. He was gone.

"Don't worry," Josh said. "I understand."

She thanked him with a smile. "Feel free to ask one of the other chaperones to dance." Josh really had been a good sport about all of this. "Do you see Kenny anyplace?"

Josh scanned the crowd. "No, I can't say I do."

Joy glanced around, looking for Tom and Michelle.

Her suspicions were instantly aroused. Without explaining, she dashed across the now-empty dance floor toward Lonny.

Lonny must have known immediately that something was wrong, because he met her halfway and reached for her hands.

"Kenny's missing," she gasped out, "and so is Tom."

Lonny released a harsh breath. "I saw Kenny leave but I thought Tom was with Michelle."

"He isn't. I just saw Michelle come out of the rest-room."

Lonny didn't wait for her to say any more. He hurried off the dance floor and out of the building. Not knowing what else to do, Joy followed. She left Josh talking to a couple of other teachers—both women.

The first thing she saw when she got outside was that a group of kids, mostly boys, had clustered in a ragged circle. Joy couldn't see what was taking place but she heard an ugly din, interspersed by girls' screams. She nudged her way through the crowd, behind Lonny.

As soon as he broke through the crowd gathered to watch, Lonny burst into the middle.

Joy saw that two boys were holding Tom down while Kenny Brighton took a swing at him. Tom kicked and bucked against the youths restraining him. Michelle stood to one side with her hands covering her face, moaning, unable to watch.

"If there's going to be a fight, it'll be a fair one," Lonny roared.

Outrage filled Joy. From the murmurs she heard around her, she wasn't the only person who objected to what was going on. She was about to interrupt Lonny and insist the fight be stopped altogether. But before she could say anything, Lonny rushed forward and tore the other boys off Tom. He flung them aside as if they were no more than flies.

Tom stood up, smudged with dirt and clutching his stomach. One eye was black, and the corner of his mouth was bleeding. Michelle ran forward, letting out a distressed cry as she saw Tom. Joy went over to the girl and placed one arm around her shoulders.

"What's your problem?" Lonny demanded, addressing Kenny.

"He stole my girlfriend," the larger boy shouted, his face twisted with rage. He raised his fists again as if eager to return to the pounding he'd been giving Tom.

"I'm not his girlfriend," Michelle shouted back.

"You were until he showed up," Kenny challenged, motioning toward Tom.

"You want to fight Tom?" Lonny asked.

Kenny nodded. "Let me at him, and I'll show you how much I want to fight."

"Tom?" Lonny asked.

Tom wiped the blood from his mouth and nodded, too.

"Fine. Then step back, everyone, and give them plenty of room."

Joy couldn't believe what she was hearing. Lonny was actually condoning the fight! "No," she cried. Not only was she against physical violence, which in her view was never an appropriate response, but she could tell that even one-on-one, this wouldn't be a "fair" fight. She felt she needed to point out the obvious discrepancies in their sizes. "Lonny, no! Kenny outweighs Tom by thirty or forty pounds."

Lonny ignored her protest.

"Stay back, gentlemen," Lonny told the two boys who'd been holding Tom down.

It seemed the entire gymnasium had emptied onto the field by this point. Joy remained at Michelle's side, still horrified that Lonny was allowing the two boys to continue fighting.

"I've got to break this up!" she said urgently.

"No," Michelle said, stopping her. "I hate it, but this is how things are settled here. Tom doesn't have any choice except to fight Kenny."

"He could get hurt." Joy knew Michelle didn't want to see Tom hurt any more than she did.

"Mr. Ellison won't let that happen," Michelle told her.

Although she'd been part of the community for two years, Joy didn't understand why quarrels like this had to be handled by such primitive means. Besides, Lonny seemed to be setting Tom up for defeat. Kenny was bigger and stronger, and poor Tom didn't stand a chance.

Kenny came out swinging, eager to take Tom down with one swift blow. To Joy's surprise, Tom nimbly ducked, and Kenny's powerful swing met nothing but air. The larger boy stumbled forward, and that was when Tom thrust his fist up and struck, hitting Kenny squarely in the jaw.

Kenny whirled back, a look of shock on his face.

"You ready to call it quits?" Tom asked him.

"Not on your life, you little weasel." Kenny swung again, with the same result.

This time, Tom drove a fist into Kenny's stomach, and the other boy doubled over.

"I'm not as easy to hit without someone holding me down, am I?" Tom said scornfully.

Joy loosened her grip on Michelle's shoulders, suspecting the fight was almost over. The girl took a deep shuddering breath.

Twice more Kenny Brighton went after Tom. Both times Tom was too quick for him. Whenever Kenny took a swing, Tom retaliated with a solid punch, until Kenny lowered his arms and shook his head.

"You finished?" Lonny asked, stepping forward.

Kenny nodded.

"Is this the end of it?" Lonny stood between them.

Tom nodded and Kenny did, too, reluctantly.

"Then shake hands."

Tom came forward with his hand extended and Kenny met him halfway.

"I don't have to like you," Kenny bit out.

"Same here," Tom said.

They stared at each other, then warily backed away.

Michelle immediately rushed to Tom's side and slipped her arm around his waist. "Are you all right?"

"I'm fine," he said smiling. "Are we going to dance or are we not?"

"Dance," she replied, and her eyes sparkled with delight. "Oh, Tom, I would never have guessed you could hold your own against Kenny."

They returned to the gym and in a few minutes, the crowd had dwindled. Kenny's friends gathered around him, but he brusquely pushed them aside and stalked to the parking lot.

"Is it over?" Joy asked Lonny, still a little nervous.

"There's nothing to worry about now," he assured her.

"I don't understand why they had to fight." Nothing like this would've been allowed anywhere else; she was convinced of that. Certainly not at a school in Seattle.

"You didn't see any of the other chaperones stopping the fight, did you?"

Joy had to agree she hadn't.

"This way it was fair and there were witnesses. Kenny learned a valuable lesson tonight, and my guess is it's one he won't soon forget."

Joy wasn't nearly as convinced of that as Lonny seemed to be.

"He'll go home and lick his wounds," Lonny continued. "Basically, Kenny's a good kid. It embarrassed him to lose, especially in front of his friends—and the girl he likes."

"What was the lesson he supposedly learned?" Joy asked, not quite restraining her sarcasm.

Lonny looked at her in puzzlement. "Kenny learned that being bigger and stronger isn't necessarily an advantage," he said as though that should be obvious.

"Yes, but—"

"He was humiliated in front of his classmates because they saw that it took two of his friends to hold Tom down in order for Kenny to get in a hit. No one wants to be known as a dirty fighter."

"But…"

"He won't make the same mistake twice. Kenny might not like Tom, but now, at least, he respects him."

Joy just shook her head. "I don't understand fighting and I never will."

"You're new here," he said with a shrug, as if that explained everything.

"In other words, I don't belong in Red Springs."

Lonny smiled. "I wouldn't say that, but I would definitely say you belong with me."

Joy walked slowly back to the dance, where she found Josh in the middle of the floor, once again the center of attention.

Chapter 21

As part of the carnival cleanup committee, Lonny got to town early the next morning. Tom accompanied him, but Lonny was under no delusion—the attraction wasn't sweeping the streets. Tom had come with the express purpose of finding Michelle Larson. Lonny was just as eager for a glimpse of Joy.

It was clear to him that Joy and Josh were completely incompatible, and he hoped she'd finally recognized it. After two years in Red Springs, Joy had become a country girl. Life in the big city was no longer right for her. According to what Letty had told him, Josh would be leaving Red Springs in a day or two. Soon, in other words, but not soon enough for Lonny.

Broom in hand, he walked down Main Street, sweeping up trash as he went. The carnival people had already packed their equipment, preparing to move on to the next town.

Red Springs was taking its time waking up after a late night. Uncle Dave's, the local café, didn't hang out the "open" sign until after seven-thirty. Their biscuits and gravy, with a cup of strong coffee, was the best breakfast in town. Whenever he had the chance, Lonny sat at the counter and ordered a double portion of the house special. Those biscuits would carry him all the way to evening.

He was busy dumping trash into a large plastic bag when he noticed Josh Howell leaving the restaurant, holding a cup of takeout coffee.

"How's it going?" Josh said, approaching Lonny. He surveyed the street, where the majority of the festivities had taken place.

"Okay, I guess." Lonny stopped sweeping and leaned against the broom. He liked the other man, but if it came to stepping aside so Josh could walk off with Joy, well, that was another matter.

"You said you love Joy," Josh murmured.

"I do."

Josh nodded soberly. "She's in love with you, too." He looked down at his feet and then up again. "The entire time we were together, she was watching you. She couldn't take her eyes off you."

It demanded severe discipline on Lonny's part not to leap into the air and click his cowboy boots in jubilation.

"I'm not sure Joy realizes it yet," Josh added.

Lonny shook his head. "She knows, all right—only she isn't happy about it."

Josh grinned as if he agreed. "I'll be heading back to Seattle later this morning. Earlier than I intended, but I can see the lay of the land. It's obvious that Joy and I don't have a future together." He met Lonny's eyes. "Good luck."

Lonny extended his arm and they exchanged handshakes.

"Are you planning to marry her?" Josh surprised him by asking next.

Lonny had thought of little else all week. "I am, just as soon as she'll have me." He didn't know how long it would take Joy to listen to reason. But with a decision this important, he could be a patient man—even if patience didn't come naturally.

Josh left soon afterward and Lonny, Tom and the others spent the better part of two hours finishing their task. He was near-starved by that time, so he stopped off at Uncle Dave's for a huge order of biscuits and gravy. Tom joined him.

When they'd cleaned their plates, Tom made an excuse to visit the feed store. That was fine with Lonny. He had personal business to attend to himself, and he was eager to do it. He just hoped Josh had already left town.

But when Lonny pulled up in front of Joy's place, he discovered, to his disappointment, that her PT Cruiser wasn't parked out front. That wasn't a good sign.

He hadn't expected to feel nervous, but he did—probably because he'd never asked a woman to marry him before. To show the seriousness of his intentions, he realized he should present her with a ring—except that he didn't have one. His mother's diamond was in the safety deposit box at the bank. Although it had minimal financial worth, its sentimental value was incalculable.

Pulling away from the curb, Lonny glanced at his watch and saw that he only had a few minutes to catch Walt Abler before the bank closed at noon, which it did on Saturdays. In his rush, Lonny forgot about the new stop sign at Grove and Logan and shot past it. A flash of red caught his attention just before a little green PT Cruiser barreled into his line of vision. Lonny slammed on the brakes, but it was too late. He would've broadsided the Cruiser if not for the quick thinking of the other driver, who steered left to avoid a collision. Unfortunately, the green car's bumper scraped against the stop sign post.

Lonny's heart was in his throat, and he held the steering wheel in a death grip, reflecting on what a narrow escape he'd had.

"What do you think you're doing?" Joy Fuller shrieked as she climbed out of her vehicle and slammed the door shut hard enough to jam it for good.

Lonny had known it was Joy the minute he saw the green car. He got out of the driver's seat and rushed over to her side.

"Are you okay?" he demanded.

"Yes, no thanks to you."

"I'm sorry. I don't know what I was thinking. I forgot the stop sign was there." His excuse was weak, but it was the truth. The irony of the situation would have made him laugh if he didn't feel so shaken.

Apparently Joy hadn't even heard him. "Look what

you've done to my car!" She sounded close to tears as she examined the damage to her bumper.

The dent was barely noticeable as far as Lonny could see. He walked over and ran his hand along her bumper and then stepped back.

"This is a new car," she cried.

"I thought you got it last year."

"I did. But it's still new to me and now you've, you've—"

"Have it fixed. I'll pay for it."

"You're darn right you will." She raised her hand to her forehead.

Fearing she might have hit her head, Lonny took her by the shoulders and turned her to face him. "Are you okay?" he asked again.

She nodded.

"You didn't hit your head?"

"I...I don't think so."

"Maybe you should sit down for a minute to be sure."

The fact that she was willing to comply was worry enough. Sitting on the curb, Joy drew in several deep breaths. Lonny welcomed the opportunity to calm his own heart, which was beating at an accelerated pace.

"Where were you going in such an all-fired hurry?" she asked after a moment. She bolted suddenly to her feet.

"The bank. But what does it matter where I was going?" he asked, standing, too.

"You can't drive like that in town! You're an accident waiting to happen."

"I...I—" He didn't know what to say. The accident *had* been his fault. Twice in the past she'd caused the same kind of mishap and he'd been the one demanding answers to almost identical questions.

"You should have your driver's license suspended for being so irresponsible." Arms akimbo, she faced him, eyes flashing.

"Now, Joy…"

"I should contact the Department of Motor Vehicles."

"Joy." He was doing his level best to remain calm. "Getting upset like this isn't good."

"Don't tell me what I can and can't do!"

"Okay, fine, do whatever you want."

"I will," she snapped and started to stomp away.

He didn't want her to leave, not like this. "I love you, you know."

She paused, her back to him. Finally, she turned around, a thoughtful frown on her face. "You're sure about that?"

He nodded. "Very sure. Fact is, I was on my way to pick up an engagement ring."

Her frown darkened. "You said you were going to the bank."

"I was. My mother's diamond wedding ring is in the vault there. I intended to give you that. You can change the setting if you wish."

Joy seemed stunned into speechlessness.

"Letty wanted Mom's pearls and insisted I keep the ring in case I ever got married. She was thinking my wife-to-be would like that diamond." He was rambling, but he couldn't seem to stop himself. "It's not a big stone. It's just a plain, ordinary diamond, but Mom loved it." He glanced at his watch again. "I'll have to wait until Monday now, and then you can see for yourself."

"A diamond ring?" From the look on her face, Lonny wondered if Joy had understood a single word he'd said.

"Now probably isn't the time or place to ask you to marry me." Letty had been telling him all along that he had a terrible sense of timing.

"No…no, I disagree," Joy said. "Continue, please."

Since she seemed prepared to listen, Lonny figured he should take this opportunity. He cleared his throat and removed his hat. "Will you?"

She blinked and craned her neck toward him. "Will I *what?*"

"Marry me." He thought it was obvious.

"That's it?" She threw her arms in the air. "*Will you?*"

He didn't see the problem. "Yes."

"This is the most important question of a woman's life, Lonny Ellison."

"It's important to a man, too," he said.

"I want a little more than *will you.*"

Annoyed with her tone, he glared at her. "Do you want me to add *please?* Is that it?"

"That would be an improvement."

"All right. *Please.*"

She motioned as if asking him to come closer. "And?"

"You mean you want *more?*" Lonny had never expected a marriage proposal to be this difficult. He wished now that he'd talked to his brother-in-law first. Chase would've advised him on the proper protocol.

"Of course." Joy didn't sound too patient. "For one thing, *why* do you want to marry me?"

That was a question he was beginning to ask himself. "I already told you—I love you."

"Okay. That's a good start."

"Start?" he repeated. "What else is there?"

"Quite a bit, as it happens."

Lonny shook his head. "Are you interested or not? Because this is getting ridiculous."

Joy folded her arms and cocked her head to one side, as if considering the question. "I might be, if the person doing the asking put a little more of his heart into it."

Lonny looked up at the sky and prayed for tolerance. "Joy Fuller, the luckiest day of my life was the day you ran me off the road last month, because that's when I discovered exactly how much I love you." He grinned. "Hey, this is our third accident—er, incident—together. And you know what they say. Third time's the charm."

She narrowed her eyes, apparently not all that charmed.

"Listen," he said hastily. "This might be news, but I'm not in the habit of kissing unwilling females. You were the first."

"And the last," she inserted.

"The absolute last," he agreed. "I kissed you because you made me so crazy I didn't know how else to react. I understand now that it wasn't anger I was feeling. It was attraction so strong it simply knocked me off my feet."

"Well, you infuriated *me*."

Lonny grinned again. "This isn't the best way to go about reconciling," he said.

She conceded with a curt nod.

Lonny stepped closer and reached for her hands, holding them in his. "I don't know that much about love. I've been a bachelor so long, I'd sort of assumed I'd always be one. Since meeting you, I've found I don't want to be alone anymore."

Her eyes went liquid with tenderness. "Really?"

"I don't need you to cook and clean and all that other stuff. I don't care about that. I've been doing those things for myself, anyway." He didn't like housework and Tom didn't, either, but between the two of them they managed.

"Then why do you want me?"

"I'd like you to sit on the porch with me in the evenings, the way my parents used to do. I like telling you my ideas and listening to what you think. I want us to be partners. If Chase and I go ahead with our guest-ranch idea, you'd be a real help because you know kids."

"*Are* you going to pursue that?"

"I haven't talked to him yet," he admitted, "but whether we do or not, I still want you as my wife."

She nodded slowly.

"Speaking of kids," he said, "I'd like a few and I hope you would, too." He should probably clarify his feelings on the matter right now. "I've seen you with the children at school, and Cricket thinks the world of you. Letty, too. As far as I'm concerned, you couldn't have any better character witnesses. They love you and I'm just falling in line behind them."

Joy gave him a quavery smile. "I want children, too."

"I was thinking a couple of kids. Maybe three."

She nodded, and the look on her face tightened his gut with a mixture of love and longing. Intent on making this proposal as perfect as possible, Lonny raised her hand to his lips. "Joy Fuller, will you marry me?"

"Yes," she whispered and tears rolled down her cheeks.

"Soon?" he asked, then added, "Please."

She smiled at that and nodded.

His heart full, Lonny put his arms around her and brought his mouth down on hers. He wanted this to be a gentle kiss, one that spoke of their love and commitment. Yet the moment her mouth met his, he thought he might explode. He wanted her with him, in his home and his bed, right then and there. Waiting even a day seemed too long.

Joy must have felt the same way, because she became fully involved in the kiss. She held nothing back, nothing at all.

By the time Lonny broke it off, they were both breathless. A car had stopped at the intersection— obeying the stop sign—and honked approvingly. Fortunately, traffic was unusually sparse for a Saturday.

"Wow," Lonny whispered, leaning his forehead against hers. "If we get a license first thing Monday morning, we can be married by the end of the week."

"Lonny, Lonny, Lonny." Her eyes were warm with love as she straightened, shaking her head. "I only intend to get married once in my life, and I'm going to do it properly."

"Don't tell me you want a big wedding." He should've known she'd make a production of this.

"Yes, I want a wedding." She said this as if it should be a foregone conclusion. "Not necessarily *big,* but a real wedding."

This was getting complicated. "Will I have to wear one of those fancy suits with a ruffled shirt?"

She laughed, but he wasn't joking. "That's negotiable."

"How long's the planning going to take?"

"A few weeks."

He groaned, hating the thought. "Weeks. You've got to be kidding."

Her look told him she wasn't. Then she smiled again, and it was one of the most beautiful smiles he'd ever seen. It was full of love—and desire. When she kissed him, his knees went weak.

"I promise," she whispered, "that however long the planning takes, it'll be worth the wait."

With the next kiss, Lonny's doubts vanished.

* * * * *

Also by Delores Fossen

Harlequin Intrigue

The Lawmen of McCall Canyon

Cowboy Above the Law
Finger on the Trigger
Lawman with a Cause
Under the Cowboy's Protection

Blue River Ranch

Always a Lawman
Gunfire on the Ranch
Lawman from Her Past
Roughshod Justice

HQN Books

A Wrangler's Creek Novel

Lone Star Cowboy (ebook novella)
Those Texas Nights
One Good Cowboy (ebook novella)
No Getting Over a Cowboy
Just Like a Cowboy (ebook novella)
Branded as Trouble
Cowboy Dreaming (ebook novella)
Texas-Sized Trouble
Cowboy Heartbreaker (cbook novella)
Lone Star Blues
Cowboy Blues (ebook novella)
The Last Rodeo

A Coldwater Texas Novel

Lone Star Christmas

Don't miss *Hot Texas Sunrise*,
the next book in the Coldwater Texas series.

To see the complete list of titles available from
Delores Fossen, please visit www.deloresfossen.com.

THE HORSEMAN'S SON

Delores Fossen

To my wonderful editor, Allison Lyons.
Thanks for everything.

Chapter 1

Greer, Texas

"Sir, we have an intruder on the grounds," the house-keeper warned Dylan Greer.

Dylan's stomach clenched into a cold, hard knot. He silently cursed, said a brusque goodbye to his business associate in London and dropped the phone back onto its cradle.

An intruder. Well, the person had picked a good day for it.

It was Thanksgiving morning, barely minutes after sunrise, and he'd given most of his household help time off for the holiday. He was understaffed. Plus, there was a snowstorm moving in. With the already slick, icy roads, it'd probably take the sheriff at least twenty minutes to get out to the ranch.

"Where is he?" Dylan asked Vergie, the housekeeper, through the two-way speaker positioned on his desk.

"The north birthing stables."

In other words, too close to the house. That meant Dylan had to take care of this on his own.

"Call the sheriff," Dylan instructed Vergie as he unlocked his center desk drawer and took out the Sig Sauer that he'd hoped he would never have to use. He grabbed his thick shearling coat from the closet and put his gun and his cell phone in the pocket.

"You want me to tell Hank to go out there with you?" Vergie asked.

"No." Hank, the handyman, was seventy-two and had poor eyesight and hearing. Besides, this might be Dylan's chance to have a showdown with the person who'd made his life a living hell.

Dylan worked quickly to get the information he needed. He used his security surveillance laptop to bring up the camera image of the exterior of the birthing stables. It wasn't the most vulnerable spot on his six-hundred-and-thirty acres, but it did have one major security flaw.

Accessibility.

Anyone could have parked on the dirt road a quarter of a mile away from his property, climbed the eight-foot-tall wooden fence and made their way across the pasture to the stables. Not an effortless undertaking in the cold, but it was doable.

And, on his computer screen, he saw the person who'd managed that feat.

There, next to the birthing-stable doors, was a shadowy figure holding a pair of binoculars. The person was dressed all in black. Black pants, bulky black coat and a knit cap. That attire and those binoculars weren't positive signs. Whoever it was hadn't dropped by to wish him a happy Thanksgiving.

Mercy, did he really have a killer on the grounds?

With everything that'd happened, Dylan couldn't take the chance that this was all some innocent intrusion.

"Lock up when I leave," Dylan instructed the housekeeper from the intercom. "And call me immediately if our *guest* moves closer to the house."

He left through the French doors of his office and stepped into the bitter cold. It wasn't officially even winter yet, but the weather obviously didn't know that— it was a good twenty degrees below normal. The wind howled out of the north, slamming right through his jacket, shirt, jeans and boots. A few snowflakes whirled through the air.

The birthing stables were on the opposite side of the house from where he'd exited, so Dylan knew the intruder hadn't seen him with those binoculars. He ran, following a row of Texas sagebrush and mountain laurel, hoping the shrubbery would conceal him for as long as possible. He wanted the element of surprise on his side. Correction. He *needed* that. Because this person might have already committed murder.

With that brutal reminder crawling through his head, Dylan took out his gun so that he'd be ready. He had to protect his son at all costs, and if necessary, that would include an out-and-out fight. He wasn't going to lose someone else he loved to this nameless, faceless SOB.

Though the cold burned his lungs and his boots

seemed unsteady on the ice-scabbed pasture grass, he didn't slow down until he reached the stables. Dylan went to the rear of the building so he could approach the intruder from behind, and peered around the corner. The person in black hadn't moved an inch and was about fifty feet away.

He checked his watch. It'd been nearly fifteen minutes since the housekeeper had called the sheriff, and there was no sign of him. Dylan decided not to wait.

The wind worked in his favor. It was whipping so hard against the stables that it muffled his footsteps, and he halved the distance before he was heard. Dylan already had his gun aimed and ready when the intruder dropped the binoculars and spun around.

It was a woman.

She was pale and trembling, probably from the cold, and she reached inside her jacket, as if it were an automatic response to draw a weapon.

"Don't," Dylan warned. He wanted her alive to answer the questions he'd wanted to ask for twelve years.

She nodded and without hesitation lifted her gloved hands in surrender. "Dylan Greer," she said.

It wasn't exactly a question so Dylan didn't bother to confirm it. "Mind telling me why you're trespassing on my property?"

She didn't answer. She just stood there staring at him.

Dylan didn't want to notice this about her, but she looked exhausted and fragile. He didn't let down his guard, though. There was too much at stake for him to do anything but stay vigilant.

He inched closer, so he could get a better look at her face. Definitely pale.

And definitely attractive.

Something he shouldn't have noticed, but it would have been impossible not to observe that about her. Her eyes were dark chocolate-brown and a real contrast to the strands of wheat-blond hair that had escaped her black stocking cap.

"I don't know you," he said.

"No."

Funny, he thought he would. Well, if she was the person responsible for two deaths. But he was beginning to doubt that she was the monster he originally believed her to be.

She didn't look like a killer.

And he hoped his change in attitude didn't have anything to do with those vulnerable brown eyes.

"Who are you?" he asked.

"Collena Drake." She studied his face as if her name might mean something to him.

It didn't.

But Dylan kept pressing. "What are you doing here?"

She looked away. "I needed...to see you."

That hesitation and gaze dodging made him think she was lying. "The sheriff will be here any minute to arrest you for trespassing."

"Yes. I figured if you spotted me that you'd call the authorities. I don't blame you. If our positions were reversed, I would have done the same thing."

Her rational, almost calm response confused and unnerved him. "Then why come? Why risk certain arrest?"

And he was positive he wasn't going to like this answer. What would make this visit *that* important?

But the answer didn't come after all. He could see that she was breathing hard. Her warm breath mixed with the cold air and surrounded her face in a surreal opal-white fog. Mumbling something that Dylan didn't understand, she reached out with her right hand, grasping at the empty space, until she managed to catch on to the side of the building. The grip didn't help steady her.

She crumpled into a heap on the ground.

Dylan didn't let down his guard, or his gun, but he rushed to her to make sure she was okay. She'd apparently fainted, and when he touched her face, he discovered that her skin was ice-cold. After cursing, hesitating and then realizing there was nothing else he could do, he scooped her up into his arms and took her into the empty birthing stables.

He deposited her onto the hay-strewn concrete floor and flipped the switch on the wall to turn on the lights and the heater. Still, the place wouldn't be warm for hours, so he grabbed a saddle blanket from the tack shelf and covered her with it.

Dylan checked the time again. The sheriff was obviously running late, and he debated calling an ambulance. Her color wasn't great, but her breathing was steadier now and she had a strong pulse. This didn't appear to be a life-threatening situation.

Since she had no purse, Dylan stooped down beside her and checked her coat pocket for some kind of ID. He found a wallet, a small leather flip case and keys. He looked inside the wallet and located her Texas driver's license.

If the license was real, and it certainly looked as if it was, then her name was indeed Collena Drake. She was twenty-eight, five-feet-nine-inches tall, and she lived in San Antonio, a good two-hour drive away. Also in the wallet were credit cards and about three hundred dollars in cash, but no photos or other personal mementos to indicate exactly who this woman was.

However, the flip case gave him a clue.

It was a private investigator's badge.

That didn't answer any of Dylan's questions, but it did add some new ones to the list of things he wanted to know about this fainting trespasser.

He pulled open her jacket and immediately saw the shoulder holster and gun. Since he didn't want to take the chance of being shot, he extracted the weapon and put it in his own pocket.

"Miss Drake?" Dylan said, tapping her cheek. He took out his phone to call for an ambulance, but he stopped when she began to stir. "Are you all right?"

Her eyelids fluttered open, and she ran her tongue over her wind-chapped bottom lip. "What happened?"

"You passed out," he informed her. "Are you sick?"

She hesitated, as if giving that some thought. "No. I don't think so."

"Are you pregnant?" Not that there were any visible signs of a pregnancy, but then it would be hard to see a baby bump behind that loose sweater.

Something went through those intense dark eyes. Something painful. "No. Not a chance." Collena Drake held on to the blanket but maneuvered herself to a sitting position. In the process, she brushed against a post, specifically a raised nail head that caught onto her stocking cap. "It's been a while since I've eaten. I'm light-headed."

Dylan shook his head. "For a trespasser, you didn't exactly come prepared, now, did you? You nearly froze to death and you're starving. Is this your way of asking for an invitation to Thanksgiving dinner?"

"No," she snapped. She pulled off her stocking cap, and her blond hair spilled onto her shoulders. She untangled the yarn from the nail and slipped the cap back on. "I didn't come here for food."

He hadn't thought for a minute that she had. "Then, maybe it's a good time for you to tell me why you did come?"

"Because you're Dylan Greer." She inched away from him. "I saw you yesterday. You were in town."

That was true. He had gone into town the day before to do some early Christmas shopping. However, during all his errands, Dylan hadn't seen this woman.

That caused his concern level to spike again.

Because Dylan wanted to make sure she understood that he didn't approve of her, her presence or what she'd done, he leaned in closer. Too close. So that they were practically eye-to-eye.

She didn't cower from him. In fact, her chin came up, and instead of fatigue and frustration, he saw some resolve in her expression.

"What's a P.I. from San Antonio doing following me around town?" he demanded.

Her resolve increased even more. "I've been looking for you a long, long time, Dylan Greer."

And it sounded a little like a threat.

"I'm not a hard man to find. I've lived in Greer all

my life. The town is named for my great-great grand-father. And I own a fairly well-known horse-breeding business. My name is even on the mailbox at the end of my driveway."

She made a soft sound of frustration. "You weren't easy to find because I didn't know I was looking for you."

He heard the sheriff's siren in the distance. *Finally.* It was about time. In five minutes, maybe less, he could turn all of this over to the authorities. But he couldn't do that until he learned more about his visitor.

Tired of answers that weren't making sense, Dylan decided to cut to the chase. "Did you kill my sister and my fiancée five years ago?"

Her eyes widened. "No. God, no."

Collena Drake sounded adamant enough, but it didn't satisfy Dylan. "Are you telling me that you didn't know about their murders?"

"I knew. I mean, I ran a background check on you. Their deaths popped up on the computer records. But the computer records didn't say anything about murder."

"Trust me," he snarled. "It was murder. Now, I want to know what you had to do with that."

"Nothing. Until three days ago, I'd never even heard of you."

Yet something else that didn't make sense, especially since she'd said she'd been looking for him for a *long, long time.* "So, what changed three days ago?"

"Everything."

The single word that left her mouth was more breath than sound.

Dylan didn't need the winter to chill him, because

that comment put some ice in his blood. He stood and stared down at her. Waiting for an explanation. And not at all sure that he really wanted to hear it.

"I'm a cop," Collena Drake said, getting to her feet.

It was another crazy twist in this crazy encounter. "If you thought that would stop me from having you arrested, you thought wrong."

"I have no expectations about how you will or won't react to me." She hugged the blanket tighter to her chest and waited a moment until her teeth stopped chattering. "Last year I took a leave of absence from the San Antonio PD so I could work full-time on the Brighton case."

"Brighton?" he repeated. Dylan shrugged. "Am I supposed to know what that means?"

"You should. I'm talking about the Brighton Birthing Center investigation. Last year, the police discovered that the center was a front for all sorts of illegal activity." She paused. "Including illegal adoptions."

His heart felt as if someone had clamped a meaty fist around it. Because last year he'd adopted his own precious son, Adam. And he wasn't just a part of Dylan's life, Adam *was* his life.

"I didn't go through Brighton to get my son," he informed her.

"No. But Brighton still supplied the newborn that you adopted through the law firm you used."

"What makes you think that?" Dylan fired back.

Her jaw muscles stirred. "Because for months I've investigated every detail, every file and every person who had any association whatsoever with Brighton. Then, three days ago, all the pieces finally came together, and I was able to figure out what'd happened."

The siren grew closer, and Dylan knew that the sheriff was now on the ranch itself and headed straight for the birthing stable.

"Are you saying you believe that my son was illegally adopted?" Dylan asked.

"Yes," she answered without hesitation.

Oh, the thoughts that went through his mind. Nightmarish thoughts. Had the birth parents changed their minds about the adoption? Did they want Adam back? If they did, it wasn't going to happen. Adam was his son in every way that mattered, and he wasn't going to give him up.

Dylan pushed aside all the emotion he was feeling and focused on one glaring hole in her theory. "If you thought the adoption was illegal, then why did you come? Why aren't the San Antonio police here instead?"

She met his regard head-on. "I came because I have a personal stake in this."

Outside, the siren fell silent. Dylan heard the tires crunch on the frozen ground as the patrol car braked to a sudden stop.

"Is this your case?" he clarified.

Collena Drake shook her head. "It's not just that I'm the investigating officer. I, too, was a victim of the Brighton Birthing Center. After giving birth there, my baby was stolen."

Dylan was about to ask what that could possibly have to do with him, but the doors burst open. It wasn't the sheriff but Deputy Jonah Burke, a hulk of a man who was armed with a semiautomatic. The deputy definitely wasn't the person that Dylan wanted to see and, judging from Jonah's expression, he felt the same about Dylan.

"Everything okay?" the deputy asked, his attention nailed to Collena Drake.

She let the blanket fall to the floor so that she could again lift her hands in a show of surrender. However, she kept her gaze pinned on Dylan.

"Sixteen months ago, I gave birth to a son," she continued. Her voice cracked on the last word and her bottom lip began to tremble.

Dylan wasn't trembling, but he felt some of that raw emotion himself.

"So?" he challenged.

"*So,* you illegally adopted him. I'm Adam's mother.*"

Chapter 2

Collena held her breath and waited for Dylan Greer's reaction to what she'd just told him.

She'd braced herself for just about anything. Shouts, accusations, violence, perhaps even an arrest. But neither violence, nor an arrest would stop her from making him understand the truth.

Dylan Greer had her son.

Just silently saying the words made Collena's heart ache. Yes, she'd found her baby—*finally*—but the man who'd adopted him was a massive obstacle who stood in the way of her becoming a real mother to her child.

Collena was prepared to make any and all compromises to be a mother. What she wouldn't do was walk away and not be part of her son's life. No way. She wouldn't do to her child what her own mother had done to her.

"Well?" the deputy prompted. "Is someone gonna tell me what in the sam hill is going on here?"

With their eyes locked, Collena waited to see what Dylan would say. He didn't make it easy on her—she had to wait several long moments.

"I'm not sure," Dylan answered. "But I'll find out."

The deputy turned up the collar on his thick wool coat. "Mind if we 'find out' someplace warmer? I'm freezing my butt off out here. And if this is some kind of lovers' quarrel—"

"It's not," Collena and Dylan said in unison.

But she did agree with the deputy on one thing. She was freezing, too. And she was dizzy. How could she have been so stupid not to eat before she set out to try to get a glimpse of her child? It was an understatement to say she'd been preoccupied with seeing her son, but fainting and feeling weak weren't good bargaining tools for what would no doubt be a major battle with Dylan Greer.

"How about we take this to the house?" the deputy suggested. "I can have a cup of Ina's coffee and you two can decide when you're going to let me know what's going on." He aimed his index finger at Dylan. "But I warn you, if you brought me all the way out here on Thanksgiving for nothing, then even Ina's coffee won't improve my mood."

The ruddy-faced deputy added a lopsided smile to indicate he was only partly joking. Dylan didn't return the smile. The tension between them was almost as thick as it was between Dylan and Collena.

Almost.

"Can you walk on your own?" Dylan asked her. He

waited just long enough for her nod before he headed out of the stables and in the direction of his house.

Where her son was.

That sent Collena's heart racing, and it was for all the right reasons. She might get to see her child.

Ahead of her, Dylan took out his phone and Collena heard him make a call. He told whomever answered to unlock his office door and to make sure Adam stayed out of there for a while.

Collena wouldn't be able to see him. Part of her understood that. Dylan Greer didn't know her at all. Judging from the questions he'd barked at her, he thought she might be a killer.

Now, that brought on more than just raw nerves. What had happened to this man to make him think a trespasser was out to murder him? And were his suspicions valid? Collena certainly intended to look into the matter, because if it was true, her son might also be in danger.

"Some advice?" the deputy drawled. "It's not a good idea to trespass on Dylan's property. Since he adopted that little boy, he doesn't pull any punches about stuff like that. He'll have your butt arrested in a New York minute."

Collena ignored the warning and brushed some snowflakes off her face. "Is he a good father?"

The deputy glanced at her as if she were mentally a little off. "Yeah. He is. A surprise, if you ask me. When the two of us were growing up, I never took Dylan for the fatherly type."

Well, the deputy was apparently the only person surprised with Dylan's fatherly attributes. In the past three days, Collena's team of investigators had dug up everything they could on the man, and from all accounts Dylan wasn't just a good father, he was an outstanding one. In addition, he had a sterling reputation and was considered to be an honest, dependable man if not a little ruthless when it came to running his business.

And it was all those things combined that had made Collena come up with her plan.

A plan that had to work. Even though she had no idea how she was going to convince Dylan Greer to do what she needed him to do.

She studied the man ahead of her. He had the looks to go along with that sterling reputation. He was, for lack of a better word, *golden*. Bronze-colored hair that fell low on the back of his neck. Naturally tan skin. And those sizzling green eyes. Amazing eyes to compliment his amazingly rugged face.

Collena hated that she noticed the last part, but it would have been impossible to ignore. If the world ever needed a cowboy cover model, Dylan Greer would be the perfect man for the job.

She'd expected to feel insecure and inferior around him, what with his money, education and power. There would always be some of that. But Collena hadn't expected to feel the slight tingle inside that reminded her she was a woman.

A hungry woman.

The tingle couldn't have anything to do with Dylan. Low blood-sugar levels were to blame. And Collena refused to believe otherwise. She had a job to do here, and she couldn't let tingling feelings get in the way.

"I take it there's a history between Dylan and you?"

The deputy didn't wait for her to answer. "Were you two lovers and then you gave up your baby for adoption?"

"Nothing like that," she muttered. So she wouldn't have to continue this interrogation, she hurried to catch up with Dylan. "Did you hear what I said about being Adam's mother?"

It was a rhetorical question, a way to get the conversation started. Because Collena was dead certain he had heard every single word she'd said back there in the stables.

He spared her a glance and kept walking through the pasture. "There was no reason to respond because I don't believe you."

Ah, skepticism. She'd expected that, too. "It's the truth. I have proof."

Another glance. This one had some fire and ice to it. He had the eyes for such a range of emotion. Those shades of green seemed both hot and cold at the same time. Right now, they were leaning toward the chilly side, and that chill was all aimed at her.

"I'll be interested in this so-called proof," he said, opening the door. He went in ahead of her and checked out the place before he motioned for her to enter.

Collena stepped inside the toasty warm room, and she could almost feel her body sigh with relief. The deputy came in, shut the door behind him and brushed the snowflakes off his clothes.

Collena soon detected the source of the welcoming heat. There was a massive stone fireplace with flames flickering inside. The place smelled of mesquite wood and the scents from the winter pasture that they'd brought in with them. There was also the aroma of roasting turkey and pumpkin pie. Someone was apparently getting ready for Thanksgiving.

Her stomach growled, but Collena ignored it. She had a more important task at hand.

Dylan Greer's office was exactly what she'd expected. Palatial and functional. Horse-themed artwork on the walls. Rich, glossy woods for the floor and desk, and on the desk was a sliver-thin computer monitor and a gleaming silver tray with coffee, raisin wheat toast, biscuits and crystal dishes of various jams and marmalades.

A photograph next to the computer monitor caught Collena's eye. It was a picture of Dylan holding a baby.

Her baby.

But before she could get a better look, Dylan grabbed the photo and slammed it facedown on his desk. He picked up his phone, punched in some numbers and requested a background check on her.

Which she'd expected. She'd certainly done a thorough check on Dylan.

"Jonah, you can go get your coffee now," Dylan *advised*.

The deputy scowled at what was obviously an order, but he headed for the set of interior doors. However, the doors opened before he could get to them.

A woman was in the doorway. Ina, maybe? She was in her late fifties, Collena guessed, and her copper-red hair was cut very short, less than an inch long around her entire head.

"Where's Adam?" Dylan immediately asked.

"Still asleep. I was about to wake him for breakfast

and then give him a bath." She glared at Collena with piercing stone-gray eyes. "Are you the intruder?"

"Yes." The woman's scrutiny suddenly made Collena feel a tad guilty. "I'm sorry that I caused such a fuss."

The woman made a grunting sound of disapproval.

"Go back to the nursery," Dylan told his employee. It was another order. "And stay there until you hear from me."

The woman's sound of disapproval became one of concern. "What's going on, Dylan?"

"I'll fill you in later." He didn't say another word until both the woman and the deputy were out of the room and the doors were closed.

"Was that the nanny?" Collena asked.

He paused so long that she didn't think he would answer. "Yes. Her name is Ruth. If you did a background check on me, then you also know she was my own nanny and someone I trust."

"Ruth Sayers," Collena supplied. "Her name did come up." And she was clean. No criminal record. In fact, not even a traffic violation.

"Just what kind of proof do you think you have about the adoption being illegal?" Dylan asked.

"More than enough." Because she was feeling light-headed again, Collena sank down into the plush saddle-brown leather chair across from his desk and tugged off her gloves. "As I said I've been investigating the Brighton case since August of last year. When I realized just how many babies had been illegally adopted, I asked for help from the pediatric community. I was able to get names of adopted babies, and I compared them to those who had been legally adopted."

He pushed the silver tray toward her and motioned for her to eat. When he motioned a second time, Collena pinched off a piece of raisin wheat toast and popped it into her mouth. Even though it was cold, it tasted heavenly.

"And you're saying that Adam's name came up on that list of adopted babies?" he asked. But he didn't just ask. It was buried under a mountain of skepticism.

She nodded. "Adam's name and one hundred and twelve other infant boys. There were a lot of them, and that's why it's taken me so long to find my son."

His jaw turned to iron. He paced a few steps in front of the fireplace, turned and stared at her before taking one of the biscuits, opening it and handing both it and the silver jam spoon to her.

With the hopes that her faintness would go away, Collena smeared some strawberry jam on one half and started to eat. Dylan didn't say anything until she had finished.

"Adam's my son," he insisted. "And I don't really care what kind of proof you have. You gave him up—"

"I didn't give him up."

Oh, that had not been easy to say. Collena had to choke back all the pain and emotion just so she could speak.

"Sixteen months ago, I went into premature labor while I was at Brighton," she explained. "Without my consent, a doctor gave me a strong narcotic so that he could steal my baby. I fought him and his accomplice as much as I could. I managed to escape…eventually. What I wasn't able to do was find my child. Until now."

He cursed. And then as if he'd declared war on it,

he peeled off his jacket and tossed it into the closet. He didn't stop there. Dylan came across the room, bracketed his hands on his desk and leaned in so he could stare at her some more.

"And why should I believe you?" he challenged.

Collena tried to keep her voice level. "In my car I have the police and doctors' reports detailing what happened to me and the subsequent arrest of the director at Brighton. I also have the original files. Both sets, the legal ones that Brighton put together, and the illegal ones they figured no one but they would ever see."

He shook his head. "Reports and files don't prove anything about Adam. So what if you had a child? It could have been *any* child."

"Adam's date of birth matches the day I delivered," she pointed out.

"That could be a coincidence. You could be confused about the date."

She took a deep breath and tried to tamp down her frustration. She couldn't say she hadn't expected this, though. In fact, Collena figured there'd be many rounds of stonewalling before he started to come to terms with this.

"I'm not confused. There were only four baby boys born that particular day at Brighton," Collena said. "And three are already accounted for."

He waited a moment, and she could almost see the thought process going on behind those eyes. "This doesn't make any sense. I want to talk to Adam's birth father."

"He's dead." And for the time being, that's all she intended to say about her late fiancé, Sean Reese. Thankfully, Adam would never have to have Sean in his life, but that didn't mean Sean's DNA couldn't come back to haunt them. Later, she'd have to explain all of that to Dylan. "Look, I know this is hard to accept—"

"You have no idea."

"But I do. Remember, someone stole my baby and tried to kill me. I have an inkling of what it's like to lose something as important as a child."

Oh, mercy. She felt the tears threaten, and she tried to blink them back. One escaped anyway, but she quickly wiped it away so there'd be no proof of the pain that had ripped her heart apart.

"Look at me," Collena requested. "Don't you see some kind of resemblance between Adam and me?"

It was a gamble, because Collena had no idea if her son did indeed resemble her.

But the gamble paid off.

Dylan combed his gaze over her. Studying her, hard. And at the end of several snail-crawling moments, he groaned and scrubbed his hand over his face. He dropped down in the chair across from her and raised his head.

"Adam has blond hair and brown eyes," he admitted. "Like you."

The relief washed over her. Not because she doubted this child was hers. No. She was positive of it. But the resemblance might go a long way to convincing Dylan of what she already knew.

It might also convince him to accept the deal she was about to offer.

"I won't believe any of this until I see DNA results," he added a moment later.

Collena had anticipated that, as well. "I already have DNA results to prove he's mine."

"You couldn't."

"But I do. You probably remember telling your adoption attorney that you wanted your baby's umbilical cord to be stored in case it was needed in the future. Since the storage facility was also owned by Brighton, the police got a search warrant to have all the umbilical cords tested. The newborns' identities were all in code, so I knew that one of the babies was mine, it just took a lot of DNA tests to figure out which one."

He pulled in his breath. "And how do you know that you unraveled the code correctly?"

"Because all the other babies have been accounted for. All except Adam. He's the last one on the list."

Collena took the small DNA test kit from her pocket, opened it and wiped the sterile swab on the inside of her cheek. She put it in the plastic bag, resealed it and handed it to him.

"You can send it to any lab you choose," Collena instructed. "Ask for a maternity study. Have them expedite it. Within forty-eight hours you should have the proof you need."

"Need for what?" He stood and dropped the kit onto his desk. He pressed his thumb to his chest. "I love him. Adam is my son."

Collena stood also, so she could make eye contact. "I love him, too. And he's my son."

He cursed, and it wasn't mild. "I can't give him up."

"Neither can I."

"I'll fight this in court." His stare turned to a glare. "I'll have to."

"Maybe not."

Dylan blinked, and his forehead bunched up. "What the hell is that supposed to mean?"

"I know you're a good father." She motioned around the room. "And I can't give Adam all the material things you've given him. Or the stability. Or the respectability."

There was more.

She'd save that for later.

On top of everything else he'd learned, it might be too much for Dylan Greer to hear that they might both lose the precious child they loved.

"And I can't overlook the fact that you're the only parent that Adam knows," Collena added, hoping that she was making her case. "To take him from you now would be as criminal as what happened to me at Brighton sixteen months ago."

His glare softened. "Are you saying you won't fight me for custody?"

"Not exactly."

The softening vanished. "Then, what are you saying?" he asked.

Mercy, she only hoped this sounded better aloud than it did in her head. But it didn't matter if it sounded insane. She had no choice.

"What I'm offering is more of a compromise," Collena explained. "When you weigh all the options, when you think about how we can both have Adam in our lives, there's only one thing you can do."

His glare returned and intensified. "And what's that one thing that I can do?"

Collena braced herself for his reaction. "You can marry me."

Chapter 3

Dylan hadn't thought there could be any more surprises today, but he was obviously wrong. Collena Drake had just delivered the ultimate surprise.

"Marry you?" he questioned.

She nodded and moistened her lips. "I'm Adam's mother. You've raised him, true, but we both love him. It seems…reasonable that we can both be his parents."

"You don't even know him," Dylan tossed right back at her.

"He's my child. *I love him.*"

He couldn't dispute that. He'd loved Adam, too, from the moment that he learned Adam was his. Dylan hadn't had to see him to know just how deep that love was. Still, that didn't mean this woman had a claim to Adam.

"Neither of us wants to lose him," Collena added as if that would change his mind. It wouldn't.

"And you think the solution is for us to get married, even though we're perfect strangers?"

She nodded.

He didn't agree with her. It was an insane proposition. He couldn't do it. Could he?

Oh, man. He hated to even consider it, but Dylan went through a mental list of reasons why he shouldn't. He had no idea who this woman really was. And even if she proved everything she'd said, it would still mean a marriage to a stranger so that he could keep his child.

Dylan wasn't sure he could go that far, nor was he sure he had to. There was rarely just one solution to a problem, even when that problem was as massive as this one appeared to be.

"And what if I say no to your marriage proposal?" Dylan asked.

She took a deep breath. "Then I'll petition the courts to return Adam to me. In my car, I have all the documentation to prove that he's mine and that the adoption was illegal. I've already retained an attorney. He could file my petition as early as tomorrow morning. In nearly all the Brighton cases, the illegally adopted children have been returned to the birth parents. And in those cases where they weren't, it's because both birth parents were dead."

Dylan felt the knot in his stomach tighten. Collena had obviously given this plenty of thought, but then, according to what she had said earlier, she'd had three days to absorb it. He was still trying to come to terms with it, and for him, it was a nightmare.

The adoption attorney he'd used had sworn to him that there were no birth parents in the picture, that they were both deceased. Well, it seemed that either the adoption attorney had been wrong or he was a criminal.

Or maybe this was simply a case of someone on the Brighton staff lying to his attorney.

"In other words, if I don't jump at the chance to marry you, you'll try to cut me out of Adam's life," Dylan mumbled. "This is blackmail, pure and simple. If it's money, you're after—"

"I'm not after your money. In fact, I'll sign a pre-nup agreement and won't use any of your income or resources for my own expenses. What I'm after is far more important than money. I want a decent life for my child. A life that includes me. You were born and raised here. You don't know what it's like to be considered trash."

That set off some alarms. Dylan stared at her. "And you do?"

"I do." She glanced away for a moment. "I had the misfortune of not being born in the right family. My son has the chance I didn't, and I don't want that chance taken away from him."

Neither did he. Nor did he want to consider what his own life would be like without Adam. Some way, somehow, he would keep him.

"I trust that you don't need an answer right now," Dylan said.

"Of course not." She stood as if prepared to go.

Dylan heard the slight static sound then, and he groaned. Someone was listening on the intercom. He'd forgotten to turn it off earlier when he'd rushed out to find the intruder.

"This is a private conversation," he called out. He

pointed to the intercom speaker so that his guest would know why he'd said that. No one confessed to the eavesdropping, but Dylan added, "Ask Jonah to come to my office. He'll need to escort Ms. Drake to her car."

Dylan turned back to face her. "I need some time to think this through."

She nodded. "What you mean, is you need to consult your attorney."

"That, too."

"Go ahead. Talk to your attorney. I'm sure he or she will tell you what I've already told you—that I have a legal right to claim the child that was stolen from me." She glanced at the picture that he'd turned facedown on his desk. "May I see Adam?"

Dylan didn't even have to think about it. "No." He wasn't ready to share Adam with this woman.

Heck, he might never be ready to do that.

She stared at him, as if she might challenge his decision, but she didn't. "When we were by the stables, you said something about a killer. Is there some kind of threat to Adam?"

Oh, hell.

Dylan didn't want to go there, because this was exactly the kind of fodder she could use if she challenged him for custody. "I'm a cautious man," he said. "Adam is safe."

"But you said your fiancée and sister were murdered," she reminded him.

"I believe they were. But they have nothing to do with Adam."

"You're certain?"

"Absolutely," he lied.

But the only thing that was absolute was that the two people he loved the most—his sister and fiancée—had been murdered.

Another girl, his high-school girlfriend, had been viciously assaulted after Dylan had taken her to the prom. The incident had so traumatized her that she'd moved away from Greer. Dylan, too, had moved away for a while. To San Antonio, right after he graduated from college.

For all the good it'd done.

A woman he'd dated there had also been assaulted one night when putting her recycling bin on the curb. The police hadn't been able to find the person responsible. Ditto for his prom date—no suspects and no arrests. And the local sheriff had ruled his sister's and fiancée's deaths accidental.

But Dylan knew better.

Those two car crashes had not been accidents. And neither had the other assaults. They were connected to him. He was the only common denominator.

Since he was aware of that, he'd learned to take precautions, and he wouldn't let anything bad happen to Adam—accidental or otherwise. In fact, that's the reason he hadn't been seriously involved with any woman since his fiancée's death five years earlier. For whatever reason, it seemed as if someone didn't want him to be happy in love.

"If there's a threat to Adam," he heard Collena say, "then I need to know about it."

And Dylan decided to turn the tables on her. "You said someone tried to kill you after you gave birth."

She nodded. And swallowed hard.

"Then maybe whoever it was will try to come after you again and finish what he started," he pointed out.

"No. The Brighton criminals were arrested. Some are dead and some are in jail."

Because he thought there might be doubt in the depths of her brown eyes, he pushed harder. "You're absolutely positive that the police rounded up all of them?"

"I'm as certain of it as you are of the fact that your sister and fiancée's killer has nothing to do with Adam."

Touché. Under different circumstances, Dylan might have liked her.

"So, why suggest marriage?" Dylan asked.

"On paper, it's the best solution. Adam will have two parents who love him. He'll want for nothing. No shared custody. No one weekend with you, the other weekend with me. And if we're married, if you legally adopted him, then there'll be no way that anyone can cut either of us out of his life."

That last part sounded reasonable, but the whole picture had flaws the size of Texas. "And what about a loveless marriage? Do you really want that?"

Collena made a soft sound of amusement. "From my experience, love is vastly overrated."

"You're too young to be so skeptical," he commented.

"I'm a lot older than my age might imply." She shifted her position. "Look, I'm not some starry-eyed gold digger, Mr. Greer. I don't want a husband, a lover or someone's shoulder to cry on. I don't even want someone to support me or pretend that I matter to him. I just want the best possible life for my son. A life where no one is pointing fingers at him because he's different."

Dylan didn't let himself react to the emotion. To the

truthful tone of that obviously painful confession. "If you wanted that, you should have stayed away from him," he challenged.

"I considered it."

And she was serious, too. Serious enough to bring tears to her eyes. It was the second time today that she'd teared up, but even with that track record, Dylan didn't think she was a woman accustomed to showing her feelings. Those tears looked out of place.

"You considered staying away," he paraphrased. "Yet, you came anyway. Lucky me."

"I tried, but I can't give him up." She moistened her lips, looked away. "I lost him once, and I can't survive if I have to go through that again."

Unfortunately, Dylan knew what she meant, but he pushed aside the camaraderie he felt. It was best to keep his feelings toward Collena Drake as detached as possible.

He checked his watch and realized it'd been a good ten minutes since he'd asked Jonah to return. Dylan hit the intercom button on his desk so he could be heard in the kitchen.

"Jonah?"

"He left," Dylan heard Ina, the cook, say. "He said he had another call."

Well, that was just great. Jonah wasn't finished with *this* call. For all the deputy knew, Collena Drake could have been a killer. At a minimum, she'd trespassed, and Jonah should have waited around long enough to see if he was going to have to arrest her for that. Not that Dylan planned to have her thrown in jail. But Jonah didn't know that.

"I can see myself out," Collena insisted. She was heading for the door before she turned back around to face him.

She probably hadn't realized how close they were when she turned around. Mere inches apart.

Both of them stepped back.

"Please think about what I've said," she added.

"Oh, I will." In fact, he would think of little else.

"I'll get my car and drive back to drop off the papers that prove Adam is my son. Or I can have someone bring them to you if you'd prefer."

Dylan didn't want anyone else involved in this just yet. He went to the closet and grabbed his coat and car keys. He wanted to see what kind of evidence she had so he could start looking for flaws in it. He didn't know what he would do once he'd found them, but he wanted all the information about this situation and the woman who'd proposed marriage and then threatened to take Adam away from him.

"I'd also like my gun back," Collena said.

"It's in my pocket. You'll get it back when you're off my property."

Figuring that he needed to go on the offensive, Dylan picked up his phone and pressed in some numbers. "Sorry to bother you on Thanksgiving," he said to the man who answered. "But it's an emergency. Call me the second you have any information on Collena Drake. And I have a DNA test kit that I need you to pick up ASAP and take to a lab."

"Your lawyer?" Collena asked when he hung up the phone.

"A P.I. I want as much information about you as you think you have about me."

And he would get it.

He needed all the ammunition possible to stop this woman who'd intruded into his life.

They went back outside, and Dylan could have sworn the temperature had dropped even more. The snow-flakes had picked up, as well. They weren't steadily falling, yet, but it would happen soon. Despite every-thing that was going on, he couldn't help but think of how Adam would react to building a snowman.

"You're smiling," Collena mumbled.

He put on the stoniest face he could manage. It was easy to do. He was riled at this woman who'd come in unannounced and threatened to tear his life apart.

Dylan motioned toward his truck and unlocked the doors. "I can walk," Collena assured him.

"I don't doubt that, but this will be warmer."

But not faster. She could actually walk across the pasture quicker than taking the roads around the ranch to get to her car, but Dylan wasn't sure how steady she was on her feet. She'd eaten a few bites in his office, but she was still pale and seemed unsteady.

And it irritated him that he was even remotely con-cerned about that.

This woman could cost him everything.

He wanted to hate her.

What he didn't want was to believe that she was tell-ing the truth. Because if she was, if someone had truly stolen her baby and left her for dead, then she'd been through hell, something that Dylan totally understood.

"I suppose Adam can walk?" she asked.

He groaned. He didn't want to talk about Adam, not to her, but it'd be petty to withhold such simple information. Still, he considered it before he finally mumbled, "Yes."

"And he can talk?"

He bit back another groan. "He can say a few things."

Collena nodded. "Thank you. I know that wasn't easy." She watched as he drove out of the wrought-iron gates that fronted the ranch. "I came today, hoping I'd get a glimpse of him through one of the windows. I really hadn't planned on intruding on your Thanksgiving day."

What could he say to that? That she'd gone about it the wrong way? Well, they both knew there was no right way to do this. If she'd come to his door with this bombshell on any day, holiday or not, he wouldn't have let her in.

He made the turn on the dirt and gravel road that snaked against the fenced portion of his property. The snow had already dusted the surface, making it hard for him to see where the road ended and deep ditches began.

Because the silence was thick and uncomfortable, Dylan decided to push her for more information. "Tell me about the father of your child," he said.

Collena took black leather gloves from her pocket and put them back on. She also took a deep breath. "Sean Reese was a lawyer. We'd been engaged nearly a year when I got pregnant."

A year. That wasn't a casual relationship. "You planned a family?"

She shook her head. "No. I was on the pill, hadn't

missed taking any, so the pregnancy wasn't planned. When I came home from work the day after I told him, he was gone. He'd moved out and left me a typed letter saying he didn't want to be a father and that he was breaking up with me." She paused. "That's the kind of man he was."

"And he's really dead?" Dylan managed to ask through his suddenly tight jaw. Because he didn't want a guy like that in Adam's life.

"Yes. About six months after he moved out, one of his drug-dealing clients murdered him when he received a guilty verdict that obviously didn't please him."

Dylan hated to feel relieved, but he was. It was bad enough having one birth parent in the picture. *If* Collena was indeed a real birth parent. It was hard to doubt it, though, especially when he looked at her mouth.

That was Adam's mouth.

Heart shaped. And capable of expressing a huge range of emotions.

So, if Collena Drake was truly Adam's birth mother, then the question was—what was he going to do about it?

He didn't get a chance to come up with any possibilities because Collena spoke before he had time to think.

"There's something else you should know about Sean Reese," Collena said. Her voice was practically a whisper now, and she looked down at her gloved hands. "I hadn't planned on telling you this soon, but you'll probably find out when you press your P.I. for a deeper background check on me."

Which he would do, especially after an opening

like that. "There really is someone from Brighton after you?" he asked.

"No. Not Brighton. The problem is Sean's father, Curtis Reese. He's been looking for Adam, too."

Well, that sounded ominous, and Dylan didn't like where this conversation was going.

"Curtis Reese is very wealthy," Collena continued. "And Sean was his only child. He loved him, and he was obsessive about it. Once he learned that I was pregnant with Sean's child, he became consumed with his unborn grandchild, as well."

Dylan quickly came to a conclusion, but he hoped he was wrong. "Are you saying that this Curtis Reese will try to get custody of Adam?"

"He'll try," Collena confirmed. "I know you don't want to hear this, but since the adoption was illegal, you don't stand much of a chance of keeping Adam."

His jaw tightened even more. "That's debatable."

"It's true. There are things in my past that Curtis Reese will try to use to challenge my own custody. Nothing criminal," she quickly added.

Dylan would have questioned exactly what those things were if he hadn't seen the smoke ahead. Collena obviously saw it, too; she pointed in that direction.

"That's where I left my car," she said.

With the snow and the wind, it wasn't a day to burn brush. Besides, he'd given all the hands the day off. Dylan took the last turn, dreading what he would see.

There, off to the side of the narrow dirt road sat a dark blue compact car, engulfed in flames.

Chapter 4

Collena saw the fire and smoke.

She felt the instant slam of adrenaline, and she reached for her gun, which wasn't there. Because Dylan still had it in his pocket.

Dylan reacted, too. He caught on to her shoulder and shoved her down onto the leather seat. Hard. Then, he drew his own weapon, threw his truck into Reverse and sped backward to put some distance between them and her burning vehicle.

It was a good decision. With the flames already eating through the interior, the car could explode.

"Do you see anyone?" she asked, trying to get up. But he merely used his muscled body to keep her in place. Protecting her.

More than likely, it was an automatic response, something he would do for anyone who happened to be in danger. And there was no doubt in Collena's mind that this was a dangerous situation.

Someone had set fire to her car.

And that someone could still be around to do even more damage to them.

"No, I don't," Dylan relayed to her. He pulled his phone and her gun from his pocket and handed both items to her. "Call nine-one-one and ask for the fire department."

Surprised, she blinked. "Not the sheriff?"

"Dispatch would only send Jonah back out."

Collena understood. The bitter and perhaps incompetent deputy obviously had some kind of personal grudge against Dylan. Besides, this was a fire, and the fire department would be able to tell whether it was from natural causes or arson.

She had a bad feeling it was the latter.

Collena made the call, and the emergency dispatcher told her that she would send a fire-response team right away.

And then she lay there on the seat, waiting for Dylan to make a decision about what to do. Unfortunately, he was practically lying on top of her. For reasons Collena didn't want to explore, she didn't want to be this close to Dylan. She could feel parts of his body that she shouldn't be feeling.

"I'm a cop," she reminded him. "Let me up so I can see if I can spot any evidence."

He did, reluctantly. "Stay low," he warned. "If someone's out there, he could be armed."

That didn't do much to steady her breathing or heart rate.

While Dylan kept his gun aimed and ready, Collena

did a visual search of the immediate area. There were trees, most of them bare from the winter, but there was also a thick clump of massive live oaks, complete with thick branches and green leaves. They completely obscured the view of the ranch. It was the main reason she'd chosen the spot, so that her car wouldn't be seen when she parked it.

Those trees could now be hiding an arsonist.

But who would do something like this?

One answer immediately came to mind. Curtis Reese, Sean's father. Collena hadn't told him that she'd found Adam, but with Curtis's resources, he could have learned that information. Maybe this was his way of warning her not to try to keep Adam from him.

But that's exactly what she was going to do.

"See anything?" Dylan asked.

"It's what I don't see that bothers me. There are no other tire tracks that lead directly to my vehicle."

"Yeah, I noticed that."

She turned her head, and their gazes met. There was plenty of concern in the depths of his green eyes. "The snow might have covered the tracks," she said.

His attention drifted toward those live oaks. "Or someone could have taken this path. Or that one," he said, shifting his focus to the other side of the road where the bare trees were.

He was right, of course. There was another dirt road less than a quarter of a mile away, and it paralleled this one. Someone could have parked there and walked over. Too bad the snow would almost certainly wipe out any tracks there.

"We need to get out of here," Dylan announced.

Collena glanced at her car and saw why. The flames were even higher now. If the gas tank blew, they were a safe enough distance away, but that didn't mean they wouldn't get pelted with debris.

Dylan began to drive in reverse down the road. He took it slowly to avoid slipping into the ditch. If an arsonist was truly still around, Collena didn't want them to be in the woods on foot.

"Both my sister, Abigail, and fiancée, Julie, died in car accidents where fires were involved," he mumbled.

"You think this is related to their murders?" she asked.

A muscle flickered in his jaw. "No one was ever arrested. In fact, the police ruled them accidents. But in both cases, the cars caught fire and that caused the accidents and their deaths. Neither was able to get out alive."

"But why would whoever killed them want to set fire to my car?"

Collena was certain he would dismiss any connection. Just as he'd dismissed the danger earlier.

However, he didn't dismiss it now.

"Most of the women I've been personally involved with have encountered some kind of violence."

"Excuse me?" And Collena held her breath.

"You heard me," he snapped. His posture and tone became defensive. "That's why I've sworn off having a relationship, and it's the reason I adopted a son and not a daughter."

She shook her head. "But Adam—"

"There hasn't been an incident since I adopted him."

Collena pointed to the fire. "What about my car? You don't think that's an incident?"

"That might not be related to the other fires." And he didn't add anything else, as if waiting for her to confirm or deny it.

Sweet heaven, she couldn't.

Dylan finally made it to the end of the dirt path and turned onto the main road that would take them back to the ranch.

"Now you understand why I can't consider your marriage proposal," he continued. "Though my past is only one of many objections I have."

Collena understood. In fact, his past terrified her. But not as much as the alternative of losing Adam. "We might both lose custody if we don't work together."

"Working together," he repeated. "I'll give you that. But marriage is out."

Not being married to Dylan would put a serious wrinkle in her plans. Besides, this fire might not have anything to do with his past or with Sean's father. "Maybe this was some kind of prank. Kids are out of school for Thanksgiving. Maybe someone was bored and decided to light a match."

Dylan didn't answer right away. "Maybe."

Collena released the breath she'd been holding and hoped they weren't deluding themselves.

Individually, they both had some old baggage, but she hoped that it wouldn't surface. Above all, she had to do whatever was necessary to keep Adam safe. And if that meant taking her son and fleeing, she would.

But she also knew an action like that would heavily impact her little boy. After all, she'd be taking her child from the only parent Adam had ever known.

That was the very thing Collena was trying to avoid.

While they sat in silence, Dylan drove through the gates to the ranch. There was still no sight or sound of the fire truck. Of course, it was winter, and the weather wasn't cooperating. Her car was gone, as was everything inside it—including the copies of the documents to prove she was Adam's mother. The only thing left for the fire department to do was tell them how the fire had started.

And then the sheriff could maybe determine who had started it.

Dylan had been with her the entire time, so she knew he wasn't the culprit. Besides, this wasn't his approach to things. He wouldn't have set fire to a car to destroy documents or to intimidate her.

He was a face-to-face kind of man.

"I have a visitor," Dylan commented.

Collena picked through the other vehicles that were near the house and spotted a black luxury car parked in the circular driveway in front. She didn't recognize the car, but she had no trouble recognizing the tall dark-haired man who was pounding on Dylan's front door.

"Oh, God," Collena mumbled.

"You know him?" Dylan asked, firing an accusatory glance at her.

She nodded. "Yes. That's Curtis Reese, Adam's biological grandfather. He's probably here to try to take him."

Well, this was shaping up to be the day from hell.

Dylan braked to a halt directly in front of the house and barreled out of his truck. He was not going to let Curtis Reese anywhere near Adam.

"I'm sorry," he heard Collena say. "I didn't know he'd follow me."

Dylan didn't take the time to respond to that. Besides, what could he say? He certainly wasn't going to give her a pass.

Yesterday, his life was as close to perfect as it could get, and now mere hours later, things were tumbling down around him.

In the distance Dylan heard the fire sirens, but he focused his attention on the man trying to beat down his front door. Dylan kept his gun gripped in his hand, and he started up the porch steps.

His visitor whirled around with his tight fist still high in the air. Dylan didn't raise his gun. He didn't issue any threats. He just stared at the man, daring him to use that fist in any way.

Curtis Reese stared back at him.

When Collena had first told him that this was Adam's biological grandfather, Dylan had expected someone who looked like a grandparent. Curtis Reese didn't. Dylan figured he had to be at least in his early fifties, but he looked much younger. There wasn't a strand of gray in his dark brown hair. The man was at least six-four, and he had a muscular build that his Italian cashmere suit didn't hide. And Curtis Reese had a formidable expression on his wrinkle-free face.

"I'm here to see my grandson," Curtis announced.

"Then you've wasted your time," Dylan shot back.

Curtis looked past him, and his equally formidable granite-gray eyes landed on Collena. "Did you think you could hide my own flesh and blood from me?"

"For a while." Collena took the steps slowly, and

Dylan hoped she wasn't having another dizzy spell. "It's Thanksgiving, Curtis. Go home and give me a chance to work things out with Mr. Greer."

"What you really want is time to figure out how to steal him from me."

Collena shook her head and slipped her gun into her coat pocket. "I don't have to steal him. You have no right to Adam."

"And this conversation is over," Dylan intervened.

Curtis's gaze snapped back to Dylan. "It's not over. I know what Collena's trying to do. She'll try to make a pact with you to stop me from getting custody. Well, you should know that Collena Drake isn't fit to be a mother. Her own mother was a drug addict and prostitute—did she tell you that?"

Dylan shrugged. "It didn't come up in conversation. Now, are you leaving voluntarily, or do I need to *help* you to your car?"

"I'm not going until I make you understand what an unsuitable mother she is. It's her fault that she was at Brighton, and it's her fault that Adam was stolen. She took a deep-cover assignment while she was pregnant. Something bad could have happened there. And it did. She endangered herself and therefore her baby. I think I can convince a judge that what she did can be construed as child endangerment."

Dylan tried not to react to that, mainly because coming from Curtis, it could be a lie. But then he glanced at Collena. He didn't think it was his imagination that she was even paler now than when he'd first seen her. Later, after Curtis was off the grounds, they would obviously have to discuss this latest allegation.

"Adam's in danger," Curtis said, his voice strained with emotion. "And it's all Collena's fault." He volleyed glances between them. "Did you know that Rodney Harmon escaped from jail last night?"

Collena actually dropped back a step, and Dylan caught her arm so that she wouldn't fall on the slippery porch. He'd never heard the name Rodney Harmon, but he figured soon he'd know why the man had caused Collena to have that kind of reaction.

"Harmon will come after you again," Curtis warned Collena. "And if you're near Adam, he'll come after him, too. You shouldn't be within a hundred miles of that baby."

Collena glanced at Dylan and stepped out of his grip. "Rodney Harmon is the man I helped arrest and put into prison. He was one of the security guards at Brighton. And among other things, he was responsible for…stopping me from going after the doctor who stole Adam."

He didn't have to guess how the guy had stopped her. Dylan had a strange gut reaction to that realization. He wanted to pound the guy to dust because he'd attacked a vulnerable woman who'd just given birth. And why? All so someone could steal her infant son and sell him.

But Dylan had lived the flip side of Rodney Harmon's diabolical plan. He'd adopted the baby that Rodney had helped steal. Dylan couldn't regret that. Ever. But he could regret the pain Collena had gone through.

But maybe that could be overshadowed by Curtis's other allegation. That Collena was responsible for what had happened.

Had Collena assisted Rodney in some way?

Since there was obviously a lot of new issues to discuss, Dylan chose the one that could cause the most serious and immediate problems. "Why would this Harmon guy come after you?" Dylan asked Collena. "Weren't there dozens of cops who helped put him away? Why single you out?"

Collena looked him straight in the eye when she answered. "He blamed me personally for his arrest because I was the only one who was able to identify him. And I testified against him during his trial."

Hell.

So, there was a new threat—a serious one. And if Harmon had escaped the night before, he could have been the one to set fire to Collena's car. But that was a stretch, since Harmon would have first had to know where Collena was and then follow her.

Still, it wasn't impossible.

But Harmon was a threat Dylan would have to deal with later. Right now, he had to get Curtis off his porch and far away from Adam.

"Look, I have zero patience for you and this visit, especially today," Dylan told Curtis. "Have your lawyer contact my lawyer, and stay away from anything that's mine. And right now, Adam is mine."

"This isn't over," Curtis insisted, though he did proceed down the steps. "One way or another, I will get my grandson. There's not a judge anywhere in the world that will give Collena custody. Nor you, Dylan Greer."

That did not sound like an idle remark. "Been digging up dirt on me, too?" Dylan calmly asked.

Curtis caught the door handle of his car, but he didn't get in. "You bet I have." The man smiled. "That's some dark cloud you got hanging over you. Two women are dead. Others are psychologically scarred for life. It could happen again. And I'm going to use anything I can to get custody of Adam."

With that threat still lingering in the freezing air, Curtis got in his car and slammed the door. Dylan and Collena watched as he sped away, kicking up a spray of snow, dirt and ice. The back end of the car fishtailed on the slick surface, but Curtis continued to speed out through the gates.

"Why don't you come in?" Dylan invited Collena. He took hold of her arm to make her realize this wasn't an invitation she could turn down. "You have some things to explain."

Chapter 5

Collena had hoped to tell Dylan about her past in her own way and on her own terms. She didn't want to have the conversation on Thanksgiving before he'd had a chance to consider her offer of marriage.

But it was obvious this couldn't wait.

He opened the front door, and they stepped back into the warm house. Dylan immediately locked it. Double locks, then he set the security system before he led her in the direction of his office.

They weren't alone in the house. Ruth, the nanny, and a younger auburn-haired woman peered out at her from what appeared to be the family room. There was no sign of Adam, but since Collena had run a brief background check on the staff, she figured the younger woman was probably Millie, Ruth's daughter who'd been raised at Dylan's estate.

There was a lot of disapproval in the women's expressions.

It matched the disapproval in Dylan's.

Oh, yes. She had some explaining to do. However, before she could even begin, her cell phone rang. After one glance at the caller-ID screen, Collena knew it was a call she had to take.

"I won't be long," she told Dylan, who walked into his office ahead of her.

He gave a look that conveyed she'd better not. He practically ripped off his jacket, shoved it into the closet and dropped down into the chair behind his desk.

Because the two women were still lurking nearby, Collena stepped inside Dylan's office, as well, and closed the door. It was a matter of picking her poison— she'd rather have Dylan overhear this particular conversation than his staff. Besides, she apparently didn't have anything else to hide. Curtis had already spilled the unsavory details of her life to Dylan.

"Collena," the caller greeted. It was Sergeant Katelyn O'Malley from the San Antonio PD.

And Collena was almost certain what this call was about.

"Rodney Harmon escaped from jail last night," Katelyn confirmed. "We're doing everything we can to locate him and put him back behind bars."

So, it was true. Curtis hadn't been lying after all. And this added a new wrinkle. "Yes. I heard about the escape. From Curtis Reese. He came to Dylan Greer's ranch a couple of minutes ago."

She risked looking at Dylan, knowing what she

would see. She was right. He was glaring at her. And waiting.

"So, Curtis knows that you found Adam?" Katelyn verified. "What about Dylan—how'd he take the news when you told him who you were?"

"We're still dealing with that. Can I call you back, Katelyn? I'm in the middle of something here."

"I'll bet you are. I'll check for updates on Harmon, and I'll also try to find out if Curtis Reese is planning to hang around the town of Greer for a while. Let me know if you need anything else."

Collena assured her that she would, thanked her old friend and ended the call.

"Talk fast," Dylan insisted. "It won't be long before the fire department arrives."

Yes, judging from the sound of the sirens, they were already by her car. Soon, they'd come to the house to do interviews and a report.

"Everything Curtis Reese said about me is true," Collena confirmed.

Judging from the way Dylan stared at her, he hadn't expected that answer.

"My mother was a drug addict, and before she walked out on me, she occasionally turned tricks to pay for her drug habit." She slipped off her coat and eased it onto the back of the chair. "And, yes, Rodney Harmon will probably try to kill me if the police don't find him before he finds me."

"What about the part about it being your fault that Adam was stolen?" Dylan asked.

Collena decided it was a good time to sit. She took the chair across from him. She also took a deep breath and prayed she could explain this without crying. This was painful enough without adding the humiliation of tears.

"When I was pregnant, I was working Special Investigations for SAPD. We got reports about irregularities at the Brighton Birthing Center, but it was out of our jurisdiction. The local sheriff didn't have the manpower or the experience to handle it so he requested our assistance. Since I was pregnant, I went in undercover. Not at Brighton. But at a nearby home for unwed mothers where I would have daily access to the birthing center. We'd had reports that Brighton officials were pressuring and even coercing these young women into giving up their babies."

"That still sounds dangerous." His eyebrows lifted.

"It was. It was also stupid."

Dylan shook his head. "Then why'd you do it?"

Ah, he'd cut to the chase. "Because my boss asked me to, and I thought I could handle the situation. I thought I could stop what was happening to those young women at Brighton."

His mouth flattened into a thin line. "You put the job ahead of your pregnancy?"

"Yes," she admitted. It wasn't the first time she'd confessed her guilt.

Collena reminded herself of it every minute of every day.

She let Dylan fill in the blanks. Someone at Brighton had gotten suspicious of her. Maybe someone had recognized her as a cop. A former witness or a person involved in a previous case. Or maybe someone at the home or the center had even had her investigated because they believed she was a prime candidate to put her baby up for adoption. It wouldn't have been that hard to find her real identity if someone was seriously looking. And Rodney Harmon had been the one to try to get her out of the picture. Unfortunately, in doing so, Collena had lost the most precious thing in the world.

Her newborn son.

She and Dylan sat there, staring at each other. She didn't attempt to read his expression, because she knew what he was thinking.

"You can't possibly be any more disgusted with me than I am with myself," she said. "I made a horrible mistake. And I paid for it. I'm still paying for it."

"And now you want me to pay for it, too?" he snapped.

She didn't have time to answer. Two sounds happened at once. There was a knock at the door, and the fax machine began to spit out a sheet of paper.

The door opened, and Deputy Jonah Burke stepped in. He was sporting a scowl, and there were snowflakes on his Stetson and jacket.

"It's Thanksgiving," the deputy greeted. "And it's snowing like crazy out there. How many more times am I going to have to come out to the ranch today?"

"As many times as it takes," Dylan informed him. He stood and went to the fax machine. "Where's the fire chief?"

"Busy with the investigation. He's shorthanded because of the holiday, so he sent me over here to let you know what's going on."

"And what is going on?" Collena asked when Jonah didn't continue. "What happened to my car?"

Jonah lifted a shoulder and couldn't have possibly looked more disinterested. "Somebody burned it."

Both Collena and Dylan shot him a flat look, but it was Dylan who responded. "Obviously. But since you're a deputy sheriff and supposedly in charge of keeping the citizens of Greer safe, I thought you might have at least a professional obligation to investigate a crime."

His disinterest turned to another scowl. "If there's something to investigate, I'll do my job, but the fire department didn't detect accelerant, and their initial impression is that it might have been an electrical problem."

"The car's engine was turned off," Collena informed him. "Hard to have an electrical fire without the engine running."

Part of her wanted to believe an electrical problem was the cause. But this didn't feel like an accident. Her cop's instincts were telling her this was a crime, and apparently Dylan felt the same.

"So you say the engine was off, but you see, I'm suspect of anything you tell me because I already know you're a trespasser." Jonah turned that scowl on Dylan. "Of course, maybe she had a good reason to trespass."

"You got something to say to me?" Dylan challenged, as he gathered up the pages coming from the fax. He took his attention off Jonah and stared down at the papers.

"I made a call when I left here," Jonah explained. "I found out that Ms. Drake here is investigating illegal adoptions. Since you adopted Adam, it's not much of a stretch to think she's investigating you. What'd you do, Dylan? You cut some corners?"

Collena got to her feet and faced the deputy. "Dylan did nothing wrong. If you check the facts, the real culprit is the clinic where Adam was born."

"I don't need you to defend me," Dylan told her.

For some reason, his cold words sliced right through her. But why wouldn't he say something like that? He despised her, especially after she'd just confessed all to him. She and Dylan weren't comrades. Not even close. And he had every reason to try to remove her from the picture.

Dylan went to his computer and typed something before he continued. Collena got just a glimpse of it. It was an e-mail requesting a background check on Curtis Reese. "Tell the fire chief that I want a report of his preliminary findings," Dylan told Jonah. "And close the door on your way out."

Jonah looked ready to explode over what was obviously another order—a rude one, at that—but he didn't. However, he did mumble something profane before he exited and slammed the door behind him.

Dylan walked closer, until he stood right behind her. What he didn't do was speak. When the silence became uncomfortable, Collena whirled around to face him. Best to go ahead and get this latest argument out of the way.

But she didn't see an argument in his eyes.

She was too close to him.

Something passed between them. A shiver of energy. Something warm.

No, it was *hot*.

Much to her disgust, Dylan could make her feel

things she shouldn't feel, and he could accomplish that by merely being close to her.

Collena shook her head to clear it. She refused to let her thoughts and feelings go in this direction. Dylan was merely her son's adopted father. That was it. There could never be anything between them.

Well, nothing except that stir of heat that wouldn't go away.

"The P.I. already sent me a preliminary report on you," Dylan said.

That drew her back to her senses.

Dylan showed her the top sheet of the papers he'd taken from the fax machine. It was indeed a report that included the basics: her name, address, age, height and weight. All bits of info taken from her driver's license, no doubt.

The next page was a copy of a newspaper article where she'd gotten an award for outstanding service for uncovering the criminal activity at the Brighton Birthing Center. There was no picture because Collena hadn't attended the ceremony. Nor had she picked up the award. She'd ripped it to bits after her lieutenant had delivered it to her apartment.

"That award should have been for my stupidity," Collena mumbled.

Dylan didn't respond to that. He simply flipped over to the next page.

There was a picture this time.

It'd been taken as part of the police report after she'd clawed her way out of those woods near Brighton and made it to the local sheriff's office. The photo showed the torn, dirty hospital gown that was practically hanging off her body. Her battered face. Her hair matted with her own blood. A busted bottom lip. And the bruises and scrapes on her hands and knees. She looked a half-step away from death, which wasn't too far from the truth.

She'd come too close to dying in the woods.

The police report indicated how close to death she'd been. It also indicated that she'd recently given birth, and that would hopefully convince Dylan that she wasn't lying about being Adam's mother.

Dylan stared at her. "I don't want to feel sorry for you."

That improved her posture. Collena snapped her shoulders back. "Good. Because I don't want you to feel sorry for me, either. I was a cop. I knew the risk before I ever stepped foot in Brighton."

"You couldn't have anticipated that kind of risk. And you didn't deserve that." He shook his head, and his nostrils flared. "What did Rodney Harmon use to put those bruises on you?"

It took her a moment to answer. No more stiff shoulders. She automatically slumped. "His fists and the gun he took from me when I went into labor. I was trying to fight him off because the doctor had just left the room with Adam."

His jaw muscles moved. "So, Adam wasn't there when you were getting the hell beat out of you?"

"No. Thank God. And the fight didn't last that long. Harmon gave me some kind of heavy narcotic, and after I escaped, I don't remember anything until I woke up in the woods." She paused a moment to gather her composure. "My advice? Shred that picture. Forget that you ever saw it. I don't want it to play a part in your decision as to what we're going to do about Adam."

"My decision," he said. He tossed the papers onto his desk and groaned. "You come here to my home and deliver a bombshell, along with a would-be killer on your trail. And as an added bonus, I've had to deal with Adam's biological grandfather, a man who can challenge us both for custody."

"I'm sorry—"

"Don't," he warned. He stepped farther away from her. "I want to hate you. But I can't. Because I can see the pain in that picture. Hell, I can see the pain in your eyes right now."

"That pain's in your eyes, too."

Dylan immediately looked away. "I won't feel sorry for you and I won't be attracted to you."

Collena blinked, certain she'd misunderstood him. Mercy, had he noticed the way she'd looked at him earlier? With lust in her eyes?

Oh, this was not good.

She actually welcomed the knock on the door. They obviously needed some kind of interruption, because there was nothing that either of them should say about his attraction remark.

"It's me," a woman said from the other side of the door. Collena recognized the voice. It was Ruth Sayers, the nanny.

Dylan reached behind him and turned Collena's photograph facedown. "Come in, Ruth."

The woman opened the door, but she wasn't alone. Her daughter, Millie, was with her, and the pair stood in the doorway.

Collena got a better look at Millie then. She was a younger version of her mom, with fiery red hair and piercing gray eyes. However, Millie had a calmness and serenity about her that Ruth lacked.

"The fire chief said I'm to tell you that he'd be in touch with you," Ruth told Dylan. "Jonah's still here, though." She pointed her finger at Collena. "Is he planning to arrest that woman for trespassing?"

Dylan pulled in a weary breath. "This is Collena Drake, and there's a very good possibility that she's Adam's biological mother."

Ruth frantically shook her head, but her daughter, Millie, had a different reaction. She merely stared at Collena. Examining her.

"Does she have any proof of what she's saying?" Ruth snapped.

"Some," Dylan confirmed. "It'll take a couple of days to get the DNA results back. Or I might be able to get the results sooner if I can get the tests from the lab where she had Adam's stem cells tested."

"Adam has her mouth," Millie whispered, nudging her mother with her elbow.

Collena was so relieved she couldn't speak. Another person was confirming that there was a resemblance between her son and her.

"Her eyes, too," Dylan added.

Just that bit of information nearly brought on the tears, but Collena blinked them back. However, it didn't stop her longing to see her child. She'd gotten only the briefest glimpse before the doctor at Brighton had whisked Adam away.

Ruth shook her head. "I don't see any resemblance. Lots of babies have blond hair and brown eyes."

"Someone used the intercom earlier to listen in on the conversation I was having with Collena," she heard Dylan say. He obviously wasn't planning to address Ruth's comments. "Any idea who would do that?"

So much had happened with the fire and Curtis's visit that Collena had practically forgotten about that. But was it even important?

"Are you accusing me of eavesdropping?" Ruth asked. And she looked as if he'd slapped her.

"I'm merely asking a question." Dylan's tone certainly wasn't accusatory, but he did sound adamant about getting to the bottom of the situation.

Unfortunately, the eavesdropping was nothing compared to other things that could be brewing. And Collena thought she knew who was behind them.

Rodney Harmon.

He was the most likely candidate for setting her car on fire. She couldn't imagine Curtis traipsing around the woods in his pricey suit. Nor could she see either Millie or Ruth doing the same.

Eavesdropping, yes. Arson, no.

But now the question was—how had Rodney found her so quickly? She'd been in Greer for the past eighteen hours, and that would have put her already there in town right about the time that Rodney was escaping.

"I don't know who listened in on the intercom," Ruth finally answered. "Ina, maybe. She probably turned it on when she told you about the intruder and then forgot to turn it off."

It seemed reasonable to Collena, but there was something in Dylan's scrutinizing stare that made her wonder if it sounded reasonable to him.

"I've got things to do," Ruth declared. "If you want to accuse me of anything else, you'll find me in the nursery."

Dylan didn't make any attempt to apologize or follow the woman. Probably because he heard the same sound she did. There were thudding footsteps making their way down the hall, and for a moment, she braced herself for yet another confrontation with Curtis. Or worse. She prayed that Rodney Harmon hadn't wormed his way into the house.

But it wasn't either of them.

It was Deputy Jonah Burke.

"Well, thanks to you, I'm stuck here at the ranch for Thanksgiving," Jonah complained, aiming that complaint at Dylan. "The fire chief just called. The road between town and here is now officially closed."

"Closed?" Collena repeated, groaning. Well, that was just *wonderful*.

She had no car and no way to leave. This day just kept adding more and more obstacles. She wanted Dylan to get that DNA test to the lab, and that wasn't going to happen with the roads closed.

"Jonah, I'll make up the upstairs guest room for you," Millie volunteered. She stopped, though, and looked at Dylan. "What about Ms. Drake? Should I get a guest room ready for her, too?"

The impact hit Collena full force. Yes, the road closure would hinder the DNA test and getting replacement copies of her documents, but if Dylan actually let her stay, then she would be under the same roof as Adam.

She might get to see her son.

But she rethought that when she and Dylan turned toward each other at the same moment. That wasn't exactly a welcoming or inviting look he was giving her.

"She'll stay," Dylan said as if he were speaking profanity. He turned to Millie. "Have Hank check the security system. I want all perimeter and internal alarms set to the highest levels. Lock all the doors and windows. Make sure no one gets in without my permission."

Millie's eyes widened, and she nodded. "Dylan, are you expecting trouble?"

"Trouble's already here," he mumbled. "There's a fugitive on the loose," he added in a louder voice, apparently for Millie's ears. "He's dangerous, and I don't want him anywhere near the house."

"What about Adam?" Millie stared at Collena when she asked that question. "What should we do with him to make sure he's…safe?"

Safe, and away from Collena.

"Keep Adam in the nursery until you hear from me," Dylan ordered.

Another nod and Millie walked away, apparently ready to do her duty by making sure Collena didn't see her little boy.

Dylan would have walked away, as well, if Collena hadn't grabbed his arm. "Adam has my eyes. My mouth. My hair. He's my son, and I want to see him."

She could see the debate start. It seemed to make its way through every muscle in his body.

Dylan glanced back at the photo of her that he'd turned facedown on his desk. He was likely feeling sorry for her again. Part of Collena despised that—she hated pity—but another part of her was willing to do anything to see her child.

That included begging.

Still, she wasn't certain that even begging would be enough to convince Dylan.

They stood there. Long, long moments. While his mental debate continued. Collena had her own. To speak or not to speak. And she decided there was nothing she could say that would help her cause.

He groaned softly. "Come with me," he finally said. "And don't make me regret this."

Collena was too afraid to hope that he was leading her in the direction of the nursery.

Chapter 6

Dylan knew this could be a huge mistake.

After the incident with the car fire and Collena's suggestion of marriage, he wanted nothing more than to distance himself from the woman who could take Adam away from him. But he also knew that distancing himself wouldn't make this situation go away.

One way or another, he had to convince Collena that he should be the one to raise Adam. He couldn't do that if they were at each other's throats. And as for marriage for the sake of them sharing custody? Well, that was an absolute last resort, but he wasn't ruling it out just yet.

Dylan led Collena through the maze of corridors in the sprawling house. Nearly ten thousand square feet was more than enough room to bring up an active child. He'd had fatherhood in mind when he made renovations several years earlier.

He stopped for a moment outside the nursery door and looked back at Collena. She was nibbling on her bottom lip and showed more nerves than she had when facing down the car fire and Curtis Reese.

"I'm scared," she admitted.

"Me, too," Dylan acknowledged.

Her mouth quivered as if threatening a smile. Dylan figured it'd been a long time since she'd made that particular facial expression. But the smile didn't materialize. Instead, she squared her shoulders and took a deep breath.

Dylan did the same, and he opened the nursery door.

The room was empty.

Because of the leftover adrenaline, he felt another jolt of concern, but then reminded himself that it wasn't unusual for Ruth and Adam to be away from the nursery. Just because they weren't there in the room didn't mean that someone like Curtis Reese had kidnapped his son. He stepped into the room and pressed the button to turn on the house intercom.

"Ruth?" Dylan called out.

It only took a few seconds for the nanny to answer. "Adam and I are in the playroom."

"This way," Dylan instructed Collena, leading her back through the corridors. He hated that edgy feel of the adrenaline and hated even more that it was now associated with his son's safety. Since he'd had five years with no incidents, he had thought they were safe.

He'd obviously thought wrong.

"Does Adam really look like me?" Collena asked.

He stopped, turned around and considered lying. But

he didn't after he combed his gaze over Collena's face. "He's the spitting image of you."

Her bottom lip trembled a little, and she blinked hard. "Thank you." But then she hesitated and stared at him. "You're being nice to me because of that picture. I asked you to forget about it."

Why, he didn't know, but he stepped closer, violating her personal space. "I'm not being nice to you. If I had my way, you wouldn't be here at the ranch and you definitely wouldn't be on the verge of going into the playroom."

She lifted her shoulder. "So, why am I? Why are you letting me see Adam?"

"Because I don't think I have a choice. We're each other's obstacles. You want what I have, and I don't want to give him up. Somehow, we have to work through that, and working through issues is something that I'm usually pretty good at doing."

"I offered a solution," she reminded him.

"I don't call that a solution." In fact, he didn't know what exactly to call her marriage proposal.

Since marriage was the last thing he wanted to discuss, Dylan turned and started walking again toward the playroom. Collena was right behind him. And with each step, he dreaded this meeting even more.

Yet, he knew it was inevitable.

If he didn't allow Collena to see Adam, then tomorrow when the roads were clear, she'd no doubt start legal proceedings to get custody. So, he wasn't being nice. He was doing what he had to do to keep things amicable between Collena and him.

When he reached the set of playroom doors, Dylan

didn't pause. He didn't dare. Because he might change his mind. It was like ripping off a bandage. Fast, but definitely not painless.

He threw open the doors.

Dylan spotted Ruth first. She was sitting in a recliner with a paperback clutched in her hand. Adam was on a toy car that he was scooting around the room. He looked up, spotted Dylan and smiled the smile that always made him feel on top of the world.

"Is there a problem?" Ruth asked. Her eyes went straight to Collena, and the nanny got to her feet.

"No problem," Dylan assured her.

Ruth made a nasally sound to indicate she didn't buy that. "Then why is that woman here?"

Good question. But Dylan kept that remark to himself. Instead, he stood back and watched as Collena took short cautious steps toward Adam.

The little boy stopped and eyed the stranger who was approaching him. Adam didn't smile. Nor did he back away as he sometimes did with people he didn't know. He simply studied Collena as she stooped to Adam's eye level.

"Hi," Adam said, using his latest favorite word. Except it sounded more like "i."

"Hi," Collena answered. Her voice was clogged with emotion.

Neither Dylan nor Ruth said a word, but their gazes met, and he could tell that Ruth saw what Dylan had already known.

This was definitely mother and son.

Collena dropped down onto the floor, sitting directly across from Adam, and the two just watched each other. Adam babbled something, reached out and touched Collena's hair, which was barely a shade darker than Adam's own.

That one touch seemed to open the floodgates for Adam. With help from Collena, he climbed off the toy car, took a picture book that was lying on the floor and toddled back to Collena. Adam thrust the book toward her, and Collena took it and began to read to the child.

The simple gesture got Dylan right in the heart. Adam was more accepting of Collena than he wanted his son to be.

However, he didn't have time to react beyond that because his phone rang. Dylan extracted it from his pocket and checked the screen. It was from Mason Tanner, the P.I. friend who'd sent him those faxes about Collena. Dylan had e-mailed the man shortly thereafter and asked him to do a background check on Curtis Reese.

Because he didn't want Ruth or Collena to overhear this particular conversation, Dylan stepped into the hall to take the call.

"Please tell me you found something on Curtis Reese," Dylan said, commencing with a greeting.

"I did. Thankfully, his life is somewhat of an open book. That's the good news. The bad news is that he's staying at the hotel in Greer and is literally less than eight miles from your doorstep. He's not alone, either. He has his lawyer and a pair of private investigators there with him. And he has power, Dylan. Lots of it. Along with a couple of judges in his pocket."

That was not what Dylan wanted to hear. "Are you saying he could actually win a custody battle?"

"Absolutely. From what I can see from the outside

looking in, he can make a case against either you or Collena Drake. Yours is a no-brainer. The adoption was illegal, and that means legally you have no claim to Adam."

Dylan felt as if someone had sucker punched him. "I've raised him since birth."

"That won't negate the fact that the adoption was illegal. I'm not a lawyer, but Collena obviously has the strongest claim for full custody."

He felt another punch. "Once she has proof that she's Adam's mother."

"Oh, there's proof already. I checked the lab where you'd stored Adam's umbilical cord. They're the ones who ran the DNA test for the police, and Collena's DNA is on file because she's a former cop. Adam is Collena's son, all right. No disputing that."

That one was more than a punch. Dylan was grateful for the brief period of silence that followed. He needed it to come to terms with the fact that Collena had been telling him the truth.

Hell.

And the truth was that he could lose Adam.

"Collena has the best claim for custody," Mason Tanner repeated. "Unless, of course, Curtis Reese is able to prove she's unfit in some way."

And Curtis just might be able to do that if he could prove that Collena had endangered her unborn child by going on an undercover assignment. A good lawyer could argue that, and Curtis would almost certainly have a good lawyer. Heck, he'd have an entire team of them.

"What about Curtis Reese himself—what kind of dirt could you find on him?" Dylan asked.

"Nothing, other than rumors that he owns those judges and a few politicians. He was born stinking rich, inherited his family's chain of hardware stores, and then added to his wealth through what appears to be legal means. He's considered a good, upstanding citizen by most. And now that his less-than-stellar son is dead, there isn't even a hint of danger in any facet of his life. He comes off like a Boy Scout, Dylan, and that's not good news for you."

It wasn't. His worst fears had been confirmed—he could lose Adam.

"Keep digging," Dylan ordered. "I want any and every thing that you can find on not just Curtis Reese, but Collena Drake and the man who recently escaped from jail, Rodney Harmon."

"I will, but you have to start looking at the likelihood of a serious custody battle. Or some kind of settlement with Collena. If you can't buy her off, then if I were you, I'd be hoping that she's a reasonable woman."

Dylan clicked the end-call button, slipped the phone back into his pocket and leaned against the wall. His lungs felt heavy, as if he'd taken in too much air, and every muscle in his body was in a knot.

What the hell was he going to do?

He turned and opened the door just slightly so he could see inside the playroom. Ruth was in the chair, and she was glaring at Collena. However, Collena was oblivious, because her attention was focused solely on Adam, who was back on his toy car. His son was grinning from ear to ear and babbling happy sounds.

Collena turned and spotted him in the doorway. She, too, was smiling, and there were tears of joy in her eyes.

Dylan didn't waste any time. There wasn't a reason to delay this.

He knew what he had to do.

He motioned for Collena to come to him. Her smile faded, probably because she anticipated that he'd gotten some bad news from the phone call. She got up from the floor and, without breaking eye contact with him, she made her way to him.

"What's wrong?" she asked.

"Everything." Dylan cleared his throat. He partially closed the door, only leaving it open a small crack. "If your marriage proposal is still good—I'm accepting it."

Of all the things that Collena had expected to hear Dylan say, she hadn't expected that.

"You're accepting my marriage proposal?" she asked, certain she'd misunderstood him.

He nodded. And he looked as if he were facing a firing squad. "The P.I. I just spoke with confirmed that you're Adam's biological mother. He also believes that Curtis Reese has a chance of getting custody of Adam."

"He does," Collena agreed, speaking around the lump in her throat. That's why she'd suggested marriage in the first place. She didn't have the resources and political contacts to fight Curtis, but Dylan did. With Dylan's help, she could get custody of her child.

Her plan was working. That was the good news, but she knew they had a long fight ahead of them. This was just the first step.

"I thought we stood a better chance of winning if we were together," Collena added.

Dylan huffed. "Of course, a judge might see right through our convenient relationship."

"I don't doubt that, either, but Curtis is a widower, and I think a judge would be more likely to keep Adam in the home where he was raised and with parents who've made a commitment to give him the best life possible. We'll just have to be honest and not hide the reason we're getting married. I'm hoping our marriage will prove to the judge that we're willing to do anything for Adam's happiness. Curtis can't compete with that."

His eyes snapped to hers. "You really think we can pull this off?"

"I don't think we have a choice. And believe me, for the past three days, I've studied all the options. If I'd been able to come up with something better, I would have gone in that direction."

"I'll bet you would have," he mumbled. He took a hard breath and opened his mouth to say something. However, Ruth interrupted him.

With Adam in her arms, Ruth threw open the door. "It's time for Adam's bath," she announced.

Collena desperately wanted to spend more time with her son, but she also needed to work out some details with Dylan.

Apparently, they were getting married.

Just thinking that sent a rush of panic through her. She'd come up with the plan before she'd met Dylan. Before she'd realized that she was attracted to him. She wanted her son, but she didn't want a relationship with Dylan. Not with her past. And not with her excess emotional baggage. She still hadn't gotten over the painful relationship with Adam's father.

Falling for him could ruin everything she'd planned.

Collena took both a step back, both emotionally and physically, and let Ruth walk past them. Adam gave them a little wave as Ruth carried him down the hall.

She and Dylan stood there in silence. He was no doubt thinking of the enormous impact of what he'd just done. Collena knew that impact, as well.

"Don't mention the marriage to anyone just yet," Dylan finally said. "I want to be the one to tell the staff."

"Certainly." Though Collena figured that wouldn't be a pleasant conversation, especially when it came to Ruth. The woman obviously loathed her and was more than just staff. She was family.

Dylan checked his watch. "I need to make some calls, and you probably want to freshen up. I'll show you to the guest room."

Collena nodded and followed him. "When you talk to your lawyer, you'll want to make sure that we can keep the custody hearings here in this county. Curtis has a lot of powerful friends in San Antonio."

"So I've heard."

No doubt he'd learned that from that phone call. "Before I came here, I sold everything I own. It should be enough to cover legal expenses. What I don't have are Curtis's contacts in the judicial system." She paused. "I'm hoping you do."

"I haven't bribed politicians and judges, if that's what you mean, but people know me in this county. Besides, losing isn't an option."

Collena believed him. She *had* to believe him. She hadn't come all this way to fail.

"You'll join us for Thanksgiving dinner?" Dylan

asked, stopping outside one of the doors in the long corridor of rooms.

It took her a moment to shift gears in the conversation. "Yes. Thank you." It would get her more time to spend with her son.

"In the meantime, I'll have Ina bring you a tray so you'll have something to eat."

Collena didn't refuse that, either. She was still feeling a little light-headed, and she didn't want that with all the critical things going on in her life.

Dylan didn't say anything else. He merely opened the door, motioned for her to go inside and walked away. Collena stood there, watching him, and praying that this plan would succeed.

She stepped inside. The light was already on, so she had no trouble seeing the guest room. Or rather, the guest suite. There was a sitting room with a bay window to her right, and the bedroom and bath were to her left. Like the rest of the house, it was tastefully decorated in warm neutral colors with a dark hardwood floor dotted with Turkish rugs.

Collena went inside and sank down onto the taupe-and-cream-colored chair in the sitting room. She felt drained and exhausted, but like Dylan, she had some calls to make. She took out her phone, just as someone knocked. She didn't even have time to get out of the chair before the door opened and Millie walked in.

"Oh, I'm sorry," Millie immediately said. "I thought you were still with Dylan." She lifted her arms to show Collena a stack of clothes. "We're close to the same size, and I figured you could use these, especially since we don't know how long you'll be here with the snow and all."

Collena stood and took the clothes from her. "Thank you."

Millie shrugged. "It's the least I could do, considering your car caught fire."

The words were right. Kind, even. But the kindness didn't make it to Millie's eyes. In fact, Collena got the same cold vibes from Millie that she did from her mother, Ruth.

The woman glanced around before her attention came back to Collena. She hesitated, licking her lips. "Is it true? Are you really Adam's birth mother?"

Collena nodded.

"Oh." And that's all Millie said for several seconds. "But you gave him up for adoption."

"Someone stole him from me," Collena corrected. She left it at that. The sanitized version was best for now. Later, maybe Dylan would explain everything to Millie and the rest.

Another "oh" from Millie. Another hesitation. Millie's breathing was suddenly uneven. "Well, if you need anything else, just ask. The phone there is a private line, in case your cell phone doesn't work out here. Sometimes, service is spotty." She went to the intercom speaker on the table next to the chair and pressed some buttons. "And if you need someone in the house, like the cook, for instance, all you have to do is hold down the talk button. Someone will answer. You don't have to bother Dylan or anything. He has enough to deal with right now."

Now, it was Collena's turn to say, "oh." There was

nothing chilly about that remark, but it was, well, territorial.

Did Millie have feelings for Dylan?

If so, this was about to get very messy.

Millie mumbled a goodbye, and as soon as the woman was out the door, Collena closed it and locked it. She didn't want anyone walking in on the phone call she was about to make.

She took her phone from her pocket, flipped it open and pressed in the numbers to her friend and former coworker, Sergeant Katelyn O'Malley.

"Katelyn," Collena said when she answered. "I hate to bother you on Thanksgiving—"

"You're not bothering me. Thanksgiving dinner is still hours away, and you got me out of cooking duty. I owe you, girl. I'm not into basting turkeys."

"We'll work something out," Collena joked. But the light tone was a facade. She was terrified of what Katelyn might or might not have learned.

"I've been doing some checking on a few of the citizens of Greer," Katelyn continued. "One thing that really stuck out was Deputy Jonah Burke. Have you met him yet?"

Collena didn't like the sound of this. "Oh, yes. Because of the snowstorm, he's stuck in the house with us."

"Well, then, you better hope the roads clear soon. He's had two suspensions from the job and even had criminal charges filed against him for stalking. The charges were dropped when the person who filed them was killed. That person was Dylan Greer's sister, Abigail."

"Dylan's sister?" Collena certainly hadn't expected

that. "Why is Jonah still on the force if he was stalking her?"

"Law of supply and demand. Apparently no one else in Greer wants his job. Still, Jonah's not well liked, and even the sheriff doesn't have much good to say about him."

Neither did Collena. "I'll make sure I lock my door tonight."

"Don't lock it just for Jonah Burke's sake. You need to keep an eye out for two of Dylan's employees, Ruth and Millie Sayers. Get this—both have been under psychiatric care since Dylan's sister was killed five years ago."

Another surprise, but it wasn't totally unexpected. "I think they were very close to her. And her death was unexpected. And suspicious."

"That, too. I plan to look a little harder at that, especially if Deputy Burke might have had a reason to kill this woman."

Katelyn was right. The stalking charge would give Jonah motive, and since he was a deputy, he already had the means. That only left the opportunity, and in a small town like Greer, there should have been plenty of opportunities for the deputy to go after the woman. So, had his involvement been covered up?

"There's more," Katelyn continued. "Millie was dating Burke at the time he was supposedly stalking Dylan's sister."

"You're kidding."

"I wish I were. I wish you'd get out of that house ASAP. I don't think it's safe for you there, Collena."

"I can't leave. I want to be here with Adam."

"I know. I know," Katelyn repeated. "Just be careful, okay?"

Collena assured her that she would, ended the call and put her phone on the table.

Mercy, what was going on here?

In addition to the tangled web between Dylan's sister and the surly deputy, there was that whole issue of psychiatric care for Ruth and Millie. Did Dylan know about this? He would almost have to with both women living under his roof. Unless they'd intentionally kept it from him.

Those issues were a lot to add to the ones she'd brought to the ranch. An escaped convict and her ex's father who seemed determined to get his hand on his grandson. Her plan was turning out to contain a myriad of complications.

And perhaps danger.

Jonah Burke definitely wasn't a man she wanted to tangle with on top of everything else.

She heard a sound behind her and automatically reached for her gun. Collena tried to force herself to calm down. After all, Millie had walked in earlier without knocking. Maybe the woman had returned.

But this didn't feel right.

Collena felt a too-familiar shiver go down her spine. A cop's shiver. A warning that she was in the presence of danger.

The doorknob turned again. Not gently. An almost frantic gesture.

"Who is it?" Collena called out.

No one answered.

With her heart in her throat, her blood pumping and

with her gun gripped in her hand, Collena threw open the door.

No one was there. And the corridor was empty. Well, empty except for the yellowy newspaper that was lying on the floor near her feet.

While keeping watch around her, she stooped and picked up the *Greer Herald*. It wasn't the weekly edition. It wasn't even recent.

The date indicated it was five years old.

During the background check she'd done on Dylan, Collena had yet to see anything from the *Greer Herald*. The small newspaper wasn't electronically stored, nor had there been any online copies. Since both the newspaper office and the town library had closed early for the Thanksgiving holiday, she hadn't been able to read any back issues.

Confused as to why someone would leave something like that outside the guest-room door, Collena glanced at the front page. The lead story was the sheriff's investigation into Abigail Greer's death.

Dylan's sister.

According to the article, there had been no witnesses to the suspicious car fire that'd killed Abigail. Collena kept reading, scanning through the lengthy article that detailed the specifics of what remained of the vehicle.

And then she realized someone had highlighted a line near the end of the newspaper report.

"Dylan Greer has been brought in for questioning and is considered a suspect in his sister's and fiancée's deaths."

Chapter 7

This was not the quiet, relaxing Thanksgiving dinner that Dylan had planned.

The table was filled with all the traditional foods that he'd requested Ina make—roasted turkey with all the trimmings, mashed potatoes, gravy and three vegetable dishes.

Everything looked perfect. It probably tasted good, too, but he doubted anyone at the table, other than Deputy Burke, knew that firsthand. Ruth, Millie, Ina, Hank, the handyman, and even Dylan himself were picking at their food and trying to avoid direct eye contact with anyone else.

Collena wasn't even making an attempt to eat, and Dylan didn't think it was his imagination that she seemed leery of him.

The sole bright spot was Adam.

He sat in his high chair eating peas and tiny bits of turkey. Each bite seemed to amuse him, because he babbled and grinned at Dylan. Despite the trouble of the day, Dylan had no choice but to smile back at the little boy. Those smiles were welcome reminders that he was well worth fighting for.

Dylan spotted Collena smiling, too, and Adam seemed pleased that he had someone else's attention. He offered Collena a pea that was pinched between his tiny thumb and forefinger, and Collena got up to take the offer.

Adam giggled when Collena ate the pea from his fingers.

"You two sure look an awful lot alike," Jonah commented. He shoveled another forkful of mashed potatoes into his mouth.

For such a simple comment, it certainly caused a reaction. Everyone stopped, as if waiting to see how Dylan would respond to that. Then, seconds later, Ruth tossed her silverware onto her plate. It made a loud clanging sound.

"Adam's tired," Ruth announced, standing. "It's time for me to get him ready for bed."

Collena looked at Dylan. "Can't he stay up just a little longer?" There was a definite motherly plea in her voice. Just as there was a back-me-up plea in Ruth's eyes.

And that's when Dylan knew he had to put a stop to this.

First, he motioned for Ruth and Collena to sit down, and because he was positive he would need it, he finished off his glass of wine.

"Collena is Adam's birth mother," he started, making brief eye contact with everyone at the table. "Someone stole Adam from her, and Collena's spent all these months looking for him." He had to pause a moment. "The adoption was probably illegal."

No one seemed shocked by that revelation, which meant it'd likely been the topic of house gossip all afternoon.

"You didn't know it was illegal," Millie declared. "The judge will understand that. You won't lose Adam."

Dylan wasn't so certain of that.

"What about Curtis Reese?" Jonah asked. "What's he got to do with any of this?"

"He's Adam's grandfather," Collena answered before Dylan could.

Dylan added to the explanation. "And he plans to fight both Collena and me for custody of Adam."

Now, that caused a reaction. Jonah stopped eating and stared openmouthed at Dylan. Millie flattened her hand over her chest and frantically shook her head. Ruth went ash pale and slowly sank back onto her seat.

"He can't take Adam," Millie said practically in a whisper.

Dylan nodded. "Collena and I have a plan to stop that from happening." That also got everyone's attention. Dylan figured he was going to get more than their attention with what he had to say next. "Collena and I have decided to join forces to fight Reese. And the best way for us to do that is get married and have me legally adopt Adam."

"Married?" Millie and Ruth said in unison.

Hank and Ina apparently decided it was a good time

to go check on dessert. He didn't blame them. Dylan waited until they were out of the room before he continued.

"Together Collena and I can make a stronger case for custody," he added.

Millie stood. "But marriage?"

Dylan nodded again. "I've gone through all the options, and this is the best one for fighting Reese off."

"So, this would strictly be a marriage of convenience?" Jonah asked while still chewing his food. Despite what had to be a shocking conversation, it'd only deterred Jonah from eating for a few seconds.

"Yes." And Dylan hoped they all understood that. After what'd happened to the other women he'd loved, he wanted to make it crystal clear that he didn't care for Collena.

That was the only way he could save her from the fate of the other women. Even then, it was still a risk. This might open old wounds that he never wanted open. Now, if he could only figure out whose *wounds* it was that had made his life a living hell.

"There has to be another way," Ruth declared. "You can't marry her, Dylan. She could take Adam and run."

"She can try to do that even if we're not married," Dylan pointed out. "Collena is Adam's mother. I have no legal or moral right to try to cut her out of Adam's life."

Ruth stared at him, and there were tears in her eyes. "Adam's tired," she repeated. "It's time for me to get him ready for bed."

Collena got up again, as well. "I want to go with him so I can say good-night."

Ruth took off the high-chair tray, picked up Adam

and turned around to face Collena. "Give the baby some time. You can't force motherhood on him."

With that, Ruth took Adam out of the room.

Dylan considered going after her, to remind Ruth that while she was a member of the family, she couldn't shut out Collena, but he decided they could all use a little breathing space. Besides, with their late start on the Thanksgiving dinner, it really was Adam's bedtime.

"I'll have to excuse myself from the table, too," Millie said. "I'm not feeling well."

Jonah smiled at Collena. "You sure know how to clear a table."

That brought Dylan to his feet. He was about to give Jonah a piece of his mind, but Collena stopped him. "Don't," she whispered. "It's not worth it." She stood and placed her napkin beside her plate. "If you don't mind, I need to get some rest. It's been a long day."

Dylan shot Jonah a nasty glare and headed after her. Collena was in the corridor, and she was already practically running in the direction of her guest room.

"Wait," he called out to her.

She didn't exactly wait, but she did slow down so he could catch up with her. "I really am tired," she told him.

"I don't doubt that." Dylan caught her arm and turned her around to face him.

He'd had some good ideas in his life, but that wasn't one of them. When he whirled her around, she practically landed against him. So close they were nearly touching. He saw the stark fatigue in her eyes. The worry lines on her forehead. The too-pale skin.

But he also took in her scent. Not warm, exactly. But

inviting. He was attracted to her in the most basic way that a man could be attracted to a woman.

Collena was beautiful. And she had both a toughness and a fragileness about her. The kind of woman who could take care of herself but was still vulnerable beneath. He was a sucker for a strong woman, but his attraction went up a significant notch when there was vulnerability involved.

"Well?" Collena prompted. She took a step back. It didn't help. She was still close enough that her scent was playing havoc with his senses.

"I apologize for Ruth's comment," Dylan said, forcing himself to speak.

"No need. I didn't think for one minute that fitting into your life would be easy. And the truth is, I'll try to stay out of their way—and yours—as much as possible."

He studied her, specifically her defensive posture. She'd folded her arms over her chest and was leaning away from him. Definitely defensive.

"Okay, what's this all about?" he asked. He motioned toward her folded arms.

To her credit, she didn't say, *What do you mean?* Nor did she deny that something was wrong. "Earlier today someone left a newspaper outside my door."

Though that didn't seem serious, Dylan wasn't ready to shrug just yet. A lot of crazy things had happened. "What newspaper?"

Collena opened the door to her room and, without turning on the light, went inside. Several moments later, she returned with the article in question. One glance at it, and Dylan didn't have to ask any more questions about what it was. He knew. It was *the* story that had implicated him in the deaths of his sister and fiancée.

"I didn't kill them," Dylan said simply.

Collena looked him straight in the eyes. "I believe you."

He was so surprised by her adamant vote of confidence that it took him a moment to respond. "Then why did that article upset you?"

"Because first of all, I don't know who left it for me. Or why. Maybe the person was trying to make me run in the other direction. But I won't run," she insisted.

No, he didn't think she would. But Dylan did want to know the answer to her questions. Who had left it? Obviously someone on his staff. Or maybe Jonah. He was in the house, too. And as for why, maybe this was a little gas-lighting, an attempt to make Collena feel unwelcome.

And unsafe.

Oh, yes. He'd question everyone in the house, and he'd get to the bottom of this.

"I also think Curtis Reese might try to use this article against us," Collena added.

Of course. Dylan should have thought of that. Even though there'd been no evidence against him and even though he was never a solid suspect, there had been questions and gossip about his innocence. Those questions had been raised in that particular story in the *Greer Herald*.

"I can't make that article go away," Dylan explained. He took the newspaper from her and tucked it under his arm. "But I can have my lawyer negate it by pointing out that I was never charged with a crime."

"Still…" She groaned softly and leaned against the wall. "Curtis already has so much ammunition. That's why I proposed."

"I know. And it's a good idea."

She blinked.

He blinked, too. "Did I just say that?"

The smile that curved her mouth was born of pure irony and frustration. "It might take a decade or two before your staff believes it's a good idea."

"They'll get used to it, because they won't have a choice. I'm not losing Adam, and if this marriage can stop that from happening, then we need to say 'I do' as soon as possible."

"How soon is that?" she asked.

Dylan couldn't believe he was about to say this, either. "I plan to call the county clerk tonight at his home. He's an old friend. I want him to expedite the licensing process, and if all goes well, I think I can have everything arranged for this weekend."

She blinked again. "That soon?"

He heard the doubts in her voice and knew they'd be in his voice, as well. "Curtis Reese will probably be filing his custody petition as early as tomorrow morning."

Collena drew in a hard breath. "You're right. We should do this as soon as the county clerk has the license." She paused. "You'll tell Ruth and the others about the hasty wedding plans?"

"Yes." Though he knew that wouldn't be a pleasant conversation. Nor would the other chat he'd have to have with Adam's nanny. "I'm not going to let Ruth cut you out of Adam's life."

Collena shook her head. "I wouldn't let that happen

anyway." She touched her index finger to her mouth. "I am concerned, though, about Ruth being under the care of a therapist."

Ah, so she'd learned that. "She is. Millie, too. My sister's death sent them both into emotional tailspins. Don't worry, though, it doesn't affect how they interact with Adam. They both love him, and they wouldn't do anything to hurt him. I'd stake my life on that."

"I can see they love him," Collena admitted. "But I can also see that Ruth is going to make it very difficult for me. She won't succeed. I've worked too hard to find Adam to allow anyone to stop me from being his mother."

Even though she probably hadn't meant that as a challenge or an order, it made Dylan feel a little defensive. He had to remind himself—again—that he couldn't have an adversarial relationship with Collena. But that did bring him to another question.

Just what kind of relationship would this really be?

They'd both already established that it was to be a marriage of convenience, but he certainly couldn't deny the attraction he felt for her.

Was it one-sided?

Dylan studied her. They were still close, and they seemed to get a whole lot closer when her eyes came to his. He saw it then. The heat. He felt it, too. And knew this wasn't a good thing.

Dylan chose his words carefully. "There's this connection between us," he admitted.

She nodded. "Conflict at first sight."

"It's not all conflict, and that's the problem."

Her stare intensified before she mumbled something

under her breath and looked away. "We feel this way because we're comrades of sorts. We've made a pact not to lose custody of Adam."

"That's part of it, I'm sure. But the other part is that we're physically attracted to each other," he added. "Don't deny it."

"I wasn't planning to. Yes, it exists. That doesn't mean we have to act on it. In fact, acting on it could cause problems for us in other areas."

"You're right," Dylan admitted. "There's that unresolved issue of my past relationships. Besides, sex would complicate things."

No more leaning against the wall. She practically snapped to attention. "Who said anything about sex?"

He lifted his eyebrow.

Just like that, her body relaxed, and Collena shrugged. "Attraction leads to sex—point taken. It can't happen, though."

"I'm sure you're right, but if this attraction gets any stronger, we might have trouble remembering why it'd be a bad idea."

"It'd be bad because it would get in the way of what we both want, being the best possible parents to Adam."

He nodded. "That's a good argument."

But it didn't stop a curl of heat from making its way through his body. It was just basic lust, he repeated to himself, intensified because of the camaraderie and because it'd been too long since he'd been with a woman.

Way too long.

His body just wouldn't let him forget that.

Nor would it let him forget that judging from the

look in Collena's eyes, she was engaged in the same battle he was.

"My, isn't this cozy?" Dylan heard someone ask.

He looked over his shoulder and saw Jonah making his way toward them. The deputy had obviously noticed the proximity of Collena and him, because Jonah was grinning as if he'd just caught them raiding the cookie jar.

"Did I interrupt anything?" Jonah asked.

"Nothing that we care to share with you," Dylan fired back.

That caused Jonah's nostrils to flare. The man stopped just several inches away from them. "You just don't learn, do you, Dylan?"

"What's that supposed to mean?"

"You don't have a real good track record with women, now, do you? I seem to recall the last one you got engaged to was killed in that car fire."

Dylan shifted his posture and glared at Jonah. "Is that some kind of threat?"

Jonah held up his hands in mock surrender, and he chuckled. "Not from me." The jovial expression quickly faded, and the look in the deputy's eyes turned dark. "But even you can't deny that you've got a problem. My advice? Watch your back and hers. I don't want to be investigating another suspicious death or two."

With that, Jonah strolled away in the direction of the other guest room.

The curl of heat was quickly replaced with anger, and followed by the realization that while Jonah was an SOB, he was also right.

Dylan *did* need to watch Collena's back.

In his attempt to keep custody of Adam, he couldn't endanger Collena's life.

It was time to reopen some of his own personal wounds and take another hard look at what'd happened years ago.

"Jonah obviously doesn't want to see you happy," Collena said. She waited until Jonah was in his room before she continued. "I learned some things about him."

"That he was stalking my sister right before she was killed." Dylan nodded. "I believe it's true, though Jonah has denied it. He said it was all a misunderstanding, that he thought my sister was truly interested in him."

"He was also dating Millie at the time."

"You've done your homework." And Dylan couldn't fault her for it. He was investigating her and her friends, as well. "Yes, they were dating, but I think Jonah was doing that only to make my sister jealous. It might have worked if Abigail had had any feelings for Jonah. But she didn't."

Collena folded her arms over her chest. "I have to ask—do you think Jonah could have had something to do with your sister's death?"

He didn't have to think long about his answer. "I honestly don't know. If he did, he certainly hid his guilt."

"Some people don't feel guilt." Collena glanced down the hall at Jonah's room and scrubbed her hand over the back of her neck. "I should get some rest. You, too. We have a long day ahead of us."

He couldn't dispute that, but after the conversation they'd just had about Jonah, Dylan didn't want to take any chances. "This is probably overkill since you're a former cop, but I'd like to check your room."

Her eyes widened. "You think…" But she didn't finish that. She merely stepped aside so that Dylan could go in.

He didn't waste any time. He turned on the lights, and with Collena trailing right behind him, he checked first the sitting room and then the adjoining bedroom suite.

Nothing seemed out of the ordinary.

Dylan turned toward her. "Lock your door tonight."

"I intend to. And I have my gun."

He nodded, though he hated the idea that Collena might ever have to use it. In fact, he had to believe there'd be no need to use it. He'd done everything possible to create the safest environment for Adam, and he had to trust that all his security measures would be enough.

However, first thing in the morning, he was getting Jonah out of there, and he would turn on the corridor security cameras to make sure Jonah didn't leave his room. In addition, he'd set the security system in the nursery so that no one could sneak in there.

Dylan considered asking Collena if she wanted him to stay in her suite with her. He briefly considered it anyway. But another look at her reminded him that would be a really bad idea.

Besides, he wasn't even certain there was a threat.

The newspaper could have been Millie or Ruth's way of trying to make Collena want to run in the other direction. And if so, they wouldn't get away with it. If he found out they were behind this, there'd be hell to pay. He'd make it clear to both women that he wasn't going to let them do this to Collena.

Dylan and she walked back into the sitting room. That's when he noticed the message light blinking on the phone. "Someone must have called you."

Collena looked in the direction of the phone and stared at the red blinking light. "No one I know has that number. All my calls having been coming through my cell."

That put a new knot in his stomach. Still, the most logical answer was that it was a wrong number. Hoping that was true, Dylan went to the phone and punched the button.

It was several moments before he heard any sound. First, there was static. Lots of it. The line crackled and hissed as if the connection was really bad.

Then, there was the voice.

"Collena," the person said through the hiss and static. The voice was muted.

No, not muted.

Disguised.

The caller had something over his or her mouth.

Collena moved closer, until they were side-by-side, and they continued to stare at the phone. Waiting.

"Collena," the voice repeated. "Are you ready to die?"

Chapter 8

Collena had experienced one of the longest nights of her life, and she wasn't holding out any hope that the day after would be any easier.

With the threatening phone call, the newspaper appearing outside her door, Curtis Reese's custody threat and Rodney Harmon's escape from jail, her stress and anxiety levels were sky-high.

What made everything tolerable was Adam.

Much to Ruth's disapproval, Collena had insisted that she feed her son breakfast. Then, she bathed Adam. The process hadn't gone perfectly, especially with Ruth shadowing her every move, but Collena ignored the woman and just enjoyed her first precious moments of motherhood.

There would be lots more of these moments.

And it would take more than a threatening call to put her off.

Collena dressed Adam in denim overalls, brushed his hair and carried him into the playroom so they could have some reading time.

Ruth followed her.

"You're getting him out of his morning routine," Ruth complained.

Collena considered ignoring her, but she decided it was time to get things straight. Ruth's criticisms had been going on for hours, and she didn't want it to continue. "Adam's my son," Collena stated firmly. "I'm going to raise him. And right now, I'm going to read him a book."

Ruth pulled back her shoulders. "You're trying to cut me out of his life."

"No, I'm not. Dylan hired you, so he obviously believes you're a good nanny." At least she hoped that was true, that Ruth wasn't still around simply because she'd become a fixture at the ranch. "I have no intentions of cutting you out of Adam's life. But I won't have you trying to do the same to me."

Ruth's shoulders relaxed a bit, and after several snail-crawling moments, she gave a crisp nod. "I'll give you two some time to read," she said as if it were a massive concession. Which for her, it probably was. And then the woman quietly left the room.

"Alone at last," Collena mumbled.

She sat on the floor, put Adam right next to her and selected a book from the large stack. Adam cocked his head to the side, studying her, before he climbed into Collena's lap. It was an amazing feeling, and it was several moments before Collena could find her voice so she could read to her child. However, she barely made it through the first page before someone opened the door.

It was Dylan.

As much as Collena hated to have her time with Adam interrupted, she wanted to see Dylan, as well, so she could find out what progress he'd made on the threatening phone call and Curtis's custody petition.

And much to her displeasure, she realized she also wanted to see him just for the sake of seeing him.

She certainly got an eyeful.

He wore faded jeans that hugged his well-toned lower body and a white shirt that did the same for his equally well toned torso. He hadn't shaved and had rather hot-looking desperado stubble.

"You found out who made that call?" Collena asked, forcing herself to get her mind back on business and off Dylan's body.

He kept his expression pleasant, no doubt for Adam's sake, and came and sat on the floor next to them. Adam immediately left Collena's lap for his, and the child gave Dylan a sloppy kiss on the cheek. Dylan returned the kiss.

"There are private lines in both guest rooms where you and Jonah were staying," Dylan explained while he played patty-cake with Adam. "Both numbers are listed so they'd be easy for anyone to get them. And there was an identical message on the machine in Jonah's room."

Collena processed that info. "So, the call could have come from anyone who knew I was staying here. Anyone, including Curtis Reese or Rodney Harmon." It sickened her to think of a man like Harmon having any contact with the ranch.

She wanted him far away from Adam.

"I tried to have the call traced, of course," Dylan continued. "But it came from a prepaid cell phone."

Collena knew what that meant. The call wouldn't be traceable. The threat was a dead end because, in addition to Rodney Harmon or Curtis Reese, Ruth or Millie could have made the call. For that matter, Jonah could have, as well. The message on the phone in his guest room could have been a ruse to throw suspicion off him.

"You look tired," Dylan said. He reached out and slid his finger over her cheek to push away a lock of hair that had strayed from her ponytail. His touch was warm. And comforting.

"You look tired, too. Probably because you stayed outside my door all night."

He nodded and seemed a little surprised that she'd known that little detail. "Since the nursery's at the end of that particular hall, I figured I could keep an eye on both Adam and you."

"Thank you for that. For Adam's sake. But since I have my gun, I feel safe."

That was a lie, but Collena didn't want him to think she was a wuss. Dylan had enough to worry about without adding her to his list.

Dylan handed Adam a toy dog. "Curtis Reese filed the custody motion this morning."

Collena had been expecting him to say that, but it still hit her hard. It took her a moment to gather her breath. "And what about Rodney Harmon? I don't suppose the police have found him?"

"Not yet. But I hired a couple of P.I.s to look for him, as well."

That was a start, and she had to remind herself that Dylan had an excellent security system at the ranch. No, it hadn't prevented that troubling call, but it would probably stop an intruder from breaking in. After all, he'd detected her with ease when she was by the birthing stables. Now that they knew Rodney Harmon was on the loose, Dylan had no doubt beefed up security even more.

Plus, he'd slept outside her door.

Collena didn't want to be touched by that.

But she was.

"There's nothing new on your car," he continued. He divided his attention between Adam and her. "The fire chief is still thinking it was an electrical problem, but he's going to continue to investigate."

Collena hoped it was an electrical fire that hadn't been spurred by human means. It was far better than the alternative, but considering that phone call, the car and the call could have been attempts to run her out of town.

"Did anyone on the staff know about the newspaper left outside my door?" she asked.

"Everyone denied putting it there." He scrubbed his hand over his face. "Obviously, someone is lying."

Obviously. "If the newspaper was only meant to unnerve me, I can live with that." Collena stopped and tried to decide the best way to continue. But Dylan had no trouble picking up on where this conversation was going.

"You think this has something to do with the deaths of my sister and fiancée. And the other attacks," he added.

She drew back her shoulders. "What other attacks?"

Dylan shrugged, but there was nothing casual about the gesture. "I figured you'd come across that in the background check."

"I didn't." And Collena braced herself for the worst. Thankfully, Adam helped soften the impact. The little boy's laughter broke the tension building inside Collena.

"It started when I was seventeen. My high-school girlfriend was assaulted. Someone clubbed her when she was getting into her car one night. She wasn't able to get a look at her attacker because the assault happened from behind."

Oh, mercy. Collena could only hold her breath while Dylan continued.

"Then, when I was in college, a woman I dated was also beaten."

"I take it the only thing these women, your fiancée and your sister, had in common was…you?" she asked.

"Yes. And I know what you're thinking—did someone I know commit these crimes."

"You mean, Deputy Burke?" She didn't wait for him to confirm that. "He certainly seems capable of doing something malicious. I don't know about murder, though."

Dylan lifted his shoulder. "Maybe the fires weren't meant to kill them."

She considered that. She also considered something else. "What if it was someone else connected to you, someone who works for you?"

He stayed quiet a moment. "I had to consider that, but then I dismissed it. The only people who were around for all the incidents were Millie, Ruth and Hank, the handyman."

Collena tried not to make the tone of her next question sound confrontational. "Both Millie and Ruth are under care of a therapist. Maybe one of them is, uh, well, a little unbalanced."

Dylan looked neither surprised, nor upset with the suggestion. "Anything is possible. But I just don't see it. Ruth's been a great nanny, and Millie practically runs the household. If either of them is a sociopath with killer tendencies, it hasn't shown up in any behavior or any incident here at the ranch."

"Maybe because you've stopped dating and therefore you've stopped giving one of them a reason to do something violent."

He stared at her. Rather than getting angry about that theory, he actually seemed thoughtful before he shook his head. "Ruth loves me like her own son. I'm sure of that. I'm also sure that she wants me to be happy."

Collena wasn't so certain of that at all. "And what about Millie?"

Another headshake. "She's not romantically obsessed with me. She sees other men. Heck, she was engaged to a guy from San Antonio just last year, but things didn't work out between them."

"Well, that leaves Hank, and I'm not about to accuse a seventysomething-year-old man of murder and assault." She paused. "Unless you think there's a reason to accuse him."

"No reason at all. My dad died when I was a kid, and Hank stepped up to do all the things that a dad normally would have done. He was also a huge help to my mom when it came to running the business. When she died of breast cancer eight years ago, Hank took it as hard as I did."

So, Hank was family. Not that being family was a good enough reason to remove him from a list of suspects.

"Hank is Ruth's father and Millie's grandfather," Dylan added.

"I didn't know that." She wondered if that bit of information was important. "I didn't investigate him before I came to the ranch."

"All three—Millie, Ruth and Hank—are Sayers. Ruth was never married to Millie's father, so that's why they have the same surname." Dylan looked at her again. "Do you want me to have them move out for a while?"

Collena wanted to jump at the chance for that to happen. But it wasn't fair. Not to them. Nor was it fair to Adam. Besides, Dylan was right. There were no solid indications that the women wanted to prevent him from being happy in love.

However, she couldn't say the same for Jonah.

She really needed to do some more digging into his past.

"What about the roads?" Collena asked. It was obviously time for a change of subject. The mood was positively gloomy. "Are they still impassable?"

Dylan shook his head. "They've been plowed."

"Does that mean Jonah is on his way home?"

"He left about an hour ago."

Well, that was something to celebrate, but Dylan didn't look in a celebratory mood. And that brought her to something she should have already suggested. "Do you want me to move to a hotel?"

"Absolutely not. We only have one hotel in town, and Curtis Reese is staying there."

"Right." She definitely didn't want to be near him.

"Besides, it's too risky for you to leave," Dylan added.

"You mean, too risky because of Rodney Harmon?" Collena knew he couldn't verify that Rodney was the only risk, but she wanted to know if he was ready to admit that someone in his household might have been responsible for the car fire and the threatening call.

"Rodney Harmon. Curtis Reese," he verified. "Plus, there's the wedding."

Yes. That.

Despite all the other thoughts and fears that'd clogged her brain and prevented her from sleeping, Collena hadn't been able to get the wedding off her mind.

When she'd first come up with the marriage plan, it'd seemed like a solid idea, but now she was having her doubts. But she didn't have another choice. Without being a married couple, they wouldn't be able to put up a strong fight to stop Curtis Reese.

Dylan scraped his thumbnail over the book that she'd laid next to her. "I've already arranged for the marriage license. The county clerk went to his office despite the holiday and expedited everything. And with the roads clear, the justice of the peace should be able to get here without any trouble. We'll be able to do this soon."

"How soon is soon?" she asked.

He cleared his throat. "This afternoon."

Of course she'd known that Dylan intended to move

quickly, but she certainly hadn't anticipated they would say *I do* in mere hours.

"You're having second thoughts," he said.

Second, third and fourth. She only hoped she wasn't inviting even more danger for all of them by becoming Mrs. Dylan Greer.

Dylan took out his gun from the desk drawer and slipped it in the leather shoulder holster hidden beneath his suit coat. He doubted many men carried a gun on their wedding day, but this wasn't any normal wedding day.

There was a killer on the loose.

And a cold-case killer who might try to make a return visit.

This obviously wouldn't be a dream-come-true wedding. But he had to stay focused on Adam. The wedding would help him keep custody.

He hoped.

There was a tap at the door, and Dylan figured that the justice of the peace had arrived. So, it was time. Which was good because his doubts were growing by leaps and bounds. It was best to get this over before he did something stupid such as change his mind.

"Come in," he offered.

The door opened, and Millie stepped inside. "I want to talk to you."

Oh, man. He didn't like the sound of that, and he didn't have to guess what she wanted to discuss. "Is the J.P. here yet?" Because if so, their conversation would have to wait.

"No. He just called. He's running a little late." Millie shut the door behind her and leaned against it as if blocking his path. "Dylan, are you sure about going through with this wedding?"

He buttoned his jacket so no one would be able to see his gun. "I want to keep custody of Adam."

"There has to be another way."

Since her comment had a hint of desperation to it, Dylan couldn't help but think back to the conversation he'd had with Collena that morning. Was Millie obsessed with him in some way? He'd known Millie all her life, since they were practically the same age. He was thirty-two—Millie, thirty-one. They'd been raised together, more like brother and sister than the nanny's daughter and the ranch owner's son. He studied her eyes, her expression, even her body language, but the only thing he saw was an old friend concerned about his well-being.

Of course, people wore masks.

"You don't know Collena," Millie continued. "You could wait and see what Curtis Reese is going to do. Who knows, he might change his mind and withdraw his petition for custody."

"You know something I don't?" Dylan asked.

"No. But people do that. They change. They do what's right. He might decide that Adam is better off with you."

"I'm not going to hold my breath waiting for that," Dylan mumbled. He went to the closet and rifled through one of the dresser drawers until he found something he rarely wore—his cuff links. It took him a few moments to get them into place.

When he turned around, Millie was right in front of him. Mere inches away.

Staring at him.

"Please," she said, trying to blink back tears. She wasn't successful. "Don't do this."

Dylan got a really bad feeling about her reaction. He stepped out of the closet. "What's this all about?"

"I'm scared," she whispered. Her bottom lip began to tremble. "What if this time the killer goes after you? What if it's your car that catches on fire? What if you're the next one who dies?"

As chilling as that was, Dylan actually relaxed a bit at the realization that it could happen. Because he'd much rather a killer come after him than Collena or Adam. Besides, he welcomed such a confrontation. He'd wanted to confront this SOB for years.

There was another knock at the door, followed by Hank's somber voice. "The justice of the peace is here," he announced. "Everybody's gathering in the family room, just like you wanted."

That was Dylan's cue to get moving. First, though, he used his thumb to wipe the tears off Millie's cheek. "Everything will be okay," he promised.

And he would do everything humanly possible to make sure he kept that promise.

With Millie by his side, Dylan went into the corridor where Hank was waiting. Hank shot him a questioning glance, and even though the man didn't voice his objection to these nuptials, the argument was there in the depths of his aged eyes.

Dylan ignored it but encountered more questioning stares as soon as he stepped into the family room and saw Ruth. The nanny was standing just inside the arched double doorway. She cast her daughter a glance, and Millie shook her head, apparently letting her mother know that she had not succeeded in talking him out of this.

With Hank, Millie, Ruth and even the sour-looking justice of the peace, the energy in the family room was tense.

Until he spotted Collena.

Holding Adam in her arms, she stood by the floor-to-ceiling white limestone fireplace, a mesquite fire flickering in the hearth. Collena wore a straight-cut pale green dress that landed just above her knees. Adam wore a dark blue one-piece corduroy suit.

Unlike the others, Adam wasn't somber. He was playing a modified peekaboo game with Collena. Collena was reciprocating with the game, but Dylan figured her efforts were an attempt to cover her nerves.

Then, she turned and looked at him.

Dylan hadn't anticipated the reaction he would have when he saw her face. She wasn't so pale this afternoon. There was a peachy tone to her skin, and that color was deepened on her mouth.

For just a moment, he forgot the marriage was a pretense.

For just a moment, he forgot how to breathe.

Man, Collena was beautiful. Definitely not the fragile pale waif that had fainted outside the stables. This was a woman with warmth, substance, and his gut reaction was intensified by the fact that she held his son so lovingly in her arms.

He went to her, and Collena leaned in to whisper in his ear. "You look ready for the firing squad," she joked.

Dylan appreciated her attempt to keep things light, but the whisper and even the joke felt too intimate. A glance around the room told him that the others had interpreted it as intimate, as well.

That couldn't happen.

He wasn't ready to concede that Hank, Millie or Ruth was a cold-blooded killer, but all three could gossip. If word got out that he was indeed attracted to his soon-to-be wife, then the killer might be tempted to come out of hiding. And go after not him but Collena. It was best to keep his lust hidden away, and that hiding started right here, right now. Then he could make sure the word got out that this was a marriage of convenience, just in case the killer thought this was real.

"Let's get this done," Dylan said to Martin Caldwell, the J.P. The short, round-bellied man gave his thick bifocals an adjustment and opened a leather folder that contained the license and other paperwork.

The J.P. glanced at both of them from over the top of his glasses. "Do you, Dylan Greer, and you, Collena Drake, assent to a mutual agreement to take each other as marital spouses?"

There it was. Dry as dust. Practically sterile. Just what Dylan had requested.

"I do," Dylan quickly answered.

Collena followed suit. "I do."

Adam tried to repeat the two words, his attempt causing them to smile. Again, it felt intimate.

"Will you exchange rings?" the J.P. asked.

"No," he and Collena said in unison. No ring. No symbol that this was a real marriage.

The J.P. glanced around the room. "Are there any objections to this union?"

With the most intense glare he could manage, Dylan dared them to object. All three stayed quiet.

"Then, I, Martin Caldwell, justice of the peace in the state of Texas, act in my official capacity in pronouncing you to be husband and wife." He looked at Dylan. "If you're going to kiss her, now's the time to do it."

"No kiss," Dylan mumbled. Though it suddenly seemed like something he wanted to do. He pushed that desire aside.

Ruth started crying. Millie stared at them as if they'd done the most horrific thing she'd ever witnessed. Hank just stared at the window.

Dylan glanced at Collena to see how she was holding up. She, too, looked a little shell-shocked, but he couldn't soothe her, not even in a friendly sort of way. He didn't want his feelings misinterpreted.

"Jonah's back," Hank announced. He left the window and headed for the front door to let the deputy in.

Collena groaned softly.

Dylan shared her sentiment. He thanked the justice of the peace, handed him some cash, and then he and Collena signed the marriage license.

With each stroke of the pen, Dylan couldn't help but wonder if he'd sealed their fate.

The J.P. headed out just as Jonah entered the family room.

"This better be important," Dylan commented.

Jonah didn't even acknowledge that he'd just walked

in on a wedding ceremony. Or maybe, with the mood in the room, he simply wasn't aware of it. "Don't look at me like that," Jonah snarled. "You think I enjoy coming back out here? I don't. This is business."

Dylan was afraid of that, and he knew that if the business required a personal trip to the ranch, it couldn't be good news.

"First of all, Curtis Reese is staying at the hotel in town. Y'all already know that. But what you don't know is that he filed a harassment complaint against the two of you because someone left a threatening message on the phone in his room."

"You mean, a message like the one left on the two guest-room phones?" Collena asked.

"Identical," Jonah confirmed. "Obviously, someone had too much time on their hands."

Dylan hoped that was all there was to it. A prank. But he didn't believe that.

Dylan's breath streamed out in frustration. "You drove out here to tell us this?"

"No. I drove out here because our fax machine's on the fritz, and the sheriff said that Collena needs to take a look at these two pictures right away."

Collena took the first photo that Jonah handed her, and both she and Dylan studied the grainy shot. Even with the lack of clarity, Dylan had no trouble seeing the tall, dark-haired man in the center of the photo.

"The camera in the ATM of the bank in town snapped the pictures," Jonah explained. "The bank manager saw 'em this morning and got suspicious since he'd never seen the man before. So, how about it, Collena, do you recognize him?"

She nodded. Then nodded again. The motion was choppy, as was her breath. "That's Rodney Harmon."

Dylan cursed. That meant the escaped felon was close. Too close. And they didn't need this complication on top of everything else.

"You're sure that's Harmon?" Jonah asked Collena.

"Positive."

Jonah looked past her and fixed his attention on Dylan. "Harmon was obviously in town just a few hours ago. I'm betting he's still there."

That meant they had a killer bearing down on them. "You said there were two pictures?"

"Yeah." Jonah didn't add anything for several seconds. Then he took the second photo from beneath his arm and gave it to Collena.

It was another picture of Rodney Harmon, but this one was clearer because he was closer to the ATM camera. In fact, the man was staring directly into the camera as if he had known this recorded image would make its way to Collena.

And it had.

In his hands, Rodney Harmon was holding up a hand-scrawled cardboard sign that was as clear as the sneer on the man's face. The words on the sign hit Dylan like a fist.

"Collena, are you ready to die?"

Chapter 9

Years earlier, before her idea of romance had turned sour, Collena had often dreamed of her wedding night. What she hadn't included in that dream was a loveless marriage and a monster out to kill her.

Added to that, both the groom and she were armed with semiautomatics and would be indefinitely, until the danger had passed.

However, there were some pluses to this particular wedding night. Well, one anyway. She and Dylan were going to spend the night in the nursery alongside Adam. With Rodney Harmon's latest death threat and with the uncertain motives of those in Dylan's household, it seemed the reasonable and cautious thing to do.

Unfortunately, when they had come up with the sleeping arrangement, Collena had failed to grasp the full impact of staying in the same room with Dylan. Alone, with a sleeping toddler.

Close quarters probably weren't a bright idea with the attraction brewing between them. Still, there weren't many options, and keeping Adam safe was their top priority.

"I had this moved from one of the guest rooms," Dylan whispered as he motioned toward the double bed with the wrought-iron headboard. "Let's hope it's comfortable."

Collena eyed the bed and the stack of bedding they'd taken from the linen closet. Then, she eyed Dylan in his hot jeans and a chest-hugging black tee. Nope. Neither the bed, nor her husband would make this situation comfortable.

"I doubt I'll get much sleep anyway." Collena kept her voice as soft as possible so she wouldn't wake Adam. Her little boy had had a long day and needed his rest.

"Try," Dylan insisted. "Neither of us will be much good to Adam if we're dead tired."

She nodded because he was right. That didn't mean, however, that sleep was going to happen.

Especially if they were in the same bed.

Since they hadn't specifically discussed the sleeping arrangements, Collena stood there and waited to see what Dylan planned to do. From across the mattress, her eyes met his. Even in the dimly lit room, she could see what he was thinking.

There was heat stirring in those eyes. Thankfully, there was also concern. Maybe the concern would win out.

"I can sleep on the floor," he suggested.

"Or we can put pillows between us."

Silence followed, a long, uncomfortable silence where they just stared at each other. "Pillows," he finally agreed after glancing at the floor.

Collena picked up the sheet, unfolded it, and they began to make the bed. "The security company delivered extra motion-activated monitors this afternoon like the one over there," he explained, hitching his thumb at the thin monitor mounted on the wall near Adam's changing table. "They'll pick up movement outside the house. I figured it'd help if everyone in the house was keeping an eye on the grounds."

Yes, it would help. Unless someone in the house was the one to watch for. "And you said something about having someone monitor the security system?"

"I hired a pair of P.I.s who'll be on monitor duty and act as backup if we need it. They're working out of my office for now, but tomorrow, they'll move into the other guest room just in case this situation lasts for a while."

In other words if Rodney Harmon stormed onto the ranch with guns blazing, there'd be at least four of them to stop him. She hoped that was enough, because Collena was a hundred percent certain that Harmon would try to come after her.

It was only a matter of time.

Unless the cops could catch him first.

Collena gave Adam a soft kiss on the cheek and walked back to the bed. Dylan did the same. Neither of them took off their shoes, and both were fully clothed.

They just stood there side by side and stared down at the bed.

"This is ridiculous," Collena whispered. "We're adults. We can sleep in the same bed. This is all for Adam."

That was the nudge that Dylan needed, because he climbed into bed. Collena got in, as well. And once again, the silence returned.

"My lawyer is still doing a thorough background check on you," Dylan whispered. "He wants to know if there's anything in your past that Curtis Reese will be able to use against us during the custody fight."

"I've already told you the things he can and will use. My upbringing, my mother's profession and the undercover assignment that resulted in Adam being stolen."

"What about lovers other than your fiancé? Curtis Reese will use whatever he can," Dylan added when she didn't immediately answer.

It took her several moments to answer. "Other than Sean Reese, I was involved with only one other man. That was…let's see, when I was twenty."

"That's it?" he asked.

"That's it."

He shook his head and gave a lopsided smile of irony. "We're some pair, aren't we? I gave up on love when it became deadly. You apparently gave up on it before you even got started."

Collena mumbled an agreement and wished that she didn't feel anything down deep within her. Because it only made her feel closer to Dylan. Despite their starkly different pasts, they had a lot in common.

Including this troubling attraction.

She wondered if she should address it or, better yet,

try to dismiss it. If they talked about it, it might make things worse.

She looked at him again. He hadn't covered up so she still had an incredible view of him. Her eyes went in the wrong direction, traveling the entire length of his body. She even paused in the zipper region, the last place she should be looking. And when she forced her gaze to stop traveling and looked up at Dylan again, she realized he was watching her gawk at him.

Collena waited for embarrassment to flush her cheeks, but it didn't come. She wanted it to come. Because if not, she would look brazen.

She certainly felt brazen.

Worse, Dylan looked it, too. That wasn't a back-off vibe passing between them.

"To hell with this," Dylan grumbled a split second before he slid his hand around the back of her neck and dragged her to him.

It happened so fast that his mouth was on her before Collena realized what was happening. Even then, she had a stupid reaction. Instead of planting her hands on his chest and pushing him away, she heard herself moan a hungry sound of pleasure, and she slung her arms around his neck.

Oh, mercy. He looked good, but he tasted even better. And it'd been a long, long time since she'd kissed a man who knew exactly what he was doing.

The kiss quickly turned hotter. Of course, it'd started out so hot that she was amazed it could get better. Still, she didn't stop it. She deepened it, letting their tongues mate, letting him nip her bottom lip with his teeth.

There was a sharp rap at the door. That was the

only warning they got before it opened. They untangled themselves from each other, but not before their visitors saw what was going on. It was Ruth, and Hank was directly behind her.

With everything going on, they'd obviously forgotten to lock the door.

"Oh." Ruth's hand flew to her mouth.

Collena didn't even try to offer an explanation. It would be useless, because she figured she looked well kissed. There was no way to disguise that.

"Is there a problem?" Dylan asked.

Hank nodded. "Millie's not feeling good—she's got one of her migraines. Ruth and I are going to drive her to the emergency room."

Dylan got up from the bed. "Is there anything I can do to help?"

"No. We'll leave just as soon as Millie's dressed." But Hank didn't move. He stood there and scratched his head. "I was in your office checking on those private detectives, and I saw the report about the fingerprints."

Collena froze, and that question cooled the rest of her passion. "What fingerprints?"

"The ones from the newspaper that you say you found outside your door," Ruth provided. She glared at Dylan. "You didn't trust me when I told you I had nothing to do with putting it there."

"I simply wanted to know whose fingerprints were on it." He turned to Collena. "In addition to a lot of smudges, there were prints from Hank, Millie and Ruth."

"Because we all read that article of lies when it was published five years ago," Hank insisted.

Dylan conceded that with a nod. "I also wanted to check and see if Jonah's prints were there."

"Jonah?" Ruth's hand went to her mouth again. "You think he's doing something to scare off Collena?"

"I don't know. But if so, the newspaper won't help prove that because his prints weren't on it."

"Jonah could have worn gloves," Hank suggested.

Collena silently agreed. In fact, as a police officer, Jonah would have taken steps to cover his tracks.

"What about security surveillance cameras?" Collena asked, wishing she'd thought of it before. She certainly wasn't putting her cop's training to good use.

Dylan shook his head. "That night, I didn't have cameras in the corridors. They only went in today. I'm having the security company install them in all the halls and the common areas."

"If Jonah's behind this," Ruth speculated, "then the cameras probably won't help because he's probably already heard about them. Besides, I doubt he'll be planting any more newspapers."

"What's this about Jonah?" Millie asked. She was squinting, apparently in severe pain.

Millie's posture, however, didn't stop her from looking at Dylan and then Collena. Like her mother and grandfather, Millie probably knew that she and Dylan had just kissed.

"Let's go," Ruth said, gripping her daughter's arm.

Even when the women walked away, Hank still didn't move. "I know I'm not one to give advice," Hank whispered, "but you two should stay away from each other. And you should watch your backs. It's a small town, and it doesn't take long for news to travel. Especially bad news."

"Are you trying to tell me something I don't already know, Hank?" Dylan asked.

"I'm trying to save your *bride's* life. You should get her out of here, Dylan. Send her far away. If not, you're going to have another death on your hands."

Dylan sat in his office and stared at the paperwork he needed to be doing. But instead of business, he was thinking about Collena.

They'd shared a restless night in the nursery. Restless, because of the kiss they'd shared. And because of their intense attraction. Hank's warning hadn't helped, either.

Unfortunately, it wouldn't necessarily be safer anywhere else for Collena and Adam. At least with them at the ranch Dylan could personally keep an eye on them. Besides, he and Collena needed to be physically together under the same roof, living as a family, so that it'd help them keep custody.

He checked the security monitor on his desk. It was a split screen that featured the north pasture, the front porch and the playroom where Adam, Collena and Ruth were.

Collena was wearing jeans and a loose red top. While Adam was playing with a toy horse, she stood and went to the window. She was no doubt checking to make sure all was well.

Even on the monitor, he could see that Collena was tired. And beautiful. He couldn't stop his brain from registering that part about her beauty, and it was futile to try. That reckless kiss had sealed his fate. He wanted to kiss her again. He wanted to hold her.

Dylan wanted her in his bed.

Regrettably, she felt the same. Every inch of him was aware of that. Which brought him to the next matter that wouldn't leave his mind. How the hell were they going to keep their hands off each other?

His phone buzzed, and because he needed a change of thought, Dylan quickly glanced at the caller ID. The caller's identity and number were blocked. Dylan answered it anyway.

"Greer," the caller snarled. "It's Curtis Reese."

Dylan instantly went on the defensive. "What do you want?"

"You mean, other than my grandson? I want your butt in jail for making that threatening phone call to my hotel room. That's harassment, Greer."

"That's paranoia, because I didn't call you."

"I don't believe you. And I don't believe this ridiculous pretense of marriage that you have with Collena."

"You know about that?" Dylan was surprised, though he shouldn't be. He knew that, eventually, Curtis would find out.

"Of course, I know. It's all over town. At lunch, that's all the waitress at the diner could talk about. Love at first sight, she said. That's what people in town believe. But you and I know better, don't we? There's no love in that charade of a marriage."

Dylan groaned. *Love at first sight.* That was not what he wanted people in Greer to be discussing. "You probably set the waitress straight, huh?"

"I didn't say a word to her. If the town wants to believe you married Collena for love, then let them. A judge will see it for what it is—a desperate attempt by two desperate people who aren't fit to raise a child."

Dylan detected some movement in the doorway, and he looked up and spotted Collena. That top and jeans looked even better in person.

It's Curtis Reese, Dylan mouthed.

She rolled her eyes and sighed.

"Unless you plan to drop this custody suit," Dylan told the man, "then any future calls should go through my lawyer. If not, I'll consider them harassment."

Dylan hung up, but he knew it wasn't the last he'd hear from Curtis.

"He's going to do everything he can to make our lives miserable," Collena said. She walked closer and looked down at him. "Ruth said a friend of a friend called to say that everyone in town is talking about us."

So, there it was—confirmed gossip. Curtis hadn't been just blowing smoke. "I heard."

She made a sound deep in her throat and stood there, almost stoically, but Dylan knew this information was causing a firestorm inside her.

"Maybe the person who killed your sister and fiancée is long gone." Her voice was a little unsteady, and she sank down onto the edge of his desk.

Because she looked as weary as he felt, Dylan stood and pulled her into his arms. Yes, it was stupid. Reckless, even. But it didn't seem to matter. To the town of Greer, they were a couple, and that news would likely get back to a killer.

If there was a killer.

Maybe, just maybe, fate would decide that both of

them had already been through enough, and the person responsible for the deaths was either already locked away for other crimes or else dead. Dylan didn't care which; he just wanted the person away from Collena and Adam.

"You want a drink to steady your nerves?" he asked.

She shook her head. "I don't drink. I have a low tolerance for alcohol." She pulled back and met his gaze. "Besides, with so much going on, I should keep a clear head."

"I agree."

But he kissed her anyway.

It was worse than the kiss the night before because this one came naturally. It was as if he'd kissed her a thousand times. Too bad that feeling didn't satiate the fire growing inside him.

He stopped, ran his tongue over his lips and was pleased to taste her there.

"I'll bet you're going to remind me that kissing you is a mistake," he said.

She shook her head. "No, but I should remind myself." Collena reached out and smoothed her hand over his face. "Maybe we knew each other in a past life or something. Maybe that's why we feel so connected."

Surprised and amused, he flexed his eyebrows. "You believe in past lives?"

"Not really. But I've gone through all the logical answers and have moved on to the illogical ones to explain why I'm so attracted to you. I want to have sex with you." She wagged her index finger at him to stop him from jumping on that. "It wasn't an invitation."

Dylan knew that. She was fighting this as much as

he was. And, like him, she was failing. Still, it was easier to think of the attraction than the other realities that were nipping at their heels.

"We could just try it," he offered, tongue-in-cheek. "Maybe we'd suck in bed together."

"Suck," she repeated, flexing her eyebrows. "You know it wouldn't suck. It would probably be the best experience I've ever had, and it would do all sorts of things to remind me that I'm a woman."

"You don't like to be reminded of that?" he asked, serious now.

"Let's just say that, as a woman, I've made choices that weren't always good. So, I'm trying to think more like a mother and more like a cop."

"Cops and mothers can still have sex."

She frowned at his smile and used her fingers to draw down the corners of his mouth. The heat rifled through his body. And he instantly wanted more. With her touching his face. With them so close that all he had to do was reach out, pull her to him and kiss her again.

But Collena put an end to that short fantasy. She moved away from him and went to the French doors that led to the side yard and pasture. Her maneuver didn't mean this discussion was over. Far from it. The attraction wasn't going away and, sooner or later, they'd have to address it.

"Adam is amazing," Collena said with her back to him. "When he wakes up from his afternoon nap, I thought maybe the three of us could do something together."

"I'd like that." In fact, that felt as inviting as the whole idea of having sex with Collena.

And that meant he was in serious trouble here.

Collena glanced at him over her shoulder. There was a hint of a smile on her face.

The moment seemed to freeze.

Dylan sensed that something was wrong a split second too late.

A bullet crashed through the glass panes of the French doors.

Chapter 10

The sound of the shot registered in Collena's head just as Dylan and she drove to the floor.

It was just in time, because the next bullet shattered the glass right in front of where she'd been standing.

The adrenaline was quick, hitting her hard and causing her blood pressure and heart rate to spike. She didn't have her gun. She'd left it in her room when she went to spend time with Adam.

That could turn out to be a fatal mistake.

Because someone wanted them dead. Rodney Harmon, probably. He'd found her, and this time, he'd come to deliver on that promise to kill her.

Dylan scrambled to the side and took her with him. He also put himself in between those bullets and her body. It was admirable. Heroic, even. But she wanted to throttle him for nearly getting himself killed to save her.

"My gun's in the desk drawer," he said. His breath was rough.

Collena knew what that meant—the desk drawer was in the line of fire. Whoever was shooting at them would be able to hit Dylan or her if they went after the gun.

The same was true f they tried to get to the door that led to the corridor.

They were trapped.

There was another shot. Then another. Both tore through the thick glass and sent it spewing across the room. Collena ducked down and sheltered her eyes to prevent being hit.

"Where's your phone?" she asked.

He shook his head. "On the desk."

Both of them cursed. Someone had to get to the phone. They had to warn Ruth to keep Adam safe and they had to call the sheriff. Of course, someone in the house had likely heard the shots by now. After all, the two P.I.s were in a guest room that they'd converted to an office. Maybe the sheriff was already on the way.

Or Jonah, if the sheriff had sent him again instead.

And that caused Collena's heart rate to spike even more. If Rodney Harmon was indeed out there shooting at them, she didn't think Jonah would do much to deter him.

Two more bullets slammed through the door, each of them taking huge bites out of the wood. Splinters and glass pelted them.

"The gunman's closer," Dylan said.

Collena lifted her head and listened. The next shot confirmed that.

The gunman was moving toward the house. Toward their son.

Oh, God.

The shooter was armed with a high-powered rifle and might start firing into the nursery where Adam was napping.

"I have to get my gun and phone," Dylan informed her. He started to move, but she latched on to his arm.

"It'd be suicide. We need some kind of diversion."

Collena glanced around the room, looking for something—anything—while the gunman continued to blast through the French doors. They didn't have much time. The shots were getting closer, and there wouldn't be much of the doors left as a barrier once the gunman made it to them.

"Throw anything you can get your hands on at the French doors," Dylan ordered.

Collena considered his plan. It wasn't much of a diversion, but it was the only one they had. She prayed it would work, and she grabbed the pillows from the cozy chairs next to the fireplace.

"Now," Dylan said.

She hurled the first pillow at the door and quickly followed it with another. Collena didn't stop there. She stood and grabbed the items from the mantel. Pictures, flowers and even a heavy brass horse figurine all flew in the direction of the doors. Hopefully, she was creating a visual barrier for Dylan.

But the gunman didn't stop.

At a furious, almost frantic pace, the bullets began to rip through the house.

Dylan sprang into action. With the objects flying

through the air, he dove toward his desk, landing amid the glass, splinters and debris.

Collena pushed her concern and fear for him aside and started to throw the books from the side shelves that flanked the fireplace. When she saw Dylan reach up, she knew he was at the most vulnerable point of this plan to retrieve his gun and phone. She had to do something more.

But what?

Out of the corner of her eye, she saw Dylan make his move to the desk. Collena looked up and spotted the painting over the fireplace. It was the only thing within her reach that was large enough to do any good. She ripped it from the wall, and while Dylan lifted his head to grab what he needed, she stuck out the painting and tried to use it as a barrier.

A shot tore through the canvas.

"Hurry!" she shouted to Dylan.

There wasn't much left of the glass, but there was enough wood in the door frame to pose a significant risk to both of them. But it wasn't nearly as big a risk as not getting the phone and his gun. They needed the items to keep Adam safe.

Dylan grabbed both from the desk and dove back toward the fireplace. Collena dropped the shredded picture and took his cell phone. Dylan rattled off the number to her so she could call the line in the nursery and playroom. A line that Ruth should have answered.

She didn't.

That did it. Collena went from being afraid to being terrified. Her son had to be all right.

She tried the number again, while the bullets continued to riddle the house. Dylan called out a new set of numbers, and Collena frantically pressed them in.

Ina, the cook, finally answered.

"What's going on? What's that noise?" the woman shouted. "Is somebody shootin' at us?"

"Yes. Stay down and try to let Ruth know what's happening so she can keep Adam away from the windows."

"I will. I already called Sheriff Hathaway and told him to get himself out here."

Thank God. But Collena immediately rethought that. "Is he bringing Jonah?"

"No. He said Jonah wasn't there so he said he'd come himself. He called in the night-shift deputy who's supposed to meet him here."

That was good. *If* they made it in time.

"Try to check on Adam," Collena instructed. "And let the two P.I.s know what's going on. Just don't come into Dylan's office. Don't even get near the door. Because that's where Dylan and I are pinned down, and it's where the gunman is shooting."

Collena ended the call so she could keep the line open in case the sheriff tried to phone them.

Dylan inched toward the gaping holes in the French doors, took a quick look and then pulled back.

"I don't see anyone," he relayed to her.

That meant the gunman was likely using the outbuildings as cover. But it didn't explain how the person had gotten there in the first place. The security monitors should have detected the movement. Or the P.I.s should have spotted someone skulking across the property. Did that mean the system had malfunctioned?

Or had someone tampered with it?

There was a lull in the shooting, and Dylan levered himself up to get a better look. Collena saw him stiffen, and he took aim.

He fired.

So did the shooter.

The bullet came so close to him that Collena could practically feel it. It slammed into the far wall near the corridor door.

Dylan started to fire again, but Collena pulled him back. It was a good thing, too, because the next barrage of bullets pelted the room, hitting everything in their path.

Collena scrambled to the corner, using the thick stone fireplace as cover—the bullets couldn't penetrate that. She also kept a firm grip on Dylan's arm and tried to prevent him from attempting to return fire. While she wanted him to do that for Adam's sake, she knew it was simply too big a risk to take. She had to hold on to the hope that the nursery was out of the gunman's reach.

They had to make sure it stayed that way.

"The sheriff will be here soon," she reminded him. And herself. She silently repeated it like a mantra.

Her heartbeat was so loud in her ears that it took her a moment to realize she was hearing the sound of a siren. Hopefully, from the sheriff's squad car.

Dylan looked at her. His eyes were wide and vigilant. And then he cursed.

Because the shots stopped.

"The gunman's getting away," Dylan insisted. He tried to rear up, but again Collena restrained him.

"You can't go out there," she warned. "It could be an ambush."

"He could be going after Adam."

That realization was like a knife to her heart.

With their gazes locked, she released the grip she had on him and got to her feet, as well. "Not outside," she whispered. "We can go through the corridors and get to the nursery."

Of course, that didn't mean the gunman wasn't waiting for them to do just that. The person could have a rifle aimed at the one spot that they would try to get to: the corridor door.

"We can dive behind the desk and use it as cover," Dylan suggested. But he didn't just suggest it. He dove, landing behind the thick oak that would hopefully shield him from any more bullets.

Collena was about to start her own dive when she heard the sound.

A sound that stopped her heart—breaking glass.

And it came from the other side of the house.

"Adam," Dylan whispered. He had to get to his son. Because that sound could mean the gunman was breaking into the nursery.

"Go!" Collena shouted to him.

Dylan did. He didn't wait for Collena, and prayed she could stay out of the line of fire. Instead, he crawled to the door, opened it and scurried into the corridor. Once there, he got to his feet and started racing toward the nursery.

He checked over his shoulder and saw that Collena wasn't too far behind him. She wasn't armed, and he couldn't take the time to find her a weapon. Every second was crucial.

There was another crash. Not a bullet. More broken glass. It'd probably come from a window where someone was trying to break in.

Dylan ran faster, and it seemed as if the siren from the sheriff's car got louder with each running step he took. He didn't even pause when he got to the nursery. Dylan threw open the door.

Adam was sleeping in his crib. There was no broken glass anywhere.

Behind him, he heard his cell phone ring, and Collena answered it as she ducked into the nursery with him.

"It's the sheriff," she relayed to him. "He spotted someone running away from the house, and he's going in pursuit."

Well, that was a start, but it wouldn't do squat for them if the gunman backtracked. "Lock the door," he told Collena. "Move the crib away from the windows and to the corner of the room."

She immediately began to do as he asked. "Where's Ruth?"

"I don't know." But he intended to find out. For now, he took up watch by one of the trio of floor-to-ceiling windows in the nursery.

Once Collena had moved the crib, she grabbed the security monitor from the changing table and began to flip through the various camera angles.

"Do you see anything?" Dylan asked. Because from the window, he didn't see either the sheriff or the shooter.

"The entire screen is nothing but static."

Dylan cursed again. He didn't think that was a coincidence. And while he was thinking, he tried to put a name to the person who'd just tried to kill them.

Rodney Harmon, probably.

But he wasn't about to rule out anyone just yet. "Call Ina," Dylan instructed. "Find out where everyone is and if they're safe."

He watched, waiting, as Collena made the call. She kept her voice low, practically at a whisper, so she wouldn't wake Adam.

"Ina's okay," she said several moments later. "But she's alone in the kitchen. She doesn't know where anyone else is."

That was not what Dylan wanted to hear. Even if Ruth, Millie and Hank were nowhere to be found, at least the two P.I.s should have heard something from the guest suite where they'd set up their office. But thankfully, he heard something that he welcomed. Sheriff Hathaway's voice.

"Dylan, it's me—don't shoot."

Dylan opened the window as the sheriff approached the exterior of the house. "Please tell me you got the gunman."

The lanky, sandy-haired sheriff still had his gun drawn, and he was still darting glances all around him. He shook his head. "Afraid not. I didn't even get a good look at him. The person was dressed all in black and was wearing a ski mask."

Hell. "Could it have been Rodney Harmon?"

"Coulda been anybody." He tipped his head toward the back porch. "I'm coming in through the kitchen. Stay put until I've had a chance to look around."

Dylan welcomed the help because he didn't want

to leave Adam and Collena until he was sure that it was safe.

He kept guard at the window and listened for any sound to indicate that an intruder was in the house.

And then he saw Ruth.

The woman was coming out of one of the barns. She was dressed in her pants and a sweater top, but she wasn't wearing a coat. Maybe she'd heard the gunfire and hidden there. But if so, why hadn't she tried to get to Adam? That should have been her first priority, even above her own safety.

"If Rodney Harmon is behind this, he won't stop," he heard Collena say.

Dylan glanced back at her. She was standing guard over the crib, but she was also looking out one of the other windows. She'd seen Ruth, as well.

"*If* he's behind this," Dylan clarified. But he couldn't be positive that he was.

Too many things had gone wrong since Collena's arrival, and while it was true that Harmon wanted to kill her, Dylan couldn't rule out that someone else might have been responsible for this shooting.

"It's me—Sheriff Hathaway," said a voice from the other side of the door.

With his gun still ready, Dylan went to the door and opened it.

"No sign of a gunman inside," the sheriff volunteered. "But someone not only shot out the doors in your office, they shot the windows in the dining room. And those two guys in that room at the end of the hall have been drugged or something. They're knocked out cold, and there's an empty pizza box sitting on the coffee table."

The pizza they'd had delivered just an hour earlier.

"Ina says there's something wonky with your security system," the sheriff continued. His attention went to Collena. "Here's what I think happened. About two minutes before I got Ina's call about the shooting here, I got a call from Marla Jenkins's boy. He was supposed to be delivering pizza out here, but he says someone sneaked up behind him and hit him with something. A shovel, he thinks. Next thing he knew he was tied up and shut in the Dumpster outside the pizza place."

"You think the man who delivered the pizza was Rodney Harmon?" Collena asked. Adam stirred, and Collena tried to soothe him by rubbing his back. Dylan wished he could do something to soothe her because Collena was pale again, and her hands were trembling.

"I think that's a strong possibility."

Dylan processed that, and he didn't come to a good conclusion. "If it was Harmon, then why didn't he just shoot his way in when the P.I.s opened the door? Why would he sneak onto the property posing as a delivery man, only to then walk at least two hundred yards away before he started shooting?"

The sheriff lifted his shoulder. "I don't have an answer for that." He studied Dylan. "But I'm guessing you might have some idea?"

He did, but he didn't have time to voice it before he heard footsteps. The sheriff turned, but immediately relaxed. "It's Ruth."

Collena moved protectively in front of Adam.

"Is the trouble over?" Ruth asked. She peered past the sheriff and looked at Dylan.

"Where were you?" Dylan asked, and he was certain it sounded just the way he meant it—as an accusation.

Ruth drew back her shoulders. "Outside, checking on that new mare. I stayed there and hid when I heard the shots. Why?"

"Are you willing to let the sheriff test you for gunshot residue?"

Her mouth dropped open. "What are you saying, Dylan? Do you think I'm responsible for what happened?"

He shook his head. "I don't know, but I know I can't risk having you here."

"What's going on, Mother?" Millie asked from the corridor. Several moments later, she joined Ruth and stood side by side with her. Both of them stared accusingly at Dylan.

Ruth didn't answer her daughter, but Dylan did. "I think it's best if you, Ruth and Hank move to the hotel in town for a while. Until we can get all of this straightened out."

"What's to straighten out?" Ruth asked. She fired a nasty glance at Collena. "You're responsible for this. You've been trying to come between Dylan and me since you stepped foot in this house."

"I only want to make sure Adam is safe," Collena answered.

"No. You don't want to share Dylan or Adam with anyone. Especially with me." With each word, the anger in her voice climbed, and Dylan could see a vein bulging on her neck. "I raised Dylan. He's as much a son to me as if I'd given birth to him. That doesn't mean I can't see when he's making a mistake."

"Let's go, Mother," Millie said, taking Ruth's arm.

But Ruth held her ground and glared at Collena. Dylan stepped between them so he could make eye contact with Ruth. "This isn't Collena's fault. I'm the one who wants you to move out."

"I'll never believe that. She's just like your sister— can't you see that? Demanding. Manipulating. Always trying to have you to herself."

Dylan felt himself freeze. "What did you say?"

Ruth stilled, and she frantically shook her head. "Nothing."

Millie tried to pull Ruth out of the room, but Dylan stopped both women. However, he directed his question to Ruth. "Do you know something about my sister's death?"

"She knows nothing," Hank said. He was in the corridor, just behind the sheriff. "And this conversation is over."

Hank brushed past the sheriff and grabbed both women by their arms.

Millie looked back at Dylan. "I need to tell you something."

"Talking time is over," Hank declared. And he hurried Millie out the door before she could say anything else.

Chapter 11

Collena glanced around her suite and made sure everything was checked off her mental list. They'd decided to stay in her suite rather than Dylan's because there were fewer windows and because his had French doors that led to an outside patio.

The crib was in place—tucked in the corner of the bedroom away from any windows and doors. Since it was already close to midnight, Adam was sound asleep, resting beneath a pale blue blanket, with his favorite stuffed horse snuggled against his chest.

All the windows were locked and the curtains drawn. Collena had checked that; so had Dylan and the two P.I.s. The security system was set for the interior and the perimeter of the ranch. Both she and Dylan were armed, and one of the P.I.s was standing guard outside the suite door to make sure no one got in. The other was in the family room on the other side of the house and would keep watch on the motion-activated security monitor.

In other words, they'd done everything they could to keep Adam and themselves out of harm's way.

It had to be enough.

Because Collena didn't even want to consider the alternative. She couldn't go through another round of shooting. It'd taken ten years off her life when she'd realized that Adam could have been hurt.

However, the shots all seemed to be aimed at Dylan and her. Or maybe the bullets had been meant solely for her and the shooter had been willing to take Dylan out during the process. Either way, it could have been a deadly situation, and they were lucky to be alive.

Collena had taken a long shower once Adam had fallen asleep around eight o'clock. The steamy hot water had helped relax her a little. So had the herbal tea and turkey sandwich that Ina had fixed for her. But Collena wasn't holding out hope that she would get much sleep tonight. She'd be listening for any sound or sign that the gunman had returned for another round.

Dylan was pacing in the sitting room while he talked to the sheriff. It was his sixth call to the man since the shooting. Collena figured there'd be many more but hopefully not tonight. Dylan was exhausted, and it was obvious that nothing was going to be accomplished at this late hour.

"No sign of Rodney Harmon," Dylan said in a whisper to her when he ended the call.

It'd been too much to hope differently. Besides, the security system was fixed now. Or rather, it was now turned on. Shortly before the shooting, someone had apparently disarmed it using the power-supply box located outside the house. Or maybe it had just malfunctioned on its own. Just in case, Dylan had given the box a new lock and had made it tamperproof.

She hoped.

Collena walked toward him. A closer look revealed his sleep-weary eyes and the way stress had tightened the muscles in his face. "What do you think Millie wanted to say before Hank forced her to leave?"

He rubbed his forehead. "I don't know—maybe that her mother is a killer. Ruth certainly let something slip with that comment about my sister."

Yes. Collena had gone over that a hundred times. "It could mean nothing."

"It could mean everything," Dylan countered. He sank down on the foot of the bed. "I'm going to contact their therapist, but it's hard for me to accept that, for all these years, I might have had a killer living beneath my roof."

"I know." Because he looked as if he could use it, she touched his arm and rubbed it gently. "But Rodney Harmon is still our number-one suspect. When he's caught, then you can decide if you want to smooth things over with Ruth and the others. In the meantime, you need to get some rest."

He turned toward her. "You know I'm not leaving this room, right?"

"I know." She didn't want him to leave. As difficult as it would be for them to spend another night together, Collena wanted Dylan close in case something went wrong.

He reached out, hooked his arm around her and

pulled her onto the bed with him. Apparently, he didn't have anything sexual in mind because he simply maneuvered them to the head of the bed so their heads were on the pillows, and then he pulled the side of the comforter over them.

Collena was still dressed in jeans and a loose shirt, but she was also wearing her shoulder holster and weapon. It was digging into her side, so she sat up, slipped it off and put it on the nightstand. In the process of removing the holster, one side of her top slipped off her shoulder. She quickly tried to put it back in place.

But Dylan noticed the scar.

"What happened there?" He traced the still-pink scar with his finger.

"Gunshot wound." She wanted to keep the explanation short, but Dylan questioned her with his stare. "One of the investors at the Brighton Birthing Center was aiming at someone else—another victim—but shot me instead. Don't worry. He's in a maximum-security prison. In addition to shooting me, he was responsible for the death of another woman."

"Did he have any part in what happened to you right after Adam was born?" he asked after a long pause.

"Probably not." She carefully put her gun on the nightstand close enough that she could still reach it. "I think that was all Rodney Harmon."

Anger went through his eyes. "It makes me sick to think that he was even in the same room with you and Adam, and at a time when you were so vulnerable. You'd just given birth, for God's sake, and he used you like a punching bag."

She heard the sympathy in his voice and could see it

in his expression. It had been there since he'd seen that photo taken of her shortly after the attack.

"I know what's going on," she said at the end of a heavy sigh. "You're not really attracted to me. You have this male need to safeguard me. You're a natural protector."

He continued to stare at her. "I wasn't able to protect Julie and Abigail."

"Not from lack of trying." She considered giving Dylan a reassuring hug. But even reassuring hugs could get out of hand. "The need to protect me is now all mixed up with what you think is attraction."

"What I think is attraction," he repeated. There was a dangerous edge to his voice, as if she'd just pushed a button that shouldn't have been pushed.

The air between them changed.

He changed.

That edge slipped into his eyes.

Collena didn't back away. She wasn't afraid of him. But she was afraid of what she'd started. So much for analyzing him and blowing off the attraction.

"Let's test your theory," he said. "Let's see if there's any lust buried beneath all that need to protect you."

And with that, he reached out lightning fast.

He latched onto a handful of her hair and pulled her to him. Before Collena could even catch her breath, Dylan lowered his head and took her mouth as if he owned her.

Of course, Dylan hadn't needed the kiss to prove that lust to him, but he wanted to prove it to Collena. Why, he didn't know. And maybe proving it was simply an excuse to do something he'd been wanting to do for hours. Kiss her. Taste her. Hold her. And then push hard and deep into her until she quit trying to dismiss the attraction between them.

But she wasn't dismissing anything.

From the moment his mouth touched hers, Collena became a willing participant. She kissed him right back. She also lifted her arms, first one, then the other. She slid them around his neck, brushing his chest with her breasts.

The contact only made him want more.

So, he took the kisses to her neck. It was a temporary stopping point, but he lingered a while when he realized it was a sensitive area for Collena. Her fingers began to dig into his back and, with gentle pressure from her palms, she urged him closer.

So Dylan got closer. A lot closer.

Pushing her back onto the bed, he shoved up her top and dropped some kisses on the exposed parts of her breasts. Collena made a sound of raw pleasure and arched against him.

It aligned their bodies, her sex against his. And as if that weren't enough, she slid her hand between them and ran her fingers over his erection.

Dylan lost his breath.

He didn't care if he ever found it.

The attraction and lust turned to a full blazing fire. He wanted her, bad, but he also didn't want to skip any of the things that he'd been fantasizing about. And one of those fantasies had been to strip her naked and kiss every inch of her.

Dylan started by unhooking the front clasp of her bra, spilling her breasts out into his hands. Now, it was his turn to moan as he kissed her and tongued her erect nipples. It was pure pleasure.

And pure torture.

Because each taste of her only made Dylan want her even more.

Still, he continued the kisses, pleasing both her and himself, and he made his way from her breasts to her stomach. He unbuttoned her jeans and slid down the zipper so he could sample the silky area around her navel. It was another sensitive spot. As he gently sucked her, she lifted her hips, offering him more of her.

That's when he knew the jeans had to go.

He peeled them off her and was more than happy to find a tiny swatch of white lace. He could see the triangle of blond hair beneath. And that lace was the only thing standing between him and Collena's sex.

Because he couldn't wait, he tasted her through the lace. That earned him some unspoken praise as Collena wound her fingers into his hair and slipped her legs over his back.

Dylan figured they were on the brink of something incredible.

He figured wrong.

Because that's when it hit him that something was missing.

He lifted his head and cursed. "No condom."

"No condom," she repeated in a whisper. And she repeated it again through her heavy gusts of breath.

"There are some in my bedroom." He got up, fully intending to leave.

But Collena stopped him. "The P.I. is outside the door."

"So?"

"So, you can't go out there with that." She ran her bare foot over the front of his jeans and damn near made him climax in the process.

"Trust me, I can go out there like this." It wouldn't be comfortable, and it'd be a little embarrassing, but at least he and Collena would get to have sex.

Unfortunately, going out there would mean leaving Collena and Adam.

And that wasn't a smart idea.

His body begged to differ, but Dylan offered his body an alternative.

"There's more than one way to go about this," he suggested to Collena. After all, he'd already started in that direction.

"No." She shook her head and tugged her jeans back up. She also redid her bra and lowered her top over her breasts. "We shouldn't even be doing this."

He knew she was right, but he wasn't ready to give up just yet. "Please remind me why."

"Adam might wake up. Also someone is after us. We need to stay focused. Somehow, I don't think we can stay focused if your mouth is...occupied."

She was right again.

Damn her.

"I should have stopped before we got started," she grumbled. "But you got me hot. And I can't think straight when you kiss me."

Dylan was still aching. Well, throbbing actually. But it made him feel marginally better that he'd made her a little crazy. "You're admitting that?"

She nodded. Then, she huffed. "I can't deny the attraction I have for you. Or the way you make me feel. I also can't deny that we'll act on that attraction. Because we probably will. But I have to wonder where sex will lead us. Once the passion is all burned out, we still need to be friends so we can raise Adam together."

He frowned. There was an argument in her logic, and Dylan would have started it, too, if there hadn't been a knock at the door.

Just like that, his heart went into overdrive. He prepared himself for the worst. So did she. Collena grabbed her gun, and Dylan barreled out of the bed to go to the suite door.

"What's wrong?" Dylan asked the P.I. without opening the door.

"The deputy sheriff is here to see you."

Dylan checked his watch. It was nearly twelve-thirty in the morning. "At this hour?"

"He says it's important."

It'd better be. "Wait here with Adam and Collena," Dylan instructed the P.I. Dylan wanted her far away from the deputy, just in case Jonah was a killer and this was some kind of ambush.

With his gun in hand and an angry expression on his face, Dylan stormed toward the front door. He found the other P.I. and Jonah waiting in the foyer. Jonah didn't have his gun drawn, but he had a perturbed expression that, no doubt, matched Dylan's.

"What's this about?" Dylan demanded.

"Business," Jonah snarled back. "There's been a murder, and I need to know if you're the one who committed it."

Chapter 12

Collena glanced at the clock.

And paced.

Dylan had been gone over ten minutes. Not a lifetime, but considering the potential danger that was all around them, it felt like forever to her.

She checked Adam, who was still sleeping. Then Collena opened the door just a fraction to make sure the P.I. was still there. He was.

"Do you know what the deputy wanted with Dylan?" she asked the P.I.

He shook his head.

And that's when Collena knew she'd waited long enough. Deputy Jonah Burke was their suspect, and by now he could have done all sorts of things to Dylan and the other P.I. She grabbed her gun and the baby monitor so she could keep an eye on Adam. She also ordered the P.I. to stay put and guard the baby while she went in search of Dylan.

Collena listened as she hurried down the corridor. There were no shouts, no sounds of violence. Nor was there any indication that Dylan was under attack. And she confirmed that once she made it to the foyer. Dylan was leaning against the wall, and he was staring at Jonah, who was only a few feet away from him.

"What's wrong?" Collena immediately asked. She knew something had happened from their bleak expressions.

"Curtis Reese is dead," Jonah announced. "Someone murdered him."

Her breath clogged in her throat, and though she had a dozen questions about whom, when and how, she couldn't ask any of them. She could only stand there and try to absorb what she'd just heard.

Curtis Reese was dead.

She hated that she felt even marginal relief over the custody issue. But Collena couldn't feel any happiness that a man had been murdered. After all, Curtis might have been a pigheaded snob, but he wasn't a criminal, and he didn't deserve to die.

"A hunter found Reese's body not far from here," Jonah continued. "Only about an eighth of a mile from where your car was burned."

Collena wondered if that was a coincidence. Had Curtis been there when he was killed, or had the killer deposited the body there as some kind of warning to them?

She walked to Dylan and touched his arm. The gesture brought his gaze to hers. Dylan was obviously as upset and shocked about this as she was.

"I was just telling Dylan," Jonah went on, "that it's hard to tell much of anything because Reese's body was badly burned. But it looks like he was shot first and then set on fire."

"He was burned?" Collena asked, though she had to say it twice for the words to have any sounds.

Jonah nodded. "Similarly to the way Abigail and Julie were killed. Except their accidents were caused by electrical fires. Reese's car had been doused with gasoline that someone siphoned from the tank."

Jonah didn't add anything else. He just stared at them, and she soon realized why he was really at the house.

"Neither Dylan nor I killed Curtis Reese," Collena volunteered.

"So Dylan already said. He also said you were both here at the house all day and night. Is that true?"

"Yes. With Rodney Harmon on the loose, it wouldn't have been safe for us to go out." She paused. "How long has Curtis been dead?"

"Don't know yet. The coroner might be able to pinpoint the time of death, but with the burns, that might not be so easy."

"But you're sure it's Curtis?" she clarified.

Jonah nodded. "The sheriff got the name of Curtis's dentist from his housekeeper, and we e-mailed him some pictures of his teeth. The dentist made a preliminary match. Plus, the housekeeper was able to ID his shoes and watch."

That wasn't one-hundred-percent proof, but on the

other hand, she knew of no reason Curtis or anyone else would fake his death.

"We're the only suspects," Dylan told her.

"Then you'd better find other possibilities," Collena insisted, talking to Jonah. "Because if you're sure this was murder—"

"We're sure. And as for those other possibilities, perhaps you can suggest some."

"Rodney Harmon," she said without hesitation. "He's out there somewhere, and he's a killer. Maybe Curtis had the misfortune to cross paths with him. After all, they're both in Greer."

"And what motive would Harmon have to kill a perfect stranger?" Jonah didn't wait for them to answer. "Because as far as I can tell, Curtis Reese didn't have any connection to the Brighton Birthing Center or to Rodney Harmon."

Collena opened her mouth, closed it and glanced at Dylan. Was he thinking what she was thinking? That maybe Ruth, Hank or Millie had done this?

Unfortunately, they had motives.

And that motive was Adam.

Collena wasn't sure she could trust the three of them, but she had no doubts about their love for Adam. Could one of them have eliminated Curtis because he was a threat to Dylan's claim to custody?

Mercy.

Was one of them a killer after all?

Dylan didn't offer any speculation about his former nanny and the members of her family. Nor did Collena. It was best for her to do some digging before she pointed a finger at anyone.

"Once the coroner's done with the autopsy," Jonah continued, "I want you both to come to the police station for questioning." He shifted his stance and eyed Collena. "Because the way I see it, there were only two people who had a reason to kill Curtis Reese, and those two people are you and Dylan."

While Dylan waited on hold for a report from his lead P.I., he continued to review the surveillance videos taken around the perimeter of the ranch.

He'd set up a makeshift office in his bedroom. It wasn't well equipped since the shooting, but he'd managed to salvage his desk and most of his computer equipment. Thankfully the security disks had been spared by the bullets so he was able to view the section of the ranch near the fence where they'd found Curtis Reese's body.

Dylan saw the flames in the distance. But not the killer. The darkness had concealed his identity, giving them nothing new.

Now, on top of everything else, Collena and he were murder suspects. Not just in Jonah's eyes, either. The brief conversation that Dylan had had that morning with Sheriff Hathaway was more than enough for Dylan to realize that since he and Collena had a motive, the authorities weren't interested in looking elsewhere.

Dylan was.

That's why he hadn't refused Millie's request when she phoned and said she wanted to come out to the ranch to talk to Collena and him. He didn't exactly relish the idea of having Millie around right now, but he wanted to question her about Curtis Reese's murder. Dylan only hoped that Millie didn't know anything about it.

He wanted this pinned on Rodney Harmon.

Dylan opened his desk drawer and searched for a mint or some gum. His mouth was parched from the central heating and the fact it'd been a while since he'd bothered to eat or drink anything. When he found nothing in the center drawer, he went through the side ones.

And he found the condoms.

They'd been there for months. He'd bought them at a time when he was certain he was ready to risk having an actual sex life. The bulk of the box was still there. Sad. And it was probably dangerous to think of Collena and condoms and then pair them in the same thought, but he did.

He took one of the foil packs and slipped it into his pocket. Dylan thought of Collena again and grabbed a second one. Yes, there was something calculating about carrying around condoms, but he also wasn't stupid. Sooner or later, they'd land in bed, and this time he was going to be prepared.

Dylan heard the doorbell and knew that one of the P.I.s would screen the visitor. He checked the surveillance monitor and saw Millie standing on the front porch. The P.I. let her in and, as Dylan had instructed him to do, the man led her toward the family room.

"Dylan," the lead P.I., Mason Tanner, said from the other end of the phone line. "Sorry that it took me so long. I was trying to gather reports from all my men. I've got six working on this, including Angelo Cardona and Ron Cowan, the two at your house."

Dylan hoped it was enough. "And has anyone found anything?"

"We're going through the security disks that the bank manager and some of the store owners let us use. No more Rodney Harmon sightings, but using the disks, I was able to verify that Curtis Reese left his hotel room about eight o'clock last night. An eyewitness saw him driving in the direction of your ranch."

That wasn't really news, considering Reese had been found on the property bordering the ranch.

"The sheriff brought in the Rangers to go through the crime scene," Mason continued. "That's good news for us since I was able to get my hands on their preliminary report. Reese had some pretty expensive surveillance gear in his car. Binoculars, video equipment and even a long-range eavesdropping device. He went to those woods to spy on you, Dylan."

And got killed in the process.

"Did the town surveillance disks show anyone leaving shortly after Curtis?" Dylan asked.

"Yeah. It could mean nothing, though. Could be a coincidence."

Dylan wasn't sure he believed in coincidences. "Who was it?"

"Your employee, Millie Sayers."

Dylan groaned softly.

"I was going to find Millie and talk to her," Mason explained.

"No need." Dylan glanced at the house surveillance screen again and spotted something he definitely didn't want to see. Millie was in the family room, all right. But she wasn't alone.

Collena was with her.

And it appeared the two were arguing.

"Call me if you find anything else," Dylan said to Mason. He hung up so he could hurry. But once he got close to the family room, he realized the women weren't arguing.

They were discussing him.

He stopped just outside the door and listened.

"So, you're admitting that you're in love with Dylan?" Collena asked.

Millie didn't answer right away. "Yes. I've been in love with him for a long time."

Well, that's the first he'd heard of it. Millie had certainly kept her feelings hidden.

Or had she?

Dylan mentally backtracked and recalled the looks she'd given him. He also recalled how upset she'd been when he announced his engagement five years ago. Still, she'd never said anything about loving him.

"Mother was always trying to push me to get together with Dylan," Millie continued. Her voice sounded heavy, as if she were fighting back tears. "I told her it was useless, that Dylan didn't see me that way, that he thought of me as a sister. But she believed I could change his mind."

Collena made a sound of understanding. "Is it possible that your mother decided to…eliminate Dylan's fiancée so you'd stand a better chance with him?"

Until Collena had asked that, Dylan had been ready to end his eavesdropping and go into the family room, but now he paused a moment longer. Because that was the question he needed answered.

"My mother wanted me to come and talk to you," Millie said. Which obviously wasn't an answer to Collena's question at all. "She said if I didn't come clean with you she'd tell Dylan *today* how I feel about him. And she would. My mother believes if you know that I love him, that you'll back away so that Dylan and I can have a chance at a real relationship."

Collena shook her head. "Dylan and I are together because of Adam. I can't back away. Besides, have you talked to Dylan about this? Because I don't think he'll back away from me, either."

"You're right," Millie said a moment later. "Still, my mother thought I should try. She wants what's best for me, and despite what you think of her, she wouldn't hurt anyone. Neither would my grandfather." She paused. "At least I hope they wouldn't."

Oh, man.

That was Dylan's cue to make himself known, and he had every intention of pressing Millie to explain why she had doubts about her own flesh and blood.

"Dylan," Millie said the moment she detected his presence in the room. "Thank you for letting me come."

"I hope you came with answers." Dylan crossed the room so he could stand beside Collena.

"Maybe." Millie suddenly looked very uncomfortable. She glanced at Collena as if she might ask her to leave, but she didn't. Instead, Millie reached in her coat pocket and took out something.

Dylan reached for his gun in the shoulder holster beneath his jacket.

Collena did the same.

Obviously alarmed, Millie's eyes widened. "It's jus

medicine." And she lifted the plastic amber bottle so Dylan could see for himself.

She handed the bottle to Dylan. "The doctor prescribed these for my mother years ago. They're antidepressants. And until this week, she'd been faithful about seeing the doctor and taking them. She stopped. And I'm worried about her."

So was Dylan. And he was worried about what Ruth could have done without that medication.

"How worried?" Collena asked.

But Millie looked at Dylan when she answered. "I'm afraid she might have killed Curtis Reese."

Dylan had to take a moment before he could speak. "Why would you think that?"

Millie volleyed nervous glances between Collena and him. "We're staying at the hotel, and I know that Mother had been trying to keep an eye on Curtis. Last night, when he left the hotel, she took Grandpa Hank's truck and followed him. I followed her in my car."

That meshed with the surveillance video, but what troubled Dylan was why the video hadn't managed to capture images of Ruth leaving. But then, maybe the woman had used the hotel's side parking lot. If so, the camera angle wouldn't have recorded her.

"Did you see your mother kill Curtis Reese?" Collena asked point-blank.

Millie frantically shook her head. "No. I had to stop for gas, and I lost track of her. For all I know, she might not have followed him after that. She might not have hurt him."

"But she might have," Dylan concluded.

Millie took his arm. "That's why I'm here. I want

you to help her. Talk to her, Dylan. Make her go back on those pills."

Dylan looked down at the nearly full bottle of prescription medicine. And then he looked at Collena. "I need to make a quick call." He waited until he had Collena's nod of reassurance before he stepped into the corridor and took out his cell phone.

But he didn't call Ruth, as Millie had probably expected him to do.

He called Dr. Finn McGrath, a friend in the nearby town of Fall Creek, Texas.

"Finn," he greeted when the man answered. "I don't have much time, and I need a favor."

"What can I do for you?"

"A friend of a friend is taking a drug called perenazine." Dylan used the label to spell it out. "She was using it for depression, but stopped—"

"That's not an antidepressant," Finn interrupted. "Well, not a normal antidepressant anyway. It's an antipsychotic drug and is normally used to treat delusional psychosis and severe cases of bipolar disorder."

Dylan refused to react just yet. "I know what bipolar means, but please explain the rest of that in laymen's terms."

"The patient was probably having problems distinguishing reality from fantasy."

Now, Dylan reacted. He wasn't happy to hear that, and he was concerned about what else he might learn from his next question. "Would this person be violent?"

"Possibly. That's why it's important to stay on the medication."

That tightened his stomach. "And if the person went off the medication?"

"Then, there'd be a serious problem."

And that's exactly what Dylan was afraid of.

He looked at the bottle again, so he could read out the dosage to Finn, but that's when Dylan noticed the problem. The patient's first name had been obliterated with what appeared to be a black permanent marker. Only the surname remained.

Sayers.

The surname of not just Ruth.

But also of Millie and Hank.

Of course, why would Millie bring this to him if it were hers? Dylan immediately thought of an answer. Maybe she'd done that to throw suspicion off herself. But would she really do that and put the blame on her mother? *That* he couldn't answer.

So, the question was—whose antipsychotic medication was this? Once Dylan knew that, he might also know the identity of a killer.

Chapter 13

Collena read through the information on the compute
screen and realized that Dylan had been right. The dru
Millie had brought over to show them was indeed ant
psychotic medication. It was too bad Millie had insiste
on taking the bottle back with her—so she could try t
convince her mother to take the pills.

Or so Millie had said.

But Collena wished she had that bottle and its con
tents to send to the police lab in San Antonio. That wa
she and Dylan might have learned whose medicatio
it really was. A call to the doctor hadn't produced th
answer because the man was out of town for the hol
day weekend.

Of course, maybe Millie was telling the truth.

And if so, they were back to square one. In oth
words, they had lots of suspects and no concrete e

idence to arrest any of them. In fact, one of them—
Jonah—was doing his best to have Dylan and her
arrested for Curtis's murder.

She glanced over her shoulder and made sure Adam
was okay. Her son was on the carpeted floor of the
playroom with Ina. Thankfully, Ina had volunteered to
help take care of Adam until things returned to normal.

Collena wondered if that would ever happen.

Adam and Collena had already played blocks and
other games. In fact, Collena had gotten to spend some
wonderful hours with her son without Ruth's watchful
eye over them. The only "low" moment had come when
Adam had noticed Collena's shoulder holster and gun.
That was when Collena decided to put the weapon on
top of the armoire that housed the television. It was still
within reach but out of Adam's sight.

Collena checked the security monitors for the rest
of the house, something she'd been doing all day. The
two P.I.s were in the kitchen having dinner. She maneuvered the camera angle to the exterior—Dylan was
in the stables with the vet. One of his prize mares was
sick. He'd promised her he wouldn't be long.

And then on the monitor, Collena saw a car approach
the house.

She got ready to alert the P.I.s, but then she recognized that car and the driver. It was Sergeant Katelyn
O'Malley, her old friend from SAPD. Katelyn had called
her an hour earlier to say she was on the way and
that she was bringing homemade chili.

Katelyn was also bringing medical access codes that
might help them find out whose prescription meds Mil-
e had brought over. Even with the access codes, it was

a long shot, but right now, the only shot they had since they couldn't convince the sheriff to get a search warrant to get that pill bottle.

"I'll be right back," Collena told Ina. "I want my friend to meet Adam."

Collena hurried down the hall and made it to the foyer just as the doorbell rang. She threw open the door and lowered her head against the blast of arctic air. Despite the cold, she greeted Katelyn with a smile. And with some confusion. Because the porch lights were out.

When had that happened?

The lights had been on when Katelyn drove up.

Katelyn didn't return the smile. But one brief look at her friend's face, and Collena knew something was terribly wrong.

And she soon realized what.

Someone was just to the side of the door, mere inches away from Katelyn. Collena caught a glimpse of the barrel of a handgun that'd been rigged with a silencer.

"Watch out!" Katelyn shouted.

That was the only warning Katelyn managed to give before the shadowy figure rammed the business end of a tiny six-inch stun gun against her neck.

Just like that, Katelyn collapsed into a limp heap on the porch.

And just like that, the figure stepped out and shoved the stun gun in his pocket. He grabbed Collena's hair. With a fierce jerk that shot pain through her entire body, he dragged her out of the foyer and to the porch.

The adrenaline knifed through her. A hard jolt triggered the fight-or-flight mode. Unfortunately, she couldn't do either because of the fierce grip her attacker had on her.

The moon was hidden beneath the thick night clouds and, with the porch lights out, it took Collena's eyes a moment to adjust to the dark.

Then, she saw him.

Oh, God.

It was Rodney Harmon.

Even though it'd been sixteen months since he'd attacked her and tried to kill her in the Brighton delivery room, that was a face that she'd never forget. He'd found her, and he was going to try to kill her.

If she didn't do something to stop him.

She fought her way through the initial panic and tried to figure out what she could do. She didn't have her gun with her. It was on the armoire in the playroom, and that meant she had to try to use her own strength to try to prevent this from escalating. It wouldn't be easy. Rodney was a hulk of a man.

There were hurried footsteps behind her. The P.I.s, she realized. They wouldn't be able to see well because of the darkness, and if they did spot Rodney, they wouldn't have an easy shot because they might hit her. Rodney must have realized it, too, because he calmly turned in their direction and fired.

Two shots fired from his gun rigged with a silencer.

She didn't see the bullets hit the men, but she heard them fall. Mercy. Rodney might have killed them.

Collena struggled to get away from him, but Rodney already had the upper hand. He shoved his right hand and gun over her mouth, to muffle the scream she was about to let rip from her throat.

Rodney didn't use the stun gun on her, but he did use his brute strength to maneuver her off the porch. Collena managed to ram her elbow into his stomach, but he was so heavily muscled there that the blow had little effect. It didn't even slow him down. Rodney dragged her down the porch steps and headed toward Katelyn's car, which he no doubt intended to use as an escape vehicle.

With her as his hostage.

Collena knew with absolute certainty what he intended to do once he had her away from the ranch.

"No one's coming to help you," he snarled with his mouth right against her ear. He stank of cheap whiskey and menthol cough drops.

He might be right. Maybe no one would help. With the P.I.s down, it was possible no one was monitoring the surveillance screens. And Dylan might not hear the struggle. So she fought, trying to dig her heels into the frozen ground.

"Keep fighting me," Rodney warned, "and I'll go inside and get your kid. That should shut you up."

The threat sparked a flood of horrible memories. Memories of Adam being stolen. Memories of Rodney nearly beating her to death.

For just a moment, the images paralyzed her, much as the physical beating had done the night she'd given birth at Brighton. Collena hadn't immediately fought back that night, either. And those lost moments had nearly cost her everything.

That wouldn't happen now.

She hadn't just given birth. She wasn't weak. And she wasn't going to let this monster get anywhere near Dylan or her son. Not again.

When Rodney reached for the door handle of Kate-lyn's car, Collena knew it was time to put a plan into motion. She dropped her weight so that her butt practically landed on the ground. In the process, she dragged Rodney down with her. It wasn't enough force to make him fall, but it did throw him off balance a little.

It was just enough.

Collena used her fists to start battering away at him. Not one jab. But as many as she could manage.

Rodney loosened the smothering grip he had on her mouth and, for a moment, she thought he was going to try to turn the gun on her. But he didn't. Instead, he merely lowered his arm and put her in a choke hold.

He tightened his grip. Squeezing hard. And it prevented her from breathing.

She gasped for air.

Felt her throat close.

Still, Collena didn't give up. She couldn't. She was literally fighting for her life and for Dylan and Adam's lives, as well. Because if Rodney managed to kill her, then he might go after them.

She clawed at Rodney, but he was wearing a heavy coat and gloves and her fingernails weren't able to dig into his flesh. With each frantic movement, Collena used more of what precious little breath she had left.

Once she was weakened from the struggle, Rodney shoved her into the passenger side of the car. With his chest still pressed hard against her back and his arm still around her throat, he tried to position the stun gun so he could hit her with it. Collena dodged it, barely, and kicked at him.

That's when her shoulder brushed against something metal.

The keys that'd been left in the ignition.

Though she had to fight through the dizziness that was starting to overtake her, she grabbed the keys, practically ripping them from the ignition. In the same motion, she thrust them behind her.

Collena sliced the keys over his face.

He growled in pain and snapped her neck so hard she was afraid he'd broken it. Still, that didn't stop her. Collena threw the keys over his shoulder, and she heard them land on the ground somewhere amid all that remaining snow. Hopefully, they'd fallen someplace where he couldn't easily reach them. Somehow, she had to stop him from driving away with her, because he would take her to a secondary crime scene that he'd probably already prepared.

Rodney cursed her and lifted the stun gun again.

Collena caught movement out of the corner of her eye. Apparently, so did Rodney. Because he looked up to see Dylan running full speed toward the car.

Rodney lifted his gun and fired.

Dylan dove to the ground just as the bullet slashed past his head.

Another half inch to the right and he would have been a dead man.

From the moment Dylan realized that something had gone wrong, he knew that it involved Rodney Harmon. That's why he'd ordered Ina to stay with Adam and sprinted to the front of the house once he realized the P.I.s weren't inside.

And his worst fears had been confirmed.

Rodney had Collena. The bastard had her. And from the looks of things, Rodney had already shot the P.I.s and incapacitated another woman on the porch. Collena's cop friend, no doubt. She was moaning and trying to move. But Dylan couldn't worry about her.

Right now, he had to save Collena.

Rodney Harmon reaimed his gun, and Dylan had no choice but to shift his position again. He scrambled toward the porch, got behind one of the massive marble columns that fronted the house and aimed his weapon at the man.

That didn't stop Rodney. Instead of shooting at Dylan, or dodging Dylan's shot, Rodney climbed into the car, crawling over Collena. Even in the darkness, Dylan could see the struggle. Collena was fighting like a wild woman.

And then she stopped.

She just stopped.

Collena fell limp onto the seat.

Dylan shouted, though he had no idea what he said. The rage and fear came tearing through him as if he'd been blasted with a hundred bullets.

Had Rodney shot Collena?

With the winter wind howling, he wouldn't necessarily have heard the shot fired through the silencer. It would have blended in with the other sounds of the struggle.

A sickening sense of dread came with the rage and fear. Dylan wanted nothing more than to shoot at the SOB, but he couldn't, because Rodney grabbed hold of Collena and pulled her in front of him like a shield.

"Come closer, and you both die," Rodney warned.

Collena still didn't move, but Rodney had her in such a choke hold that Dylan figured he might have strangled her unconscious. At least he prayed that's what had happened. Collena couldn't be dead. And she didn't appear to be bleeding.

Still using her as cover, Rodney dragged her several feet from the car. He stooped and began to feel around the yard. He was looking for something. But what? Dylan couldn't take the chance that he might find it. And he couldn't waste any more time, either.

Collena and her cop friend needed medical attention.

Dylan watched Rodney and tried to calculate the best time to make his move. Anything he did could be dangerous for both Collena and him, but doing nothing was equally dangerous.

When Rodney looked down at the ground, Dylan knew it was time. He sprang from his position and, while trying to keep his gun ready, Dylan charged the man. Rodney looked up, cursed and tried to take another shot at Dylan.

But Dylan got to him first.

Hoping that he didn't hurt Collena any more than she already was, Dylan launched himself at Rodney, and all three of them went down to the frozen ground.

Dylan tried to move Collena out of the way, but she was totally unconscious. Her deadweight was to his advantage because Rodney was beneath her and unable to maneuver his gun so that he could shoot.

Moving fast, Dylan shifted to the side and dragged Rodney with him. Rodney outsized him by a good forty pounds, but Dylan had something that Rodney didn't—the overwhelming need to protect Collena.

Dylan drew back his fist and slammed it into the man's jaw. Rodney's head fell back, and he didn't try to put his hands up to defend himself. In the back of Dylan's mind, he realized that wasn't good.

But he realized it just a second too late.

Dylan felt the jolt. As if a million tiny needles had been shot into his body.

He tried to reach for Rodney, but he couldn't make his hands or legs move. He couldn't make anything move. Dylan couldn't even break his fall when he landed face-first on the ground next to Collena.

The world collapsed around him.

And Dylan could only lie there as Rodney carried Collena away.

Chapter 14

For Collena, everything was off kilter.

She couldn't move, and it took every ounce of her mental energy just to hold a brief thought in her head. Only one thought kept repeating—Rodney Harmon had kidnapped her.

And he'd used a stun gun on Dylan and her.

Collena forced her eyes open, but her vision was blurry. Still, she could tell that she was riding in a car. A glance over to the driver's seat, and she confirmed what she already feared.

Rodney was behind the wheel. He had apparently hot-wired the car, and he was driving her to her death.

"Don't think about doing anything stupid," Rodney snarled.

She looked down to where his right hand held a gun pointed directly at her rib cage.

"You're going to kill me anyway," she managed to say, though her words were slurred. "Why should I co-operate?"

"Because I'm not going to kill you at this exact moment." He said it almost gleefully. "Well, unless you don't give me a choice. I'll kill you now if I have to."

She needed to escape.

Collena glanced around, not moving, using only her eyes. Everything was white, still covered with snow, but she recognized something. Thanks to the clouds moving from in front of the moon, she saw the remnants of an old barn. She'd been here before. She had checked out this area days earlier when she was trying to figure out the best way to get onto Dylan's property and hopefully get a look at Adam. In fact, if some live oak trees hadn't been in the way, she probably could have seen the wrought-iron gates that fronted the property.

Did that mean Dylan would follow them?

Yes, of course, he would.

Once the effect of the stun gun wore off. Which could be five minutes from now, maybe more. But by then, it might be too late.

"You thought you could outsmart me," Rodney taunted. He shoved the gun even harder against her ribs, causing her to grimace in pain. "But I proved who's the smarter one, now, didn't I? I got out of jail. And then I got me a plan to come after you. The plan worked, too. Well, with a few hitches."

"You mean Dylan," she mumbled.

"No. I figured he'd get in the way. I'd counted on

him and was ready to kill him if necessary. But I hadn't counted on having to kill Curtis Reese."

Collena turned her head and stared at him. "You killed Curtis?" She saw it then, the bloodstains on the sleeve of his parka. She also saw the wild, insane look in his eyes. Judging from his strong body odor and scraggly beard, he'd probably done nothing but stalk her and commit murder since he escaped from jail.

"Had to kill him," Rodney verified. "When I went to park over in that spot next to the ranch last night, he was there. You shoulda seen him. He had all this fancy equipment to spy on you and jam your security system. I borrowed it to make sure your boyfriend wouldn't see me coming."

So, that's how he'd managed to get onto the ranch. Curtis, too, apparently. It was too late to wonder, but had Curtis planned on kidnapping Adam if the custody hearing hadn't gone his way? If so, she could thank Rodney for stopping it.

Yet another ironic twist.

"I didn't leave the ranch after I fired those shots at you," he continued. "I hid from the sheriff and lay low in one of the stables. It wasn't hard to do because there weren't many ranch hands around. When I saw that woman drive up, I knew that was my chance. She never even heard me coming when I sneaked up behind her when she was on the porch."

Katelyn would be riled about that. Hopefully, she would help Dylan come after her. Too bad Collena couldn't leave a proverbial trail of bread crumbs for them to follow.

They wouldn't have a clue where Rodney had taken her.

And that's why she had to do whatever she could to save herself. She had to accept that help might not come.

"Why did you kill Curtis?" she asked while she checked out the surroundings. The road had narrowed considerably, and Rodney had to slow down on the slick, snow-covered gravel. "Why didn't you just use the stun gun on him?"

"Things kind of got out of hand. I figured it was best not to leave any witnesses at that particular stage of the game. I wouldn't have wanted him to get loose and go blabber to you where he'd seen me. You'd have had your cop friends combing all over those woods looking for me. And I couldn't get caught. Not until I'd kept my promise to kill you."

But Rodney had left witnesses with Katelyn and Dylan. He'd probably thought she'd be dead and he would be long gone before they found her body.

"I'd read newspaper articles about the car fires with Dylan Greer's sister and girlfriend. I just copycatted what I'd read about them and decided that was the best way to get rid of Reese."

Well, he wouldn't let her off so easily. If he had his way, this would be slow and painful. It turned her stomach to think what he had in mind.

He took a turn onto a side road that was lined with thick woods on the right. She didn't recognize it, but she thought it was one of the roads that flanked the ranch. If so, then perhaps he was taking her to the outbuildings that Dylan used to house seasonal workers. Collena had noticed them when she was studying the property and trying to figure out the best way to get a look at her son. If she'd been able to find them, then Rodney no doubt had, as well. Those buildings would be exactly the kind of isolated place he'd want to use to hold her until he could kill her.

Collena tested the muscles in her hands, feet and legs. They weren't a hundred percent. But she had enough strength to do what she needed to do.

She mentally counted to three, waited until Rodney took the next turn that would lead him to the back of the ranch. He slowed down, just enough to make the turn, and Collena knew that it was the best opportunity she'd get.

Slapping her hand against Rodney's gun so it would get it away from her rib cage, she jerked back the door handle, opening it, and dove out into the cold darkness.

She hit the ground hard, knocking the breath right out of her. Still, she forced herself to move. She *had* to move. Because there wouldn't be much time. Rodney slammed onto the brakes, and she heard his door open.

Collena got to her feet and began to run toward the thick woods blanketed by the night and the snow.

She was still weak from the stun gun, and her hands and knees stung from where she'd hit the ground. It was déjà vu. This was what she'd experienced the night she'd escaped after Adam's birth.

Behind her, she heard Rodney shout. He cursed at her, calling her vile names. And then she heard his footsteps. Followed by a shot.

He was coming for her.

Again.

* * *

The cold helped revive him.

Dylan could feel that bitter chill seep into his body. And then he heard the woman's voice.

Not Collena's.

It was her friend Katelyn. She had him by the shoulders, and she was shaking him and repeating his name. But both her voice and touch seemed miles away. The only thing that seemed real was the numbing cold.

"Rodney Harmon has Collena," she yelled. "He shot both of the P.I.s so we don't have backup. They're alive but need an ambulance. And we need to save Collena. Get up!"

That penetrated the numbness and registered in his brain. Rodney Harmon had Collena, and he had to get her back before the man killed her.

Dylan forced himself to move from the ground. He wasn't successful on the first try, but he managed to get to a sitting position with Katelyn's help. He was exhausted. Zero energy. So, he pulled in several hard breaths, hoping that would help clear his head.

Katelyn hurried things along by practically dragging him to his feet. "I need a car so we can go after her. Rodney took mine. He used it to escape with Collena."

Dylan shook his head, cursing the damn fog in his head. "We don't know where he took her."

"Yes, we do." She showed him the screen of her cell phone. "I drove here in an unmarked squad car. It has a GPS tracking system built into it. Headquarters is sending me the coordinates of where Rodney and Collena are."

Dylan grabbed the phone and looked at the tiny backlit screen. "He's still close to the ranch. But the car's not moving."

"No." And her voice was so strained on that one word, that Dylan knew exactly what'd happened.

Rodney had stopped so he could kill Collena.

She was fighting for her life at that exact moment.

That got Dylan running as fast as his weakened legs would carry him. He raced toward the garage and tried to figure out the best way to get to the west side of the ranch. It wasn't far through the pasture. Less than a mile. But it would be a lot longer than that if he followed the roads as Rodney had.

"Stay with Ina and Adam," he yelled to Katelyn, who was following him.

"But I want to help Collena," she protested.

"I want you here in case Rodney backtracks and tries to get into the house."

There was no way she could argue with that. Ina wouldn't be much of a defense against an escaped felon, especially since the two P.I.s were apparently out of commission.

Katelyn had probably already called the sheriff and requested an ambulance. But it would take twenty minutes or more to reach the ranch, Dylan couldn't wait for them to arrive. Every second counted.

Dylan opened the garage door, jumped into his four-wheel drive, backed out and floored the accelerator. He didn't drive toward the road but instead cut across the pasture. It was a gamble. A huge one. With the snow covering the ground, he wouldn't be able to see a hole or any potential debris that could slice through his tires. Still, it was a risk he had to take.

He pushed the vehicle hard, and he kept his focus on the fence that he could barely see in the distance. There was a shallow ditch on the other side of that fence, and if he was reading Katelyn's coordinates correctly, her car was just beyond that.

Hopefully, Collena would be, as well.

And while he was hoping, he hoped she was still alive.

He couldn't think differently. He couldn't even let the possibility of failure cross his mind. Dylan simply sped toward an encounter with Rodney. One he had to win to save Collena.

Thankfully, there was no livestock in this part of the pasture. No trees, either. Just flat land that lay between Collena and him.

He slowed a little as he approached the fence, and put on his seat belt so the impact wouldn't throw him through the windshield. Dylan did one more calculation of the position of Katelyn's car, and adjusted his own vehicle, driving it just slightly north.

Then, Dylan aimed at the fence and rammed it with his vehicle.

The speed helped. So did the sheer size and power of the four-wheel drive. There was a fierce jolt. But he tore through the chain-link fence and came out on the other side—right on the gravel road, less than twenty feet from Katelyn's car.

Both doors of her car were wide-open. The engine was running. The low-beam lights pierced the darkness, creating an eerie, foggy effect.

But neither Collena nor Rodney were anywhere in sight.

With his gun ready, Dylan jumped from his vehicle and, using his door as cover, he turned on his own high-beam lights. Still, he saw no sign of her on the side of the road near the ranch. Or the woods. Of course, those woods were thick, and if Rodney had taken her in there, even the high beams wouldn't help him see her.

"Collena?" he called out.

The wind was howling, and in the distance, he could hear the sirens from the sheriff's car, but Dylan also heard something else. Something human. A man's voice.

A second later, the bullet shattered Dylan's windshield.

Dylan welcomed the shots because that meant Rodney was aiming at him and not Collena.

But where was she?

The sirens drew closer, and Dylan hoped that Katelyn was navigating the sheriff in the direction of the road. Dylan would need backup if he had to go into those woods. Besides, the sound of the sirens might flush Rodney out.

It might also make him panic.

Dylan shouted Collena's name again. Waited. With his heart pounding and his thoughts running wild, he cursed. More than anything he wanted to race out into the darkness and pound Rodney into dust. But Rodney had a better vantage point and could ambush him. If that happened, he wouldn't be able to help Collena.

"Collena?" Dylan shouted one more time.

That generated another shot aimed at him. This one ripped through the top of his vehicle and sliced right through the metal. It also helped him pinpoint Rodney's general direction.

He was in the woods.

Dylan tried to pick through the area lit by his high beams. He looked for any movement or any indication of Rodney's exact position.

And then he saw him.

Just as Rodney leaned out from behind a massive oak and fired another shot at Dylan.

Dylan got only a glimpse of him, but it was enough to let him know that Rodney didn't have Collena with him. Well, he didn't have his hands physically on her anyway. Dylan couldn't discount that she was there nearby. Maybe unconscious. That might have been why she hadn't answered him.

But he prayed for the alternative.

That Collena hadn't answered because she was hiding and hadn't wanted to give away her position.

Dylan focused his aim and his attention on the oak that Rodney was using for cover. The seconds seemed like an eternity. But still, Dylan waited. Until Rodney leaned out a second time to take another shot.

Dylan fired first.

Rodney jerked back, and howled in pain. Dylan had hit him. And hopefully stopped him.

There was some movement in the woods to Rodney's right. There, among the dark shadows of the trees, Dylan saw Collena.

She was alive.

And then he saw something else that terrified him.

Just as the sheriff's vehicle pulled onto the road, Rodney came out from cover and took aim.

At Collena.

Dylan didn't have to re-aim. He already had his gun

trained on the spot where he'd last seen Rodney. And Dylan didn't hesitate. He shouted for Collena to get down, and he fired at Rodney twice.

And he watched as both shots went into the man's chest.

Chapter 15

"The medics just pronounced Rodney Harmon dead," Jonah Burke announced from the doorway of the family room.

Collena didn't feel guilty. In fact, it was the news she'd wanted to hear. Yes, a man was dead, but that man had come within a hair of killing both Dylan and her. If Dylan hadn't stopped Rodney with those bullets, she would have spent the rest of her life in fear that he would come after her again.

This way, she was free.

And she could thank Dylan for that.

Of course, Dylan wasn't in a receptive mood. She could see the tension still straining the muscles in his face. Heck, she could see that tension in his every movement, even though he was trying to be gentle as he cleaned the scrapes on her hands and knees.

"What about the P.I.s?" Collena asked.

"They were both taken to the hospital. You'll get an update as soon as there's an update to give." Jonah's voice was edgy, and Collena suspected he wasn't thrilled about making another trip out to the ranch.

"Your cop friend, Katelyn O'Malley, is okay. She's with the sheriff out at the crime scene," Jonah continued, his voice gaining edginess with each spoken word. "And I'm here with you two. Lucky me."

Collena tried to suppress a wince when Dylan dabbed antiseptic on the scraped knee. She wasn't successful. And Dylan noticed. "Sorry," he mumbled.

"It's okay. It doesn't hurt much."

Dylan made a sound to indicate he didn't believe that, so Collena caught his chin and lifted it to force eye contact. "I'm *really* not hurt. These scrapes are minor. And everything will be okay."

Judging from the set of his jaw, Dylan didn't believe that, either, and Collena understood what he was going through. He was blaming himself, even though he'd done everything humanly possible to stop the kidnapping.

"Could we cut the tender moments," Jonah snarled, "and get back to business? I'm supposed to collect Collena's clothes and interview the two of you about what happened. Oh, and that's a separate interview from the one I still need to do about Curtis Reese's death. You two are just racking up the dead bodies, aren't you?"

Collena ignored the jab and pointed to the paper bag near the door. "My clothes are all in there. Everything is bagged and tagged."

She'd anticipated that the items would be needed

for evidence. Besides, she hadn't wanted to wear them. They smelled of Rodney Harmon. As soon as Dylan had brought her back to the house, she'd changed into a loose blue dress so her scraped knees could be cleaned.

Jonah leaned down and glanced inside the bag. He didn't seem pleased that she had done a small part of his job for him. "And what about the interviews? Let's get them done, too."

Collena glanced at the clock on the mantel. It wasn't that late, just past ten at night, but she was beyond exhausted.

"You're leaving now, Jonah," Dylan insisted. He set the antiseptic and gauze aside on the coffee table, stood and walked to Jonah. "Any statements and interviews can wait until morning."

Jonah put his hands on his hips, and his nostrils flared. "I have to do my job."

"If you'd been doing your job, Rodney Harmon wouldn't have had the opportunity to kidnap Collena."

His nostrils flared even more. "Don't try to pin it on me. That man was on Collena's tail before she even came to the ranch. She brought him here."

Dylan didn't say a word. He glared at Jonah, and the deputy must have decided it wasn't a good time to pick a fight with Dylan.

"I'll be back bright and early in the morning," Jonah snapped. He grabbed the bag from the floor. "And you're going to give me those statements." He turned and nearly ran into Ina. He didn't offer her so much as a hello before he stormed away.

"You doing okay?" Ina asked them.

"Yes," Collena lied. "How's Adam?"

"Sound asleep. He doesn't have a clue what happened."

Good. Collena wanted to keep it that way. If she could erase the memory of Rodney Harmon from her own memory, she would.

Ina looked at Dylan. "I moved Adam's crib back into the nursery. I figured you two had enough to handle so I'll stay in there with him tonight."

He nodded. "Thank you."

"I'll also reset the security system and make sure all the doors are locked." Ina didn't linger, probably because she, too, looked exhausted. It'd been such a long, horrible night, but maybe, just maybe, they would get some peace.

Dylan went to the security monitor and checked the nursery. Collena got up from the sofa and went to his side. Ina had been right—Adam was sleeping.

"You need some rest," Dylan insisted, looping his arm around her waist. He led her in the direction of her suite.

Collena almost protested, because she didn't want to be alone tonight. Not after what'd happened. But she went anyway since Dylan probably didn't have the energy to play nursemaid for her. He'd tended her scrapes. He'd bullied Jonah into leaving and waiting on those statements. Now, he probably wanted time alone to try to come to terms with the fact that he'd killed a man.

"Rodney's dead," Dylan said. He opened her suite door and eased her just inside the room. "He can't hurt you again."

Not trusting her voice, she nodded. "Thank you for saving my life."

Something went through his eyes. Not gratitude for her thank-you. It was something dark that went bone deep. Probably something to do with this latest incident bringing back old memories of his sister's and fiancée's deaths.

He reached out and skimmed his fingers over her chin. "Try to get some sleep."

She nodded. But didn't move.

Dylan didn't move, either. Nor did he take his fingers from her chin. His touch was warm.

Comforting.

He groaned, the sound rumbling deep within his chest. "I should go," he added. "You're hurt, and you're tired."

But he didn't go.

Collena just stood there, waiting, to see where this was leading. She didn't have to wait long.

Dylan stepped closer. So close that she took in his scent. Sweat mixed with the cedars from the woods. And Dylan's own scent was there, too.

She felt the shiver of heat before his hand moved from her chin to the back of her neck. She saw matching heat in the depth of his searing green eyes.

"This is wrong," he admitted. Right before his mouth came to hers.

He kissed her gently, his lips shaping hers with soft pressure. His touch was equally gentle. A real contrast. Since she could feel his strength beneath the clever fingers that glided over her skin.

"This is wrong," he repeated. "But unless you say no, I won't stop."

With that, he kissed her again, and Collena melted

against him. Dylan was probably right—this was wrong. But she wasn't going to say no. She wasn't going to stop, either. She wanted him in her bed. In her arms.

She just wanted him.

So, Collena didn't resist when he backed her into the suite and shut the door. And why should she resist? His looks alone could have seduced her. The bronze-colored hair tangled around his perfectly chiseled face. Those eyes, filled with longing and need.

Everything slowed down. Her heartbeat. Her breathing. Her thoughts. Even the emotions that'd had felt so raw and damaged just moments earlier spiraled down until they simply faded away.

Her body relaxed, and the pleasure of the kiss went through her like sips of fine, warmed whiskey.

Dylan didn't hurry things. He took his time. Kissing her. Savoring her. Building the fire inside her by small degrees until it wasn't enough. That was the problem with good, thorough kisses—ultimately they only made her want more.

Collena stepped closer to him. Pressing her body to his. She put her arms around him, to draw him closer, so that she could feel the solid muscles of his chest. That satisfied her for several moments, but then Dylan took his kisses to her neck.

He didn't stop there.

Dylan eased off his shoulder holster and dropped it onto the table. Then, he slid his hand down the side of her body, all the way from her neck to her right breast. To her waist and to her hip. That's when Collena knew it was time to do something about touching him.

She went after the buttons on his shirt.

"The scrapes on your hands," he reminded her. "I don't want you to be in pain."

"Oh, I'm not in pain." Though the scrapes and bruises were probably hurting, Collena couldn't feel them. Need and passion were apparently great at numbing the body to anything unpleasant. And right now, the only thing she could feel was the ache of pleasure.

Collena opened his shirt. Found a solid man beneath. He was everything she thought he would be. Toned, naturally tanned pecs and abs. You couldn't get that kind of body in a gym. This came from years of physical labor on the ranch.

A cowboy's body.

Her cowboy, she said to herself. And she smiled at the thought of Dylan being hers, if only for tonight.

His shirt came off. He reciprocated by unzipping her dress and easing it off her shoulders. It fell to the floor.

He skimmed his gaze down her body, and the look in his eyes let her know that he appreciated what he saw. Collena did the same to him.

And she unzipped his jeans.

She kissed him on the chest that she'd been fantasizing about, and while she was kissing, she decided to sample his stomach, as well. She felt his muscles stir beneath her tongue and lips. She also felt his erection and knew that while the foreplay was incredible, that's what she wanted from him.

Her stomach kisses obviously had an effect on Dylan. The intended effect. He made a husky sound of pleasure and sank down to her eye level. He went to his knees, gripped her waist and eased her down on the floor beside him.

The thick carpet was soft beneath her. That was the only thing her mind had time to register before he kissed her and everything went a little crazy. No more slow, soothing pace. Not this. His French kiss nearly caused her to climax.

But the heat was just beginning.

With one hand, he unclasped her bra, and with the other, he removed her panties. It was an incredible sensation. Her bare breasts and sex on him.

But his jeans and boots had to go.

"Condom," he mumbled, when she tugged off his boots and pushed the jeans down his hips.

Collena groaned.

Until he produced the wrapped condom from his pocket.

Dylan had obviously come prepared, and she rewarded his preparation with the best kiss she could manage. And she rewarded herself by running her hand into his boxers.

He was hot and hard. So ready. And she was ready, too. She stripped his jeans off him and arched her back so that their midsections would meet, his erection against the wet folds of her body.

Oh, mercy.

This had to happen now.

He put on the condom and entered her slowly. It was torture. She wanted all of him, and she wanted it now. Yet, Dylan held back. And he stayed gentle.

She had the feeling that he was treating her like fine crystal because of her injuries. And it was costing him big-time. She could see the battle going on beneath those clever touches and easy strokes inside her.

He wanted to take her hard and fast.

Which was exactly what Collena wanted.

So, she lifted her hips and wrapped her legs around his lower back. He made eye contact with her. His eyebrows lifted, questioning her about how far he could go.

"As far as you want," she offered.

He understood her, and Collena nearly laughed that they were on the same wavelength, even when it came to the specifics of sex.

The next stroke inside her wasn't exactly gentle.

But it was thorough. And extremely pleasurable.

Because she was watching his face, she saw the change in him. The savage was free, and she could feel the difference in the way he moved. The way he looked at her. The way he smelled. It was something primal. Something wild and untamed.

Something she wanted.

He plunged his left hand into her hair so that he controlled the movement of her head. He hooked his right arm beneath her thigh, lifting her so that she could take him deeper inside her. And he made sure that it was deep with each long, hard thrust inside her.

Her body reacted. Wanting more. Wanting it *now*.

Collena dug her fingers into his back, trying to force him to get closer to her, but the truth was, they couldn't get any closer.

The sweat of Dylan's body was slick now. It added to the friction already there. Wet body against wet body. Man against woman.

His grip tightened on both her hair and thigh. He moved faster. Harder. Deeper. Until the intensity and the pleasure was overwhelming.

Collena wanted to hang on to every second of the ecstasy. She wanted it to last. And the same moment, she thought she would die if he didn't give her that final release.

Dylan didn't disappoint her.

When he could take and give no more, he thrust into her one last time. Collena felt her body surrender. Dylan lowered his head, kissed her and surrendered right along with her.

Dylan lay there, trying to level his breathing. He didn't even try to pretend he had regrets about what had just happened. The main thing he was thinking was that he had a sated body and the taste of Collena still in his mouth. He wouldn't regret it.

But he was afraid she would.

She'd been through a horrible ordeal and had nearly been killed. Having sex was probably the last thing she'd planned. Still, it had happened. There was no turning back. All that was left were the consequences.

"That wasn't good," she mumbled.

It took Dylan a moment to process what Collena had said. "Excuse me?"

"That wasn't good. It was phenomenal. And that's a problem."

Yeah. He knew exactly what she meant. Where did they go from here?

"Let's just not analyze it," Collena insisted, snuggling against him. "In fact, let's have sex again tomorrow and not analyze it then, either."

He bunched up his forehead, but he wasn't about to

veto the plan. In fact, he wanted her again tonight. "So, we just...float?"

She nodded. "It's better than the alternative."

It would probably be nice for a while, especially since they had a mountain of other problems to deal with.

Still, they couldn't *float* forever.

"Will you want a divorce?" she asked.

Stunned, Dylan looked down at her. It was definitely an odd thing to ask a man while she was still naked in his arms. "What?"

"A divorce," she said as if that clarified everything. He just kept staring at her until she continued. "Because with Curtis dead, there won't be a custody battle. At least not between him and us."

"There won't be one between us, either," he assured her. But he wasn't the only one driving that, now was he? Collena had a huge say in it, and he wondered if that's what she was trying to tell him now. "Do you want a divorce?"

Collena didn't answer.

Because the lights went out.

There was the slight beeping sound that came from the security monitor. The entire system had a backup generator so the monitor stayed on, and its milky-blue screen practically lit up the room.

Dylan got up and, in the same motion, he reached for his jeans. The monitor beeped again. It was soft. Hardly alarming. But he had a bad feeling that those two little beeps meant big trouble.

"What is it?" Collena asked. She got up, as well, and reached for her clothes.

Dylan hurried to the monitor and switched it to the

main panel so he could see which alarm had been trig-gered. It was the back door that led from outside into the kitchen.

According to the monitor, the door was open.

He pushed the intercom button into Ina's room. "Did you leave the back door open?" he asked softly so that he wouldn't wake Adam.

"No," Ina answered immediately. Her voice was soft too, but not so soft that Dylan didn't hear the concern in it. "And I hear footsteps in the kitchen. Dylan, I think we might have an intruder in the house."

Chapter 16

"Lock the door, take Adam and go in your bathroom. Lock that door, too," Collena heard Dylan tell Ina. "And call the sheriff. Call me immediately if anyone tries to break into the room. I'll be there as soon as I've checked things out."

Collena's heart went to her knees. No, no, no! This couldn't be happening. They'd already been through so much.

"It's probably nothing," Dylan told her. He pulled on his boots and grabbed his gun. "Some of the ranch hands might have come back from the Thanksgiving break. They're probably looking for a late-night snack."

"Would they have known the code to disarm the security system?" she asked.

"One or two of them do."

She latched onto that hope. But Collena knew it could

be something sinister. After all, there'd been violence in Dylan's life before she'd come into it. Violence associated with his personal relationships. It hadn't surfaced in years, but then, he hadn't been in a relationship in years, either.

Until now.

It was all over town that they were a couple. The wrong person could have heard that information and decided it was time to kill again.

While he shoved his cell phone into his pocket, Dylan scanned through the various camera angles of the house. Collena stood by him and watched, as well, hoping she would see something to help soothe their concerns. He went through each area, including the kitchen, but because the electricity was off, it was impossible to see if anyone was hiding in the shadows.

"Wait here." Dylan reached for the doorknob, but Collena stopped him.

"You need backup in case that's not a ranch hand out there." A ranch hand would have called out to let Dylan or Ina know that he was in the house.

An intruder, or a killer, wouldn't do that.

For a moment, she thought Dylan might argue with her and insist that she wait there, but then he nodded, probably because he knew that he did indeed need backup. "Stay behind me, and don't you dare take any unnecessary risks."

Collena returned the nod. "We'll do what it takes to protect Adam."

That was all she had to say to get him moving.

The kitchen was on the other side of the house, but

it was much closer to the nursery. Too close. "Does Ina have a gun?" she whispered to Dylan.

"She does. And she knows how to use it. But I don't know if she has it with her or not."

Collena prayed that she did but that the woman wouldn't have to defend Adam and herself. They had to make sure that didn't happen.

Moving quietly and staying close to the wall, they started down the pitch-black hall. Unfortunately, the corridor was open on both ends, and both ends had L-shapes that opened into other halls or rooms. That meant the intruder could come at them from either direction. Collena turned and walked backward so she could cover one end of the area and Dylan could cover the other.

Outside, the wind was battering against the row of windows that lined the corridor. Shrubs rustled. Even her own breath contributed to the sounds. It was uneven and came out in rough gusts. She could even hear the swish of the pendulum of the grandfather clock in the foyer.

What Collena couldn't hear were footsteps other than their own.

That wasn't necessarily a good sign. If the intruder knew the layout of the house—and he or she likely did—then there were many ways to ambush them without being heard.

But who would do this?

Jonah, maybe. Or Ruth, Millie or Hank? Of course, there was another possibility—a killer that had already struck twice with Dylan's fiancée and sister. A killer whose identity they didn't even know.

The moonlight bled through the bare vein-shaped limbs of the shrubs outside the windows and cast eerie shadows on the walls like a skeleton's fingers. The shadows moved and slashed with each new gust of wind.

Dylan stopped and lifted his hand so that she would stop, as well. Collena looked and listened, trying to pick through all those other shadows and sounds to see what had alarmed him.

And then she heard it.

Footsteps.

They were coming from the end of the hall that she was facing. Dylan whirled around in that direction and aimed his gun.

But just like that, the footsteps stopped.

They stood there waiting. Collena tried to figure out the best way to neutralize this person. The simple approach might work, especially if this was some ranch hand who'd come into the house and then gotten spooked by the electrical failure.

"Call out to the person," Collena whispered.

Because Dylan's arm was touching hers, she felt his muscles stiffen. But he obviously agreed with her idea because he stepped in front of her.

Get down, he mouthed.

She did. Collena crouched and then steadied her shooting wrist with her left hand. She didn't want her aim to be off in case things turned ugly.

"Who's there?" Dylan said. It wasn't a shout, but his voice practically echoed through the corridor.

Silence.

There were no footsteps to indicate the person was

running away. Nor was there any acknowledgment. So, they had their answer.

This wasn't a ranch hand.

And whoever it was waited just around the corner, less than thirty feet away. But what did this person want?

For Collena, the answer was simple: the killer wanted her because she'd gotten involved with Dylan.

But so far, the other attacks hadn't involved Dylan. So, if this was his blast-from-the-past killer, then why try to do this here at the house?

Unless the person fully intended to kill Dylan, as well.

"If you're after me," Collena called out, "then leave Dylan out of this."

That earned her a nasty glare from Dylan.

It also earned her some movement from the intruder. There was a shuffling sound. Followed by a slight bump against the wall. And someone mumbled something. Collena's comment had definitely caused a reaction.

Hopefully, it was the right reaction.

Collena saw the shadow then. The person didn't step out from cover, but she saw the hand.

And the gun.

Just as the person fired at them.

The nightmare had returned.

But this wasn't a dream, and the bullet that'd slammed into the wall just over their heads wasn't some unconfirmed fear over what had happened in the past.

That bullet was real.

And it'd come damn close to hitting them.

Dylan shoved Collena to the floor, and he maneuvered himself so that he was in front of her. That way, if the intruder shot at them again, he'd be in a better position to protect her and return fire.

Judging from Collena's muffled protest, she didn't like that idea. But Dylan wasn't giving her a choice. He'd already lost two women in his life, and he wasn't about to lose another.

While he was there, crouched over Collena, he went through the other possibilities, none of them good. He might have a killer in his home. Or maybe a kidnapper who'd come for Adam. After all, he was a wealthy man, and anyone who'd heard about the recent shooting in the woods might have thought this was the perfect time to commit another crime.

But that didn't make sense.

If this was a kidnapping, why hadn't the person just gone after Adam? And why try to kill him, the person who would be paying the ransom for the child?

Part of Dylan was elated that this might not be connected to Adam. But he couldn't be that happy, because Collena's life was on the line, and they almost certainly had a killer in the house.

He saw the gloved hand jut out again. The shooter didn't aim or peer out from around the corner to determine their position before firing.

This shot smashed into the window a good ten feet away from them, and the wind howled through the now gaping hole left in the glass. But that shot told Dylan exactly what he needed to know.

That Collena could escape.

Because the shooter wasn't aiming. That would have

required the person to leave cover and be exposed to gunfire.

"Crawl to the opposite end of the hall," he whispered to Collena. "And get into the family room. I'll be right behind you."

Until he'd added that last part, Collena had been shaking her head. But that stopped her, and after a few moments of hesitation, she started inching her way backward.

Dylan did, as well.

However, he kept watch to make sure the shooter didn't jump out with guns blazing. He also listened for the sound of footsteps in case this SOB decided to backtrack and sneak up behind them. Of course, that would mean the person knew the layout of the house.

Collena and he crawled back. Inch by inch. Dylan's adrenaline level was sky-high, and with each passing second, it got even higher. It didn't help that the wind was screaming now. Muffling sounds that shouldn't be muffled.

He cursed himself, for not doing more to prevent this. Collena wouldn't blame him. She wasn't the sort to do that. But he was. And it would take him a lifetime or more to get over the fact that he'd endangered her and Adam.

They made it to the end of the corridor. Just as another shot came at them. It tore off a piece of the ceiling, and the plaster came raining down on them. Dylan used the diversion to get to his feet. He dragged Collena around the corner and out of the line of fire, just in the nick of time.

The next shot splintered the wood floor where they'd been seconds earlier.

"We can double back around," Collena whispered. "That way, we can make sure Adam and Ina are okay."

Yes, and while he was at it, he could leave Collena with them. That would serve two purposes. It would get her out of the immediate path of this killer, and it would give Ina some much needed backup if this shooter got past Dylan.

He didn't intend to let that happen. But he could use the backup plan to convince Collena to stay where she stood the best chance of surviving this.

Dylan took off his boots, so that they wouldn't be heard on the hardwood and tiled floor. Collena did the same with her shoes. Once they were done, they started to move again, quickly, so they could get to the nursery.

Just in case the shooter had the same idea they did.

Dylan kept his ears and eyes open for any movement or sound.

Unfortunately, he heard one, even over the winter wind.

Someone was running down the corridor that Collena and he had just left. The shooter was coming after them, and once he or she rounded the corner, the bullets would likely start flying again.

Collena grasped their situation, as well. With Dylan right behind her, she began to run for the nearest cover—the dining room. Dylan calculated that they had just enough time to dive inside before they became targets.

But he miscalculated.

He saw the figure at the end of the hall. Just a

shadow, camouflaged by other shadows that the moonlight and the shrubs had created.

And he realized it was too late for Collena and him to take cover.

The figure stepped out, a bulky, awkward movement that seemed to involve some kind of struggle. He had a split-second realization that there might be not one shooter but two. However, that realization came a little too late.

Someone fired.

And fired.

And fired.

That's when Dylan got a better look at the person who was trying to kill them.

Chapter 17

Collena aimed her gun to return fire.

Only to realize she couldn't.

The person coming down the hall toward them was none other than Ina. But Ina wasn't the one who was shooting. There was someone behind her.

Someone was using Ina as a human shield.

Collena yelled for Dylan to keep down, and they tried to scramble out of the line of fire.

It wasn't easy. The bullets seemed to be flying everywhere. She wasn't even sure the shooter was aiming. Just blasting random shots through the air. Still, stray bullets could be as deadly as aimed ones.

Collena dove into the dining room and tried to drag Dylan to safety with her.

Of course, that left Collena with one terrifying question.

Where was Adam?

Oh. God.

Where was her son?

"Ina, are you okay?" Dylan shouted.

He grabbed Collena when she started to get up. He knew that she was in a panic now that she'd realized Adam might not be safe. But she had to get to her son.

Ina didn't answer right away. "I'm alive."

"And Adam?" Collena asked. She held her breath and prayed.

"Still sleeping in his crib. I'm sorry, Dylan. I couldn't get him in the bathroom in time to lock us in there like you said."

"I wouldn't hurt Adam for anything," someone added.

It was Millie.

Dylan cursed under his breath. Collena cursed, too, because she realized they had a very unstable woman on their hands. This situation could easily turn more deadly than it already was.

"You're sure Adam's all right?" Collena demanded, and she listened for any hint of a lie in Millie's response.

"He'll be okay as long as you cooperate and do as I say."

Millie's threat was chilling. And convincing. That meant Adam was okay, for now.

"Put down your gun, Millie," Dylan insisted. "And let Ina go. We need to talk."

"Yes, we do," Millie agreed. "But Ina and my gun stay put. For now, anyway. Toss out your guns and step closer so I can see you. If you don't, Ina dies right here."

Millie might be bluffing, but it was a huge risk to

take, especially if she was off her antipsychotic medication. Still, if Dylan and she surrendered their weapons, they'd be defenseless against Millie's gun.

"Collena's not armed," Dylan said, and he motioned for her to hand him her gun. Because she didn't have a better plan in mind, Collena cooperated.

Dylan tossed his weapon onto the corridor floor and tucked her gun in the back waist of his jeans. "I'm coming out."

"Collena, too," Millie insisted.

"No. This isn't about her."

"But it is. It's about both of you. Come out, or Ina dies."

"We need to stall her," Dylan whispered to Collena. "The sheriff will be here soon."

That might or might not be a good thing. Once Millie heard the sirens, she might just shoot them and then try to escape.

"Come out now!" Millie yelled. Her voice was so loud and shrill that Adam woke up.

From the end of the hall, Collena heard her son begin to cry and only hoped that Adam was safe in his crib. She didn't want her child getting out of the room and coming anywhere near this.

"Try to stay behind me," Dylan told Collena. Then, he raised his hands in the air and stepped out.

So did Collena, and when she went into the corridor, she came face-to-face with a woman who obviously wanted her dead. Judging from Ina's dire expression, she'd already accepted her death and was just waiting to see how all of this would play out.

"I'm in love with you, Dylan," Millie said. Her voice

was trembling. Her whole body was trembling. And that meant her trigger finger was, as well.

"You don't know what love is," Dylan fired back at her.

Millie frantically shook her head. "Oh, but I do. I killed for you, Dylan. That woman you asked to marry you wasn't right for you. I thought you'd figure it out for yourself, but you didn't. Collena isn't right for you, either. She only wants you so she can keep Adam. You're too good for her."

There it was. Motive and confession. All along, the killer had been under Dylan's own roof.

"Did you kill my sister, too?" Dylan asked.

Millie nodded. She didn't seem eager to finish her confession. "She found out what I'd done. I couldn't let her go to the police. I couldn't let you know what I did because I knew you wouldn't understand. You wouldn't have forgiven me."

"No. I wouldn't have." Dylan took a step toward the two women. "You're a killer, plain and simple. That has nothing to do with love."

"Don't come closer," Millie warned.

Dylan took another step anyway and, even in the pale, shadowy moonlight, Collena saw Millie's index finger tighten on the trigger. "You don't want to hurt Ina." His voice was calm. Unlike the storm of emotion swirling around them. "You want to let her go. I can arrange help for you."

"You mean a psychiatric hospital. I won't go. Mother's been trying to make me go to a place like that for years, and I won't. I'm not crazy. I'm only trying to protect you." Millie's eyes turned on Collena. "She's trash. Can't you see that?"

"She's not trash. She's Adam's mother. And remember, our marriage is one of convenience. For Adam's sake. There's no reason for you to feel threatened by Collena."

Collena knew he was probably just trying to negotiate, to buy some time until he could distract Millie enough to get that gun away from her. But she also knew it was true. Despite the fact they'd had sex, this was a relationship based on providing the best for their son.

Unfortunately, Millie, with her delusions and sick love for Dylan, could take that all away. And Dylan was taking a huge risk with every step he took toward her.

He didn't stop, despite Millie shaking her head and backing up. Collena's cop instincts made her want to shout for Dylan to stop. He was pressing too hard. But she also knew he didn't have a choice. They wouldn't let Ina die, and they couldn't allow Adam to be put at further risk.

Collena moved closer, as well, in case she had to help.

"Put the gun down," Dylan told her.

"No." Twin tears spilled down Millie's cheeks. "I can't. It can't end this way."

The words had hardly left her mouth when she gave Ina a fierce shove. Right at Dylan and Collena. Ina collided with them, and the impact sent the three of them crashing to the floor.

Millie didn't waste any time. While Ina, Dylan and Collena were untangling themselves from one another,

Millie turned and sprinted down the corridor away from them, and headed right for…

"The nursery," Dylan said. He picked up his gun and tossed Collena hers. "We have to get to Adam before she does. Millie might try to use him to escape."

Or worse.

Collena and Dylan jumped up from the floor and raced to save their little boy.

Dylan's heart was pounding against his ribs. He had a dozen horrible thoughts that he didn't want to have. Still, he didn't let those thoughts distract him.

Adam was in danger, and he had to get to the nursery.

Because his pulse was pounding in his ears and because of their collective footsteps on the hardwood, Dylan couldn't tell Millie's position. But he guessed that she was using the west hall to get to the nursery. Collena and he were using the east.

Millie's route was slightly shorter.

But she didn't have as much at stake as Collena and he did.

Dylan turned the corner, mere feet away from the nursery door. He could hear Adam's soft sobs, as if he were trying to go back to sleep, but Millie was nowhere in sight.

However, the nursery door was wide-open.

Collena tried to bolt past him, but Dylan restrained her just in case Millie was inside the doorway, waiting to ambush them.

There was another problem, as well. The door directly across from the nursery was open, too. That was Ruth's room, and Millie could easily be hiding there.

Either way, Dylan couldn't risk her firing any more shots. One way or another, he had to get that gun away from her.

He heard the sirens from the sheriff's car and knew there wasn't much time. Millie would know it, too, and she might already be in the nursery. She could even escape out the window with Adam.

Dylan hated to put Collena's life at further risk, but he didn't have a choice. He tipped his head to the nanny's room. *You go there,* he mouthed. *I'll go into the nursery.*

She swallowed hard and then nodded. Collena looked as if she wanted to say something to him, but both knew there wasn't time for that. Aiming her gun, she slipped around him and eased into the room.

Dylan went in the other direction.

Adam stopped crying. Dylan preferred the tears. It let him know that his son was okay and that he was nearby. Without the sounds of the little boy's cries, Dylan had no idea if he was still in the nursery.

He stepped cautiously into the room. Watching his back. And trying to watch Collena's. He went to the crib. Adam was indeed there.

Thank God.

His son's eyes were closed, and he was sucking his thumb.

Dylan checked the windows next. They were all shut tight. It was harder to tell if all was well in the room because the moonlight was scarce on this side of the house. The only illumination came from the battery-backed-up night-light near the crib. There were a lo of shadows in the room, and Millie could be lurking, waiting to strike.

A soft sound put him on alert. Not a footstep. More like a swish of movement across the hall.

Where Collena was.

He didn't dare call out to her. It might give away their positions. Dylan eased his way back to the door and looked out.

What he saw caused his blood to turn to ice.

Millie was there. In the hall. Collena's back was to her. And Millie already had her weapon raised and aimed.

She was about to kill Collena.

In that flash of a moment, things became crystal clear. He was in love with Collena and desperately wanted her in his life. Not just as Adam's mother. Dylan wanted *her*. He couldn't lose her.

"Get down!" he yelled to Collena. And then he launched himself at Millie.

She fired the shot anyway.

The sound and the bullet ripped through Ruth's room, but Dylan had no idea if it'd hit Collena. The impact of the collision with Millie threw them off balance, and they crashed into the wall.

Unfortunately, she kept control of her gun. Dylan didn't. Millie kicked his hand, sending Dylan's gun flying across the hall.

Millie fought like a wild woman. She clawed at him, bashing his head and face with her gun.

"I loved you!" Millie yelled. "You had no right to do this to me."

He managed to catch her right hand and pin it against

the wall. She continued to fight, her finger still on the trigger. They weren't out of danger yet.

Collena went to him. He couldn't tell if she was hurt or not, but she grabbed Millie's left arm while Dylan wrenched the gun from her right hand.

So that Millie wouldn't hurt herself or him, Dylan dragged her back to the floor and held her down so that she couldn't move.

"Anybody here?" someone called out. It was Sheriff Hathaway. Just in time to arrest a killer.

"Back here," Dylan shouted. And then he looked over his shoulder to see if Collena had checked on Adam.

But Collena was still in the corridor leaning against the wall.

And there was blood streaming down her forehead and onto her face.

Chapter 18

Collena winced when the doctor flashed the light in her eyes.

"Got a headache?" Dr. Finn McGrath asked her.

She nodded. The movement made her head hurt. So did her knees, hands and her right arm. She'd injured it somehow in that scuffle with Millie. Heck, she hurt all over, so she quit trying to identify each source of annoying pain.

Dylan sat in the corner of the examining room. He looked worried, but he was okay. So were Adam and Ina. She'd made the medics check them out at the ranch before she would get in the ambulance and come to the hospital. And Collena would gladly go through a million headaches or more if that meant everyone was safe.

"You have a mild concussion." The doctor turned off the light and stared down at her. "A cracked rib, multiple cuts and contusions, a sprained wrist and you're going to need stitches in your forehead where that bullet grazed you."

"All minor stuff," she concluded, and she sent Dylan a reassuring glance to let him know just that. It didn't appear to reassure him, though. His jaw was clenched like iron, as it had been during the entire ambulance ride to the hospital and the examination.

Dr. McGrath turned and looked at Dylan. "I don't suppose it'd do any good to suggest an examination for you?"

Dylan shook his head. "I'm fine. Take care of Collena."

"Already done that. The prodding and poking is over, and all that's left is for the nurse to come in here in a minute to do some stitching and bandaging. While she's taking care of that, I'll write Collena a prescription for some nice painkillers, and leave written instructions about how to deal with that concussion. But I have to figure, if she has injuries like these, then you're probably hurting some, too."

"Just some bruises," Dylan assured him.

The doctor grunted. He paused as if waiting for Dylan to change his mind. A couple of seconds later Dr. McGrath huffed again and headed out.

"You should be examined," Collena insisted. "Just in case."

Dylan pushed himself away from the wall and walked to her. Slowly. Almost cautiously. He eased down on the examining table beside her. "I'm so sorry."

Collena blinked and tried to brace herself for more bad news. "For what?"

"For Millie."

"Oh." *That.* She shrugged and realized she should have anticipated that he would react this way. "What Millie did wasn't your fault."

"But it was. I should have figured it out before she attacked us."

Even though it was painful, Collena managed a smirk. "You don't have ESP." She pressed her fingertips over his mouth when he started to say something else.

"Millie's in jail?" Collena asked, sliding her fingers from his mouth to his chin. She held the touch a moment longer before she dropped her hand back into her lap.

"Yes. Hank called me on the way over. The sheriff's going to transfer Millie to a psychiatric hospital in San Antonio as soon as the paperwork is done." He paused. "Millie confessed everything."

That included the murders of Dylan's sister and fiancée. Dylan would probably still blame himself for that, as well. It would take time for him to heal. Far more time than it would for her superficial wounds.

Would he allow her to help him heal?

Perhaps not.

Collena hated to think of the future. Even though it certainly looked rosier than it had just two days ago. Curtis Reese was no longer around to try to claim custody of Adam. Rodney Harmon was dead. And Millie, the person who'd made Dylan's life hell for years, was in custody and would be locked away for the rest of her life.

Still, there were so many things left unsettled between them.

What the heck were they going to do now?

Collena made eye contact with Dylan, but he looked away. He scraped his thumbnail over her plastic hospital bracelet. "Hank told me that Millie admitted to the threatening phone call and to putting the newspaper outside your door."

"So it was her and not Rodney," Collena said under her breath. "I thought he might have been the one to make the call."

The silence returned. It was filled with tension, on her part anyway. Dylan seemed to be in a dark mood. Since the danger was over, she had to wonder if she was the reason for his state of mind.

"It'll be okay," she assured him.

Now, his eyes came to hers. Oh, they were intense. Something was obviously on his mind, and Collena thought she knew what it was. Instead of putting him through the agony of how to say what he wanted to say she decided to get everything out there so they could hopefully deal with it.

"We can start fresh," Collena began. "Without the threat from Curtis, we can get—" She stopped when she heard a wonderful sound coming from outside the room.

It was Adam, and he was chattering.

"I had Ina drive Adam here for a short visit," Dylan explained, standing. "I thought he'd cheer you up. Are you up to seeing him?"

"I'm always up to seeing him. But I'm not the one who needs cheering up."

If he heard that last part, he didn't react to it. Dylan opened the door and motioned for Ina to come inside She was holding Adam in her arms. But not for long

Adam immediately reached for Dylan, and he took the little boy and brought him to the examining table.

"Hi," Adam greeted. And he almost got the *"h"* sound in there.

Despite the twinge of pain it caused her, Collena grinned from ear to ear. She'd never grow tired of this precious little boy. Just seeing him made all the pain worth it.

Dylan sat next to her again so that Collena could kiss Adam's cheek. Unfortunately, Adam wasn't interested in the kiss. He was interested in the now-cleaned bullet slice on Collena's forehead. Adam frowned and tried to touch it, but Collena took her son's hand instead and kissed his fingers one by one.

Adam laughed.

"Ruth called on the way over here," Ina said, walking closer. "Hank and she are leaving town. Once they're settled, she'll give you a call, but she wanted you both to know she's real sorry for what happened. She didn't know what Millie was up to, and Ruth hopes one day you'll be able to get past all this hurt. She's gonna try to get past it, too, and start seeing a doctor again."

Collena was about to suggest that Dylan call them, especially since neither Ruth, nor Hank appeared to have been involved in Millie's criminal activities. But maybe it was best if they had some time apart.

"We'd better not stay much longer," Ina said, eyeing the wound on Collena's head. "Besides, I need to get this little one back. He's probably wanting some breakfast by now."

Collena grabbed one last kiss from Adam, and Dylan did, as well, before Ina whisked the baby away.

"Breakfast," Collena repeated. "Maybe if this wound gets stitched up in time, we'll be able to make it back to the ranch before Adam's morning nap. It'd be nice to spend some quiet time with him."

He nodded. That was it. His only reaction. Which brought her back to what they'd been discussing before Ina and Adam arrived. However, Dylan spoke before she could continue.

"A fresh start, you said before Ina got here." He paused a moment. "I think that's a good idea."

She was afraid of that, but Collena had no intention of holding him to the vows they'd made in desperation. "I can start the paperwork."

His eyebrows lifted, and he studied her. "What do you mean?"

She had to clear away the lump in her throat first. Mercy, this wasn't easy. "There's no need for you to stay married to me. We'll work out a custody arrangement with Adam."

Dylan just stared at her.

"And I was thinking about moving to Greer," Collena continued. "That way, I'll be closer to Adam."

His stare turned to a scowl. "You call that a fresh start?"

"Why, what did you have in mind?"

He looked on the verge of answering her. But he didn't say a word. Instead, Dylan leaned in, cupped her chin gently and kissed her. Even with all her aches and pains, it was potent.

"I like your plan better than mine," she let him know.

"That wasn't a plan. That was foreplay." He shrugged.

"But we'll have to wait for you to mend before we carry that any further."

Collena disagreed with another kiss, one that left her breathless.

"Will you marry me?" Dylan asked with his mouth still against hers.

That left her breathless, too.

"We're already married," she pointed out.

"We entered into an arrangement for Adam's sake. I don't want that now. I want more. A lot more."

Collena felt her heart swell. "How much more?" she whispered.

"I want everything. You. Adam. A marriage. A real family. Maybe even more kids."

Now, she was breathless and speechless, and all those aches and pains seemed to melt away.

"Well?" Dylan prompted. "What's your answer?"

As if trying to convince her, he kissed her again.

But Collena didn't need convincing. "I was ready to say yes the minute you kissed me."

"Why?" he asked.

Ah, this was easy. Collena didn't even have to think about it. "Because I'm in love with you. Because you're Adam's dad. And because you're great in bed." Despite the light comment, she had to blink back tears. Happy tears, though. "What about you? Why did you ask me to marry you?"

"Because I love you."

That was it. Nothing more. And Collena realized that was the only thing she needed to hear.

* * * * *

We hope you enjoyed reading
The Wyoming Kid
by #1 *New York Times* bestselling author
DEBBIE MACOMBER
and
The Horseman's Son
by *USA TODAY* bestselling author
DELORES FOSSEN

Both were originally Harlequin® series stories!

From passionate, suspenseful and dramatic
love stories to inspirational or historical,
Harlequin offers different lines to
satisfy every romance reader.

New books in each line
are available every month.

Harlequin.com

SPECIAL EXCERPT FROM

HQN™

*Thanks to his dark past, Deputy Judd Laramie
has built walls around himself that most people
have difficulty penetrating. But Cleo Delaney isn't most
people. Although his childhood friend has always held
a special place in his heart, will the big favor she's
asking him for summon old ghosts...or rekindle
everything they once shared?*

Read on for a sneak preview of Hot Texas Sunrise,
part of the Coldwater Texas series from
USA TODAY *bestselling author by Delores Fossen.*

"You know, that look you're giving me feels like a truth serum,"
he said. "You really don't want me to start spilling all, do you?"

Judd stayed quiet, maybe considering her question. Considering,
too, that her spilling might involve talking about this heat that was
still between them. Heat that sizzled when her eyes cleared enough
to actually see him.

He looked away from her.

Obviously, he wasn't in a spilling or hearing a spilling kind of
mood. Too bad, because a quick discussion of sizzle, followed by
some flirting, might have washed away her dark film of thoughts.

"How are you?" Cleo asked, but what she really wanted to
know was why he'd felt the need to call his sponsor.

His mouth tightened enough to let her know he didn't want to
discuss it, but it did get his gaze back on her. A long, lingering,
smoldering gaze. Though Cleo had to admit that the smoldering
part might be her own overly active imagination.

Or not.

Judd said a single word of really bad profanity, grabbed her
shoulders and dragged her to him. His mouth was on hers before

Cleo could even make a sound. It turned out, though, that no sound was necessary because she got a full, head-on slam of the heat. And this time it wasn't just simmering around them. It rolled through her from head to toe.

Now she made a sound, one of pleasure, and the years vanished. It was as if they'd picked up where they'd left off seventeen years ago, when he'd been scorching her like this in his bed.

His taste. Yes. That was the same. Maybe with a manlier edge to it, but it was unmistakably Judd. Unmistakably incredible.

Cleo felt herself moving right into the kiss. Right into Judd, too. Unfortunately, the gearshift was in the way, but she still managed some more body-to-body contact when she slid against him and into his arms.

Judd deepened the kiss, and she let him. In fact, Cleo was reasonably sure that she would have let him do pretty much anything. Yep, he'd heated her up just that much.

Apparently, though, he hadn't made himself as mindless and needy as he had her, because he pulled back, cursed again and resumed his cop's stare. Though she did think his eyes were a little blurry.

They sat there, gazes connected, breaths gusting. Waiting. Since Cleo figured her gusty breaths weren't enough to allow her to speak, she just waited for Judd to say something memorable.

"Damn," he growled.

Okay, so maybe not memorable in the way she'd wanted. Definitely not romantic. But it was such a *Judd* reaction that it made her smile. Then laugh.

She leaned in, nipped his bottom lip with her teeth. "Don't worry, Judd. I'll be gentle with you."

Don't miss
Hot Texas Sunrise *by Delores Fossen,*
available April 2019 wherever
HQN Books and ebooks are sold.

www.HQNBooks.com

Need an adrenaline rush from nail-biting tales
(and irresistible males)?

Check out **Harlequin Intrigue®**,
Harlequin® Romantic Suspense and
Love Inspired® Suspense books!

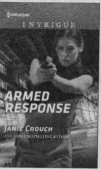

New books available every month!

CONNECT WITH US AT:

Facebook.com/groups/HarlequinConnection

Facebook.com/HarlequinBooks

Twitter.com/HarlequinBooks

Instagram.com/HarlequinBooks

Pinterest.com/HarlequinBooks

ReaderService.com

H HARLEQUIN®

**ROMANCE WHEN
YOU NEED IT**